A CAPITAL OFFENSE

A CAPITAL OFFENSE

GARY E. PARKER

THOMAS NELSON PUBLISHERS
Nashville

Published in Nashville, Tennessee, by Thomas Nelson, Inc., Publishers

The Bible version used in this publication is THE NEW KING JAMES VERSION. Copyright © 1979, 1980, 1982, 1990, Thomas Nelson, Inc., Publishers.

Library of Congress Cataloging-in-Publication Data

Parker, Gary E.
    A capital offense / Gary E. Parker.
        p.   cm.
    "A Janet Thoma book."
    ISBN 0-7852-7786-2 (pbk.)
    I. Title
PS3566.A6784C36   1998
813'.54—dc21   97-46995
                                                                              CIP

Printed in the United States of America.

1 2 3 4 5 6 QPK 03 02 01 00 99 98

CHAPTER

1

Determined to carry in all the groceries in one trip, Connie Brandon pinned one bag against each hip with an elbow, gripped another in the fingers of each hand, and dangled one from her teeth. So loaded down, she rushed toward the side door of her modest but comfortable white stone home. Though unable to glance at her watch, she knew she was almost late picking up Katie, her seven year old, from the baby-sitter.

Usually, being a few minutes late wouldn't matter. Mrs. Everhart, the retired woman who kept Katie for three hours after school every day while Connie finished up her last semester at the University of Missouri Law School, generally had nothing pressing to do. But today she had an appointment at the beauty parlor and had kindly informed Connie she needed Katie picked up no later than 6:30. Connie had promised to get there on time. Unfortunately, an automobile accident a half mile from the grocery store had created what served in Jefferson City, Missouri, as a traffic jam. On the scale of one to ten, it didn't amount to that much, but car wrecks in the state capital were as rare as trees in the Sahara Desert and a number of rubberneckers had slowed Connie far too much. A stickler for punctuality, she typically arrived at appointments at least ten minutes early.

Easing the groceries in her right hand to the floor of the garage, she yanked open the door, grabbed the sacks again, staggered inside, and dropped all the groceries except the sack in her mouth onto the small dining table that sat just inside in the kitchen. Opening the refrigerator, she shoved the bag that had hung from her mouth, the one holding ice cream, into the back of the freezer. In spite of her hurry, she had to smile.

Jack would thank her for the ice cream. Early in their courtship she had learned how much he loved it. He ate a bowl of vanilla almost every night, mixing it with milk and sometimes a banana, making a milkshake unmatched by any fast food restaurant or ice cream shop.

Thankfully, Jack could afford such caloric extravagance. For that matter, so could she. Both of them were small people, Jack no more than five-eight and a hundred fifty pounds and she barely five-two and one hundred five. Even though he had inhaled a bowl of vanilla practically every night of their seventeen-year marriage, Jack hadn't gained an ounce.

Brushing off the front of her cream-colored blouse and gray pleated slacks, she hurried to Katie's room. Library books were due today, and Connie refused to let them run late.

As she grabbed the books off Katie's bed, the phone rang. She held the books to her chest and rushed back to the kitchen. The phone, sitting on a counter by an open window, rang a second time. She glanced at her watch. Unlike so many other people, she hated for a call to go unanswered or for an answering machine to respond. Such deliberate disregard for the caller seemed rude to her, like passing someone on the street and not speaking. The phone rang again. Connie almost reached for it but then thought of Mrs. Everhart. She couldn't let that good woman down. Just this once, the answering machine could get the phone. She would call back as soon as she got home.

Connie headed to the door, listening with one ear as the voice of Daniel, her fourteen-year-old son, clicked in on the machine: "Hello. This is the home of Connie and Katie and Daniel and Jack. Leave a message and we'll call back."

Connie reached for the doorknob. After a beep, she heard Jack's strong bass boom through the phone.

"Hey, Sunset, it's Jack."

Connie stopped in her tracks. Jack! The only person who called her Sunset, the color of her hair as he described it. Every time she heard him say it, she melted. She had to take Jack's call, even if only for a moment. She stepped back and grabbed the phone. A soft breeze from the crisp April day outside brushed across her face.

"Yeah, Jack, I'm here, but I've got to hurry."

"Okay, just wanted you to know I'm at the bookstore now, but I'll be out late. The city council is meeting in a special session at 7:30 with some gambling people from Las Vegas. I won't speak or anything, but I want them to know I'm there."

Connie shuddered and the air from the window suddenly felt chilled. Goose bumps rose on her arms. She sensed a threat of some kind in the breeze, a force as unpredictable as the Missouri River that snaked below the bluffs less than a hundred yards from the back of her house. She pushed her hair from her eyes, then squeezed the phone tighter. "What time will you get home?" she asked.

"Don't know. The vote is just a few weeks away and everyone's a little on edge. We'll talk when I get home . . ." His voice trailed off.

Connie wanted to ask him more but knew she didn't have time. For the past year Jack had waged a campaign to convince people to reject riverboat gambling in Jefferson City. In response, the gambling interests had stooped to personal attacks against him. They had labeled him a religious bigot, an intolerant stick-in-the-mud who wanted to control the lives of the citizens of Jefferson City. To her shock, a series of nasty phone calls had invaded their home. The anonymous calls, always made past midnight and always spoken in clipped, short tones by the same male voice, told Jack to stop meddling.

"This whole thing has gotten too mean," Connie said.

Jack laughed. "It shows I've scared them. If they didn't think people were listening, they wouldn't bother me."

"But the phone calls, Jack, what about them?"

"Harmless," he said. "I expected this kind of thing. A person doesn't speak out on moral issues without stirring up a few enemies."

Connie knew he was right. Christians often found themselves at odds with culture. Nothing new about that. But that didn't make her any less upset about the calls. Angry and protective of her family, she wanted the calls to stop and she wanted them to stop now! Though small in stature and often shy, she had never backed away from a confrontation if someone pushed one on her. The only child of an army sergeant who tended to treat her and her mom like one of the recruits he trained, she knew something about toughness, even if she seldom practiced it.

But Connie's anger hadn't stopped the calls. They continued to come, sporadically, but never ending. She never knew when to stay awake and when to fall asleep. She and Jack left the phone off the hook several times, but the instant they put it in place again, the caller inevitably rang.

"You think we ought to call the police again?" Connie asked.

"I don't know. Like they said last week, all they can do is put a tracer on the phone."

"I like that idea."

"Don't you think that's overreacting?"

Connie bit her lip. *Maybe so.*

"Look," Jack continued. "The election is June fourth. After that, one way or the other, the calls will stop. If we lose, the guy might call to console me, but that'll be all. If we win, he'll know the game's over. Either way, the calls will stop."

Though Connie didn't necessarily agree, she decided to let it go. The police could deal with the man if they identified him, but only a trace gave them a chance to do that, and Jack didn't want a trace.

"Hey, I've got to run," she said, remembering Mrs. Everhart. "See you tonight."

"Late tonight."

"Late, then."

"I love you, Sunset. And don't worry."

"Love you too."

She hung up, rushed to her five-year-old van and jumped in. Rolling down the driver's side window, she spun onto the road and tried to calm herself. Her shoulder-length red hair whipped out in the breeze, a cascade of scarlet billowing in bangs around her brown eyes. She gunned the gas. If she hurried, Mrs. Everhart might still make her hair appointment on time! As she rounded the corner and headed down the hill below her house, she thought again of the nasty calls that scared her so much. The calls had touched something primal in her, raised her antennae of emotions to a level she'd never before experienced. She now knew how a mother bear felt when something threatened her young.

With her newly discovered senses, she detected something unusual going on with Jack. He had seemed quieter over the last few weeks, less given to the humor that usually poured out of him like overflowing water from a faucet. He hadn't popped Daniel with a towel or told a corny joke in weeks, and that disturbed her. She couldn't quite put her finger on it, but she knew more was going on than he had confided to her.

He had a tendency to do that—try to protect her, not tell her things if he thought them worrisome. Connie swung left at a light and remembered the day after their marriage. They were traveling from Jefferson City to St. Louis for their three-day honeymoon. They stopped at a gas station to fill up. Spotting a hamburger franchise across the road, Connie kissed Jack on the cheek and told him she wanted to get a soft drink. His face instantly changed, his blue eyes growing cloudy.

"Will you be okay?" he asked, concern etched in the deep notes of his voice.

At first Connie didn't understand. "Why wouldn't I be?" she asked. "I'm just going across the street. I've been crossing streets by myself for a long time now."

Though he smiled, Jack's voice still sounded anxious. "Well, you know . . . it's just . . . well, I just got you. I don't want anything to happen to you, that's all."

"I'll look both ways," Connie promised, kissing him again and walking away.

Stopping at a yield sign, Connie checked her watch. About six more minutes to Mrs. Everhart's.

The day of their marriage had been the first hint of his protectiveness. Other experiences had followed. From time to time, she had argued with Jack over it, told him he didn't need to play guardian over her. Most of the few marital disagreements they had centered on this issue. More than once she had told him, "Look, I know you're trying to protect me and I love you for that. But I'm a grown woman. What bothers you bothers me. I don't like it when you don't tell me things, even if you are taking care of me. I'm asking you to change this for me, change it and let me help you when things happen."

"I'll try, Sunset," he always said. "I'll really try. I know you'll stay after me if I don't."

She smiled. How well he knew her. She gave up on very few things in life. Over the years, Jack had improved. But lately, he seemed . . . well . . . too quiet, almost as if he didn't want to say anything lest he open himself up to questions. His involvement against gambling had caused an anxiety in him she hadn't seen for a long time.

Mrs. Everhart's house loomed just ahead, and Connie forced her thoughts away from Jack and his involvement with the gambling battle. She had to let him do what he thought right. He certainly told her that often enough.

"I'll do what I think is right," he kept saying. "For Katie and Daniel and the rest of the kids in this town." When he said it so simply, how could she argue?

With a hard left, she spun into Mrs. Everhart's driveway and ground to a stop. Directly ahead, she spotted Katie running down the sidewalk, her red hair blowing in a thousand directions. Behind Katie, Mrs. Everhart trudged at a much slower pace, her ample girth and arthritic knees slowing her down. Seeing the gray-haired saint, Connie smiled. She'd never known anyone quite so sweet.

Connie climbed out of the van and rushed across the yard, bending low toward Katie. How blessed could one person get, she wondered? She had a loving husband, a maturing teenage son, and a daughter who looked just like her mother, right down to the color of her hair; the row of freckles across her button nose; her high, rounded cheekbones; and her eyes the color of chocolate milk.

Katie rushed into her mother's arms. Connie grabbed her and squeezed. Mrs. Everhart waved, turned left, and walked toward her garage.

"Sorry I'm late," yelled Connie.

"No problem, child," called Mrs. Everhart, apparently unconcerned. "Hairdressers always make you wait anyway." She disappeared into the garage, and Connie heard her car door open.

Connie chuckled. What a blessing Mrs. Everhart was. Like a grandmother to Katie.

"See you tomorrow," she yelled, picking Katie up and climbing back into her van. Mrs. Everhart didn't answer.

Back on the road, Connie pointed the van toward town. A pleasant thought occurred to her. She would stop at the bookstore on the way to the library and catch Jack by surprise, see him before his busy night began. "You want to go see Daddy?" she asked Katie.

Katie nodded. Connie leaned over and took her hand. Jack would love to see them. The April breeze blew in off the river and through the window. Connie squeezed Katie's hand and thought again of Jack, the only man she had ever loved.

CHAPTER

2

His elbows propped on his cluttered metal desk, Jack Brandon clutched the phone to his left ear and concentrated on the voice of the man on the other end of the line.

"I need to see you tonight, Jack," the man said, his voice insistent. "Sometime past ten."

"But that's too late for me," said Jack. "I don't know if I can make it."

"You've got no choice but to make it. This can't wait."

Jack gritted his teeth, an anger he seldom felt and even more rarely displayed rising up in his chest. "But a person always has choices," he said.

"Guess again, my friend. I'm telling you, your options are few."

Jack wanted to argue but then caught himself. That wasn't his way. He closed his eyes and counted to ten, letting the worst of the negative emotion pass. He had to stay focused if he wanted to deal with this situation. A decision made out of anger would most likely end up the wrong choice.

He opened his eyes and pulled a baseball from the top drawer of his desk. Tossing the ball into the air, he watched the names written on it spin around and around as it rose. He knew the names—Musial, Schoendist, Brock. All written on his St. Louis Cardinals ball, the ball autographed by a slew of famous Cardinals and given to him by Daniel, Connie, and Katie this past January on his fortieth birthday. Daniel had saved money from cutting grass for months to pay his part, and Katie had contributed a dime a week from her one-dollar allowance. Connie had paid the rest. The ball fell into Jack's right hand, his left one still holding the phone.

Jack knew if he wasn't careful with this caller, everything could go down the tubes—everything he'd spent more than a decade trying to build.

He tossed the ball a second time, then caught it as it dropped. He loved baseball, had played it all through his childhood, second base. His coach at Miller High had described him as tough on the double play and fast on the bases. Only his lack of size kept him from playing past high school.

Calmer now, Jack rolled the ball onto his desk. It skipped across several sheets of scattered white paper, then came to a stop against a stack of books with a black spiral notebook laying on top. Jack focused on his call again.

"What time past ten?" he said.

"What about midnight?"

Jack rubbed his forehead. Staying out that late would require an explanation for Connie, but he couldn't tell her the purpose of this late-night rendezvous.

"Can we do it any earlier?"

"Not really. I like it late. That way no one can see us together."

Jack would have laughed if everything weren't so serious. Lately, lots of people had worked hard to stay away from him in public. Since the gambling interests had chosen Jefferson City as a prime target for a floating casino, scores of normally sane people had gone off the deep end, diving for the dollars the gamblers so freely threw around. Lawyers, builders, bankers, and merchants—all seemed hypnotized by the gambling green.

Jack knew all these people, considered them his friends. For years, they had bought newspapers, the latest novels, and cards and gifts from his shop. On cold winter mornings, he served them steaming cups of coffee, which they took to one of the tables he had set up in the back of the store. There, sipping their coffee, the people read the morning paper and spilled out the latest city gossip.

When one of them got sick or suffered a death in the family or married off a child or earned a promotion, Jack acknowledged it with a card or a gift certificate for a book. From time to time, as opportunity arose, he engaged different ones in conversation about religion, his deep voice and gentle demeanor a strong advocate for the Jesus he loved. Pastors in a number of the city churches filled their baptismal pools and received new converts more than once as a direct result of Jack's steady efforts to live out his faith. Over the years, clients and others in Jefferson City spoke often of the "good man" who owned the Good Books Store.

In the last few months, though, things had changed with some of those people. The changes were subtle to be sure, but noticeable nonetheless. Many seemed cooler toward him, at times even standoffish. Though he tried not to get paranoid, it seemed that some crossed the street when they saw him coming. Others, when they talked to him, kept their conversations short. People treated him as if he had the flu and they wanted to keep a distance so none of his germs spewed onto them.

Jack sighed, resigned to their attitudes. He knew when he got into this fight that a lot of people might respond negatively. But he hadn't known how lonely it would make him feel.

"Where do you want to meet?" he asked, pushing away his unpleasant thoughts. "I don't know many late-night spots. I'm usually in bed by 10:30."

The caller laughed, but it sounded forced. "You imply that I do know those spots?"

"Let's just say the odds are better for you than me."

"But I thought you weren't a gambling man, my friend."

"I'm meeting you, aren't I?"

The man laughed again. "Indeed. You know the parking area for the Katy Trail on the north side of the bridge?"

Jack nodded. "Sure, I know the spot. Take the family over there from time to time for a walk or a bike ride."

"Meet me there at midnight."

Jack leaned forward, grabbed his baseball again, and squeezed it. Though not exactly scared, a ripple of unease washed over him. The Katy Trail, a bike path converted from an old railroad line, came to an end in a dark, secluded area on the opposite side of the Missouri River from Jefferson City. Not the safest of places at midnight.

"Isn't that a bit dramatic?" he asked.

"We can't go anywhere public."

"What about a parking lot somewhere, a grocery store maybe?"

"You want the cops to find us, think we're a couple of teenagers doing drugs? I don't think so."

Jack tossed his baseball, then caught it again. Might as well go to the Katy Trail. If two people needed a place where no one would see them, then he couldn't think of a better location. Midnight was far too late, but that might actually help. With Connie asleep, he might manage to sneak in without her knowing exactly when he got home.

"Okay," he agreed. "The Katy Trail at midnight."

"Thanks, Jack. You won't regret it." The line went dead.

Jack hung up and stared at his baseball, but he didn't really see it. His mind had already skipped away, moving forward to the night about to unfold. So much came down to tonight.

Standing, he stepped around his desk and stared through the door at his bookstore. Almost all his dreams lay just beyond that door. The Good Books Store, opened fifteen years ago. Thousands of books lined the white wooden shelves. He had fought hard to make his store succeed. Worked sixteen hours a day those first few years. Sold books at cut-rate prices, making just enough profit to put food on the table and clothes on his family. Provided service to his customers that made shopping at the chain stores feel like a visit to a dentist with bad breath.

Gradually, he had made progress. The last few years had actually seen real growth. Not that he didn't have some worries yet. One good recession and any independent retailer could go down. But things were better. Another two or three good years and he could begin to relax a bit. He could finish the novel he currently had under construction and spend more time with Sunset and the kids.

Jack's eyes moistened as he thought of his family. Even his love for the store paled in comparison to his love for his wife and children. An orphan since the age of ten, he knew better than most that nothing meant as much as flesh and blood. His family completed him as surely as a beach completed an ocean. Without them, he couldn't exist. With them, he could survive anything life brought.

With Connie beside him, he had sunk his roots in the rich soil of Jefferson City. The town—his home ever since he finished his English degree at the University of Missouri—had a solid feel to it, an enduring quality like the cliffs that bordered it on the north side of the Missouri River. In Jefferson City, children could safely ride their bikes on the streets and elderly women could walk alone to shop. Not many places like that left in the world.

Jack didn't want that quality of life to disappear, to crumble like a weak wall under the wash of a flood. But, from what he knew and believed, gambling threatened to do just that—to rumble through the city, flushing away the underpinnings of the community in its wake.

That's why he had begun to speak out when he learned the gamblers had set their sights on the state capital, why he had gathered a coalition of people who agreed with him into an organized group, why he had spent hours at city council meetings and on the phone talking to people in hopes of convincing them that gambling was a dangerous parasite that gobbled up its hosts. That's why he refused to give up and go away in spite of the fact that former customers no longer bought their newspapers and books in his store. He had to do the right thing. For him, it boiled down to that simple thought. *If he wanted to sleep well at night, he had to do what was right.* A bit of homespun poetry his granddaddy had taught him a long time ago.

The memory of his granddad's wisdom lifting his spirits, Jack dropped his baseball into the desk drawer, grabbed the stack of books, including the black spiral notebook, off the edge of his desk and jammed them into a denim backpack. Then, without saying a word to either of his two coworkers, he stepped out the back door.

Tossing his backpack onto the seat, he climbed into his white pickup and drove straight down the alley that ran parallel with his store. His mind clicking a thousand miles a minute, he came to a stop sign, turned right, then left again onto Main Street. There, deep in thought, he missed his chance to see Connie and Katie as they drove in the opposite direction toward the Good Books Store where they fully expected to find him.

CHAPTER

3

T hough not really hungry, Jack drove to a fast food restaurant and picked up a chicken sandwich with some fries and a soft drink. Then, looking for a place to think for a few minutes before the council meeting, he parked under an oak tree beside the Governor's Mansion and tried to eat. But not much went down.

After a couple of forced swallows, he gave up, dropped the sandwich back into the bag and leaned his head against the seat. The phone call at his office concerned him more than anything he could ever remember, more than anything since the death of his mother and father thirty years earlier. It reminded him of the fragility of life, the utter weakness of everything he thought strong. In a way he'd never grasped before, he came to understand that an entire life could get swept away as easily as a spiderweb hanging in a busy doorway. It didn't make sense, but it was true. His response to the phone call would determine the outcome of at least two entire families: his own and that of the man on the other end of the line.

Considering his options, Jack desperately wanted to talk to Connie. Everything in him cried out to tell her his dilemma. Better than anyone else, she would know how to advise him. Keeping with her steady approach to life, she would assess the predicament, logically outline every option, and make a calm decision. Though she did get feisty at times, even then she never seemed flustered, and her analytical abilities astounded him.

Jack admired Connie's tough-minded qualities and often kidded her about them. "If Connie found herself at dinner on a cruise liner and the ship began to sink," he told their friends, "she'd insist on washing the dishes before she took to a lifeboat. Then, once on the lifeboat, she'd know exactly how far to the nearest shore." Sadly, he couldn't take advantage of Connie's advice on this. Not today and, based on what decision he made, maybe not ever.

He took a sip of soft drink and felt a sense of grief in his gut. Through persistent effort, he had worked hard to share more with Connie, even that which he feared would upset her. But to tell her what he knew would bring something more tragic into her life than he wanted her to experience.

Jack glanced at his watch. The sky had darkened and the breeze had picked up. Five minutes later, he arrived at the council meeting and sat down quietly in the back. A number of people turned and nodded to him as he took his seat, but no one said anything. Everyone was too intent on the events unfolding in the front of the auditorium.

Pushing away his worries, Jack also focused on the proceedings. Everything moved according to the agenda—a final meeting to determine if Casino Royale would receive city approval for a state license to set up a gambling boat on the shores of the capital city. Cedric Blacker, the front man for the Casino Royale, rolled out his presentation—complete with a slick video showing a majestic paddle-wheel riverboat steaming down the Missouri. After the video, he unfolded a full-color chart depicting projects the city could accomplish using the five million dollars a year the gambling taxes would provide. Finished with that, he unveiled an artist's rendition of the riverfront—complete with a dock and a slew of shops that would follow a successful boat.

Biting his tongue, Jack studied Blacker. The man did have style. Though in his early fifties, he had hair the color and consistency of motor oil, and he kept himself trim and well-tanned. He wore a double-breasted gray suit over a white shirt so creased you could cut bread with it. Blacker's ability to turn a phrase matched his sharp appearance.

"The Casino Royale will be a good neighbor," Blacker said, smiling at the council. "We'll put down roots here. We want the same thing you do. We want Jefferson City to thrive. If the city thrives, so do we. We'll bring our families here too. If we didn't think this boat was good for this community, we wouldn't bring it here. Together we'll make a difference. . . . "

Though Blacker continued to talk, Jack's mind wandered. He had heard it all more times than he cared to remember. Representatives of the Casino Royale and other gambling interests had spent almost two years and $400,000 making the same speech to anyone who would listen. Bring in the gamblers and grow. Raise tax dollars for the schools. Provide occupants for the hotels.

Jack studied the members of the city council, wondering what they thought of Blacker's sales pitch. The council members knew about the dirty underbelly of gambling; Jack had made sure of that. He had given them enough nasty statistics to choke a good-sized horse. They knew that gambling inevitably created crime—from petty thievery to loan-sharking. They were aware of the economic negatives—the increased money spent on police personnel, the additional funds necessary to pay for social problems, including gambling addictions. They had seen the statistics; people would spend their money in the casino and therefore have less to spend in other recreational pursuits like restaurants, movies, and bowling alleys.

Sure, the gamblers who came to town would spend money, but not in the local shops and establishments. They would spend their cash on the riverboat—shove it into slot machines, lay it down on roulette wheels, wager it on crap tables and blackjack hands. Though gambling promised prosperity, it brought pain and anguish, cannibalizing the local economy and sending the money back to Las Vegas.

Jack knew the one truth about gambling that the owners of the casinos never told: The house eventually wins and the people who gamble inevitably lose. That's the way the owners of the boats stacked the odds. Otherwise, how did they make money?

The council knew all this, but that didn't make Jack any more confident. Knowledge didn't guarantee a person would respond reasonably. The people on the council came to the table with their own agendas.

People like the mayor, Johnson Mack, a gravel-voiced, gray-haired real estate developer who had moved to Jefferson City about seven years ago. A mover and a shaker, Mack had gotten involved in the community in a hurry. Spending money, throwing parties, building residential and commercial buildings, meeting and winning over the old guard of the city with large contributions to their favorite charities and local schools. Before too long, he ran for school board, then city council. Only last year, he became mayor.

The owner of several old buildings near the site of a proposed convention center just off Main Street, Mack had offered Jack a price for his store. Apparently, he needed the property to complete his package for the convention center.

Jack knew Mack wasn't on his side and that what Mack wanted on the council he almost always got. So, Jack knew he wouldn't win in these chambers. That didn't surprise or bother him. Though he had asked for it in two meetings just like this one, he never expected the council to follow his advice and pass an ordinance against gambling. He wasn't that naive. But, what he wanted from the city council he had already received. And what he wanted was press coverage.

Though an amateur in its practice, Jack had long been an astute observer of politics. Living in the capital city, he had studied the tricks of scores of public officials. Gradually, the lessons he had learned from others became ingrained in him. Intuitively, he now understood what every political pro in the world knew as well as he knew the names of his children: The media loves controversy and will cover the person who can provide it for them.

With that knowledge as his ace in the hole, Jack had used the city council and its public forum as a way to create and stir a full-blown conflict. For the normally quiet town of Jefferson City, the public battle over gambling made for days and days of headlines. With the media as his unintentional ally, he communicated his message over and over again.

His message? Simple. Gambling makes promises it can't keep. Like a mangy dog, it brings fleas. Crime, corruption, poverty, despair, even suicide. Jack had the facts and the studies from numerous reputable universities to prove it, and he pumped those facts to the media over and over again. More times than not, they repeated what he said. Jack and his supporters didn't have much money, but that didn't mean they came to the fray without weapons.

Jack smiled as he reviewed the last few months. His tactics had thrown the gambling interests on the defensive. He had pointed out the negatives of gambling, and the riverboat proponents, not quite sure how to counterattack against a well-liked local guy, fell off their message. Instead of having free rein to talk about all the benefits of gambling, they had to spend time and money to disprove "Jack's Facts," as his supporters had begun to call his avalanche of statistics.

Watching Cedric Blacker's seamless report, Jack wondered if any of it would matter. Yes, he believed with all his heart that the Lord wanted him in this fight, that Jesus disliked it when people gambled away money they should use to buy food and clothing for children, that trying to get something for nothing contradicted the whole notion of living out of dependence on God. Yet, people often chose to ignore the life God preferred for them. In a democratic system, if the people wanted gambling, then God or no God, the government would give them gambling. And, with plans to spend another $300,000 to "get the vote out," the gambling interests had enough money to convince the people they wanted a casino.

Jack rubbed his eyes. His group, the Coalition for the Future, had spent about $25,000—pocket change for the boys from Vegas.

As Blacker finished speaking, Jack stood and made a hurried exit, not stopping to chitchat with anyone. Outside, he checked his watch. Almost ten o'clock. He thought about calling Connie, then decided against it. She would want to know where he was, what he was doing, where he was going. But he couldn't tell her.

He climbed into his truck and pulled off, headed left. Fifteen minutes later, he parked in front of the River City Community Church, an interdenominational congregation of just over two hundred members. For a second, he sat still and stared at the red-brick building. He had loved this church since the day he first saw it nineteen years ago. Though different in worship style, the church architecture reminded him of his granddaddy's Lutheran church in Miller, Missouri, the church in which he became a follower of Jesus.

A bell tower pointed to the sky. A wooden door, painted a dark red, was the front entrance. Most remarkable of all, the pastor of the church, the Reverend Rodney Wallace had a voice that sounded almost identical to that of Justin Longley, the grandfather who raised Jack after his parents' deaths.

Jack rolled down the window and took a deep breath, inhaling the moist air of a spring still pulsing, the breeze heavy with the blooming of the redbuds, tulip trees, oaks, and maples that dominated the city. The smell of spring carried him back to his childhood, to the farm outside of Miller, to the good days after the bad ones, the eight years with Justin that helped him recover from the year before, the year a house fire snuffed out the lives of his mom and dad.

Jack climbed out of the truck. Then, hoisting his backpack over his left shoulder, he walked up the sidewalk, pulled a key out of his pocket, and unlocked the side door. Glad his volunteer position as church treasurer gave him such access, he stepped through the door, down the hall, and into the sanctuary.

A glint of approval sparked in his blue eyes as he surveyed the place. Plain wood pews, unadorned by cushions. The simple but elegant communion table in the center up front, a silver chalice in the middle of the table, and a golden candelabra on either side of the chalice. Underneath his shoes, he felt the church's stone floor, worn by almost a hundred years of use.

Walking softly, Jack eased into the third pew from the front on the left side, the pew where he sat every Sunday with Connie and Daniel and Katie. He had met Connie in this very pew eighteen years ago, the second year after he moved to Jefferson City.

Jack slid his backpack off his shoulder and rubbed his hands across the pew bottom. So much rested on what he did or didn't do tonight. If the worst happened, and he knew full well it might, he and his family would probably have to leave Jefferson City. Bending at the waist, he leaned forward until his head rested on the back of the pew in front of him. Then, as fervently as he knew how, he sought the face of God.

*****

Instantly awake, Connie Brandon popped up from the bed and shivered violently. For a second, she wondered what had awakened her. One of the kids calling? She leaned forward and listened but heard nothing. Then, fingering a bit of sleep from her eyes, she spotted the curtains to her right billowing inward, pushed by a breeze that had turned icy in the night. Pulling the covers under her chin, she twisted sideways to see if the cold had bothered Jack. He wasn't there.

She rubbed her eyes again and stared at the clock that sat beside the bed on a nightstand. 12:35 A.M.

She tilted her head and looked at the clock again. The red letters stared back. For a moment, she thought it must be mistaken but then remembered Jack's warning he would get home late. But this late? It wasn't like him.

Wrapping herself in the bedcovers, she eased down and padded her size-five feet over to the open window, pulling it closed. She climbed back into bed, stretched out comfortably, and snuggled down. It wasn't like Jack to stay out late, but he had warned her. She had no reason to worry. He would get home soon.

Half-expecting to hear his old pickup pull up any second, she lay still and listened for several minutes. She imagined him walking in, getting into bed, and warming her up with a strong snuggle. They would talk a few minutes, hugging closely. He would explain the mysterious evening. Satisfied with his explanation, she would fall asleep in his arms.

Connie smiled and reached for her Bible on the nightstand. Then, flipping on a lamp, she turned to the Psalms and began to read.

"Rejoice in the LORD, O you righteous! For praise from the upright is beautiful. Praise the LORD with the harp; Make melody to Him with an instrument of ten strings. Sing to Him a new song; Play skillfully with a shout of joy. For the word of the LORD is right, And all His work is done in truth. . . . "

Relaxing into her pillows as she read, Connie's eyes grew heavy. Beside her the clock's face showed 1:02. Jack should get home any minute. Until he did, she wouldn't quite go to sleep. But she would doze.

Her eyes closed, and the Bible fell onto her chest. Connie snuggled into the covers. The clock beside her clicked off another number. Her mind drifted . . . Jack would come home soon . . . Jack would . . . She dreamed of him and she smiled.

CHAPTER

4

J ust over six and a half hours later, a sixty-seven-year-old fisherman named Sammy Sanks rubbed his unshaven face and sat back in his johnboat as it eased through the gently flowing waters of the muddy Missouri River. With a bright sun warming his shoulders, he yawned and stared toward the unkempt shoreline of Adrian's Island. The island, an undeveloped strip of often-flooded real estate, sat over a hundred feet below the majestic Capitol Building of Missouri and to the left of the railroad tracks that ran north of Jefferson City.

Sanks loved this tiny island and fished this spot often. The driftwood that caught on its uneven shoreline provided excellent feeding ground for the catfish he loved to catch there. He marked the seasons by its foliage and enjoyed seeing the changes the river brought to it day by day. New driftwood, fresh undergrowth, unexpected washes and gullies—all kept the place constantly fresh to him. He knew every nook and cranny of the island, and when something changed his sharp eyes picked it up immediately.

The water lapped quietly at the bow of his boat. He scanned the shoreline with his keen gray eyes. The trees, mostly maples, hickory, and oak, had just begun to bud. Rainfall had been sparser than usual this year and the river was down. The island lay placid and quiet, dried out more than usual for April.

Staring at the island, Sanks wondered if the city would ever develop the strip. Over the years, lots of folks had suggested it. Build a walkover for people to access it, place picnic tables and walking trails in key spots, and take advantage of it as a tourist attraction. Sanks hoped the development would never happen. It would ruin the whole—

His eyes stopped moving. He spotted something that didn't fit the naturally wild shoreline. Sanks leaned forward and shaded his eyes with his hand, blocking out the sun's glare. There! Wedged between a soggy piece of driftwood and a maple tree about to bloom. What was that?

He nudged the rudder on his twenty-five-horsepower motor, and the boat eased closer to the shoreline. The odd object began to form up into something recognizable. It looked like a . . . goodness, it looked like a body!

Sanks took a deep breath and steered closer to the still form lying in the water. He ran the back of his hand across his mouth, then spat over the side of the boat. This didn't look good. He saw it more clearly now, a navy piece of cloth, a . . . a shirt, a . . . yes, he hated to see it, but the object was a man's body, half-submerged in the muddy water.

His boat slipping through the wash, Sanks cut the engine and grabbed an oar. Sticking the oar into the ground, he pulled the boat to shore, hooked it to a tree with a thin rope, and rushed to the body. Wanting to help but wary of touching anything, he leaned down and examined the man for signs of life. The water behind him lapped softly against the shore, slightly moving the body. Sanks took a deep breath, looked around quickly, then touched the man's neck with his right hand. Carefully, he searched for a pulse, but found none. The man was definitely dead.

Satisfied he couldn't do anything to help and determined to leave everything as he found it, Sanks twisted back to his boat and lifted a cell phone from a dry compartment under the steering wheel. Feeling a bit queasy, he flipped open the phone and called 911. Then, with nothing more to do, he sat down on a stump by the body and waited. As he waited, he tried to figure out the identity of the slightly built man who lay facedown and dead in the muddy Missouri.

*****

Connie woke up at almost the same moment that Sammy Sanks first threw his fishing line into the water. That was normal for her on a Saturday, to sleep in a bit from her usual 6:30 A.M. starting time. Catch up on the rest that a woman finishing law school and taking care of a family hardly ever managed to get. For just an instant, she started to stretch, to enjoy the luxury of not having to climb out of bed. But then, before she quite knew why, she felt something out of place. She turned to her right, expecting to see Jack but knowing instinctively he wasn't there.

Briefly, she wondered if he had come home last night, then gotten up early and left again. But the smooth surface of the bed covers on his side told her that hadn't happened.

More curious than concerned, she climbed out of bed, slipped a blue-green checked robe over the extra-large T-shirt she wore at night, and padded down the hallway toward the den. Perhaps he had come in late and decided to sleep on the sofa. Always considerate, he'd done that a few times during their marriage to keep from disturbing her.

She passed the small living room at the front of the house. No Jack there. Flipping her hair from her eyes and biting her upper lip, she moved to the den. Again, no Jack. Okay. She paused to think. Where to look next? Katie's room?

Her stride longer and more deliberate, she moved back down the hallway to the last room on the left. Sticking her head inside, she saw Katie, sun streaming in on her freckled face, sleeping deeply. But no Jack. Only one more place to check. Daniel's room.

Though knowing it wasn't likely, she moved across the hall to the room on the back side of the house. Her hand trembling slightly for reasons she couldn't quite identify, she twisted the doorknob and walked into the clutter of her teenager's domain. Basketball shoes and dirty clothes lay all over the floor, and she made a mental note to make him clean up the place after she woke him. Daniel himself, all five-feet-nine of him, his right arm thrown over the bed like a loose string, snored slightly. A baseball lay on the floor near his hand. She smiled. Daniel kept a baseball in his hand most of the time.

Jack was nowhere to be seen.

Working to control the fears now building inside, she leaned against the wall and rubbed her forehead. Where could Jack be? What could keep him out all night? Business? Certainly not the store. The city council? No, that meeting had ended about nine or so. She had watched the reruns last night about ten. Had even seen Jack for a second as the camera focused on the scattered audience.

If not busy with the store or the council, then what? He said he had to meet someone, but he never identified anybody. Had that meeting lasted all night? If so, why hadn't he called? He always called when his plans changed. Jack would have called unless . . . unless something kept him from calling . . . unless—

Connie remembered the anonymous phone calls that had invaded their home over the last few weeks. Did those calls have anything to do with Jack's absence? Had someone—?

She shook her head, trying to push away the thought, but it refused to leave. Her mouth suddenly dry and her heart picking up pace, she backed out of Daniel's room and rushed to the kitchen. Once there, she grabbed the phone book off the counter by the refrigerator, looked up the number of the police department, and dialed. A woman answered.

"My husband is missing!" Connie panted. "He was supposed to come home last night, he—"

"Slow down, honey," said the woman on the other end. "Give me your name."

"Connie Brandon," she said, her words gushing out. "My husband is Jack Brandon, he was supposed to get home last night, but he's not here yet, he—"

"When did you last talk to him?"

"At around five yesterday. He said he'd get home late, but he never said all night. I just know something's wrong, it's not like Jack—"

"Men often stay out longer than they say they will, honey. Then they come traipsing in the next day with a story they stick to no matter what. Maybe you should calm down and wait on him to show up."

Connie gritted her teeth. She didn't want to sound rude, but this woman didn't know Jack like she did. And the honey reference—well, that was certainly less than professional. If the cop was right and Jack had simply stayed out without giving her a reason and without calling, then something was terribly wrong with her marriage. But if the dispatcher was wrong, then . . .

Connie didn't even want to think about that possibility. To her horror, she found herself hoping that Jack *had* deliberately disappeared for a night without telling her why. At least then she could be sure of his safety.

"Jack wouldn't do that," she said, though hoping he had. "If he said he'd come home at midnight, he would unless something happened. You see, we've had some threatening calls in the last few weeks, anonymous calls. You should have a record of them. We reported the problem a few weeks ago."

"Calls?"

"Yes, threatening phone calls. Check your records."

"Hang on a second."

Connie took a deep breath and twisted the phone cord in her hands while she waited. She couldn't imagine Jack staying out all night without calling her.

"We've got a record here," said the policewoman.

Connie stood up straighter and dropped the phone cord.

The woman continued. "Says here you got some anonymous calls about your husband's antigambling activities. But your husband wouldn't allow us to put a trace on the phone. That right?"

"Yes, he figured the calls were harmless, said they were just pranks, nothing more. I tried to tell him—"

"You say you last talked to him when?"

"About five yesterday."

"And he said he'd get home late?"

"Yes, but he's not here."

The officer hesitated for several seconds. Connie heard a door close. She almost dropped the phone, but then saw Katie poke her head into the kitchen. Connie put her finger over her lips, giving Katie the "shush" sign. Katie padded across the room and snuggled up to her. Connie pulled her close.

"I'll get an alert out," said the woman, her voice more understanding. "The patrol officers will keep their eyes open. You just stay calm. Mr. Brandon will probably come home any minute now and explain it all to you. If he's not home in an hour or so, call back. We'll see what the situation is then. That okay?"

Connie nodded and patted Katie's head. "Sure, okay. I guess there's nothing else we can do."

"Not for now. Just stay calm if you can. We'll be in touch if anything turns up."

Connie hung up the phone and, not knowing what to do next, turned to Katie. No reason to go off the deep end. Stay calm like the dispatcher suggested. Go about your normal routines. When Jack came home he would clear up all the mystery. Convinced for the time being, Connie forced herself to smile. Then, lifting Katie to her hip, she trudged down the hallway to wake Daniel from his slumbers and put him to work cleaning up his filthy room.

*****

It took the police almost fifteen minutes to get to Adrian's Island. To reach it, they parked at the railroad station and picked their way across the tracks and over the narrow strip of temporarily dried ground between the tracks and the island. In wetter springs, they would have taken a small boat. Immediately behind the cops, four ambulance attendants and a coroner arrived, wearing puzzled expressions on their tightly drawn faces. The lead cop, a burly man with a mustache the color of corn silk and a head as bald and round as a volleyball, stepped through the thick underbrush and shook Sanks's hand.

Sanks nodded toward the body. "I didn't touch anything but his throat," he said. "Thought I should check the pulse."

The cop nodded. "He's dead?"

Sanks checked the policeman's name tag. "Garner." "Yeah, I think so," Sanks said.

Garner motioned to the EMTs behind him. "Check him, guys," he said.

He turned back to Sanks. "You just find him?"

"Yeah, less than an hour ago. I was checking my trotlines, trying to bring in a few catfish. They love these shoots here between the river and the island. . . . Saw something I didn't recognize, you know it just didn't fit. I eased my old boat a bit closer, spotted the body . . . thought I should help if I could."

"You did the right thing," said Garner.

Sanks took a deep breath.

"He's got identification!"

Sanks and Garner turned to the EMT working over the body. The EMT, his hand sheathed in a rubber glove, held a wallet over his head. Walking away from Sanks, Garner yanked a pair of gloves from his back pocket, slipped them on, and stepped to the EMT. He took the wallet from the technician and, with deliberate care, held it by one corner and flipped it open. Inside, he found a Missouri driver's license. Ever so cautiously, he pulled out the license and studied the man in the picture on the license. After several seconds, he reinserted the license and handed the wallet back to the technician. Then, his wide hands rubbing his bald head, he sank down onto a stump and sighed heavily.

"It's Jack," he said to no one in particular, his voice tinged with sadness. "Jack Brandon."

"The guy who's so set against gambling?" asked Sanks.

"The same," said Garner. "You know him?"

"Nope, just read his name in the paper. What about you?"

Garner dropped his head and studied his boots. "Yeah, I know him. I go to church with him. His wife and my wife are best friends, and he's the finest Christian man I've ever known."

*****

Looking out her bedroom window, Connie saw Tick Garner turn his squad car into her driveway. She slipped a kelly green blouse over her head, smoothed down the front of her khaki slacks, and pushed her hair off her forehead. Then, her breath coming in short gasps, she hurried to the front door. For a moment, she thought of calling the kids away from the television in the den, then decided against it. If Tick had some news about Jack, good or bad, she should hear it first, then tell Katie and Daniel. No reason to disturb them until she knew what was going on.

She opened the door just as Tick stepped up to ring the bell. As the door swung open, he averted his eyes from hers and studied the tips of his shoes.

"Come on in, Tick," she said, her voice thin with nerves. "Have a seat." She gestured toward a gold wing chair that sat across from a flame-stitched sofa in her small living room.

Tick quickly followed her instructions, dropping his stocky frame in the chair, his eyes still busy with his feet. Placing herself squarely across from him, Connie took a deep breath and waited for Tick to speak. It took him a couple of seconds, but he finally raised his eyes to meet hers. Connie read them instantly, their dull sadness communicating as clearly as a blaring head-line from a newspaper. Connie's heart skipped.

"I . . . I don't know what to say," Tick stammered. "Tess is on the way . . . I started to wait for her, but she . . . well, she's on the way."

Connie bit her upper lip. Tick rubbed his head, and Connie saw he couldn't say what she already knew. She swallowed hard, her emotions going on a kind of sabbatical, momentarily leaving her without feelings. For a second, she felt like a nine year old in a new school again, that feeling that dominated her early years—the result of moving five times in ten years—a turtlelike urge to go into a protective shell of neutrality, to feel nothing lest the loneliness and fear destroy her. Her mind blank, she heard herself telling Tick to get it over.

"Go ahead, Tick. Say what you came to say."

Tick's words destroyed her shield.

"I'm sorry, Connie," he said, his eyes moist. "We found Jack."

Connie caught her breath, her hands wrapping around her stomach. "You found him?" she asked. "Is he . . . ?" She couldn't bring herself to finish the question.

Tick dropped his eyes and rubbed his head. "I don't know how to say this, but . . . but I guess I just say it, Connie . . . Jack's dead."

Connie doubled over and fell toward the floor. Jumping from his seat, Tick caught her as she fell, her bright red hair spilling softly against his thick arms. For an instant, she thought she would lose consciousness. Black dots swirled before her eyes, and a feeling of numbness moved through her legs. Gasping for air, she briefly craved the black void a faint would bring, the escape from the hurt that closing her eyes and never opening them again would offer. But then two faces replaced the black dots, and she knew she couldn't give up so easily. She couldn't give up because a son named Daniel and a daughter named Katie needed her now more than ever.

With her children's faces calling her back, Connie found a surprising strength. The words of Philippians 4:13 rushed through her head, and she seized them as a starving woman grabbing a piece of bread. "I can do all things through Christ who strengthens me." Fortified by the words, she pushed away from Tick and squared her shoulders. Tears dripped down her cheeks, but she didn't feel faint any longer. She eased back down into her seat, and Tick sat across from her.

"Tell me everything you know," she said, her voice weak but audible. "What happened?"

"A guy out fishing this morning found him on Adrian's Island."

"Adrian's Island? How in the world would he get there?"

She thought instantly of a car accident. Had Jack somehow driven off the bridge, climbed from his truck, then drowned?

"We don't have many answers yet," said Tick. "I just left him. The coroner was taking him to the . . . well, to the city morgue. As soon as we can, we'll get him up to Columbia for an autopsy. That will give us the details."

Connie found herself amazingly composed. She had always had an ability to do this, calm herself in the midst of chaos, but to manage it in the aftermath of this news stunned her somewhat. Though she suspected she would fall apart later, she stared at Tick with a clarity that seemed almost supernatural. Of course, she thought to herself, it was supernatural. Then she reached a most logical conclusion.

"They murdered him," she said, her voice routine.

Tick's silken mustache twitched downward. "You think somebody killed Jack?" he asked.

Connie didn't flinch. "I have no doubt," she said. "Everyone believes these gambling people have Mob connections. Blacker, their lawyer, represents suspicious clients. The newspapers reported it. Jack's arguments have convinced a lot of people. The gamblers are afraid they might lose in a few weeks."

"You think they'd go this far, murder a guy just because he opposed their plans to bring a casino to Jefferson City?"

"You're the policeman," said Connie, but without animosity. "You know that boats like the one they want to bring here can gross fifty to sixty million dollars a year. Wouldn't they kill for that kind of money?"

Tick shrugged. "Sure they would."

Connie nodded, sure of her conclusions. She stared hard at Tick. "You know they did it," she insisted.

He paused for a beat, then shook his head. "It's too early to jump to those conclusions," he said. "We just found him a few minutes ago. I came right over here."

"I know the gamblers did it," said Connie, her voice rising as her words picked up pace. "They've been threatening Jack for weeks! You go after them, Tick, they're the only ones who would want Jack dead! They did it, I know it, go after them—"

"We'll find the killer," Tick cut her off. "If that's what happened. But that's not what we need to worry about right now. For now, we need to get you to Jack and take care of the kids. Let the other stuff sort itself out in due time."

Though not mollified, Connie knew Tick was right. The police would take care of the murder. She had to take care of her family.

"You said the coroner had Jack," she said, forcing herself to calm down.

"Yeah, at the morgue. Later today, they'll most likely take him to Columbia. Better investigation facilities there. Probably start an autopsy Monday morning."

"Can I see him now?"

"Whenever you want."

Connie bit her lip, then said, "Give me a minute here."

He nodded, and she stood and walked away, through the dining room on the back of the house to the deck just past the back door. Stepping onto the deck, she stared off toward the Missouri River. On most days, the view of the river made her happy, helped her mark the passage of life. She loved the gentle flow of the water in late summer, the gradual cooling off in the fall, the sharp ice of winter white, and the wild rush of spring flood. Today, though, the river seemed strange to her, its dark water a symbol of mystery and danger.

Connie stared down at the water and thought of Jack. He had meant everything to her, encouraging her in ways no one ever had. He saw strength in the brown eyes of the young woman behind the big black glasses. He saw her hair and called her Sunset instead of Carrot Top like others. He saw thoughtfulness behind her shyness and power in her small-frame body.

"You're not a truck," he joked on the occasions when her temper flared at him or one of the kids, "but you're not a Tinkertoy either."

With his encouragement, she had gradually come to agree. Though not tall, neither was she frail. Daily walks of three to four miles with Jack toned her legs, and light arm weights, pumped as she walked, firmed up her arms. Lean, tight muscles rippled on her one hundred five pounds, giving her strength greater than her stature suggested.

Again, with Jack's eager support, she had resumed her education the year Daniel started kindergarten. Though coming to Jefferson City from Ft. Leonard Wood to begin her schooling at Lincoln, she had stopped after two years to marry Jack. But then, after Daniel started school, she took it up again. Attending classes primarily in the morning so she could meet Daniel when he came home, she made steady progress. By the time she became pregnant with Katie, she had finished her history degree.

Though not having any specific plans to work outside the home, she continued to look ahead after Katie's birth. The year Katie turned two, she made the surprising choice to attend law school. She liked the logic of legal argument, the intricacies of the discussion of what words meant and could mean.

After a couple of months studying for the law boards, an even bigger surprise came her way. She took the test and made a score in the ninetieth percentile of all who took it. Acceptance at the University of Missouri Law School followed, and the years rolled by as she balanced family and education. With Jack's help, she managed to take enough early morning and night classes to minimize her time away from the family.

Though it had taken almost six years, her scheduled graduation loomed only a few weeks away, and the bar exam waited in the fall. What happened next, she didn't know. One local law firm had suggested she work half-days for them or even do consultation from home. She didn't know if either would prove feasible, but she did know she wouldn't accept any job that demanded she cheat her children or Jack.

Through it all, Jack had encouraged her to do what she thought the Lord wanted. Raising the kids was holy work, but since they were now well into their schooling, she had some free time and she should use it to utilize her gifts fully. If that meant staying home, then wonderful. If that meant a job outside the home, and she could work and still serve her family, then so be it. He simply wanted her to know he stood behind her whatever she decided.

Connie sighed and tears welled up in her eyes. The Missouri River rushed on. She knew she would never again hear Jack's eager laughter, feel his warmth, smell his skin. Jack was dead, and she had to live with it.

She wiped her eyes, turned from the river, and stepped back inside. In the living room, she faced Tick again. "I need to tell the kids before I do anything else," she said.

Tick nodded. "You want me with you?"

"No, this is my job."

Tick rubbed his head. "You want me to stay until Tess gets here?"

Connie rubbed her eyes again and thought of her best friend. Skinny and bleached blonde, Tess was as sassy as Connie was shy and had been like an older sister to her ever since she and Tick moved from Sedalia and joined their church. Though Tick and Jack weren't as close as she and Tess, that didn't matter. She admired the lead-with-the-chin way Tess attacked life and laughingly appreciated the bright clothes Tess always wore, the rings on three fingers of each hand. You knew when Tess Garner entered a room and noticed when she left. But, even with all the flash, Tess's heart pulsed pure gold.

Through Tess, Connie knew and loved Tick. Grateful he had come to her instead of some stranger, she opened her arms and walked to him. Tick stood up and opened his arms too. Connie leaned into them, and he hugged her, his burly arms strong but gentle. Connie relaxed for a second and then began to cry harder, her body shaking with the grief that suddenly overwhelmed her. As the tears cascaded down her chin, she thought of her children. With a silent prayer for strength, she rested against Tick for one more minute, knowing it might be her last minute of solace for a long time to come.

CHAPTER

5

The funeral, delayed an extra day to allow completion of the autopsy, was held on Wednesday afternoon at three o'clock at the River City Community Church. Dressed in a solid black dress and jacket, Connie sat on the front row, two rows up from her normal spot. She kept her arms around Daniel and Katie and fought to maintain her composure. Over the last four days, she had cried enough to bring the Missouri River to flood stage, most of it within the hour after she told the children their daddy would never come home again. That had been the worst of it.

Since then, her tears had fallen sporadically and with much less power than the initial outburst. At the moment, she felt cried out, as if something told her to postpone the rest of her mourning until a less demanding time. To be honest, she accepted that feeling, liked it even. She wanted to hold herself together, not because she thought that showed any more strength than wailing her eyes out but because circumstances demanded it, and she didn't want to run from the circumstances.

Content with her emotions, Connie listened as the choir began to sing:

"O God our help in ages past, our hope for years to come, A shelter from the stormy blast and our eternal home. . . . " With the words echoing in her soul, she let her thoughts drift back to the awful experience of telling Daniel and Katie that their daddy was dead . . .

Leaving Tick in the living room, she had wiped her eyes, taken several deep breaths, and stepped into the den. After flipping off the television, she directed Daniel and Katie to the sofa and pulled up an ottoman between them. Katie stared at her with her big bug eyes, the picture of naive curiosity. Daniel, on the other hand, slouched his lean frame down in the sofa, his blond head with its buzz cut tilted onto his right shoulder and a baseball in his left hand. For a second, Connie just looked at him. Though already taller, he looked as much like Jack as Katie looked like her. Jack loved his son's size and so did she. It made it possible for him to star in sports, baseball especially. A left-hander, he pitched for the Babe Ruth League team and won almost every game he started.

With her right hand on Daniel's knee, she reached out with her left and patted Katie's arm. Biting her lip, she inhaled deeply again, breathed a silent prayer for courage, and then began to speak. Her voice stayed steady at first.

"I don't know how to say this," she began. "But something bad has happened to Daddy." She paused, but neither of them interrupted her. She swallowed, then continued. "Daddy won't be coming home. . . . Daddy is, well, Daddy is with the Lord. He's . . . he's dead."

Daniel jumped involuntarily, as if someone had stuck a needle into his back. One lone tear climbed into Katie's left eye. It hung there like a piece of crystal balanced at the corner of one of her chocolate eyes. Neither of them said anything. Connie waited several seconds for them to speak, but neither did. She spoke again. This time her throat weakened, and she began to sob.

"Tick . . . Tick told me . . . He found Daddy a little bit ago."

"What happened to Daddy?" It was Katie who asked, her voice tiny in the face of such horrifying news.

Connie lowered her eyes for an instant, then faced Katie again. No use hiding the truth. She would hear it soon enough. Better to come from her than anyone else. "It's really sad, honey," she said, her eyes beginning to seep tears. "But I think . . . I think . . . a really bad person killed Daddy."

"But why would they do that?" Katie asked, her curiosity momentarily overcoming her anguish. "Everybody likes Daddy."

For the first time, Daniel spoke. His voice was choking, but strong, filled with grief and anger. "Not everybody liked him!" he moaned. "The people who want gambling here don't like him! They wanted him to shut up. I bet they're the ones who did this, they killed Dad, I know they did! They're the ones the cops need to go after, Tick needs to go after them and kill them just like they did Dad, they—"

Connie let go of his knee and pressed her index finger to her lips. "Shhhh." She tried to calm him, and herself as well. "Shhhh. We'll get through this, I don't know how . . . but somehow, with the Lord's help . . . somehow we'll get through this."

Daniel closed his eyes and dropped his chin to his chest, obviously trying to hide his emotions. Watching him, Connie bit her lip, forcing herself to hold back her own suspicions. The easiest thing in the world would be to blow up in front of her kids and spew out the bitterness she felt for those she suspected had murdered her beloved husband. No one would blame her if she did. But she wouldn't do it. Not because she wasn't as prone to such anger as anyone else, and not because she didn't think she knew who had killed Jack. But because she didn't want her children's lives scarred by her own desire for revenge. The way she reacted to this would help teach Daniel and Katie how to respond to the worst life could bring. Hatred in her would sow hatred in them. She didn't want to plant that seed. Who knew what it would produce in the years to come?

She rocked forward and took Daniel's chin in her hands, lifting his head and staring into his blue eyes. For a few seconds, her tears stopped, and she managed to speak clearly.

"You're right, honey," she agreed, her voice soothing. "Those people didn't like Daddy. And I suspect they're involved in this. But we don't know that for sure. So we'll just have to wait and let the cops handle it, let Tick see to it. We've got other things to worry about right now, don't you think?"

For a long second, Daniel didn't respond. Connie tried to read his expression. His eyes were wet with tears, but his chin was set. She wasn't sure what she saw in his face, either cold hatred or grim determination, she couldn't tell which.

Then Daniel nodded. "Okay, Mom," he said, his voice choking. "We'll let Tick . . . Tick can handle it. But we've got to tell him what we know. We've got to find who killed Daddy."

Connie stroked his cheek, then rose from the ottoman, lifted Katie, sat her on her lap and took a spot beside Daniel. Reaching again for Daniel's hand, she lay her head against the sofa back. Silence came over all three of them. Not knowing what else to say, Connie simply prayed to herself. God promised believers strength beyond all understanding. God promised believers they would never receive more than their shoulders could bear. God promised believers grace sufficient for every need.

As her eyes began to gush again, Connie realized she would now discover the truth or the lie of each of those promises. Still praying, she squeezed her baby girl, held her teenage son's hand, and let the tears roll out. For almost the whole next hour, the minutes before Tess came, the three of them remained there, a trio of misery, locked together in a mutual sadness, the three of them crying and wailing and shedding tears until the sofa turned wet with their grief.

That hour had been the worst of it so far, and she had held her tears in check for the most part since. That didn't surprise or concern her. She had learned a long time ago to balance her emotions, to let them loose for a season and then chain them up again. As a military brat, she skipped from place to place with her mom and dad like a rock skipping water, and her education included more schools than she could remember. The lessons of living as the new kid became ingrained in her soul. By the time she graduated from high school and her mom and dad divorced, she had learned to handle whatever life brought, to cry when allowed, but to take care of business when circumstances demanded it.

The last four days had forced her to take care of business, and she did. Identifying the body. Tess, who instantly took leave from her state job in the Social Security Department to stay with her, helped her through that. Making sure someone stayed with the kids. Miss Everhart, bless her sweet soul. Handling funeral arrangements. Reverend Wallace made that job easier, putting his forty-five years of ministry experience at her disposal. He sat with her all day Saturday, even though he had a sermon to preach the next day. He prayed with her time and time again, his sixty-six-year-old voice asking God for grace and strength. He held her with his gnarled hands—the hands aged by long hours in the sun as he worked his garden each summer. He contacted the remains of her scattered family.

That job didn't take long. Neither she nor Anita, her mom, knew where her father lived. Though not an official orphan like Jack, Connie had felt like one most of her life. Anita, drawn to the bottle to escape the loneliness of one too many army bases, provided little nurture to her only child. Having remarried and settled in Seattle the year after Connie moved to Jefferson City, she hardly ever called. When Reverend Wallace informed her of Jack's death, she agreed to come to the funeral only after Connie assured her she could leave the evening of the burial. Her husband didn't want her away any longer than necessary.

Fortunately, Connie's friends made up for her mother's lack of support. A whole gang of church ladies came over to manage the normal household duties. Setting up a chart, Tess organized them into an efficient brigade. They established shifts to cook, clean, wash clothes, and stay over for the night. Tess, carrying a small suitcase into the only unused room in the house, set up shop and glued herself to Connie, leaving her only to oversee the work crew. Grateful for the companionship, Connie let Tess run the house, and Tess didn't let her down.

Neither did Tick. Protecting her from the brunt of the police investigation now fully under way, he led her through a series of questions about Jack's disappearance—when she saw him last, talked to him last, expected him home—all the questions the authorities need to ask. On Sunday a group of lab technicians and a detective named Luke Tyler came to search through her house, but she was at the funeral home at the time and didn't even meet them.

"No problem," Tick told her when she came home and found out she had missed the detective. "I asked you the same questions Tyler will. He said for you to get through the funeral, he'll see you the next day."

"Is he finding anything?" she asked.

Tick shook his bald head. "Not yet, but we're just getting started. Tyler will come back here before the week ends. With the funeral and all, he didn't want to upset people by tearing things up too much here or at the store. But something will turn up, I know it will."

Her energy directed elsewhere, Connie had worried little about the investigation. She would focus on it after the funeral. For now, the kids consumed her every thought.

Spending all her free time with Daniel and Katie, Connie somehow made it through the days that separated her from the moment she learned of Jack's death and the moment she now faced, the moment of his burial. Gritting her teeth, she held back the tears and forced herself to pay attention to Reverend Wallace's concluding remarks.

"I cannot answer the question that plagues all of us today," he said. "I cannot answer the question 'Why?' That question is beyond the human mind to answer. But I can point you to the One who knows the answer to all the questions. I can point you to the Lord's grace, a grace we are told is sufficient for all our needs.

"In times like this we find out the truth of that great promise. My prayer is that you will do just that, that you will discover its truth and hold tight to it in the days to come. May you hold tight to the truth that Jesus Christ is the resurrection and the life and those who believe in Him will never die. With that truth you will find your hope and your comfort. Shall we pray."

Connie bowed her head, and the pastor prayed. Behind her, she heard muffled sobs. Friends filled the church—merchants and city workers from downtown Jefferson City who came into the store every day; fellow elders and deacons from the church, all arranged in a row, their faces heavy with grief; government officials of all levels.

Directly behind her sat Tick and Tess, a steady reminder of their love and care. Beside Tess sat Anita, her eyes bloodshot from one too many drinks. She had arrived alone at ten that morning, informing Connie immediately that she had to leave on a nine o'clock flight. *So much for maternal love,* Connie thought. She knew she needed to forgive her mom. Life had dealt Anita a tough hand. But right now, Connie couldn't do it. Right now she simply mourned the estrangement and vowed to do whatever necessary to keep it from happening to her and her children.

Behind Anita sat Wilt Carver, one of Jack's best friends. Wilt, the state attorney general, had come by the house on

Saturday afternoon, his handsome face creased with sadness. Telling Connie to call if she needed anything, anything at all, he stayed for almost an hour and grieved with her. With his wife on one side and his mother and father on the other, his presence assured her Jack's murder would receive all due attention from people in high places.

Feeling Daniel on her shoulder and Katie snuggling against her side, Connie tried to focus on Reverend Wallace's prayer, but her mind continued to wander. In the next few days she had to talk to Detective Tyler, though she didn't know what she could tell him. He already knew about the phone calls.

Reverend Wallace concluded his prayer, and Connie jerked her thoughts back to the present.

"So keep us strong, O Lord. In the name of Jesus who loves us all, we pray. Amen."

Opening her eyes, Connie stood and waited while the pall-bearers moved to the coffin. Then, holding tightly to Daniel and Katie, she followed Jack's casket to the hearse. Everything seemed to move in slow motion, as if a movie producer had deliberately altered the film to make the moments creep by. Climbing into the backseat of a silver limousine, she saw people moving past her, but none of them looked real. People she had known for years appeared waxen to her, pale imitations of human beings, clones of people she once knew, but clones without personalities, false figures with no insides. She watched the clones climb into their cars and felt like a clone herself.

She spotted Cedric Blacker crossing the street, wearing a dark black suit with a crisp white shirt underneath. His presence shook her out of her stupor. She bit her lip to keep from rolling down the window and blasting him with her suspicions. How dare he come to Jack's funeral! Digging her fingers into her stomach, she held back, choking the emotion threatening to spill out in white heat.

The funeral director slid into the front seat and turned to her. "You ready, Mrs. Brandon?"

Connie nodded, grateful he had distracted her from Blacker. The funeral director pulled the car out of the lot. Connie wrapped her arms around Katie and held Daniel by the hand. None of them spoke. The limousine fell in behind a police car and turned left, headed to the cemetery.

Resting her head against the seat, Connie closed her eyes and prayed for her children. They had stayed so quiet the last three days. In a way, Connie expected as much. Not knowing how to react, they pretty much kept to themselves. Several of Daniel's friends came and parked themselves at the house, sleeping on the floor, hovering over Daniel like defenders of a wounded member of the herd. Though Connie saw him talking to them, he kept silent around her. That didn't really bother her. She had more than enough to do and his friends kept him busy. But, as soon as this funeral ended, she planned to create more time with him, make sure he knew of her support.

To her left, Connie noticed a milk truck pull over and stop. She sighed, wondering if the man in the truck knew the identity of the one he honored by his small act of respect. Probably not. Just a gesture, a tip of the hat from one life to another, an acknowledgment that we're all tied up in this together, even if we don't know one person from the next. The funeral limo left the truck behind and turned right, moving through a row of maple trees just beginning to wear their spring green.

Connie hugged Katie closer. Her dark blue dress, starched tightly, crinkled against her shoulder. Connie bit her lip. Little Katie would forget so much about her daddy. The passing years would wash away most of what she now remembered. Connie hated to think of that, but knew she could do little to change it. Her only solace came from knowing that the same years that wiped away Katie's memories would also wash away the worst of her grief. In many ways, her age gave her an advantage. Katie was plenty old enough to grieve but still young enough to recover from it.

For a second, Connie thought of her own childhood. She had done that a good bit over the last two days. No deep ties to her parents, no grandparents alive, and no aunts or uncles close enough to know. Somehow though, in spite of the loneliness of her childhood, she had survived those years. Her father's military stoicism gave her a strong dose of discipline even if it lacked the tempering of much love. Given the circumstances, Connie knew she had received as much care as many children did, and her sadness over her youth had dimmed over time. She trusted Katie would do okay, too, but she didn't know for sure.

After all, her parents hadn't disappeared because of the act of another human being. What happened to them happened because of their own choices, their own failures. But Jack, she felt certain, had died at the hands of another human being, through an act of pure evil. A murder could make a child afraid to live.

The funeral car turned right and passed through a stone gate. Seeing the wrought iron over the gate, Connie suddenly realized they had reached the cemetery. She gulped, then bit her lip. The car pulled past a number of headstones, then made a final left turn and came to a stop.

"Wait here a minute," said the funeral director. "We'll let everyone else get out; then we'll come for you."

Connie watched him climb out. She cleared her throat.

"This part is almost over," she said, looking first to Katie and then to Daniel. "Just the committal service left."

"What's a committal service?" asked Katie.

Connie inhaled, then breathed it out. "It's where we commit Daddy back to God," she said. "We leave Daddy here in the cemetery, and God takes care of him."

"Didn't God always take care of Daddy?"

Connie paused, the question taking her off guard. Though not sure if Katie saw the implications of what she asked, Connie certainly did. If God always took care of Daddy, then what happened the night Daddy died?

"Yes, God did take care of Daddy," she said, trying to formulate her answer as she talked. "But some bad people didn't do what God wanted them to do. They did something God doesn't like."

"Does God let people do that?" Katie pressed.

"Yes, God lets people do bad things. Not because God wants them to do the bad things, but because the people don't love God like they should."

Katie scrunched her face, obviously pondering Connie's response. The door on her left suddenly opened and the funeral director stuck his head inside.

"Are you ready?" he asked.

Connie glanced at Daniel. He nodded, his shoulders erect in his navy suit, white shirt, and yellow tie. She took Katie's hand. "It's time to go, sweetheart," she said. Daniel slid across the seat and stepped out of the car. Katie followed him. Connie trailed them both. Then, hand in hand, they moved over the soft grass, one step at a time behind the funeral director, who led them to Reverend Wallace. At a nod from the pastor, they took their places behind the casket, trailing it as it moved closer and closer toward a green canopy that covered four rows of folding chairs.

At the chairs, they took a seat in the front row and stared straight ahead. Around them, a circle of friends made a protective barrier, as if by their circle they could block out the hurt of the world beyond their enclosure. In the center of the circle and directly in front of Connie, Jack's casket rested on a quartet of silver bars raised about three feet off the ground. Connie knew what lay below the bars—a hole big enough to bury the box that held the body of her precious Jack. She dabbed her eyes with a handkerchief and forced herself to think of something else.

Reverend Wallace began to read Scripture. "The Lord is my shepherd; I shall not want. He makes me to . . ."

Connie quietly began to sob. Daniel tightened his grip on her hand. Katie shook against her shoulder.

The preacher read, "Yea, though I walk through the valley of the shadow of death, I will fear no evil; For You are with me; Your rod and Your staff, they comfort me. . . . "

Connie slipped a pair of sunglasses from her jacket pocket and placed them over her eyes. The preacher finished the twenty-third Psalm and began to pray.

"Now, O God, we leave this believer in Your hands. Just as You created him forty years ago for life upon this earth, so You have now re-created him anew for life in Your own heavenly kingdom. We need no longer concern ourselves with his destiny. We know that he is alive forever.

"We pray now for the future of his wife and children. Grant to them Your eternal presence and divine strength. Without these, they cannot go on. With them, they will not falter. Give them now the abiding and comforting and consoling word that in Jesus Christ there is life and life eternally. In the name of the Father and the Son and the Holy Spirit. Amen."

With a collective sigh of relief, the crowd opened its eyes. Connie felt the people watching her. For an instant, she didn't move. She stared around the circle of her friends, nodding ever so slightly to first this one and then another. She recognized all of them, good people, people who had attended church with them, who had shopped at Jack's store, who had made their lives peaceful and happy in this gentle community. Not every one of these people had agreed with Jack about gambling, of course. A few had even challenged him openly, in public forums when he had made his position clear.

A scary thought occurred to Connie. A number of these people stood to make money if gambling moved into Jefferson City. Did any of them have enough at stake to want Jack out of the way? She searched the crowd for Cedric Blacker, then noted with relief that he hadn't come to the graveside. Good. She didn't want him here.

She gazed across the crowd again. Was it possible someone here had done a despicable deed from a purely selfish motive? Shuddering, she dropped her eyes and decided the time had come to leave. The time to walk away, to trust Jack to the God he loved, the time, somehow, to get on with her life. Help the police find Jack's killer, take care of her children, start her law practice, run the Good Books Store . . .

She stood up, Daniel and Katie moving with her. Her black pumps slipping a bit on the green astro turf under her feet, she stepped to the casket. Then, standing by the coffin, she leaned forward and whispered, her voice so low no one but the dead could hear it.

"Jack, this is Sunset," she choked. "I loved you the day I met you in church, and I'll love you until the day I die. I'll do my best to take care of the kids. I'll teach them what you tried to teach them. I'll try my hardest to keep them close to God. I'll insist that no matter what, they do what's right."

She paused one final second. It didn't seem right to leave just yet, to turn her back and walk away, to abandon Jack to the deep hole under the coffin. But what else could she do? Death did this to people; it separated them, cut asunder their relationship, destroyed the unity they shared.

A sense of panic hit her and she swayed for a moment. What else could she say? A sudden inspiration came to her and a bemused smile tickled her face. The notion seemed out of place, but, at the same time, it somehow fit what Jack might have wanted. Steadying herself, she bent close to the casket. Her lips almost touched the finely grained cherry wood that enclosed Jack's body. She whispered to him, speaking again the words he spoke to her the night of their first date when he took her to the grocery store after church to get ice cream.

"Just think, Jack," she said, her eyes wet with a strange combination of grief and remembrance. "Just what you've always wanted. In heaven, you can eat all the ice cream you want and never get fat."

Hoping with all her heart that Jack's often-stated joke about heaven was now proven correct, she moved away from the coffin, Daniel and Katie in tow. Within seconds, she reached the funeral car and sagged into the backseat. Exhausted from holding in her emotions, she hardly moved as friend after friend came by to offer last-minute words of encouragement, last-minute prayers for comfort, and last-minute commitments to help her when she needed it. For only a few did she really rouse herself.

When Wilt Carver stepped to the car, she raised up and greeted him warmly. Jack cared for this man, a friend since high school days in Miller. Wilt, his dark hair now streaked slightly with gray, hugged her tightly.

"I'm going to miss him so much, Connie," he moaned, his eyes moist. "He and I have known each other a long time."

Connie's heart hurt for the man. Though the son of one of the wealthiest families in Missouri and on track to serve as governor or senator of the state, Wilt Carver had his own set of problems. His wife, though with him today, had left him recently, then returned. Rumor was their problems hadn't ended. She resented the influence Wilt's father allegedly imposed on their marriage and wanted some space between the two families. But, given Wilt's obvious political dreams and his family's even more obvious power and finances, such independence seemed impossible.

Her threats to leave again kept the political corridors buzzing. That kind of trouble could dim a man's political star, even one with the advantages Wilt enjoyed. To add to that, a good friend turned up murdered.

"Jack really liked you, Wilt," she said. "He prayed for you often."

Wilt nodded. "I need those prayers," he said. "Now more than ever. What with Vicky leaving me and all."

Though unsure about the timing, Connie felt a sudden urge to do what she thought Jack would do in this kind of situation.

"You know what you need, Wilt," she said. "You need the grace the Lord gives us. Nothing else can give us the peace we all want, the sense of comfort."

"You sound like Jack," he said. "He told me that over and over."

"He was right, you know. That's what we all need."

Wilt raked his fingers through his hair. "I'm thinking about it," he said.

"Good, I'll pray for you to do more than think."

Wilt moved away, and the line of people shuffled ahead another step. Gradually, the crowd eased past Connie, its chatter dying in the afternoon sun. In like fashion, a succession of car engines coughed to action, then moved away, carrying their occupants back to the normalcy of lives untouched by the grim specter of a murdered loved one. Connie heard them leaving and her mind slipped away. She mouthed expressions of thanks and comments of appreciation, but the faces ran together and she noticed only a few of them. Then she heard a familiar voice and made herself focus again. Dabbing her eyes, she saw Tick Garner stick his head into the door. Behind him stood Tess, wringing her hands, a distant look in her eyes.

"Can I see you just one minute?" Tick asked, a scowl creasing his bald head.

Her senses dulled, Connie didn't understand at first that he wanted her to step out of the car. But something in his posture nudged her to attention, told her he wanted to say something for her ears only.

"I'll be just a minute," she said to Daniel and Katie, sitting by her. Neither of them argued. They were as worn out as she.

Stepping from the limo, she followed Tick to a spot a good twenty feet away. Tess walked beside her, a comforting hand on her back. When they stopped, Tick began to scuff his shoes at the ground, his eyes evasive. Connie waited, giving him time to say his piece. From his manner, she guessed it had to do with the investigation. Did they have a suspect? Maybe even an arrest?

Her adrenaline surged and she stretched forward, almost on her tiptoes. She glanced at Tess, looking for a clue, but she revealed nothing.

"Okay," she pressed, her impatience getting the best of her. "You got me out here. What's up?"

Tick cleared his throat and rubbed his head. "It's hard, Connie," he started. "But . . . but it looks . . . looks like Jack committed suicide."

This time, she couldn't stop herself. She collapsed to the ground as if dead, her last thought that a black miracle had occurred, that somehow by a strange twist of evil someone had killed her husband a second time.

CHAPTER

6

When Connie regained consciousness, she found herself under the bedcovers, still wearing her funeral dress. Tick and Tess and Reverend Wallace sat in straight chairs at her side and Daniel perched at her feet. Unlike others she had heard about who couldn't remember what happened when they fainted, she vividly recalled everything. At first, she didn't move, just closed her eyes against the light that burned overhead. But her escape didn't last long.

"Mom?" It was Daniel who spoke. "Are you awake?"

Though not wanting to wake up, Connie couldn't resist the concerned tones of her boy's voice. She didn't know how long she'd been blacked out, but she did know she didn't want Daniel or Katie to worry about her any longer than necessary.

Opening her eyes, she reached for Daniel's hand. He shifted and lay himself at her side, his head beside hers on her pillow.

"You fainted, Mom," he said as if surprised such a thing could happen. "We carried you to the car, me and Tick and Reverend Wallace. Got you home about fifteen minutes ago." He paused, and Tick took up the story.

"We started to take you to the emergency room, but you kept fading in and out, so we figured it was just the strain of the last couple of days. You feeling better?"

Connie lifted her head and focused on Tick, her eyes searching his face, wondering if he had told anyone else what he told her.

"I'm okay," she said, her voice weak. "Just a shock, you know?"

Tick narrowed his eyes and shook his head ever so slightly. Connie glanced quickly at Daniel, then back to Tick. Apparently, he hadn't said anything to the rest. She adjusted her pillow and sat up taller.

"Daniel would you get me some water?" she asked.

"Sure, Mom," he said. "Anything else you need?"

"Yeah, where's Katie?"

"She's in her room with Mrs. Everhart. They're playing dress-up."

"Check on her for me. Tell her I'm fine."

Obviously glad to have something to do, Daniel jumped off the bed and left the room.

Knowing she didn't have much time, Connie turned instantly to Tick. "I take it you didn't tell them."

"Nope, no one but you and Tess." He tilted his head toward Reverend Wallace. "Not even the pastor here."

Connie swallowed. "I'm sure the word will get out soon."

"Yeah, the paper will carry the story in the morning."

Connie faced Reverend Wallace and spoke matter-of-factly. "Tick told me they think Jack committed suicide."

Reverend Wallace grunted. "I find that hard to believe," he said, facing Tick. "Jack Brandon had no reason to do anything like that."

Tick threw out his hands, a gesture of defenselessness. "I'm not the one who said it," he offered. "But the guys downtown say they found a note."

"What kind of note?" asked Connie. "Where'd they find it?"

"Apparently, it's off his computer at the store. They found it this morning in his truck, wedged under the seat."

Connie thought a second. She knew the police had found Jack's truck Saturday morning, parked at a concrete company just past the bridge on the north side of the river.

"Jack never used that computer," she said. "Everyone else at the store used it, but not him. He was old-fashioned. Still liked to write with a pen and paper."

"Well, the guys downtown say he used it at least once," insisted Tick. "You can see it for yourself as soon as you like."

Connie paused for a beat. Was it possible Jack took his own life? She didn't think so, but he had been unusually distant in the last few weeks, remote, as if hiding something. Had he given off signals she should have seen and confronted? Was he indeed hiding some dread secret to protect her as he had done more than once in the past? Did that secret haunt him to the point he couldn't deal with it?

But what about her and the kids? Suicide gave a clear message that a person had given up hope, had no reason to live. Surely, Jack hadn't come to that point, had he? Didn't he love her and Daniel and Katie enough to face whatever troubled him?

Driven by her desire to know the truth, she moved quickly to action. "I need to see the note," she said, rolling the bedcovers off her legs. "So, if you gentlemen will excuse me, Tess will help me change. Then I want to go downtown. Is my mom still here?"

Reverend Wallace shook his head and took a deep breath. "She said to tell you she had to go. It's two hours to St. Louis and her flight is at nine."

Connie nodded, but sadness bit at her. Maybe someday, when she finished with all this, she would go see her mom and try to build some relationship again. But for now, she had to move. She dropped her feet to the floor.

"You sure you're ready to get up?" asked Reverend Wallace.

Connie moved toward the bathroom. "No, but ready doesn't matter." She closed the bathroom door and grabbed her toothbrush.

Ten minutes later she walked out wearing a pair of well-worn blue jeans, a pullover tan shirt, and a pair of cross-trainer walking shoes. With Tick in tow, she left Daniel and Katie with Tess and Mrs. Everhart and drove to the police station. Inside, she took the elevator to the second floor. Tick stayed close to her, his bulky presence an encouragement. He had called in as they drove downtown, alerting the authorities he was bringing her to see the alleged suicide note.

Still weak from her fainting spell, Connie felt glad for his presence. Without his familiarity with things of this nature, she didn't know how she could endure it. Forcing herself to stay strong, she gritted her teeth. If Jack did indeed kill himself, she might as well deal with it.

Stepping off the elevator and turning left at the end of a narrow hallway, she entered the offices of the Jefferson City Police Department and nodded to a receptionist.

Tick spoke for her. "This is Connie Brandon, we need to see Luke."

"Sorry about your loss, Mrs. Brandon," the receptionist said, grabbing a phone and punching in an extension. "I've kept you in my thoughts all day."

A pained smile crossed Connie's face. People really did seem to care. "Thank you," she said. "I appreciate your kindness."

The receptionist spoke into the phone. "Mrs. Brandon is here."

She put the phone back in its hook and tipped her head to Tick. "Go on back," she said. "Luke's waiting for you."

Scared, but eager to see the note, Connie eased past the receptionist and followed Tick to a small office two doors down the hall. Stepping back to let her pass, Tick motioned for her to enter. With a deep breath, she walked through the door.

Immediately, she felt herself in the presence of power, but not from the room itself. No, the room held no particular strength at all. No more than twelve-by-fourteen and decorated only minimally, with a bland green drape, a couple of diplomas—one from the University of Missouri and one from the Missouri Bureau of Detectives—and a plastic plant in the back corner, the office looked like the habitat of a man with no sense of style and a budget to match. But there, bulging out of a government-issued chair right in the middle of the shabby decor, sat a man anything but off the rack.

Connie noticed his size first. She was not accustomed to big people, and he looked huge to her, his shoulders as wide as a refrigerator and so tall he dwarfed the desk in front of him.

"I'm Connie Brandon," she said, wrapping her arms around her waist.

Tyler stood and thrust a paw at her. "Luke Tyler. Sorry about Jack."

Connie tipped back her head, took his hand, and stared up at Tyler. Suddenly, she realized his size wasn't the source of the power she felt flowing from him. No, even as big as he was, it was his eyes that dominated the man. She couldn't really tell the color—something like a storm cloud just before it dumps its rain. But they were bigger than any eyes she could remember and they seemed to swallow her up in one glance. Below his eyes, his nose jutted out square but not big, and his teeth, straight and white, fit snugly in the center of a beard as black as coal. He wore a denim shirt without a tie and a pair of khaki slacks.

"You knew Jack?" she asked, pushing down her anxiety.

Tyler smiled slightly. "Sure, most everyone downtown did. Not well, of course, but I bought newspapers in the store from time to time."

"You and a million other people," said Tick.

Tyler kept his gaze on Connie. "From all I knew of him, Jack Brandon was a good man, an honest man. Not enough like him."

For a second, no one said anything else. Connie felt a rush of tears coming. Tyler cleared his throat.

"Here, have a seat," he said, obviously noticing her distress and pointing her to one of two chairs opposite his desk. "I'm sure you're tired and don't want to stay here any longer than necessary."

"I came to see the note," said Connie, her voice no more than a whisper.

Tyler lowered himself into his chair again and leaned back. The seat groaned under his bulk. Connie and Tick took the seats across from him, their posture more erect. Tyler pulled a toothpick from a box on the windowsill beside his chair and stuck it into the corner of his mouth.

"You sure you're up to seeing the note?" he asked. "It can wait if you're not." He locked his hands behind his head, and his black hair curled into his fingers.

Connie didn't hesitate. "I want to see it," she said. "I don't think Jack killed himself, but I can't know for sure until I see the note."

"It's not much," cautioned Tyler. "May not tell you enough to make that kind of decision."

Her patience wearing thin, Connie placed her hands on the edge of Tyler's desk. "I don't know what it'll tell me," she said. "But I need to see it."

Tyler rocked forward and reached for a desk drawer on his right. "Okay," he said. "Just wanted to make sure." He pulled a blue folder from the drawer and flopped it on his desk. "Here's a copy," he said. "Original is entered into evidence." He opened the folder and flipped to the second page.

Turning the page around, he pushed it across to Connie. Her hands shaking, she pulled the paper closer, then stared down at the printed words. She heard herself catch her breath, but it sounded far away, as if someone else had done it. She read the first word of the note:

"Sunset."

She choked, jerking her palms up and over her face. Jack alone called her that. He had given her the nickname on their second date eighteen years ago, a late afternoon hike on a trail near the Lake of the Ozarks. Just as the sun slipped below the western horizon, they had paused for a breather. Jack faced the sun and she faced him. The sun's last rays fingered her auburn hair, making it glisten and shine. Jack stared at her as if in a trance.

"It's a sunset," he said softly.

Connie turned and faced west. "Yep, it happens every day about this time," she joked.

"That's not what I meant," he said.

She turned back to him. He reached out his hand and touched her hair. "This is a sunset," he said.

"You should be a writer," she murmured, mesmerized by his sensitivity.

"I am a writer," he told her. "But nobody knows it yet."

"I do."

"You're the first I've told. One day I'm going to write the great American love story." He kissed her then, and she belonged to him from that moment. From that moment, too, the name "Sunset" belonged to her, but only he used it.

She felt a hand on her shoulder, then turned and saw Tick staring at her, a worried scowl creasing his bald head.

"You okay?" he asked.

Slowly, she nodded, reminding herself she had to do this. Lowering her hands, she turned back to the note.

I don't know what to say. But I can't go on like this, too many secrets. Can't face you and the kids. Please remember—I love you and always will. Take care of Daniel and Kate and ask them to forgive me.
Jack

For several long moments, Connie stared at the note. She reread it three times, digesting the words one at a time, trying them on, testing them to see if they sounded real or not, if they carried the tone of Jack's thoughts. She tried to hear him saying them, tried to inflect each of them with the sound of his voice. Though she couldn't quite identify why, she found something false in them, something different from the way he spoke, something alien, other than Jack.

She raised her eyes and found Luke Tyler staring at her.

"What's your verdict?" he asked, rolling his toothpick from the left to the right corner of his mouth. "Is it legitimate?"

Connie tried to imagine Jack in his last minutes, hoping to get some sense of what would have made him do such a thing, if indeed he had. Time slowed down as she pondered Tyler's question. The seconds dripped by, one torturous moment after another. But no clear answer rang out at her.

"Jack didn't use a computer," she said, clinging to the one answer she knew for sure.

"He didn't know how?" asked Tyler.

"No, that's not it. He knew how, at least a little. But he didn't use one. Used to say that the first time a computer sold a book to a customer, he would get ten of them. But until then, he wouldn't, he'd let someone else do that part of the work."

"But he knew enough to use it if he wanted?"

Connie thought a moment, not wanting to admit the truth. But she couldn't avoid it. "Yes, if he wanted, I guess he knew enough."

"So it's possible for him to have written the note."

Though she hesitated, Connie knew Tyler was right. Jack could have written the note.

"It's possible," she admitted, feeling as if she had betrayed him. "But I don't think he did."

"Why not?"

A bite of anger rolled up in her throat. Did Tyler really think her husband killed himself? Was he going to take this note as final proof of that and pronounce the case closed? But that didn't make sense. Why would Jack take his own life? After all, he had her, didn't he? Wasn't that enough reason to live? Wasn't she enough, their life together, the love they shared?

Her face flushed, but a sense of determination surged through her, and she glared at Tyler.

"I don't think my husband killed himself because he loved me!" she insisted, her teeth clenched. "He loved me and the children he fathered! He loved this town, he loved his church and his God. He loved his work. When you add it all up, it makes no sense. Jack worked all his life, through all kinds of hardships to achieve what he achieved in the last few years. Why in the world would he give it up now?"

Her emotion spent, she exhaled deeply and rested against her chair. Tick stayed silent, his eyes focused on Tyler. Tyler played his toothpick on his tongue and studied Connie as if she were under a microscope. After a couple of beats, he reached for the folder on his desk again.

"What if I told you Jack was having financial problems?" he asked, his voice measured.

Again Connie heard herself gulping. "I wouldn't . . . wouldn't believe, believe you," she stammered.

Tyler pushed a sheaf of papers from the folder across to her. "Read these."

Feeling like a fighter hit with too many blows, Connie lowered her eyes to the papers. Though not clear what she held at first, she recognized the logo of the Capital City Bank at the top of the first page. She glanced up at Tyler, then over at Tick. Neither of them moved. She studied the papers again, hurriedly reading them. It didn't take long to grasp the gist of the documents. The first paper detailed a loan for $25,000 Jack had taken out near the middle of February!

Connie gulped. She knew nothing about this loan! Jack hadn't told her about it. What in the world did this mean? Jack didn't operate this way, taking out loans behind her back.

"Did you find this at the house?" she asked, trying to divert attention while she gathered her thoughts.

"No. The bank . . . well . . . the bank gave us the information."

Not wanting Tyler to know of her confusion, Connie ignored her question about the legality of such an act and turned her focus to the second page of the papers. Though not particularly adept at numbers, she recognized the sheet as a summary of an accounting ledger for the bookstore for the first quarter of the year. From all she could figure from the numbers, sales had nose-dived after Christmas, and Jack's business reserves had dropped to almost nothing. Other than the inventory of the store and the equity they held in their home, the Brandon family owned little else. In hard terms, she was broke.

"Did you know about these problems?" Tyler asked softly. "The loan . . . the financial condition of the store?"

Connie didn't answer for a couple of seconds. She couldn't read Tyler. Was he just doing his job? Or did she read a hint of satisfaction in his voice, almost as if he wanted to find out something bad about a genuinely good man? Not knowing the answer to her own questions, she decided to evade Tyler's.

"Jack took good care of our business," she said, her words clipped.

"The loan tells a different story. And the balance sheet shows he's had some tough months."

"You're suggesting he killed himself because the store had a bad first quarter?"

"It's been known to happen."

"Not with Jack."

"You sure of that?"

Connie took stock. She had to acknowledge Tyler had shown her some shocking news: Jack took a loan without her knowledge, the store balance sheet disclosed some low numbers, and someone wrote a note and addressed it to Sunset. None of it made sense. But she wouldn't let Tyler see her doubts.

"Jack simply wouldn't do it," she said.

"Tell me why you say that. Convince me."

Staring at Tyler, she thought him sincere. "Well," she started, "I've already told you the things he loved. He wouldn't give those up so easily. He's had tough financial times before this and he made it through them. But it's more than that. You see . . . Jack hated killing of any kind. He didn't hunt because he didn't want to kill. He only voted for politicians who took a pro-life stance because he saw abortion as the death of a child. He thought Jack Kervorkian insane, a dangerous madman. He stood against the death penalty, even though everyone else seems to want it. Jack didn't believe in killing in any form or fashion. It would go against everything he ever believed for him to kill himself."

Confident in what she said, Connie paused and stared across the desk at Luke Tyler. Let him argue with that!

Tyler chewed hard on his toothpick for a second, then rocked forward in his seat. "You make a convincing case, Mrs. Brandon. But we still have the note. And, in cases like this, a note often swings the vote."

"Does this mean you're going to stop your investigation?"

"Unless we get some evidence that points us otherwise, it could happen."

Connie's eyes flashed. Tyler couldn't quit so easily! Someone had killed Jack! She knew it, no doubt in her heart at all! But Tyler was telling her that wasn't enough. She had to find something to convince him to keep searching until they found Jack's killer. A sudden idea hit her.

"Did you check the computer?" she asked.

Tyler's eyes held steady, but Connie thought she saw new respect in them.

"We're doing that now," he said. "Brought it in on Monday, but didn't have it too high on the priority list until we found the note. A couple of computer guys are checking it now. But I doubt if Jack saved the note on his hard drive."

"But if he did, it will tell us when he wrote it."

"Apparently you know more about computers than your husband," Tyler suggested, chewing on his toothpick.

Connie shifted in her seat. Computers happened to intrigue her. She had taken several computer classes in college, had a knack for it. But she didn't want to tell Tyler all that. For some reason she couldn't identify, she decided to minimize her understanding of computer technology.

"You could say that," she said. "I've been in school off and on for the last several years. Law school at MU. You don't get an education these days without knowing something about a computer."

"You're thinking that maybe this note was written sometime when Jack wasn't around and the internal clock in the computer will show that to us."

"It's worth a try."

Tyler slowly nodded his head, obviously thinking. "If your husband didn't write the note, then who did? And why?"

Connie didn't hesitate. "Certainly, I don't know who. But I have no question about why. If somebody else wrote the note, they did so because they wanted you to stop searching for a murderer."

"We have no indication anyone killed your husband. But we do have a note that indicates he killed himself."

Though she didn't want to admit it, Tyler was right. Until some evidence came to the surface to contradict it, the police had to deal with what they had in hand. And right now, until the autopsy report came back, that wasn't much. With the death on Friday, the medical examiner hadn't gotten to Jack's body until Monday morning. With the examiner's office in Columbia, that slowed the process down a bit, and they didn't want to report anything until they could report everything.

"When will you have the complete autopsy?" she asked.

Tyler pulled his toothpick from his mouth and twirled it in his fingers. "We expect a preliminary report in the morning. Some of the lab stuff will take a few more days. By the end of the week, we ought to know enough to make some kind of determination about cause of death."

Connie cleared her throat and faced Tick. "I guess we've done all we can here." Tick nodded, then looked at Tyler.

"Yeah, I think so," Tyler said. "I'll need to talk with you again soon, but I don't think today is the right time."

Connie locked eyes with Tyler. He sounded so compassionate, so different than a couple of moments ago when he seemed to want to argue with her about the note. What kind of man was he?

Tyler stood, breaking her stare and giving her permission to leave. "Take care, Mrs. Brandon," he said. "I'll call you as soon as the autopsy comes back."

CHAPTER

7

C onnie wanted to keep Daniel and Katie out of school the rest of the week, but on Friday Daniel insisted the time had come for him to go back. Katie, learning what her big brother planned to do, said she wanted to go to school too. At first, Connie argued with them. They had stayed so quiet since their dad's death, and she wondered if they were dealing with their grief in an appropriate way. But, since neither of them were particularly loud children under normal circumstances, she couldn't really tell. Thoroughly confused, she gave in when Daniel told her he just wanted to get back to normal. Though knowing "normal" would never truly come again, she relented. Not much to gain staying at home anyway. Having given in to their desire to return to school, she refused to yield when Daniel said he wanted to ride the bus.

"Not today," said Connie. "Today, you ride with me." Daniel didn't argue any further. Now, having dropped them off at their schools, Connie stood by the den window in khaki slacks and a white top and thought about her children. Daniel wanted life to find its pattern again, and, though she thought he was rushing it a bit, she had to let him go. After school, he would go to baseball practice. After practice, he would come home, eat supper like a starved wolf, do his homework, and take a shower. Following that, he would spend some time on the phone, then join her and Katie for the family devotional. Finally, in bed he would read his Bible for at least fifteen minutes, then say his prayers. Afterward, he would fall hard asleep.

Connie smiled slightly and walked to the kitchen. She and Jack had taught Daniel and Katie so well, they couldn't go to sleep without their Scripture reading and prayers. Hopefully, no matter what they faced, they would never get away from that discipline.

Tess, still in bathrobe and without makeup, greeted her from the kitchen table and handed her a cup of hot tea. Connie took the tea and pulled up a chair.

"You get them delivered?" Tess asked, sipping her own tea.

"Yes, they're back at it."

"It's as good for them as sitting at home," said Tess. "Routine means a lot. What about you? What are you doing about your classes?"

Connie slurped her tea a second, then sighed. "I don't have a clue. I called my professors yesterday. Both of them agreed to tape the last of the lectures for me. Told me to keep up with my reading and show up for the exams."

"When are they?"

Connie did a quick calculation. "About six weeks from now, right before Memorial Day weekend."

"You going to be ready?

"No way to tell. I'm so worried about the kids, Daniel especially, that I can't even think about me yet. I can't tell how he's doing. He seems so quiet, so anxious to get back into everything."

Tess didn't respond.

"Can you go back to the old patterns so easily?" Connie asked, her voice disbelieving.

Tess shook her head. "I don't think so, not really. But it's his way for now. He wants to stay with his friends, keep his mind occupied. He's dealing with it, just differently than you think he should."

Connie stood and found a sugar bowl in a cabinet by the stove. Then, spooning the sugar into her tea, she sat down again.

"All my routines are shattered," she whispered as if talking to herself. "Like so much broken china. No more early morning walks with Jack, come rain or shine or Missouri winter. No more shoulder rubs . . . man, he loved giving me shoulder rubs, and his hands were so strong . . . stronger than you'd think for a man his size. I remember so many times I'd come home from school and he would massage away every stress I had. He used to tell me, 'Honey, you make sure I always have ice cream and I'll make sure you always have a masseur.' But no more ice cream while he reads or writes in bed. No more pillow talk . . . no more . . . "

Connie paused and suddenly seemed to see Tess again. An embarrassed smile on her face, she sipped from her tea and pushed her hair from her eyes.

"I'm rambling," she said. "Sorry."

Tess patted her hand. "No problem, girl. I'm glad I'm here to let you ramble. You need that, more than either of us realizes."

Connie placed her other hand over Tess's. "I guess you're right," she said. "And you've been such a help over the last few days. Heck, for that matter, you've been a help for years. I couldn't have made it—"

The phone rang, interrupting her. For a second, she considered letting it ring. But, like always, she had to answer.

Rolling her eyes at Tess, she stood and picked up the phone.

"Hello, Mrs. Brandon?"

"Yes, this is Connie Brandon."

"This is Luke Tyler."

Connie squeezed the receiver and her eyes darted to Tess. Tess stood up and walked over to her.

"Yes, Mr. Tyler," Connie said. "Anything new this morning?"

She heard him clear his throat.

"You want me to come to your house?" he asked.

She thought about it, but for only an instant. "No, you can tell me over the phone."

A pause came on the line. Connie could tell Tyler didn't want to tell her something.

"I'm okay, Mr. Tyler," she encouraged him. "I've got a good friend here."

"Okay," Tyler said. "Two things you should know. One, the note was saved on the computer, which surprises me. Saved under 'Connie.' It was entered at 10:34 on Friday evening. As I understand it, Mr. Brandon wasn't home at that time, is that right?"

"That's correct," said Connie. "I talked to him about five or so, but not again. He never came back that night."

"So he could have written the note."

Connie wanted to argue the point but couldn't. "He could have written the note, that's true." An idea intruded into her thoughts.

"Any sign of forced entry at the store?" she asked. "Someone else who came in, wrote the note?"

"Nope, none we can see. Jack had a dead bolt on the back entrance, but nothing indicates any tampering with it."

Connie's eyes widened. "Was the dead bolt locked?" she asked.

Tyler paused, obviously unsure about the implication of her question. "Well, now that you mention it, it was. We checked it Monday when we first went over the store."

A look of satisfaction crawled onto Connie's face. "But Jack never locked that dead bolt. He was funny that way. Trusted people. Clicked the lock on the inside of the door and left the dead bolt alone."

"Maybe one of your clerks locked it," Tyler said.

"Not likely. We haven't opened since Friday, the day before Jack's death. No one there to lock it."

Tyler hesitated. Several seconds ticked by. Tess raised her eyebrows at Connie, obviously curious about the conversation. Connie held up a finger, indicating she would tell her in a minute.

"You said you had two things," she said, leaving Tyler to stew about the locked dead bolt.

Tyler cleared his throat. Connie wondered if he had a toothpick in his mouth.

"Yeah, well, the second thing is most suspicious," he said. "Most suspicious." He stopped and left her hanging.

"I'm listening," she said, trying to stay calm.

"Well . . . we can't find a fingerprint on the computer keyboard."

"What?"

"No fingerprints on the keyboard. None at all."

Connie understood the implication immediately. "Jack's fingerprints should be there if he used the computer last!" she said.

"Exactly, but they're not there. Not his, not a clerk's, nobody's."

"Then somebody wiped the keyboard," suggested Connie. "Somebody deliberately cleaned it off so their fingerprints wouldn't show up."

"Makes sense to me," said Tyler. "Question is, who did it? And why?"

"You know the answer," said Connie. "Whoever cleaned off that keyboard killed my husband!"

"Don't jump to that conclusion," said Tyler. "Maybe a clerk cleaned up late Friday and wiped the keyboard."

Connie reconsidered. That was a possibility. "You better talk to Andy or Leslie," she said, naming Jack's primary employees. "They'll know if anyone cleaned up."

She shifted direction. "If someone deliberately cleaned the keyboard, then maybe they think their fingerprints are in a file somewhere."

"You know something about all this," he said, obvious surprise in his tone.

"I'm about to graduate law school, remember? I've studied some criminal defense. A person takes care about leaving fingerprints if they think they are on record in somebody's computer."

"Could be a military person," said Tyler. "Or an airplane pilot."

"Or a government employee."

"Or a doctor, lawyer, or politician."

Connie considered Tyler's words, knowing some states had even started registering fingerprints as they gave out driver's licenses.

"Tons of people have their fingerprints on file," she said. "Most of them aren't criminals. So where does that leave us?"

Tyler grunted. "Well, it leaves me with a mystery. A note your husband could have written, but no fingerprints on the keyboard. A door locked, when you say he always left it unlocked. A body shot up with drugs, but a husband who supposedly used no drugs."

Connie staggered against the kitchen cabinet. "What do you mean?" she demanded, her face turning red. "I've heard nothing about drugs!"

"They didn't tell you about the autopsy report?"

"No, nobody called me."

"I'm so sorry, Mrs. Brandon, I thought you knew. We got the report last night. Your husband had an armload of cocaine in his veins. From all indications, that's what killed him."

"He didn't drown?"

"No, not at all. The only water in his lungs is the fluid caused by the drugs. No Missouri water there. I'm sad to say it, but your husband was probably dead by the time he hit the water."

Connie pressed her head against the wall. A rush of sadness clutched at her stomach, and she started to weep. For the first time since Tick first came, she allowed herself to wallow in her weakness again. She simply couldn't do it. She couldn't go on. Not with this new shock—the word Jack had taken drugs.

Though she couldn't believe it, she saw no reason for the medical examiner to lie. Sure, somebody might have injected the drugs into Jack's veins to make the murder look like an overdose, but she had no way to prove it. The public would believe what the police reported. If they said Jack injected drugs, people would accept it.

Sagging against the wall, she dropped the phone. She just couldn't face it, the stares of the people in Jefferson City, the whispers as she passed. She just couldn't do it. She would have to sell the store and the house and get what she could from them. Then, she would take the kids and move. She knew how to do that. Had done it all her life. No way around it. She would become a vagabond on the highways, a refuge from the ghosts of the past, a human grief wave trying to escape the tragic truth that her husband, a good man in everyone's opinion, carried some demons in his soul that only his death had revealed.

CHAPTER

8

The word about the drugs stopped Connie cold. Though she wanted to keep going for the kids' sake, she just couldn't manage it. Her system had reached its limit, as worn down as a shoreline eroded by a summer hurricane. With apologies to Tess and the other women from church who took shifts at the house, she went to her room after the phone conversation with Luke Tyler and fell into bed.

Tess encouraged her to do it. "You've made it far longer than any of us expected," she said, tucking Connie under the sheets. "You need to get off your feet for a few days, get some rest, give yourself time to settle down. Between me and Mrs. Everhart, we'll take care of Daniel and Katie, and the church has sent enough food to feed us for a year. If we need more, Reverend Wallace will see we get it."

Too frazzled to fight, Connie collapsed and lay her head on her pillow. Except for a few minutes on Friday when Daniel and Katie came home from school, that's where she stayed as Saturday passed and Sunday came. She told Daniel and Katie the truth: she was just tired and needed some rest. She didn't really feel depressed, just depleted, a husk of a person, a shell with no inner substance.

The kids said they understood but then immediately began to talk in quieter tones, whispering like a family around someone about to die. Not wanting them to get the wrong idea, but unsure how to explain herself, she let it go. Better to wait until she had a better grip on her own emotions than to try to help them with theirs when she felt so confused.

On Sunday morning, she awoke at eight and told herself to get up and get dressed for church. Climbing out of bed, though, she began to tremble, her mind running ahead, imagining the moment she would enter the front door of the sanctuary and move down the aisle. People would stare at her and the children. They would point behind her and the children's backs. Yes, their interest would come from concern, but it would bother her nonetheless. She didn't like the notion of so many people focusing that kind of attention on her family.

She couldn't just walk in, sit down on the third pew from the front on the left, and participate as if nothing had happened. She had met Jack in that pew. As he later told the story, he spotted her as she came through the door. Her auburn hair, longer then, cascaded around her black glasses and made her appear just a bit owlish. But that didn't put him off: behind the glasses he saw the face and figure of a petite doll.

He watched her as she came in alone. Then, when he finished his work as an usher, he walked straight to the pew and took a seat on the opposite end. Through the worship, she noticed him glance over occasionally and tilt his ear as if listening to her singing. The sermon seemed to last forever that night, but eventually it came to an end.

Jack moved with dispatch across the pew and introduced himself. Within two weeks, he took her out to eat. A trip to the Lake of the Ozarks followed. By the end of a month, he took his spot right beside her each week when she sat down on the third pew. Just over one year later they married, with the Reverend Wallace performing the ceremony.

Now she wondered—how could she sing without Jack, his right hand holding the hymnal while his left hand touched her lightly in the small of her back? How could she give her offering when the ushers passed the plate, knowing that Jack always passed it down their row, winking to her each and every week as she dropped in their envelope? How could she go back so soon after seeing his body before the altar, lying so still in the coffin just four days ago?

To make it worse, the newspaper had reported the discovery of drugs in Jack's system. Yes, they had parroted the police department's declaration that the investigation continued, that no one had made a final determination about suicide or homicide yet. But, that disclaimer wouldn't stop the talk. Those who knew and loved Jack would never believe he killed himself with drugs, but those who didn't would reach their own conclusions. And, though she hated to admit it, even in church, gossip would happen. Even with God's grace, people still sinned, and she knew it.

Unable to face the people, Connie crawled back into bed and stared at the open window to her left. The curtains hung limp there, lifeless, empty of any breeze. With a sigh, she realized that's the way she felt without Jack—lifeless, cut off from that which filled her up. Before she met Jack, she felt that way often. Droopy and flat, really unattractive. She disliked her small size, so tiny she shopped in the preteen clothing section. Her red hair and freckles and big black glasses made her stand out as a child and she hated that. Given all she disliked about herself, it was no wonder she grew up as shy as a newborn deer.

Jack, though, helped her get past the worst of her timidity. He was small too.

"Small doesn't mean weak," he often said. "No more than big means strong. You measure the size of a person from the neck up and from the heart in."

Staring at the window, Connie felt none of that mattered now. Jack was dead and so was she. She heard the door open and saw Tess standing there. She motioned her closer, and Tess took a seat on the bed. Connie patted Tess on the hand and shook her head.

"I can't do it," she said, her voice weary. "I'm just not ready to go back."

Tess took her hand. "It's okay, doll, no one expects you in church today anyway. What about the kids?"

"I'll leave that up to them. If I'm not going, I sure can't make them go. But if they want to go with you, it's okay."

"I'll ask them," said Tess, getting up. "Either way, I'll leave someone here with you."

"No reason for that," said Connie. "I'll be fine."

"You know better than to argue with me, girl. No reason for you to stay alone. I expect Mrs. Everhart will want to stick around. She tells me she can't hear the service anyway, and her hearing aid squeaks when she turns it up."

Connie smiled weakly, grateful for her friends. When she got on her feet again, she would have to do something for all of them. But for now, she couldn't do anything for anyone.

She waved Tess off. "Whatever you think," she mumbled. "Tell the kids I'm still tired. But send them in to see me before they go . . . if they go."

The kids didn't go to church either. Instead, Connie heard them turn on the television in the den as Tess drove out of the driveway. She started to call out to them, to tell them they had watched too much television lately. But she had no energy to argue, and she let it go.

She slept the rest of the day and into Monday. As the new week started, Connie stayed bedridden, too tired to rise. She dozed fitfully in and out of sleep, twisting and turning, wrapping the covers around her legs in a tangled mess. The bed seemed huge to her as she slept in it, far too big for someone her size with no partner to help fill it. Like a shipwrecked passenger on a deserted island, she moved from one side of the bed to the other, never feeling comfortable on either end.

She dreamed as she tossed, and she sensed she had a fever, though she didn't bother to check. Her dreams focused entirely on Jack; she saw him first in one place and then in another, in the church sitting in their pew, in the Good Books Store by the cash register, on the road where they walked every morning. He reached for her in each of the dreams, his arms open and enticing and she always reached back, stretching her small body to its limits, but she could never get to him. Her hands stretched out to him, stretched, stretched, but his fingers always fell just beyond her grasp.

He called to her in the dreams, over and over, first from above, then from behind, then from far off in front. She strained to hear his voice, to understand what he said, knowing as she leaned forward that his message carried something vital in it, something she desperately needed to hear. But his words sounded garbled, as if spoken underwater. Try as she might, she just couldn't make out what he said. When she woke up, she clenched her teeth, frustrated at her inability to reach him, saddened she couldn't understand his words. Sadness covered her every time she awoke, a sadness deeper than a tunnel and as black as a cave.

Tess brought her food on a regular basis, but she barely touched it. In the mornings she got up to shower, but she didn't get dressed or put on any makeup. She tried to pray, but found her words empty and tired. Giving up on words, she moaned in her soul and cried out to God. Like Jesus on the cross, she felt abandoned, and the cross of her abandonment was the death of her precious Jack. Her only solace came when she remembered that the Spirit prayed for her even when she couldn't pray for herself.

Through Monday and Tuesday nights, the dreams continued and she stayed in her room, unable to pull out of the lethargy that wrapped itself like a tightening noose around her heart. As Tuesday dawned, Tess brought her a tray laden with cereal and juice, her concern evident in her face.

"You've got to eat, Connie," Tess insisted, setting the tray on her nightstand. "You've probably lost ten pounds this past week, and that's too much for you. You get any skinnier and we'll lose you down the drain the next time you shower."

Connie tried to smile, but her face refused. She knew she looked awful. A glance into the mirror as she passed through the bathroom told her Tess had it right. She had lost weight. Her eyes sunk into her skull, and her face, never heavy, now looked gaunt. Her hair had lost its luster too, its usual bright sheen reduced to a dead rust. But somehow her appearance didn't seem to matter much. Without Jack, what difference did it make? She left the food on her tray, untouched.

On Tuesday afternoon Reverend Wallace came by, his third visit since Jack's funeral. Connie barely moved as he sat by her and held her hand.

"We have a prayer vigil going for you at church," he said, his voice compassionate. "Twenty-four hours a day. We can't do much else for you, but we can do that. We know you're going through the worst pain anyone could have. But we believe our prayers will get you through this."

She mumbled her appreciation but not much else. Reverend Wallace prayed for her, promised to come back soon, then left the room. She heard him talking quietly to Tess in the hallway outside the bedroom door but didn't pay much attention to what they said. It didn't matter, really. In her state of mind, nothing mattered.

Jack was dead, and she had died with him. The only man she ever loved had apparently committed suicide. Her love for him and his love for her wasn't enough to overcome whatever ate at his soul. She might as well admit that. But, it hurt so much to reach that conclusion. To admit that cut at the very core of her own sense of self, her own fragile confidence, her own value as a woman and a wife. If Jack's love for her couldn't give him the power to fight through his problems, then what worth did she have?

Her weariness worsened. On Wednesday evening, one week after the funeral, she refused again to eat any of the food Tess carted into the bedroom and set before her.

"I'm not hungry," she said, pushing the tray away and burying her head in her pillow.

Obediently, Tess lifted the tray. But this time, she didn't turn and leave the room. Instead, placing the tray on the floor, she eased herself down on the bed beside Connie. When she spoke, her voice was caring but firm.

"Connie, look at me."

Connie didn't move. Her face stayed in her pillow, her eyes closed. Tess touched the back of her head, then stroked her hair.

"Look," she soothed. "I can't imagine what you're feeling. I know it's got to be awful. . . . Hell on earth. And I'm sorry you're having to deal with all this hurt. But I've got to tell you something, even if you don't want to hear it. . . . " She paused for a moment as if gathering courage.

"I'm sure the last few days are normal, even helpful, for someone facing what you're facing. You'll probably have more of them in the months to come. Lord knows, I'm no counselor, I don't know how long or how often something like this needs to happen as a body heals from all this grief. So don't hear this as any kind of criticism." Again, she waited, giving Connie a chance to respond. Connie said nothing.

Tess continued. "I'm not saying you don't have a right to hurt. But I got to tell you, your children need to know you're okay. They need to talk to you, see you eating something. . . . These last few days they've seen you before school and when they come home, then right before they go to bed. And every time they see you . . . well . . . you seem a little worse, you know, and it . . . well . . . it scares them. . . . "

The muscles in the back of Connie's neck stiffened. Though Tess couldn't see it, the mention of her kids hooked her soul like a barbed lure sinks into a fish. Tess was right. Her condition surely frightened Daniel and Katie. She knew that, had considered it over the last few days, but didn't know what to do about it.

As if sensing the tightness in her neck, Tess paused, waiting on Connie to speak. But Connie remained quiet.

"I can't tell you what to do," Tess said, worry in her voice."But I pray you'll soon find enough strength to talk, I mean really talk, with those precious kids of yours. We're taking care of them for now, doing the best we can, but I got to tell you, they need their mama."

Connie's eyes teared up. She had pretty much grown up without a mama or a daddy. Loneliness played with her like a pet played with other kids. Nothing hurt so much. Was she creating the same feeling in her own children through her bout of self-pity?

Tess kept talking. "You may think you've got nothing right now, no reason to go on. Forgive me for saying this, but that's wrong, that's just pure, out-and-out wrong. You got that good-looking boy and that beautiful little girl, and that's plenty of reason to fight through all this and make a go of it."

Scalding tears poured out of Connie and gushed into her pillow. She was pitying herself, she confessed that, and though she believed she had a right to do it, given what had happened, she couldn't drown in self-pity forever. Not if she wanted Daniel and Katie to survive all this.

Tess pressed on. "Those kids are what you have left of Jack, and I have a feeling that if he could talk to you right now, he'd tell you to grieve, sure, to hurt until you think your heart will snap. But then I think he'd tell you to take Daniel and Katie and your trust in the Lord and live your life, live it to the best of your ability, live it for them and for Jesus. Live it and find joy in it. I think Jack would say, 'Connie, in the world you will have sadness, but joy comes in the morning.' That's what I think he would say. . . . "

Her pillow soaked with salty tears, Connie bit it, unable to respond. Tess had hit her right where she needed to get hit. She couldn't go on like this. Her children needed her. But, at the moment, she didn't know how to meet their needs.

Tess wound down. "So, there, that's my speech. . . . I'm praying for you, lots of people are. . . . " Her voice trailed off, and, without another word, she patted Connie on the back one more time, picked up the tray, and headed for the door.

Hearing her leaving, Connie made a decision. She might not know how to meet the needs of her kids, but she had to do something. Maybe the thing they needed most was her, pure and simple. Her presence, her hugs, her tears even, mingled with theirs. She lifted her head.

"Tess?"

Tess froze and twisted around. "I'm here, doll."

"Would you bring Daniel and Katie to me?"

A grin as wide as Tennessee creased Tess's face. "Don't you go anywhere," she called, already moving out the door. "I'll have those kids here in a jiffy."

Kicking the covers off and climbing out of bed, Connie almost staggered. For several seconds, she leaned against the wall, her legs weak. Black dots swirled before her eyes, but she didn't black out. Instead, she steadied herself and moved to the bathroom, stopping at the sink and staring into the mirror. Surveying her appearance, she understood why Tess had gotten worried. She looked a mess! But enough of that. Hurriedly, she brushed her teeth, combed her hair, and washed her face. Finished, she rushed back to the bedroom. Too late. Katie and Daniel had already arrived.

They sat side by side on the foot of the bed, both of them in jeans, T-shirts, and tennis shoes. They watched stiffly as she eased toward them. Their eyes were rounded wide, and Connie read the fear in them. She almost choked at the sight. Her kids feared for her! They had just lost their dad to death, and now they feared something equally bad for their mom!

Seeing their fear, Connie felt a switch flip on in her soul. Perfect love casts out fear. Well, her love wasn't perfect, but God's love was. She would raise her children to know the love of God. Just as she and Jack were doing before his death. From this moment, she would do everything in her power to remove fear from their lives. Though evil had taken their dad, she would see to it that nothing took away their mom. She would stay with them. No matter how much she hurt inside, she wouldn't give up again. She would show them her hurt and let them share it with her. As a family they would hurt, and as a family they would grow stronger.

At the bedside now, she opened her arms. In one motion, Katie and Daniel jumped off the bed and ran toward her. She bent to pull Katie into her arms, then stood to hug Daniel close to them both. All three of them were crying now, but their tears were mingled with joy.

"Are you . . . are you okay, Mom?" asked Daniel, his voice protective, so much like Jack's it made Connie's chest ache.

"Yes," she sobbed, her arms around his shoulders. "I'm going to be okay."

Katie stood on tiptoe and kissed her wet cheek. "You're back, Mommy," she whispered. "Daddy told me in a dream you would be."

Connie smiled hugely. Daddy told her in a dream. Maybe that's what Jack had been trying to tell her. Go back. Go back and care for the children. Well, she was back. Thank God for holy grace, she was back.

Holding Daniel and Katie as tightly as she could, she made a vow to herself and to God. If she had anything to do with it, she would never go away again. Daniel hugged her on the left. Katie kissed her on the right. She thought of Jack. Yes, he was dead. But he was still with them.

Then it hit her. Right there in the bedroom. The suicide note from the computer, the note that supposedly came from Jack's hand. Something about it had bothered her from the first moment she read it. But she couldn't quite put her finger on the problem. Now she did. The note had referred to Daniel and Kate. There you had it. Daniel and *Kate*, not Daniel and *Katie*. Never once had she heard Jack refer to Katie as Kate. He had never done it while he lived and Connie knew, as surely as she knew that the Missouri was muddy, he would never do it the day he died.

Somebody else had written the note. Which meant that somebody killed Jack Brandon.

Snuggling against her kids, Connie decided she had three reasons to live. One, Katie. Two, Daniel. Three, a murderer out there somewhere, a murderer she would do everything in her power to see come to justice.

CHAPTER

9

On Thursday morning, Connie woke up early, threw on a red sweatshirt, a pair of jeans, and her walking shoes, and helped Tess fix breakfast for the kids. When everyone finished, she hugged the kids, then walked them to the school bus, Daniel first, Katie thirty minutes later. Watching the second bus drive away, Connie wrapped her arms around her waist and turned slowly back to the house. More tough days would come, she knew that. But for now, she had weathered the storm.

Moving inside, she saw Tess at the kitchen sink, her ringed fingers wet with soap and water as she worked on the morning's dishes. A warm sensation overcame Connie as she watched her friend. Tess had stayed with her through the worst of it. But now the time had come for her to take her first steps alone.

"Why don't you go on home for a while?" she said gently. "You've been here over a week. Tick's going to start charging me rent on you, and I'm not sure I can afford it."

"Oh, I know you can't afford me." Tess smiled without turning. "At least Tick tells me *he* can't. But I work a lot on credit."

"I'm sure I've reached my limit on that too," said Connie. "A long time ago."

"Nonsense, friends never run out of credit with friends."

Connie walked over and stood by Tess. Taking her by the arm, she spun her around and took hold of both her hands.

"Look, my dearest friend, I'm going to make it now. You helped me get a toehold last night. I had just about slipped away there for a few days, but what you said about the kids gave me the courage I needed to dig in. I know I'm not over this, not by a long shot. I won't ever be over it, not really. But I can cope with it, at least for now. So, I want you to go on home to Tick. I don't want to wear you out so much now that you won't come the next time I need you. You understand what I'm saying?"

Tess stared back at her, her lips curling upward in a slight grin. "You're throwing me out of here," she said. "Throwing me out like a worn-out shoe."

Connie grinned too. "You got it, kid. You're done here. Now go home to your husband before he forgets your name."

Tess's face turned serious. Her eyes glistened. She squeezed Connie's hands.

"Welcome back," she said. "I knew the Lord would get you through this."

"The Lord and a whole lot of friends."

Tess let go of her hands and wrapped her arms around Connie. For several moments, the two embraced each other, neither of them wanting to let go. Connie relaxed and allowed herself to soak up the strength she felt in Tess, a strength that flowed as naturally from the good woman as water from a spring. A lot could go wrong with a life, but a good friend could provide enough comfort to survive it.

The phone rang, and the intimacy of the embrace ended. Tess and Connie stepped back from each other. The phone rang a second time.

"Call me if you need me," said Tess, pulling off her apron.

"I'll call you even if I *don't* need you," said Connie, reaching for the phone. "Like I always have. No reason to change that."

"None at all." Tess walked away to retrieve her things.

Connie focused on the phone. "Hello," she said.

"Yes . . . Mrs. Brandon?"

"Yes, this is Connie."

"Yeah, well . . . this is Johnson Mack, Mrs. Brandon. I'm sorry about your loss."

Connie immediately recognized the man's distinctive voice, the sound of sandpaper scratching on concrete. "Thank you, Mayor, it's not easy but lots of people and our faith are getting us through it."

"Good, I'm glad the community has stuck by you."

"They really have, Mayor. You can be proud of Jefferson City."

"I am, Mrs. Brandon, I am." Mack cleared his throat. "Look, Mrs. Brandon, I know you're still under a lot of stress and strain and probably haven't had time to do much thinking about any of this, but I thought I needed to talk with you about something. Have you got a minute?"

Curious, Connie pulled a chair from the bar by the sink and sat down. "Sure, Mayor, I'm okay."

"Good. Well . . . you see, Mrs. Brandon, your husband and I didn't always agree with each other, especially not on this gambling project, but I always admired him, appreciated his honesty, the integrity with which he carried on his arguments."

"Thank you, Mayor, Jack tried to treat people like he wanted them to treat him."

"Yes, exactly. A good man for sure. Now . . . let me . . . well, I . . . um, want to ask you to consider something."

"What's that, Mayor?"

"Well, I want to make you an offer on your property."

Connie swallowed hard, momentarily confused. What did he mean? Her home? That made no sense. He wanted to buy the store!

"You mean the bookstore?" she asked.

"Sure, that's it. You see, I think that's a good piece of real estate and I . . . I think I could do good things with it. I tried to get your husband to consider this a couple of times, but he wouldn't talk about it."

"You want to keep it a bookstore?"

Mack laughed quickly, then cut it off. "Oh, well, not . . . not really. You see, that's . . . that's not my business. I wouldn't know what to do with a bookstore. No, I want to develop the property. I own the three properties to the left and the four to the right of Jack's place. With his piece, I have the whole block. The block right where most folks think a convention center would fit best in Jefferson City."

Connie took a minute to catch her breath. Mack had offered to buy the store from Jack? Jack never told her. Of course, if he never considered it, why should he tell her? She refocused on Mack.

"You want the store so you can build a convention center?"

"Sure, progress, you know . . . I mean we've tried to get a convention center here for years. Now, with gambling almost sure to come, a convention center will become quite a revenue source . . . for the city, of course."

Her blood pressure rising, Connie's face turned red. Selling the store might make all the sense in the world, but right now it made her angry to consider it. How dare Mack call her so soon after Jack's death and offer to buy the business he had worked so hard to build? Worse, he did so based on the assumption that gambling was certain to come to Jefferson City, in spite of Jack's best efforts. That infuriated her!

She opened her mouth to tell him what she thought of his offer, but then the image of the $25,000 loan and a poor statement of accounts at the store rose up before her eyes. She bit her tongue, realizing she couldn't afford to burn a bridge she might one day need to cross.

"I'll need to think about this," she said, forcing herself to stay calm. "Did you have a figure in mind?"

Mack grunted, then spoke, his voice rock on rock. "Well, I . . . you see . . . I offered your husband $230,000. But I'm willing to increase that offer today. Offhand, I'd say . . . oh, I don't know . . . I think three hundred and ten would make a tidy sum for you."

Connie almost swallowed the phone. Jack had paid only $68,000 for the store fifteen years ago. Struggling to keep her composure, she forced herself to sound strong. "Like I said, I'll need to think about this."

"You do that, Mrs. Brandon. I'll be back in touch soon."

The line went dead. Connie placed the phone in the receiver.

The second she did, it rang again. Connie jumped back, then stared at the phone for a second before picking it up.

"Mrs. Brandon, this is Luke Tyler. You doing okay? I heard you were under the weather."

Connie took a deep breath. "Oh, I'm feeling better, just been real tired."

"I can't imagine how you're making it."

"Well, it's not easy, but I've got a church full of friends, and their praying makes a difference."

Tyler paused and Connie shifted her focus from Mack's offer to the detective. She wondered about the man's faith, if he had any. She considered how to ask him about his beliefs, but he spoke before she could say anything.

"I'm sure it does," he said quickly. "Look, you said you wanted to see the autopsy when we got it. Well, I've got a copy here at the station. I called Monday, but some woman there said I shouldn't disturb you with it. I thought I'd try again this morning. Glad I caught you. You still want to see this?"

Connie leaned against the counter. Reading an autopsy didn't rank high on her favorite things to do today, and she didn't know if she could face it quite yet. But, if she really believed someone else had written the suicide note, she needed to talk to Tyler anyway. Tell him about the *Kate* vs. Katie problem. See what he thought of that.

"Yes, I still want to see it," she said, determined to move ahead with her original plans.

"You want me to come out there? I'll gladly do it."

Connie weighed his offer, then decided against it. "No, I'll come downtown," she said. "I need to run a few errands anyway. What time you want me to stop by?"

"You tell me."

"An hour from now okay?"

"Sounds good to me."

She started to hang up, but Tyler interrupted her. "Mrs. Brandon?"

"Yes."

"Glad you're feeling better. The Baptists at my church have been praying for you too."

"See you in an hour."

It actually took her twenty minutes longer than that to get showered, dressed, and drive downtown. When she stepped out of her van at the police station, she felt almost like a normal person—her hair pulled back in a neat ponytail, her khaki slacks topped by a long-sleeved beige sweater, and her face made up for the first time in a week. Though not sure she should trust the feeling to last very long, she decided to ride it out as long as possible. She suspected she would go through a number of mood swings over the next few months as she dealt with the reality of Jack's death. Surely, gloom would come again, and periods of normalcy would follow. For now, normalcy ruled, and she decided to rejoice and be glad in it.

Tyler stood and held out his hand when she entered his office. She took his hand and shook it firmly, her eyes again surveying the cramped quarters. His gray eyes studied her for several seconds as she sat down. He took a seat, too, his desk between them.

"You didn't have to come down here," he began, propping his hands behind his head. "I would have come to your house."

She waved him off. "No, I needed to get out. I've been in the house too much lately. Time for me to stir again. This gave me a good excuse."

Tyler nodded, then raised up, taking a blue folder from his top right desk drawer. "The autopsy," he said, pushing it across the desk. "If you're sure you want to see it."

Connie inhaled sharply. For several days she had planned to read this file, to search it for some flaw, to find something in it to explain away the drugs. But now that it lay before her, she didn't know if she could read it without breaking down.

Tyler apparently sensed her hesitation. "You want me to sum it up for you?" he asked kindly.

Connie almost accepted his offer. But then she thought of the suicide note. Someone else had written it. She knew that as surely as she knew she had red hair. If she wanted to catch the person who wrote the note, she needed to read this report, no matter how painful.

She shook her head. "No, I'll read it myself." She reached for the folder, pulling it to her lap. Opening it, she clenched her teeth and narrowed her eyes. Tyler perched forward in his seat, his eyes not leaving her face. Connie began to read, deliberately moving slowly so she could digest the information. Though unfamiliar with the forms, she knew it was standard stuff.

Name of deceased.

Name of examiner.

Date of examination.

Reason for autopsy.

Clinical and laboratory data.

Connie bit her upper lip and took a deep breath. This was Jack's body she was reading about with such a clinical eye. The body that had held her close on cold winter nights, walked with her in the mornings while dew still hung on the grass, sat beside her in their pew at church. She stopped, wondering if she could continue. But then an encouraging Scripture came to her. The words of Paul to the church at Corinth.

> *The body is sown in corruption, it is raised in*
> *incorruption.*
> *It is sown in dishonor, it is raised in glory.*
> *It is sown in weakness, it is raised in power.*
> *It is sown a natural body, it is raised a spiritual body.*
> *There is a natural body, and there is a spiritual body.*

Thinking of the Scripture, a comforting realization hit Connie. Jack's body, though important, no longer contained him. His essence, the center of what made him unique, had achieved another form by the power of God. She could look at this autopsy clinically because it told the story of what happened to the outer, temporary frame of Jack Brandon. No matter what happened to that frame, God now took care of the inner person, the eternal soul of the man she loved. A sense of peace washed through her and she refocused on the report.

Gross anatomical protocol.

Case summary.

In medical jargon, the summary spelled out the condition of Jack's body at the time of the examination. Though ignorant of some of the terminology, Connie gathered the key points.

Time of death: best estimate: between ten P.M. and two A.M.

Cause of death: overdose of cocaine. A needle prick in his right arm at the left elbow joint, the obvious entry point of the deadly injection.

"Jack was right-handed," she said, looking up from the printout. "Wouldn't it make sense for him to have used his right hand to inject the drug, put it into his left arm?"

Tyler arched his eyebrows, his gray eyes puzzled. "Makes sense," he agreed. "But people don't always follow normal patterns when they're suicidal."

Feeling she had won the point, Connie turned back to the report.

"A lump on the back of his head," she said, talking out loud. "What caused that?"

Tyler shrugged, then pulled a toothpick from his denim shirt and popped it into his mouth. "Don't know. Maybe a piece of driftwood. Or maybe he jumped from the bridge, hit his head as he entered the water. Either is possible."

"Or someone knocked him out from behind, injected the drugs into his veins, then threw him in the river."

"Yeah, that's possible too."

Connie studied the report another moment. "It says he had river water in his nose, mouth, and throat. But none in the lungs or stomach. Like you said, he didn't drown."

Disturbed by another notion, Connie lay the report in her lap and sat up straighter.

"I can't see it," she said. "Why there's absolutely no river water in his lungs and stomach."

"Like I told you, the drugs killed him, he didn't drown. No reason for water in the lungs or stomach."

"But that makes no sense. Think about it. For the sake of argument, let's assume Jack did commit suicide. At what point did he take the drugs? Before he left his truck? Then why not just sit there and die?"

Tyler shrugged. Connie pressed ahead. "Did you find the needle in the truck?"

"No, we haven't found the needle anywhere."

Connie nodded, then continued. "If he took the drugs in the truck, planning to walk to the river, how did he know he'd even make it? He could have died at any point or someone could have seen him. Did you get any report that anyone did?"

"It was late, not that many people on the road."

Connie shrugged as if to give him the benefit of the doubt, but she knew lots of people crossed the bridge, at all hours of the night.

"Okay," she continued, "your scenario says Jack parked the truck, took the drugs with him and walked to the water, unseen by anybody because it's late and few people are out. Then, he injected the drugs and jumped into the river, probably from the bridge. Is that it?"

Tyler nodded. "Something like that, yes."

"Then he should definitely have some Missouri River water in his system."

Tyler leaned forward, his chair squeaking, his toothpick gripped in the center of his teeth. "I see what you're saying," he agreed. "Unless he was completely, totally, stone-cold dead when he entered the water, he would've swallowed at least a little water as the drug took effect. He would have involuntarily tried to survive even though he wanted to commit suicide."

"Exactly!" said Connie, slapping the folder onto Tyler's desk. "Water should be there!"

"Unless we see it another way," said Tyler, considering the options. "One, he did the drugs in the truck, then moved to the river, taking the needle with him. There he stood, literally until his heart stopped and he fell in. Two, he waited until he reached the water, then he took the drugs, waited until the dosage killed him, then fell into the river."

"If it was a suicide, it had to happen in one of those two ways."

"And if it wasn't?" Tyler asked.

"Simple. Someone knocked him out, injected the drugs, waited until he died, then carried him to the river and threw him in."

Tyler tickled the underside of his toothpick with his tongue. "You paint an interesting picture," he said. "But it's all conjecture. No proof of anything you suggest. Some evidence does, however, point to a suicide."

"The note," said Connie.

"And bad finances."

Connie had to agree. "Okay," she said. "Let's accept your assumption for the moment. Finances were tough. But that's not enough to make a man like Jack kill himself. A man with as many friends as he had, in spite of this gambling fight. He loved life too much, other people too much, his family too much—"

She stopped, realizing she had already given him this speech. "Okay, back to my point. Even with a bad quarter at the store, Jack wouldn't do it, no way."

Tyler shrugged, then nibbled again on his toothpick. "So," he said, his voice softer. "Who's your suspect?"

Connie's brown eyes widened, and she perched higher in her seat. "You really want me to tell you?"

"Sure, you're full of ideas. Tell me what you think."

Sucking in a deep breath, Connie thought a few moments. Surely, Tyler knew what she would say. But he did ask.

"The gambling people," she said. "They hated Jack. Knew they might lose because of him."

"You suggesting Cedric Blacker had something to do with this?"

"Not directly, of course. But his people have connections . . . the Mob . . . Have you talked to him?"

Tyler chewed his toothpick. "Sure I have, over a week ago. It seemed obvious I should talk to him. But, as I'm sure you expect, he claimed no knowledge of any of this, and three people gave him an alibi. Seems he had late drinks at the Capital City Club."

"But you *are* checking the possibility of the gambling interests?"

"Absolutely, I'm checking every possibility."

The room fell silent for a moment. Another idea occurred to Connie. Johnson Mack. He wanted the store so he could develop the property for a convention center. Though she didn't know the finances, she suspected he stood to make a couple of million dollars or more from such a deal. Jack had turned him down flat when he made his offer to buy the property. Could Mack have paid a killer to get rid of Jack so he could make an offer to his desperate-for-cash widow? Connie started to tell Tyler about Mack's call but then remembered she had no proof of her suspicions and decided to keep quiet. Spreading unsubstantiated stories cut against her beliefs.

"Any other suspects?" Tyler asked.

Connie shook her head.

Tyler leaned forward, his thick torso centered on his desk. "Mrs. Brandon—"

"Call me Connie."

"Okay, Connie, let me ask you a personal question."

Connie tilted her head, sensing a shift in his demeanor. "What kind of personal question?"

"Well, this kind." He lowered his eyes for an instant, then looked back at her. "How was your relationship with Mr. Brandon? . . . You know . . . any problems between you two? Recent fights? Marital issues that sometimes come up after a man and woman have been married for a few years?"

Not liking the tone of the question, Connie immediately felt defensive. How dare he ask her that? Her face reddened and her heartbeat notched higher. But then she realized Tyler had to ask such questions. A man with problems at home *and* a failing business would more logically consider suicide than one with only a failing business.

Quickly, she evaluated her marriage. Any unresolved issues that might have upset Jack, confused him, made him so despondent he would kill himself? None that she knew. But she couldn't answer for Jack. Perhaps the issues she thought minor seemed larger to him, more serious. But she couldn't imagine that any of their day-to-day disagreements drove him to his death. She answered Tyler.

"Jack and I were like most couples, I guess. We had our tiffs from time to time, usually over little things, but nothing major that I can recall."

"What kind of things?"

Connie pursed her lips. "Oh, I don't know. He tended to run late all the time and I liked to arrive early. We've had that as a running battle ever since we've known each other. And I'm neater than he is, constantly harping on him to put dirty socks away, things like that. You know what I mean. Plus, I stayed on him to tell me more about certain things. He had a tendency to try to protect me."

"Give me an example."

Connie furrowed her brow. "Well . . . several years ago, a couple of years after we married, Jack opened the store. But, without much capital to get him through the lean times, the first years were tougher than he anticipated. The store almost went bankrupt. But Jack never told me."

"How did you find out?"

"By mistake. At the tenth anniversary of the store, the banker who loaned Jack the money to start the store made a comment about the early problems as I handed him a glass of punch. He assumed I knew. Not wanting to appear ignorant, I just listened. He told me Jack had almost gone bankrupt, but he renegotiated the loan two different times and kept working at it."

"Did that upset you?"

Connie smiled briefly. "It didn't make me too happy, I can tell you that. When I told Jack my feelings that night after the party, he made light of it at first. He said, 'You were pregnant with Daniel at the time. You had enough on your mind.' I told him that didn't matter. I could have gotten a job. Brought in some extra money."

"How did he respond?"

"He promised to do better. Remember, we were young then, barely married two years. He did do better too."

"Anything else like that between you two?"

Connie rubbed her forehead, trying to think. "Not really, no big issues. The times we did have fights, we worked hard to move past them. We're both strong believers, you know. Jack since he was about twelve, me since I was sixteen. We tried to forgive each other our faults, just as God gave forgiveness to us. We had a good marriage, not one that would cause him to end his life."

"You're sure of that?"

"Positive."

A heavy silence fell over the room. Tyler stared at her, his gray eyes locked on her face. Then, as if reaching for bad medicine, he pulled out a blue folder from his desk. The toothpick in his teeth suddenly snapped in two.

Connie's shoulders clenched, and a knot the size of a grapefruit filled her stomach. As if programmed over the last thirteen days to expect bad news, she detected another knife wound coming.

Instinctively, she searched her heart for a word of strength, and one jumped to mind. Tyler opened the folder and studied the papers in it for a second. Bracing herself, Connie rolled the words of Paul through her head.

"We are hard pressed on every side, yet not crushed; we are perplexed, but not in despair; persecuted, but not forsaken . . . "

"I hate to tell you this," said Tyler, turning the folder and pushing it across his desk to her. "I hoped I wouldn't have to do it. But I don't see any way around it."

Connie searched his eyes, testing them for sincerity, not sure if she could trust his expressed regret or not.

"Tell me," she said, wanting to read his eyes, to see the pleasure or pain they would communicate as he spoke. "Tell me what's in the folder."

His gaze didn't waver. "A woman came in," he said. "A woman came in and said she and Jack Brandon were lovers."

CHAPTER

10

T hough Tyler's words shocked her, Connie didn't wince. She had faced so much the last few days that even something this bizarre failed to knock her off her feet. Like a fighter conditioned to take a blow and keep on moving, she now felt toughened against anything.

Hearing this new twist, she looked at Tyler, her stare as intent as his. For several seconds, she churned the idea around, wondering if it could be true. Did Jack have an affair? Did that explain his recent silences? Was he dealing with his guilt, the conscience that would surely have ripped a man of his convictions apart? It made a certain kind of sense. An affair would have eaten Jack up inside, maybe pushed him to the point that suicide seemed the only escape.

But where were the signs of his infidelity? Connie searched her mind for any clues she might have missed. The smell of a woman's perfume on his clothes, a smudge of lipstick somewhere, unexplained absences from home, guilty eyes? She found nothing amiss as she pondered the possibility. If Jack had fallen into an adulterous relationship, he kept it covered extremely well.

"I don't believe it," she said, her voice strong. "The woman is lying."

"Why would she do that?" asked Tyler. "She gains nothing by telling us this."

"Then why did she come forward? Why not keep it to herself and spare me this added pain?"

Tyler popped a fresh toothpick into his mouth. "I think it's plain. She came in because she thinks Jack did commit suicide and she wanted us to know why. She said he had been agonizing over the last few weeks, trying to decide what to do. He didn't want to leave you and the kids, but he wanted to be with her too. She had given him an ultimatum—either divorce you and marry her or she was going to break off the affair. As she sees it, he broke down under the strain."

"So she came in, exposing herself to public ridicule as a home wrecker, to save you the hassle of a murder investigation. Is that it?"

Tyler leaned back. "Yeah, that's it. She read the stories in the papers, knew we were trying to decide whether to declare Jack's death a suicide or a homicide. She thought her story would help us."

"A real public servant, that's what she is," said Connie, her disbelief becoming more pronounced by the second.

"We do have a few of those out there," said Tyler. "What's the problem with that?"

"No problem with her being a public servant, but I think she had another motive."

"And what would that be?"

"It's simple, unless you're already leaning toward the suicide theory. She wants the death declared a suicide because she doesn't want a murder investigation. As easy as that."

"So you think it's a smoke screen?"

"It makes as much sense as the suicide notion."

"If you're already leaning toward the murder theory."

Connie smiled, but only slightly. "You've got as much evidence for one as the other."

"I think you overstate that. We don't have any solid evidence of a murder, but we do have some evidence pointing to a suicide. We have this woman's statement, the bad loan, the note from the computer, and the drugs found in the body. I think we can make the suicide case fairly strongly."

"The note was a fake," said Connie, surprised at the confidence in her voice.

"How so?"

"It referred to Kate, not Katie. It came to me last night. Jack never called his baby Kate in her whole life."

"But the note did call you Sunset, a name nobody else used but him."

"You know that?"

"Sure, I do my homework."

"Then if you know he called me Sunset, other people obviously do too. Whoever wrote the note simply knew us well enough to know Jack's pet name for me."

"How many people could that be?"

Connie did a quick calculation. "Heaven only knows. A few close friends, but they might tell a few close friends, who tell . . . you know how that happens. Hundreds of people could know. If someone wanted to make a note look authentic, a touch like the name 'Sunset' makes a lot of sense. We didn't keep it a secret."

"So you're saying whoever wrote the note knew your nickname but blew it with Katie's."

"Exactly. Even in a distressed state, Jack would never refer to his baby girl by anything but her real name."

"It could be a simple typing mistake."

"It could be, but I just don't believe it. One thing Jack was neat about was his writing. If he put his name to it, he wanted it right. I can't believe he'd leave a typing mistake in his last words."

Tyler rocked forward and locked his hands together, his elbows on his desk. "If you're right, then the woman was lying—plain and simple—lying to make us look away from a murder."

Connie nodded. "Makes sense to me. Who's the woman?"

Tyler grunted at her. "I can't tell you that!" he said. "For obvious reasons."

"Does she live in Jefferson City? Somebody I might know, can you tell me that much?"

Tyler stared at the ceiling for a moment, then sighed. "I guess that won't hurt. No, she doesn't live around here."

"Then where? Jack didn't travel much. It had to be someone fairly close by. Columbia maybe? He goes over there fairly often."

She raised her eyebrows, silently asking Tyler for confirmation. He shook his head. Connie swallowed, then waited for several more seconds. Tyler stayed quiet. Convinced he wouldn't say anything more and anxious to get moving, she stood to leave. If Tyler wouldn't help her, she would try another tactic. She wanted to talk to this woman.

"Hold on a second," said Tyler, motioning her back into her seat. "I know we need to see this woman again. If she is lying, then maybe she can lead us to the person who put her up to it. But before *you* go running all over mid-Missouri trying to find her, let me see what I can do. I'll call her back in, go over her statement again."

Pleased, Connie obeyed and sat back down. Tyler pulled the folder back across the desk, rifled through it until he found the page he was looking for, then punched a number into his phone. Several seconds passed while he waited on a response. Connie watched him, grateful for his quick action. His toothpick rolled to the center of his mouth and stayed there, hanging on his bottom lip. Another ten seconds passed. He lay the phone back in its cradle, then raised his eyes to Connie.

"Well?" she said.

Tyler spoke softly. "The phone number she gave me has been disconnected."

"The plot thickens."

Tyler rubbed his hands through his beard. "Indeed it does. Maybe she moved."

"Or maybe she didn't pay her phone bill," said Connie, more than a bit of sarcasm in her voice. "Look, I don't know why you don't just admit it, this woman is bogus. Somebody paid her to come in here and say what she said, and now she's disappeared."

As Connie spoke, her frustration mounted and the anger created by the adultery charge, anger she had bottled up until now, boiled over.

"I bet you a dime to a doughnut that if you call Columbia, and I'm sure that's where she is, and get a patrol officer to go by whatever address she gave you, you'll find either a false address or an empty apartment! Go ahead and call, get someone by there!"

Leaning forward, she grabbed Tyler's phone and handed it to him, her brown eyes flashing. "Go ahead," she insisted. "Call the authorities in Columbia!"

Tyler stood from his chair, his body looming over her. A smile crawled out of his beard, and the corners of his eyes crinkled.

"Just relax, there, Mrs. Brandon. Don't go blowing a gasket. I'll check it out, and yes, in Columbia. If you're right, and I think you might be, we'll start a search for this woman. In the meantime, I advise you to go back home and let us do our work. I'll keep you up to date. Is that a deal?" He reached for the phone.

Breathing heavily, Connie handed it to him. "I want to know what you find out about this woman," she said, still not quite satisfied.

"You'll be the first one I'll call."

A disturbing possibility hit Connie. "Do you know if this woman is married?"

Tyler stroked his beard. "She said she wasn't, but she might have lied. If she had an affair with Jack, she would have motive to lie."

"And her husband would have motive to murder Jack."

Tyler nodded. "We'll check that possibility too."

"Who else knows about the woman?" Connie asked.

"Not many people, my boss and me, that's about it."

"Can you keep it that way?"

Tyler stared at her. Her face showed distress, her eyes narrowed, her neck red with tension.

"I can keep it quiet for a few days," he said. "Maybe longer. If we decide it's a suicide and the investigation ends, probably no one else will ever know."

"But if it's murder?"

"Well, then everyone will eventually know. The investigation will continue, the story will stay hot. Things like this do get out."

Connie bit her lip. What a mess. To protect her husband's reputation she now had incentive to call his death a suicide. Without another word, she stood and stalked out of Tyler's office, realizing as she did that he watched her every step of the way.

*****

With Connie out of the office, Tyler pulled his toothpick from his mouth, picked up his phone, and punched in a number.

Waiting for an answer, he swiveled his chair around and peered through his window, scanning the parking lot below. He spotted Connie as she moved across the lot. When she reached a blue van, she paused and glanced back at the police building. Tyler sighed. The woman had a tough row to hoe. A man on the other end of the line picked up the phone. Tyler swiveled back around and focused on the call.

"You said you wanted me to keep you up to date on the Brandon investigation," he said.

"That's right."

"Well, I just saw Mrs. Brandon, and she definitely believes someone murdered her husband."

"What do you think?"

"I'm not sure. It's getting trickier by the minute."

"It still looks like a suicide to me."

"Maybe, maybe not. I've got a few items to sift through, a few calls to make."

"Good, make those calls. And keep me informed."

"I'll do it."

Tyler put down the phone. He didn't like calls like the one he just made. But in a political town like Jefferson City, he sometimes had to make them. Nothing really wrong with it, just outside the lines a bit. Just so long as it didn't hurt anybody, he didn't mind keeping the powerful in the know.

Rubbing his beard, he thought once more of Connie Brandon. A remarkable woman, he decided. Smart as a whip and a backbone as tough as tungsten steel. Any other woman would still be in bed, crying her eyes out. But she was in his office, busting his chops about a woman who had disappeared after claiming an affair with her husband.

Tyler picked up the phone again. If he didn't want Connie Brandon to take a chunk of his hide the next time he saw her, he better get some Columbia guys to check out the woman who claimed the affair with Brandon.

*****

When Connie left Tyler's office, she drove immediately to the Good Books Store. It had opened again the Friday after Jack's funeral. Andy and Leslie Starks, a husband-and-wife team, were keeping the place going until Connie decided what to do with it. Right now, she had no idea. If the numbers on the accounting sheet reflected any kind of long-term trend, she definitely needed to sell. With the equity in her home her only nest egg, she couldn't pour any more money into an enterprise that even Jack couldn't make successful.

Parking behind the store, she hustled inside the back door and into Jack's cramped office space. Immediately, she saw Andy, a tall man with glasses as thick as silver dollars and clothes that never seemed quite long enough, at Jack's desk, his thin frame hunched over a stack of papers. Excellent with people and a lover of books, Andy had worked for Jack for seven years and did everything he could to make sure every customer found the one thing he or she liked to read.

"How's it going today, Andy?" Connie asked, her words cheery.

Andy jumped up quickly and opened his long arms to embrace her.

"Okay, Connie—actually a lot of people in the last few days. They're all buying something. Leslie and a couple of high school kids are busy as bees. Seems like everyone wants to make up for the business we lost while we were closed, like they want to help us get over this slump."

Connie stared past the open office door into the store. She started to go in for a quick look around, then decided against it. She had other things on her mind today. She motioned for Andy to sit again. He did, and she pushed some books off a chair by the desk and sat down too.

"Tell me about the slump, Andy. How bad is it?"

Andy took off his glasses and wiped them with his tie, then slipped them over his ears again. "Oh, it's pretty bad, but it always is around tax time. From Christmas until Easter or tax day, whichever comes first, we're slow. It's the nature of retail. People start buying again when they get their refunds. From now until Christmas, with only a short lull in August, we'll do fine."

"Is it any worse than usual this year?"

Andy thought a second, then answered. "Nope, not at all. Fact is, the numbers are actually about 8 percent ahead of this time last year. If we keep that up through December, we'll have an excellent year."

Connie sat straighter in her seat, her mind working fast. "So the first quarter report was actually pretty good?"

"Yeah, not bad at all for the first quarter."

Quickly, Connie switched gears. "Have the police talked to you or Leslie?"

"Sure, a couple of times. First on the Sunday after they found Jack, then again Monday morning for about an hour. Came out to the house. Wanted to know what we thought of Jack's state of mind over the last few weeks, whether we saw anything different in him."

"What did you tell them?"

"Nothing much. Jack seemed like Jack, if you ask me. A bit quieter maybe, but he got that way when he had something on his mind. You know how he was."

"What do you think he had on his mind, Andy?"

Andy took off his glasses and cleaned them with his tie again. "Oh, I don't know . . . that gambling thing more than anything else. What a casino would do to the city if it came here."

"Anything else?"

Andy put his glasses on again, then tugged at his tie. Connie could see his mind clicking, sifting what he thought important, worthy of saying.

"Nope, nothing I can remember.

Deciding to skip any questions about the alleged affair, Connie moved to another topic. Her voice picked up pace, like a prosecutor in a criminal trial.

"What about the computer? Did you see Jack use it in the last few days before . . . before his . . . death?"

"Nope, Jack practically refused to use it. We had to beat him with a stick to get him to put it in here for us to use."

"And the dead bolt? Did you or Leslie lock it the night Jack died?"

"Nope, the cops asked us that already. We left the place like Jack always did. Door locked from the inside, but no dead bolt."

"And the computer keyboard, anybody clean that?"

"Well, that one we can't answer. We had a computer guy in here on Friday to install some new software, but what he did to the keyboard we can't say. I know I didn't clean it and neither did Leslie."

"What about the drugs they found in Jack's body? You see any signs that Jack used drugs at any time or in any form?"

Andy paused and tugged his tie down as if to stretch it to his belt. He exhaled quickly, a gasp of air pouring out.

"Andy, what about the drugs?"

He looked up from his tie. "Well, that's a funny thing," he said. "First, let me say I don't think Jack had a thing to do with drugs. Never did and never would. But on Saturday morning before they found Jack, I came in about eight o'clock. As I walked back here to pull some petty cash from the safe," he pointed to a small metal safe standing in the corner, "I opened the desk drawer to get a paper clip. And there, big as you please, I found this."

Andy opened the bottom right drawer of Jack's desk and pulled out a plastic bag the size of a piece of bread. Inside the bag, a powdery white substance lay glistening in the office light. Handing the bag to Connie, Andy took off his glasses and wiped them.

Connie held the bag at arm's length as if afraid it would bite. "Why didn't you call the cops?" she asked him slowly, her voice barely above a whisper.

"Well, I didn't know what to do. Remember I found this before they found Jack and before they said he had drugs in his body. I didn't want any stink at the store, you know . . . bad publicity or anything. Business is okay, but this kind of thing could shut you down for days. So, I just kept this to myself. Then, when they found Jack, I was afraid. You know . . . I didn't know what it meant, so no need to go forward. When I saw the story about the drugs, well . . . at that point, I just couldn't say anything. You and I know Jack didn't die of an overdose, but not everyone knew him as well as we did. I didn't want his reputation hurt by a bag of planted drugs."

Connie nodded, then reached out and patted Andy on the hand. "Thank you, Andy," she said. "You'll never know how much this means to me. Jack would bless you for it."

Andy smiled widely, and his teeth seemed to reflect in his glasses. "What are you going to do with that?" He pointed to the drugs.

Connie bit her lip and lay the plastic bag in her lap. "I think we'll keep this our secret for now, Andy. That okay with you?"

Andy smiled again and tugged at his tie. "You're the boss," he said. "Whatever you think."

Satisfied she had learned as much as she could from Andy, Connie stood to leave. As she did, Andy leaned to his left and lifted a small cardboard box off the floor. Standing beside her, he handed her the box.

"Jack's things," he said. "Just a few personal items . . . pictures, a few loose papers . . . you know the stuff."

Taking the box, Connie smiled briefly, tossed the bag into it, then hugged Andy one more time. Ten seconds later, she headed out the back door. She would go through Jack's things later. Right now, other chores demanded her attention. In three hours or so the kids would get home, and she wanted to have the house cleaned and a good meal fixed for them for supper. They needed to see their mom in top form again, and she planned to see that they did.

CHAPTER

11

For the next two days, Connie busied herself with a thousand and one errands, things she had neglected in her days in bed, items she had to complete as part of the after-the-funeral-process. She wrote thank-you notes to scores of people—the ladies from the church who had stayed so faithfully at her house, all the people who brought food or sent memorials to the church in Jack's name, the workers at the funeral home, the Main Street merchants who closed their shops the day of the funeral in honor of Jack.

In addition, she had legal matters to attend—papers to sign at the coroner's office, at the bank, and at the funeral home. Plus, she had to visit the lawyer Jack used occasionally to handle matters at the store. The lawyer, a man she barely knew since Jack used him so seldom, told her the store was established in her name as well as Jack's and that he would immediately begin the process to get it listed in her name only. To her surprise, he knew nothing about a will. If Jack left one, another attorney had drawn it up. Distressed but unable to do anything about it, Connie left his office and moved to her next task. Though knowing she didn't have to do everything all at once, her tendency to get loose ends tied up drove her to do as much as possible as soon as possible.

Consumed by everything else, she found it easy to put off the thing she most dreaded doing—going through Jack's personal belongings, including the box Andy had given her. Telling herself she needed some space before she faced the emotional wringer that chore would create, she shoved the box onto a shelf on Jack's side of their closet and put off the whole job.

On Friday morning, she drove to the funeral home and asked if she could have a few days to get her finances in order before she settled up the bill. The owner, a man she had known for almost ten years, graciously told her not to worry, she could take as long as she wanted. Grateful for his understanding, but scared her finances might not improve soon, she left and headed for the bank. She needed to know exactly how much equity she held in the house and how much more she owed. Plus, she planned to change the names on the accounts she and Jack kept there—one money market for the store, one checking account for her and one for Jack. To this point, they were in both their names. Might as well get that fixed. She knew all this could wait, but she couldn't let it rest. Get it done, she kept telling herself. Get it done.

An officer at the bank gave her the first word of good news she'd heard in days. Jack, true to his dislike of debt, had been paying extra on the house principal for several years and had almost paid it off. The original loan of $59,000, taken out eleven years ago, had shriveled to only $18,000. Knowing that property values had escalated in the last decade, she figured the house would bring close to $100,000 on today's market. If worse came to worst, she could either sell the house or take out an equity line on it to pay the funeral home and take care of the loan Jack had taken out.

Comforted somewhat, she worked through the stack of papers she had to sign to remove Jack's name from their accounts. Signing the last document, she dropped her pen and smiled at the bank officer. Then, glancing at her watch, she stretched and stood to leave. A stop at the grocery store and she could get home in time to fix a good meal for the children again.

Last night had gone so well. She and Katie and Daniel had eaten their first meal alone together since Jack's death, and the evening turned out wonderfully. When she grabbed their hands to lead them in prayer before eating, she saw that both Katie and Daniel had gotten misty-eyed. Unsure whether to say anything or not, she had simply gone on and prayed.

"Lord Jesus, as we sit down to eat tonight, we feel a real loneliness. We might as well admit that. There's an empty seat at our table, and so long as we live, we'll notice the absence of one we love. But, even as we feel Daddy's absence, we know that he would want us to move forward. He would tell us to mourn him but not to forget you in our sadness. So I pray tonight that we'll do that, that we'll always remember Daddy. At the same time, though, I pray that we always remember you too. Daddy believed in you with all his heart and he wants us to do the same. Help us tonight, Jesus, help us trust you as much as Daddy did. Amen."

As she opened her eyes, Daniel squeezed her hand and she squeezed Katie's.

"Daddy's in heaven, isn't he?" asked Katie, her eyes wet with tears.

Connie nodded and leaned over to hug her. "Yes," she said. "Daddy's with the Lord."

"I miss Daddy," she said.

"We all miss him," Daniel said softly. "He was the best dad ever."

"We'll never forget him," said Connie, still holding their hands.

"And we'll never forget Jesus," said Katie. "Will we, Mom?"

Though close to tears herself, Connie smiled at her precious child. "No, Katie, we won't forget Daddy or Jesus. They'll be in our hearts forever."

Thinking of the meal, Connie decided she wanted to duplicate it tonight. She knew her family required lots of nights like that in order for them to heal. With a gaping hole in their family unit, they needed to redraw the shape of their relationships. Though they didn't talk about Jack after the prayer, the very fact they were together without him made his presence so much more real. Evenings like that would give them a chance to note his presence *and* his absence and so begin to live with both.

Anticipating another good night, Connie pivoted and headed out of the bank.

"Mrs. Brandon!"

She faced the bank clerk. "Yes?"

"I wondered if you wanted to change the safety deposit box too, since you're here and all."

Connie gulped. She didn't know she had a safety deposit box! Another secret from Jack. Not wanting the bank officer to see her ignorance, she walked easily back to the desk and had a seat.

"Sure," she agreed. "Let's do everything we can today. No use leaving anything hanging."

It took about fifteen minutes to fill out the forms. Just like everything else, Jack had the box in her name and his, so he wasn't trying to hide anything. But he hadn't told her about it. Staring at the documents that detailed the rental of the box, she tried to figure why he kept it a secret. He had opened the box only four months ago, on his fortieth birthday.

Curious about the contents, but not sure if the bank would open it for her without her having a key and hesitant to ask, she hurried through the paperwork and skipped out quickly when finished. No time for any small talk. Gunning the van and ignoring a few speed limit signs as she headed home, she jumped out the second she pulled into the yard and rushed into the house. She assumed she'd find the key to the bank box inside.

She searched through his dresser first. With no desk at home, she assumed he kept the key in one of the drawers with his clothes. But, pushing aside his socks, shirts, jeans, underclothes, and shorts, she found no key. Okay, where to look next?

His truck? Sure, his glove compartment! But wait. The cops still had the truck downtown. She hoped Jack hadn't put the key in the truck. She suspected it would require a good bit of hassle to get anything from it so long as the police held it.

Disappointed, she racked her brain. Where could it be? She looked under the bed and spotted Jack's penny jar. She smiled. Jack kept a mason jar under the bed and emptied his spare change into it every night when he came home. When the jar filled up, he gave it in alternate possessions to Katie and Daniel. With a real good jar, one heavy with more quarters than pennies, the kids made ten to fifteen dollars when he emptied the jar into their laps.

With loving tenderness, Connie slid the jar from under the bed. Filled about half full, she decided to split it at supper between the kids. She rolled the jar over in her hands, wondering how much money the kids would get, not that it would matter. They would count it out evenly, one quarter for Daniel, one for Katie, one here, one there, a penny to a penny—

Connie stopped rolling the jar. She saw a red wrapper in the middle of the pennies—a wrapper about the size of a tea bag. Instantly, she recognized the wrapper as a key container, a key for a safety deposit box.

Moving fast, she twisted off the lid of the jar, plucked out the key, and resealed the lid. The kids would still get their money tonight, but she would find out right now what, if anything, Jack had in the rental box at the bank.

She drove even faster back to the bank than she had driven home. Within twenty minutes, she had parked, signed into the vault room, pulled out the box, and taken it to the private room the bank provided for people to examine their valuables. The box sat on the one table in the room. She inserted the key and held her breath as the tumbler clicked. Her hands trembling, she pulled open the box. There, she saw a plain manila envelope.

She pulled out the envelope and dumped its contents into the bottom of the rental box. For a second, she simply stared at the document that had fallen from the envelope. Without examining it, she knew it detailed something pivotal. Her neck reddened with anxiety, and she took a deep breath. Her eyes narrowed, and she lifted the document off the table and began to read. It didn't take long to figure out it was an insurance policy, dated the day before Jack's fortieth birthday.

She wondered about the timing. Had Jack taken out the policy because he had turned forty and wanted to make sure his family had financial security if he had a heart attack or something? Or did he buy it because he had a premonition that something else might happen to him, something not nearly so natural as a heart attack? But, if he thought he was in danger, wouldn't he have warned her in some way, left behind some clue to what happened to him?

Overwhelmed by questions, but unable to reach any conclusions, Connie decided to deal with the mystery later. For now, she needed to know more about the policy. Quickly, she scanned the document, looking for the most important factor, the face value of the policy. The numbers leaped out at her from near the bottom of the first page. One million dollars! Jack had taken out an insurance policy for one million dollars!

Stunned, Connie pulled out a chair and sagged into it. What a relief! Now she and the kids could stay in their house! They could even keep the store if she wanted, not sell it to Johnson Mack and see it leveled to make way for some over-sized convention center. She could keep the store and let Andy and Leslie run it while she stayed at home to care for the children or went to work part-time with a law firm. All the options opened to her like a door on a beautiful spring morning, and she felt a rush of gratitude toward Jack for providing this support for his family, even in his death. A huge wave of tension rolled from her body, and she leaned back in the chair and closed her eyes. She would never get over losing Jack, but with this she could at least take care of her kids.

Her eyes popped open, and a jab of terror struck her. She bounced forward again, every nerve in her body alert. Wait a minute! Insurance policies usually carried a stipulation, a rider that made her as nervous as the discovery of the policy had made her relieved. Running her eyes through the fine print, she searched the document for the stipulation paragraph. Nothing on the first page. Nothing on the second page. On the third page she saw the paragraph she feared.

Her breath coming in short gasps and her face red, she digested the legal jargon. Just as she suspected. The policy would pay under any circumstances except suicidal death.

Her mind clicking a thousand miles a minute, she envisioned what would happen next. The insurance company, a national firm with a good reputation, would naturally want to know the manner of death. Not only did they have the right to know, they had an obligation to their other clients to know. If they could avoid paying, they would. Business worked that way, and Connie didn't begrudge them their right to do business. But that didn't make her situation any easier. If the policy paid, she could take care of her kids for the rest of their lives. But, if it didn't . . . well she could still sell the store, but she would definitely have to go back to work full-time. Though she knew scores of mothers who managed to work and raise children, she didn't want to leave her children at such a vulnerable time in their lives.

Stuffing the policy into her purse, Connie closed the rental box and walked back into the bank vault. With a deliberation she hoped concealed her anxiety, she pushed the box back into place and left the bank. Behind the wheel of her van again, she reached a sobering conclusion. More than one person had reason to want her husband's death declared a suicide. The murderer himself and the insurance company that would have to pay her one million dollars if a murderer was found. Yet, she now had another reason to want her husband's death declared a murder. Though a murder trial would mean an alleged affair would almost certainly come to light, it would also mean financial security for her family. Getting the money might mean sullying Jack's good name. Letting it go meant she might manage to protect it.

CHAPTER
12

Not wanting to act until she considered all her options, Connie kept the information about the insurance policy to herself. No reason to tell anyone yet anyway. The company wouldn't pay until the police made a determination about Jack's death, so she saw no rush to go yapping to anyone that Jack had left her a million dollars in insurance.

On Saturday afternoon Luke Tyler called and told her some Columbia cops had stopped by the address of the woman who claimed the affair with Jack. As Connie suspected, they found no one home. But, to her surprise, the woman's apartment gave every appearance of occupancy, right down to a flowerpot full of pansies by the front door and a pair of muddy boots by the pansies. Though Connie felt in her bones the whole thing was a setup, Tyler wasn't ready to concede that.

"The Columbia guys said everything looked pretty normal, like the woman had just gone for the day. Maybe she's just got phone problems," he insisted. "A disconnected line is no guarantee that someone has skipped out."

"Just wait," argued Connie. "This time next week, everything will still look normal, and she will still be gone."

"We'll stay on it," said Tyler.

"You do that."

Connie spent Saturday night stewing over the mystery woman's identity. Who could she be? A stooge hired by whoever killed Jack? Someone ignorant of everything but how much money she'd receive to do someone else's dirty work? Or someone deeply involved in it all, someone directly tied to the murder?

She went to bed wondering about it, but no word of revelation came to her, and she awoke Sunday morning as much in the dark as the previous night. Climbing out of bed, she slipped on her bathrobe and padded to Katie's room to rouse her for church. Though still dreading it, Connie knew she had to go back. Regardless of the emotion the experience would tear out of her, she knew that to deal with her grief, she had to go straight through it. She wouldn't sit in their old pew, of course. That would cut too deeply. Instead, she would take Daniel and Katie and find a quiet spot in the back.

To her surprise, she found Katie already out of bed and in the bathroom she and Daniel shared at the end of the hall. But she wasn't taking a shower. Instead, she sat in a chair by the commode, her head bent over her stomach, a wet washcloth on her lap.

"What's wrong, precious?" asked Connie, kneeling by Katie.

"I've got a stomachache, Mommy," moaned Katie. "I threw up." She pointed to the toilet.

Her heart skipping a beat, Connie grabbed the washcloth from Katie's lap and gently wiped her baby's face, feeling for the hot flesh that signaled a temperature. To her relief, Katie's forehead felt normal.

"Are you feeling any better?" Connie asked.

"Not too much. My stomach hurts."

"Do you need to throw up again?"

"No, I think I'm finished, but I feel bad."

"Come on, let's get you back to bed."

Lifting Katie off the chair, Connie carried her back to her room and eased her under the covers.

"Stay here, precious, I'll get you something for your stomach."

In her bathroom, Connie grabbed a bottle of stomach medicine and then got a spoon from the kitchen. Back by Katie, she spooned out the medicine and placed it on her lips. Katie slurped it down, made a face of disgust, then lay her head back on her pillow.

"I think I just need to stay here for a while," said Katie, sounding like a doctor giving a diagnosis.

"You do just that," agreed Connie. "I'll clean up the bathroom and come right back."

The bathroom cleanup didn't take long. Katie's aim at the toilet had been good. Back with Katie, Connie watched quietly as her daughter hugged a Beanie Baby to her chest and breathed softly, her eyes closed. Obviously, she was headed to sleep again.

Not wanting to disturb her, Connie made a quick decision. She would stay home from church one more week. No reason to haul Katie out of bed if she felt bad. Everyone at church would understand. Though feeling slightly guilty, she left Katie asleep and headed toward the kitchen. Passing by Daniel's door, she didn't stop. Let him sleep, too, she thought. An extra day's rest would do them all some good.

*****

Seven miles away, Sammy Sanks dropped a trotline into the water not far from the same bank on which he had found Jack Brandon's body. A good Catholic, Sanks took his Mass on Saturday night for just this reason—some of the best fishing he did came on Sunday mornings.

More attentive than ever to the driftwood and debris the island routinely caught in its branches and brambles, he kept his eye peeled to the shore as the sun warmed his back. Once a man finds a body in the water, he stays eternally vigilant. Letting his boat glide slowly with the current, he moved west to east down the island. Within a couple of minutes, he passed the spot where Jack Brandon had come to rest. What a tragedy, he mused. A good man with a precious family. Sanks had noted the pictures in the newspaper in the last few days. He sure did hurt for those kids.

He spotted the denim caught in the branches of the underbrush before he knew how to identify it. But it didn't take him long to whip his boat to ground, tie it up, and climb out. Seven quick strides and a grab and he had the object in his hands. A blue denim backpack like all the kids carried to school.

His curiosity overcoming his caution, Sanks unhooked the straps on the bag and peeked inside. Books? But what else should he expect in a backpack? Books.

Not knowing whether the books had anything to do with Brandon or not, he nonetheless decided he better get them to the police right away. But this time he wouldn't call the cops to the island. This time he would take his catch to the police himself.

*****

At two o'clock, just as she finished cleaning up the lunch dishes, Connie heard the doorbell ring.

"I'll get it," yelled Daniel, jumping from the sofa where he was reading a book.

Figuring it was someone from church, Connie continued to work, wiping off the counter by the sink. At least a half dozen phone calls had come from church friends since noon, so it didn't surprise her that someone had dropped by. In a town like Jefferson City, people still did that, even without calling ahead.

Drying her hands on the flowered apron that covered her yellow cotton blouse and blue jeans, Connie started toward the door. She appreciated the congregation's concern, but it made her feel a bit guilty that she hadn't returned to services yet. She hoped the people understood. Reverend Wallace, who had called about one, assured her they did.

"You can't rush these things," he said, his voice genuine. "With Katie sick and all, the Lord just gave you another week to get things in order. We're not going anywhere. Take care of yourself and those good kids, and I'll drop by early this week to check on you."

She didn't find a church member standing with Daniel as she walked into the living room.

"Mom, it's the detective working on Dad's case," said Daniel, his tone excited. "He said he needs to talk to you."

"Good afternoon, Mr. Tyler," she said, wiping her hands on her apron again. "You're working on Sunday?"

Tyler shrugged. "Please call me Luke," he said. "Yes, I'm working on Sunday."

Connie noticed his clothes. A dark gray suit, a light blue shirt, a yellow tie. No toothpick in his mouth.

"You've been in church?" she asked.

"I started there," he said. "But I got called out." He glanced briefly at Daniel.

"Have a seat," said Connie, indicating the sofa. She turned to Daniel. "I think Mr. Tyler and I need a couple of minutes of privacy. Why don't you wait in the den?"

Daniel's blue eyes narrowed. "I want to stay here, Mom. I want to hear what Mr. Tyler has to say."

Connie looked at Tyler.

"It's up to you," he said. "What I have to say will be in the paper tomorrow anyway."

Connie nodded to Daniel. He immediately took a seat in the wing chair by the sofa. Connie perched on the ottoman by his feet. Both of them looked at Tyler.

He rubbed his beard a couple of times, then began to speak, his tone matter-of-fact. "The same guy who found Jack was fishing in the same spot this morning. As he was checking his trotlines, he spotted a denim bag, a bag filled with books. Jack Brandon's name was inside the bag."

Connie almost jumped off the ottoman. Jack's backpack! He carried it everywhere. Kept it filled with his current reading list and notepads for his writing. She hadn't even noted it missing. Of course, she realized as she considered it, she hadn't noted it missing because she hadn't gone through his belongings yet. Though she knew she needed to face that task, she just hadn't managed to do it.

"Did it help you any?" asked Connie, focusing on Tyler. "Tell you anything useful?"

"Well, it's hard to say. We've checked it out, but we need to send it to the state crime lab, see what they find, but that'll take a few days. It's been in the water for quite a while now. Don't know what, if anything, we can pick up. But every little bit helps."

Connie wondered about the backpack. What was Jack reading at the time of his death? Even if she knew, what difference would it make?

"Can you tell us what was in there?" she asked.

Tyler reached under his suit coat and tugged at his waist in the back. A second later, he produced a blue folder from the small of his broad back. Connie almost smiled. Tyler produced a blue folder for every occasion.

"I've got a list," he said. "Seven books in the backpack." He handed Connie the folder. She took it and flipped it open. A computer printout lay inside. She quickly scanned the list of titles—a biography of Billy Graham, four recent novels, a book of daily devotions, and a reference work on the effects of gambling in a community.

Finished with the list, she handed it to Daniel, then raised her eyes to Tyler again. "It's just a list of his current reading," she said. "Nothing significant I can see."

Tyler rubbed his beard and licked his lips as if searching for a toothpick. "I hoped you might see something there," he said. "Something out of place, I don't know . . . something to get us—"

"Mr. Tyler?"

"Yes." He faced Daniel, who had interrupted him.

"There's one book missing."

Connie stared at Daniel. "What do you mean, son?" she asked.

"One book isn't there. Dad's book is missing, the black notebook he used for his writing."

Connie grabbed the list from him and studied it again.

"He's right!" she said to Tyler. "Jack had a black notebook he kept with him all the time. Never went anywhere without it. It contained his own work, the novel he'd been writing for the last five or six years. It should be on the list, but it isn't."

"So where is it?"

"I don't know."

"You think it's here at the house somewhere? Or down at the store?"

"I don't know about here, but I don't think it's at the store. Andy gave me Jack's things from there a couple of days ago."

"If it's here, then everything is fine. He just left it out of his backpack for once. But if it's not—"

"If it's not, then someone else took Jack's book out of his backpack and they did so for a specific reason." She handed the folder back to Tyler.

"You think Mr. Brandon left something in the book, some kind of warning or something?" he asked.

Connie rubbed her forehead a second. Should she tell Tyler about the insurance policy? If Jack had taken it out because he felt he was in danger, she felt certain he would have left a clue, some kind of final statement to help her know what happened. But she didn't know if that's why he took out the policy.

"I don't . . . don't know for sure," she stammered. "But it's possible."

"Do you have any reason to think he did?" asked Tyler.

Connie stared hard at Tyler. Did he know about the policy? Had the insurance company contacted him to find out about the investigation? That made some sense. As far as she knew, the insurance company had every right to make such an inquiry. But if they had, why didn't Tyler just say it plain out? His gray eyes told her nothing.

Not sure if she should trust him, Connie decided to stay quiet. If he already knew about the policy, she didn't need to tell him. If he didn't know, then she needed to see where this led before she said anything. Making sure she spoke honestly, she responded to Tyler.

"I don't know if Jack left anything behind or not. But I do need to find his black book."

Tyler scratched his beard. Connie thought he started to say something else but then chose to let it go.

"Okay," he said, pulling himself off the sofa. "I won't keep you any longer. Hope you two enjoy the rest of the afternoon." He moved toward the door.

Daniel and Connie stood, too, and walked him out. On the stoop, he suddenly turned back to them, rubbed his beard, then blurted, "By the way, I got a call from an insurance company Friday. A woman there said something about a policy they had written on Jack. I guess they'll get in touch with you."

Connie almost fell backward. Her face reddened. Tyler knew about the policy! But did he know its value? Did she dare ask? Unsure how to respond, she chose silence again.

"I'm sure they'll call," she said.

"I'm sure they will," said Tyler, a slight grin on his face. "If it's a big payoff, maybe I can investigate you." With his blue folder under his arm, he walked to his car.

Pivoting to go back inside, Connie thought a strange thing. Wives had been known to kill a husband for a million dollar payoff. As crazy as it sounded, when word of the policy came out, and it surely would, some people might actually see her as a suspect.

*****

Back in his squad car, Luke Tyler took a deep breath and picked up his cell phone. Within thirty seconds, a man responded on the other end. Tyler gritted his teeth.

"I don't like this," he said. "It's close to the line for me, you know what I mean."

"Easy, detective, easy. You're not hurting anyone here. I'm trying to help Mrs. Brandon, you must believe me when I say that. She needs to let you do your job, keep herself out of the mix. She's too fragile for things like this. I'm protecting her. So what did you find out?"

Tyler frowned, then said. "I'm not sure. She didn't say whether she knew about the policy or not."

"You couldn't tell?"

"No, she played it pretty straight."

"Interesting."

"I don't know if I can call you again."

"Oh, you'll call me again."

"I don't think so."

The man on the other end paused. Tyler wished he had a toothpick.

"She knows about the policy," said the man.

"What makes you say that?"

"Oh, let's just say a surveillance camera in the vault room at the bank told me. You don't think I'd put all my eggs in your basket, do you?"

Tyler flushed. He was a good cop. Keeping this guy informed seemed like the right thing to do at the time. No harm in it. The man had insisted his intentions were good and, from all he knew, Tyler suspected they were. A man with an influential position and a good reputation. Besides, with the power the man held, Tyler couldn't just dismiss his request out of hand. But this was going too far. Spying on a defenseless woman, prying into her business. No matter what the motive.

"I'm out of this," he said. "I'm just going to do my work, nothing less, nothing more."

"All I want is information," said the man.

"Get it from someone else."

"I'll call later."

"I won't answer."

"We'll see."

Tyler shut off his phone and reached for the box of tooth-picks sitting in the passenger seat. Sometimes he hated the demands that came with his job.

*****

By three o'clock, Connie had comfortably situated the chil-dren—Daniel with a friend from next door and Katie at Mrs. Everhart's house. Determined to do the one thing she had put off until now, she took off her apron, pushed her hair into a ponytail, and took a deep breath. Whether she wanted to face it or not, she had to sort through Jack's belongings, had to decide what to keep and what to throw or give away. With the discov-ery of the backpack and the realization that Jack's novel was missing, she now had enough motive to make her act.

Deciding to begin in the den, she moved to the wall of bookshelves that covered the right wall of the room. Jack owned a lot of books. Though the house had no study as such, a condi-tion he often vowed to change, Jack had stacked a huge assort-ment of novels, biographies, and inspirational titles onto the wall of bookshelves.

Knowing she didn't have time to search them closely, Connie nevertheless leafed through a few of the most current ones, hoping against hope Jack left a message in one of them. Without knowing what she hoped to find, she quickly became frustrated with the task. No way could she look through all these volumes! Anxious to move ahead, she gave the remainder only a cursory glance. Nothing jumped out at her. Though she lingered for a couple of seconds over Jack's high school year-book, she saw nothing that grabbed her attention.

Giving up on the books, she trudged to the bedroom, her shoulders sagging but her chin set firm. She edged around the bed to Jack's side of the room. His dresser came first. Top drawer on the left. She opened it and peeked inside. Old handkerchiefs he hadn't used in years. Keys left over from heaven only knew where. Three golf balls and a few tees, though he only played a couple of rounds a year. A box containing his high school ring.

Connie opened the box and held up the ring. Miller High School. The Wildcats. The ring wasn't big, but neither was Jack.

She supposed Daniel would want it. She rolled the ring around in her hands for a second, then dropped it back into the box. She didn't know much about Jack's high school days. He had said so little about it. For that matter, he said little about his early life period. An orphan since ten. His parents killed in a house fire. He grew up with his grandfather who died the year Jack left for college. Other than that, she knew almost nothing.

Connie put the ring back and moved to the next drawer. Underwear filled it almost to the brim—simple white, size medium. Nothing fancy about Jack when it came to the essentials. She searched through all the drawers one by one but found nothing unusual in them. Just clothing, all the normal stuff a normal guy wore every day.

Finished with the dresser, she pondered what to do with all the clothes. Give Daniel what he could wear, then the rest to the church's clothes closet.

Leaving the dresser, she moved through the bathroom to the adjoining closet they shared. Inside the closet, she moved to the belongings on Jack's side. With the house too small to have separate closets for husband and wife, she and Jack shared the space. Better said, Jack had carved out a small niche from the lion's share she used. But he never seemed to mind. He usually wore the same thing anyway—a pair of khaki slacks with a blue or white button-down shirt. Usually, he refused a tie during the week, dressing up his shirts only with a vest or a sweater in the winter. Simple lace-up black shoes covered his feet during the week.

Only on Sunday did he dress more formally, and he had two suits for that—a navy one and a charcoal gray pinstripe, which he wore with a pair of black tasseled loafers. Jack never saw a need for any more than two suits. She had buried him in the navy one. The pinstripe looked lonely hanging by itself in the closet.

Connie ran her fingers down the sleeve of the pinstripe. Jack looked so handsome in it, a starched white shirt underneath, one of his many ties giving it color. She pushed the suit back to see the ties and smiled. Jack enjoyed ties. She bought the rest of his clothes, but he bought his ties. Stripes and paisley and geometric and cartoons—he loved them all.

"A tie is a man's plumage," he often joked. "Wear a good-looking tie and no one ever notices the suit."

Connie ran her fingers through the silky-feeling ties. They included colors from every stripe of the rainbow. A tear edged into her left eye. She took a deep breath and fought to bottle her emotions. No one would ever know how much she missed him. For several seconds, she stood still and remembered the joy of those Sunday mornings when Jack stepped out of the closet wearing a new tie. That happened often in their marriage, and every time it seemed like heaven. But no more. Connie's shoulders slumped. She would let Daniel pick out the ties he wanted to keep, then give the others away. No reason to let them hang in the closet.

Exhaling, Connie left the ties and began to sort through the rest of Jack's possessions. Shirts, sweaters, vests. A couple of pairs of walking shoes, an old pair of golf shoes, and the two black pairs. Four hats sat on the top shelf—two baseball caps, one golf visor, and one straw job he wore when he worked in the yard.

As she surveyed Jack's belongings, a thought came to Connie that she had never previously registered. Jack didn't own much. In fact, as she thought about it, he owned almost nothing. Except for his collection of books, you could practically toss everything he owned into a . . . well . . . into a suitcase if you wanted. When they got married, that's exactly what he did bring—one suitcase, no furniture, no television, nothing but a few clothes like the ones that now hung in his closet. As long as she had known him, he had been that way.

Connie recalled Jack's office. Though Andy had given her the box, she would still need to check there too. But, even before she did, she knew she wouldn't find much. It, too, would offer only sparse evidence that Jack had ever lived there. If people knew Jack by what he left behind, they wouldn't know much about him. He could vanish in a day, carrying everything he owned as he went.

Reaching to the shelf to pull out the box from the store, another notion intruded. She knew almost nothing about Jack's family background. What kind of childhood had he had? Jack said so little about his parents. She had passed it off over the years as a child's vague memories. But was that all?

What about the fire that killed his parents? He seldom spoke of it and then only briefly. She had always assumed he didn't like dredging up sad memories. But was that really it?

Connie pulled out the cardboard box and told herself to calm down. Her imagination was getting away from her. Or was it? Was it her imagination running amok or was something deeper going on here, something she couldn't imagine, something evil?

With a shiver, she sat down in the floor of the closet and placed the box in her lap. Opening it, she searched inside. The bag containing drugs rested on top. She pushed it aside, pledging to get rid of it as soon as possible. But where? She would deal with that later.

She started to thumb through the rest of the stuff. She found a stack of newspaper articles, several yellow with age, others more recent. She smiled as she read the articles—one about the tenth anniversary of the Good Books Store, one telling of a prominent author signing books there. Another stack chronicled Jack's battle with the riverboat people, the formation of the committee to oppose gambling, his appearances at city hall.

Eager to finish, Connie didn't take time to read all the articles. Instead, she dug underneath the newspapers and touched something round and smooth. Jack's baseball!

She yanked the ball out and held it up for inspection. Jack truly loved this ball. Though she and the kids couldn't really afford this gift, a man celebrated a fortieth birthday only once, and it fit Jack so well.

Reading a few of the autographs, another tug of tears threatened, and she rolled the ball around in her hands for a moment, then flipped it back into the box. Within five minutes, she had moved through the rest of the collection without turning up anything significant. A whistle, a new golf glove, half a pack of chewing gum, a framed eight-by-ten of the family taken a year ago at the church, and a smaller picture of Jack and Wilt Carver on a fishing trip last fall. Nothing more.

Disappointed, Connie stood, shoved the box back on the shelf, and left the closet. Walking deliberately, she reentered the bedroom and moved to the nightstand by Jack's bed. She had intentionally saved this for last. Jack left his ice cream bowls here when he finished eating every night. He lay whatever book he happened to be reading on it when he turned out the light. He kept his Bible here, pulling it out to read every morning before he took his walk with Connie. If memories weighed a pound apiece, Jack's nightstand would weigh at least a ton.

Gritting her teeth, Connie stepped to the nightstand and opened its one drawer. She saw his Bible first—frayed at the edges. She lifted it out and thumbed through its marked-up pages. Every day of her married life, she saw Jack reading it. Yellow marker highlighted so many pages she wondered if he left anything unmarked.

Gently, she lay the Bible on the bed and riffled through the rest of the drawer. Nothing else of importance there. Pennies, a couple more golf tees (did those things breed or something?), a broken watch, a pad for phone messages.

More and more frustrated at not finding anything helpful, she squatted and opened the twin doors on the front of the nightstand. Behind the doors, she found a stack of books. A few recent best-sellers. Beneath the books, a pile of magazines, *Publishers Weekly, Christian Retailing, Writer's Digest,* some of them now outdated. Quickly, Connie pushed the magazines aside, eager to get the search over.

To her dismay, she hadn't found Jack's notebook. But it made no sense for anyone to have taken it. It had no value to anyone but Jack and his family. Had it somehow fallen out of the backpack and dropped to the bottom of the Missouri? But how had it gotten out and not the others? Weren't the clasps on the bag still hooked when they found it? She would need to ask—

She spotted a manila folder in the back page of the last of the magazines. Yanking out the folder, she tossed the magazine aside. Hurriedly, she tore open the sealed top and pulled out the contents. It contained a second envelope, this one smaller with a bank logo printed on the front. For a short instant, Connie studied the name of the bank. The Bank of St. Louis. They didn't have an account at the Bank of St. Louis. Or did they? Nothing would surprise her anymore.

She wondered why the police hadn't found this. But they hadn't spent too much time at the house. Already convinced they had a suicide on their hands, they had no reason to really tear the place up.

Carefully, but not calmly, she concentrated on the envelope, opening it and unfolding the one page she found inside. It was a bank statement with her name and Jack's printed on top. One canceled check fell onto the bed. She picked up the check and studied it. It was written on February 22 and payable to a "Mr. Reed Morrison" in the amount of $10,000.

The check in one hand, she read the statement again, checking the balance in the account. $15,072. The money left over from the loan, plus a touch of interest. It had to be.

Connie relaxed slightly. At least she could pay off a large part of the loan with this. But why had Jack taken it out in the first place? And why a secret account in St. Louis?

Puzzled, she rested against the bed. Who was Reed Morrison, and why did Jack pay him $10,000? Only Reed Morrison could answer that. But where could she find him?

On a whim, she flipped the check over. Reed Morrison's signature and an address and phone number stared back at her just as she had hoped. The bank had made him give an address and phone number before it cashed the check.

Her heart thumping like a piston in a race car, Connie rushed to the phone on her side of the bed. Dialing information, she reached an operator.

"Yes," said Connie. "Can you tell me what the 702 area code is for?"

"Sure, hold a second."

Connie bit her lip.

"That's Nevada."

"And a 207 exchange?"

"That's Las Vegas."

Connie put the phone down. Nevada, Las Vegas! Jack wrote a check for $10,000 to a man living in Las Vegas! What in the world did that mean?

Stunned, Connie forgot the search for Jack's notebook. Instead, she picked up the phone again and dialed the number on the check. The phone rang four times and then a computerized voice spoke.

"The number you have called has been disconnected. Please hang up and try again. If you think there is a problem with the number, please call your operator."

Hanging up, Connie didn't even blink. Somehow, it all made sense. It would have shocked her more if Reed Morrison had actually picked up the phone.

CHAPTER

13

onday morning dawned bright and sunny, the first real warm day of the spring. By the time the kids left for school, the temperature had reached sixty and the Weather Channel said to expect a high of seventy-eight. Glad for the warmer weather and strangely energized by her Sunday afternoon discovery, Connie decided to make a fast trip to St. Louis to the bank. If all went well, she could get there, close out the account, and return to Jefferson City by the time Daniel and Katie came home from school. Her plans set, she threw on a black skirt, a blouse the color of a sunflower, and a pair of black flats, and headed her van east.

By the time she reached Interstate 70, she had rehashed her options several times. Until she knew more, she wouldn't tell Tyler about the bank account or about Reed Morrison. Since neither necessarily related to Jack's death, she didn't want to cloud Tyler's work with extra details. Most important, she didn't want Tyler to know about the money in the St. Louis bank. If he decided to shut down the investigation, she needed that money to hire someone to find Jack's killer.

Wondering how to do that, Connie watched the miles speed by, one highway stripe after another. She could call a private detective. But how? Just go to the phone book and find one in the yellow pages? She didn't know, but she would find out if Tyler backed out on her.

She had made that decision Sunday night. No matter what Tyler did, she planned to keep the investigation going. She couldn't drop things the way they currently stood—Jack dead and his reputation in danger. Thank God the word about the alleged affair hadn't escaped yet. A charge like that could destroy a person's name forever, no matter how innocent the accused.

Grateful for that blessing, Connie sped east, St. Louis drawing closer and closer, less than an hour away now. Her mind kept churning, considering her next steps. Though hazy in specifics, she had a direction. She would take the $15,000 out of the bank in cash and hide it at home. The police might get curious if they heard she had opened a new account in Jefferson City and dropped that much money in it.

The next step called for her to tell Tick about the alleged affair and ask him for the name and address of the woman who claimed it. She hated to take advantage of a friendship, but she saw no other option. If he wouldn't give her the information, she would simply ask him to take her to the woman so she could confront her. If nothing else worked, she would do something she didn't want to do. She would ask Tick for his password into his police computer. With that password, perhaps she could find the woman without his help. She hoped she wouldn't need to put her friendship on the line that way. But a dead husband made a woman consider unusual means. Though not sure what she would discover by visiting the Columbia address—she didn't believe for an instant she would find the woman there— she still had to try. She had to meet her alleged rival face-to-face.

Past those two steps, Connie imagined herself doing one more thing. She saw herself going to Las Vegas to visit Mr. Reed Morrison. If she didn't find the woman, and she suspected she wouldn't, then Reed Morrison gave her one final chance to unravel this mystery. She didn't know if he had anything to do with Jack's death, but her instincts told her he did. More than her instincts really, her logic.

Looking back, she could see that Jack had gotten awfully quiet in the last weeks before his death. Obviously, something preyed on his mind. Averse to debt, he took out a big loan and wrote a check to a man from Las Vegas. In addition, he bought an insurance policy worth a million dollars the day before his fortieth birthday. Something foul seemed afoot, and Reed

Morrison wore the only shoes that could take her to the source of the riddle.

The sign to Lake St. Louis loomed ahead, and Connie glanced down at the address on the envelope lying in her brief-case beside her. The address on the envelope registered a west side location, 2264 Old Lindbergh Lane. Apparently, Jack had pulled into the first bank he found on the side of St. Louis clos-est to Jefferson City. Glad she didn't have to drive downtown, Connie took the exit and turned right onto Old Lindbergh. Reading the numbers on the buildings on both sides of the road, she spotted the bank's towering form several blocks ahead.

Within minutes, she parked, smoothed down her skirt, repinned her bangs from her eyes, and checked her makeup. Then, taking a deep breath, she climbed from the van and walked inside. With the account statement in her briefcase, she moved quickly through a short line. At the bank window, she smiled at the teller and wondered if a cash withdrawal for $15,000 required any special forms. Maybe not. Large to her probably meant little or nothing to the bank.

"Can I help you?" asked the teller.

Connie nodded. "Yes, I need to close an account." She opened her briefcase and read off the account number. "The account is 7694762."

The teller clicked a computer keyboard. "I show the bal-ance as fifteen thousand one hundred and four dollars and sixty three cents."

"That's right."

"You want to withdraw it all?"

"Yes, in cash, if possible."

"Can I see some identification?"

"Sure." Connie pulled out her driver's license and handed it to the teller.

After a quick examination, the teller handed back the license. "How do you want this? Hundreds, thousands, what?"

It took Connie a second to realize what he meant. "Oh, well, whatever . . . hundreds I guess."

"It'll take one hundred and fifty hundreds," the teller said, obviously wanting to do something else.

"Uh, well, give me ten thousand in thousand-dollar bills and the rest in hundreds. Can you do that?"

"Sure, that'll be fine. It'll take a minute. I need to go to the vault." The teller stepped away from the window and disappeared around a corner.

Connie exhaled quietly and propped on the counter, trying to relax. She noticed sweat had popped out on her forehead and she felt a bit light-headed. For some reason she felt like someone might be watching her, then realized someone was. Banks used surveillance cameras on a regular basis. Scanning the walls behind the teller windows, she spotted a number of small black lenses staring down. She stared back, wondering if she appeared as scared as she felt. She hoped not.

The teller returned from the vault and placed a stack of money on the counter.

"Okay," he said. "Lets count these for you. One, two, three, four . . . Going to Vegas?" The counter stopped to lick his thumb.

"Huh?" Connie asked. How would he know that?

"Getting all this cash. Must be going to Vegas."

Connie laughed. "Yeah, something like that."

The teller counted again, flicking through the cash one bill after another. "Five, six . . . "

He finished with the thousands, then started with the hundreds.

Connie jerked and glared at the walls behind the teller! The surveillance cameras! They should have Jack on them the day he came in and opened the account!

Glancing side to side, she wondered how long a bank kept their videos, if they put them in a vault or taped over them. Could she somehow get the tape of Jack? She didn't know who to ask, but she definitely planned to find out. She might learn nothing from it, but it would at least give her one more chance to see her husband. If for no other reason, she had to get—

"Okay," said the teller. "That's the full amount. All ready to go."

Her mind rushing, Connie raked the money into her briefcase.

"Thank you so much," she said. "You've been a big help."

"Don't lose it all in one place."

Connie pivoted and started to walk out. But then she twisted back to the teller, a sheepish grin on her face.

"Look . . ." she began. "I know this sounds crazy, but could you see if you have a safety deposit box in the name of Connie or Jack Brandon? My husband opened this account, and I can't remember if he said he opened a safety deposit box as well."

The teller didn't hesitate. "Sure, hold on a second."

It didn't take him long to return. "No Brandon with a safety deposit box," he said. "Anything else?"

Connie shook her head, then headed out. Okay, no safety deposit box in St. Louis. But maybe a tape, and she knew who to ask to get it. Wilt Carver. As the attorney general, he would know who to ask and would have the power to get his questions answered. She would call him. He told her to get in touch if she ever needed anything. Well, now she did.

*****

As Connie walked out of the bank, a security officer in a black chair in a back office enlarged her image on one of four video screens mounted on the wall before him. Wanting to make sure, he rewound the video, then watched it a second time, comparing it to the eight-by-ten-inch picture he had lying in an open folder on his desk. Certain that the video and the picture matched, he picked up a cell phone and buzzed his boss.

"Yeah, the woman in the photo you gave me . . . she just came in."

"What did she do?"

"Picked up a bit of cash. Walked out of here with a briefcase full of money."

"Thanks. You can throw away the picture."

"What about the video?"

"Bring that to me. Then forget you ever saw it."

"Ever saw what?"

"Exactly."

*****

Within an hour after returning to Jefferson City and stuffing her briefcase onto the closet shelf that held Jack's personal effects, Connie arrived at Wilt Carver's office on the third floor of the Capitol Building. Wilt met her in the reception area and immediately ushered her past a room full of people who apparently had been waiting for some time. Steering her into his office, he offered her a soft drink, and she gladly took it. Without food since morning, she needed something on her stomach.

"Sit down, Connie," said Wilt, a bright smile on his face. "You look exhausted."

She sipped her drink and sagged into the deep brown leather of the chair he offered. Quickly, she scanned the room. Dark wood shelves lined the two walls behind her seat, a huge window overlooked the Missouri River on the north end, and the flags of Missouri and the United States hung on brass poles in the corners of the window. A thick rug decorated with the seal of Missouri covered the center of the hardwood floor. The room demonstrated the power that came with the office of attorney general.

Wilt took a chair across from her, sinking into the leather. His appearance matched the room. Dark slacks. Starched blue shirt. A red tie with navy horizontal stripes. Black shoes with a tassel, shined so well you could see yourself in them.

Connie smiled. "Thank you for seeing me so soon," she said. "I hope I didn't upset those folks outside, skipping past them like I did."

Wilt waved his hand. "Believe me, they come every day and they get paid well for waiting. They enjoy it. Tell me how you're doing."

She shrugged. "Oh, I don't know. Getting by okay, I guess. The sadness comes and goes . . . you know, you can't cry all the time. So, I keep going. I've got the kids to raise, so I try not to give up."

"You lost a wonderful man."

Neither of them spoke for a moment. Connie sipped her drink. Wilt fingered the cuff links on his shirt. Connie broke the silence.

"Look, Wilt, I don't know you that well, but I know you and Jack go back a long way."

"All the way to high school. The good old Wildcats. Jack and I hung around together all the time. Debate club, English classes, double dates, you name it, we did it and we did it as a team. After high school, when I entered Washington and Jack MU, I missed him terribly. Then, I moved to Kansas City and Jack moved here. I was so glad when I got elected and came to

Jefferson City. Gave me a chance to reconnect with Jack. I . . . I miss him."

"I know you do. We all do." Connie's eyes moistened.

Wilt bent toward her, his elbows on his knees, his hands clasped under his chin.

"What can I do for you, Connie?" he asked. "I feel awful about all this. Let me help you if I can."

Connie squeezed her soda can with both hands. "I'm worried about the investigation," she started. "I know Jack didn't kill himself."

Wilt straightened up. "I thought the police had pretty much decided he did. You know . . . the note and everything, the drugs."

"But I don't see it that way. Not with Jack. You knew him, Wilt. Did he seem like the kind of guy who would take drugs, kill himself?"

Wilt patted the side of his chair, obviously considering her question. His dark eyes narrowed and his forehead wrinkled. After several seconds, he spoke.

"No, not really. But he had changed some lately, become more withdrawn. Jack always had those quiet tendencies, artist's tendencies I always called them. He could get pensive in a hurry, he thought so deeply about things. Not like me. I try not to get too pensive about anything. That's why I became a politician."

He smiled at his own joke, and Connie laughed for a moment with him. But the laughter quickly died, and she thought of Jack's last weeks again.

"I noticed his withdrawal too," she agreed. "Or at least I do now. I passed it off as worry about all this gambling mess. Still do for that matter. But some other things have come to light, too, and I don't know . . . don't know what to think anymore."

She stopped, trying to decide how much to say. Her secrets about the drugs and the insurance policy and the $15,000 in her closet and the check to Reed Morrison weighed on her like an anvil on an ant and she wanted to let someone else carry part of the load. But she needed someone who couldn't get hurt by it all.

That's why she hadn't told Tess. If someone did murder Jack, then the less anyone else knew, the better. No reason to bring Tess into any danger. But Wilt? Maybe he could take care of himself. Maybe she could tell him and feel reasonably sure no one could hurt him.

She studied Wilt's face. He came across as a man on the fast track to the top. No one thought he would stop with his current position. Most pundits said he would go higher. Many said he was *destined* to go higher. With his father's money, estimated at just less than half a billion dollars, he could run for any office in the nation. Speculation said he would too. Said his father would see to it, even if Wilt didn't want it.

Robert Carver, never a king, but time and time again a king maker, wanted his son on the throne. Either senator or governor in the next election cycle, then maybe a run on the White House. If a poor but bright kid from Arkansas could do it, then a rich, bright kid from Missouri surely could too.

For Connie, though, all that mattered little. For her, it boiled down to one question: Did she trust Wilt Carver? If she wanted help, she had to trust somebody. She made a decision: She would tell part of the story, enough for Wilt to help if he wanted, but not enough to get him in any real danger. That would be fair to them both.

Reaching into her lap, she opened her purse and took out a dollar. "I want to retain you as my lawyer," she said, holding out the money. "Then you have to keep confidential what I tell you."

"I'm a representative of the state," said Wilt, refusing the money. "I can't take your money. But no one can make me repeat what you tell me. You have my word on that."

Connie withdrew the dollar. "I need you to get something for me," she said. "A video from the Lake St. Louis branch of the Bank of St. Louis."

"What kind of video?"

"A video of Jack. Back in February he opened an account there. I want to see the surveillance tape of that day."

"How do you know it's there?"

"I don't. But I know he opened the account. And I know that bank has the cameras."

Wilt patted the side of his chair. "What's the point?" he asked. "You see Jack open a bank account. What does that tell you?"

Connie slumped deeper into her chair. "I don't know," she admitted. "Maybe nothing. But I need to see the film. Somehow, I think it'll help me know his state of mind, what he was thinking. You see, Wilt . . . I don't know why Jack set up that account; he kept it a secret. I trust he did it out of a pure motive, but it still hurts to know he went through all this without me, he got himself into something and couldn't get out, and that video shows him doing some of that. If by some slim chance he did kill himself, then I believe the video will show me what he was feeling, his posture, his body language, I don't know, I just need to see it, that's all. It's . . . well . . . it's the last picture I'll ever have of him and I just want to see it!" Her voice trailed off.

Wilt rose and began to pace.

"I don't know if the banks keep those tapes," he said. "I'm certain they don't keep them for long. No reason. A day passes, nothing happens, they file the tape for a few days, then bring it out and tape over it. I'm sure that's what happens. Chances are slim the tape's still there."

"But you'll check?"

Wilt stopped pacing and stood framed in the floor-length window behind his desk. He stuck his hands into his pockets and faced Connie.

"Yes, Connie, I'll do what I can. I'll make a few calls. When I find out something, I'll get in touch, one way or the other."

Pleased, Connie stood and crossed the floor to him. Her eyes smiling, she shook his hand warmly. "Jack thought so highly of you," she said. "I think now I know why."

Wilt dropped her hand and opened his arms, inviting her into an embrace. As she hugged him, he said, "Don't compliment me too highly, Connie. I'm a politician, remember."

Standing in his office with a panoramic view of the Missouri River flowing below, Connie didn't know whether Wilt Carver, state attorney general and rising superstar, was joking with her or warning her.

*****

Two floors down, a man with an earplug and a microphone attached to his head flipped a switch and spoke into his mouthpiece.

"Did you get that?" he asked, his voice little more than a whisper.

"Yeah, taped and labeled."

"He'll want the video."

"I'll get him the copies."

"You do good work."

"Glad you noticed."

*****

Knowing she didn't have much time before the kids rushed in, Connie sped home, hustled inside, and picked up the phone book. Looking up the number for Trans World Airlines, she wondered what a direct flight would cost. She didn't know for certain she would go. After she saw the tape from the bank she would make that decision. Reed might have moved for all she knew. But she needed to keep all her options open. Within a couple of minutes, she dialed the number and reached an operator.

"Yeah, I need some information on flights from St. Louis to Las Vegas."

"What dates did you want to fly?"

"Well, I'm not sure yet, just wanted to find out the daily flight times."

"Okay, let's see. We have an 8:05 then a 11:10 in the morning and a 1:20 and a 6:35 in the afternoon. The evening flights are 9:20 and 11:10. Any of those work for you?"

"Yeah, I think so. Now I just have to get my dates straight."

"Call us back when you do, and we'll gladly make your reservations. Anything else I can do for you today?"

"Yes, how much are the tickets for those flights?"

"That depends. What time of day you want to leave, how long in advance you make your ticket, whether you stay over on Saturday or not. Anywhere from 138 to 479 dollars. As soon as you know when you want to fly and how long you'll stay, we can make your reservations."

Satisfied, Connie thanked the agent, hung up, and scooted to her bedroom. Changing into jeans and a light sweatshirt, she got busy. The kids would get home in less than an hour, and she needed to get supper on.

CHAPTER
14

That night at just past 9:30, after tucking the kids into bed, Connie joined Tick and Tess in the den for a cup of hot tea. Though exhausted from the day's events, she had one more thing to do. She had to tell them about the alleged affair and ask Tick to help her find the woman who claimed it.

Taking a seat on the sofa by Tess and leaving the rocking chair for Tick, she blew on her tea and decided to go right to the point.

"Tick, I need a favor," she said, staring him straight in the eyes.

"Anything I can do, you know I'm your man."

"I thought you were my man," teased Tess.

"You better treat me better, or I might make a trade," he said, laughing. "What can I do for you, Connie, my dear."

Connie cut the levity off at the knees. "You can get me the name and address of a woman who claims to have had an affair with Jack."

Tick gulped and spilled tea on his jeans. Tess instantly set her tea on an end table and turned to Connie.

"What woman?" she exclaimed. "Who told you something crazy like that?"

Connie stayed calm. "Luke Tyler did. I don't know many details. But Tyler said this woman from Columbia came in and said she and Jack were lovers."

"No way!" shouted Tick, his blond mustache wiggling violently. "Jack loved you more than anything . . . he wouldn't . . ."

wouldn't hurt you . . . take a chance on losing you and the kids doing something like that."

"I told Tyler the same thing," said Connie. "But he didn't seem to believe me. Saw this as a reason for Jack to commit suicide. You know, conscience-ridden man involved in adultery ends his life rather than face his family, that kind of thing."

"He didn't know Jack Brandon!" Tess insisted. "Of all the crazy notions, this one takes the cake."

"But I need to prove that for Tyler to keep the investigation going," said Connie. "Right now, he's leaning toward declaring it a suicide and shutting it down."

Calmer now, Tick sipped on his tea, then said, "You're right, Connie. That's the talk downtown. Most take the suicide note pretty seriously. An affair gives him a motive. Men have done themselves in for far less than this."

"That assumes the charge is true," said Tess.

"Sure it does," agreed Connie.

"But with Jack, we know it's not," said Tick.

"But how do we prove that to everyone else?" asked Tess.

"We go see this woman," said Connie. "See her eye-to-eye. Make her tell us the truth."

Tick placed his tea in his lap, steadying it with one hand while he twirled his mustache with his other. "You say Tyler told you this?"

"Yes."

"And he interviewed her?"

"Yes. He said she came forward when she saw the story in the paper. Didn't want people going off on wild goose chases if she caused the problem."

"That was kind of her." Sarcasm dripped in Tess's words.

"Tyler's pretty good, though," said Tick. "If this woman said she and Jack had an affair and Tyler believed her, she had to do a pretty good acting job."

Connie licked tea off the edge of her cup. "I asked him to reinterview her. Try to tie down her story. Where did she and Jack go? Did they spend time in hotels? Any record of that? You know . . . the kinds of things we can check."

"What did he find out?"

"Nothing. Her phone is disconnected, and no one is home."

Tick twitched his mustache. "That's interesting. Patrols checking her out?"

"Yes, Tyler said the Columbia guys go by every day. She rents an apartment and everything looks normal, but they never find her."

"You want to go by there yourself? Is that it?"

Connie shrugged. "Sure. I want to see the woman who says she slept with my husband. Since she's lying, someone had to put her up to it, maybe paid her to tell the lie. She obviously wants the murder investigation to go away. If the police declare it a suicide, she accomplishes her goal."

"You think she's connected with Jack's killer?" It was Tess who asked, her normally boisterous voice reduced to a whisper.

"She may not know she is, but that's the way I see it."

"So we find this woman, and we find Jack's murderer?"

"I'm not sure, but possibly."

"That sounds dangerous," said Tick. "If somebody did murder Jack, they won't take too kindly to somebody digging around in that. This isn't work for a mama."

"It's police work," said Tess, sliding over to Connie and taking her hand. "You need to let Tick and Luke Tyler take care of this. You could get in trouble, get hurt. If they killed Jack, then—" She stopped, not willing to follow her logic to its conclusion.

"Then they will kill again if necessary." Connie completed the sentence.

"You think it's the gambling people, don't you?" asked Tick.

"I can't imagine anyone else."

For several long seconds, no one spoke. Tick took another sip of tea, and Tess patted Connie over and over again on the hand. The ceiling creaked, and Connie noticed the wind had picked up outside. She stared at Tick.

"Can you get me the woman's name and address?" she asked.

Tick rubbed his head. "I don't know. I'm sure only a few folks know that information."

"It's in Tyler's computer," Connie said.

"That's secure."

"Don't you have clearance?"

"Sure, but not at that level. I'll need Luke's password."

"Can you get it?"

"I'm not sure I should."

"Will you think about it?"

He twirled his mustache.

Tess spoke for him. "He'll think about it."

*****

Stepping back to let Wilt Carver enter his office, Luke Tyler studied the man. Handsome if you liked the real polished kind of guy. Not much taller than a broomstick, but he seemed taller because he carried himself with such a confident air. Black hair peppered at his temples with gray. Fine facial features. Thin without being skinny, brown eyebrows neatly trimmed and resting over an alert set of brown eyes. One barely noticeable scar on his left cheek, obviously the work of a good plastic surgeon, but once a major cut or scratch of some kind.

"Have a seat, sir," said Tyler, remembering his manners. "This office isn't much, but it works for me."

Carver glanced around, his eyes darting, taking in everything. "It looks good, functional. Thanks for seeing me on such short notice."

Dropping a briefcase to the floor, he plopped down into the straight chair in front of Tyler's desk.

Tyler took a toothpick from a box in his top drawer. He offered the box to Carver.

"What brings you slumming at my place this time of the evening?" Tyler asked.

Carver patted the side of the chair, then cleared his throat. "Well . . . you are the lead man on the Brandon situation and something has come to my attention I think you should know. I'm leaving town tomorrow and wanted to deliver it before I left."

Tyler bit on his toothpick. He didn't like all this attention from such powerful people. How had Carver gotten involved in this? Then he relaxed a bit. Carver had contacts in places he could only imagine. Someone had apparently come to the attorney general with some information. Nothing unusual about that.

This case had gotten play all over the state, even a bit beyond. Wild speculation about gambling and Jack Brandon's opposition to it poured from scores of media outlets. Connie Brandon didn't stand alone with her suspicions that the gambling industry, with its alleged ties to the Mob, had snuffed Jack Brandon to win a local election in the state capital. People all across the country were calling this election a key to the Midwest. If Jefferson City, conservative center of middle-America morality, passed gambling, then every city and town bordering the Missouri and Mississippi River became an open target.

With that kind of national play, information about Brandon's death might come from anywhere. Someone might go to the attorney general with their story. Tyler shrugged. He didn't care. No sweat off his nose.

"I'm all ears, Mr. Carver."

"It's Wilt, detective. Just Wilt. Look, here's what I've got." He reached to his side, pulled up his briefcase, and opened it. Inside, he grabbed a videotape and held it up for Tyler.

Tyler reached across the desk and took the tape.

"What's on it?"

"A bank surveillance video. Routine these days."

Tyler nodded. "Brandon?"

"None other."

"Local?"

"Nope. St. Louis. Opening an account."

Tyler bit into his toothpick. "Twenty-five thousand dollars in that account?"

Wilt's eyes darkened. "I don't know about that. I've got no authority at that point. You'll have to check that for yourself."

Tyler nodded. "I expect I will. What's special about the tape?"

Wilt lowered his eyes. "It's Jack," he said. "Jack Brandon and a woman."

Tyler cracked his toothpick, then picked it out of his mouth. Slowly, he opened the top right drawer of his desk and pulled out a blue folder. Opening the folder, he slid it over to Carver for his inspection. "Does this describe the woman?"

Carver studied the page for almost a minute. It described a blonde woman. Five feet seven inches tall. Blue eyes. One hundred fourteen pounds. As he read, he began to nod. "It sounds like the same woman," he said. "The one in the video."

Tyler stroked his beard. The woman, Sandra Lunsford, listed at 110 Maple Road in Columbia, Missouri, had her name registered in three hotels in Jefferson City between January 15 and April 1. Having interviewed her, Tyler knew the description in his folder didn't do her justice. Almost forty years old, she had naturally blonde hair, eyes the color of a robin's eggs, and a body that made men get neck cricks when she walked past. Andy Starks said she had visited the Good Books Store on at least two occasions. Once, Starks remembered, she stayed alone with Jack in the back for at least fifteen minutes.

Not wanting to stress Connie Brandon until he knew more, Tyler had asked Starks to keep this information quiet, and Starks agreed. Now, though, the truth had to come out. He hated the thought of it, but he had a job to do.

"Can I keep this video?" he asked.

Carver nodded quickly. "Sure, I brought it for you to keep. For the investigation."

"One of us needs to tell Connie Brandon."

"Connie already knows about the tape. But she doesn't know the woman is on it."

Tyler's eyes widened. "She knows about the tape?"

"Yes, fact is, she came to me and asked me to get it for her."

"Then I assume she knows about the account also."

"She's the one who told me."

Tyler leaned back and cradled his head in his hands. "She's a remarkable woman."

"I think so."

Tyler raised back up. "Why are you bringing me the tape? Shouldn't you take it to her?"

Carver sighed and lowered his eyes. When he looked up again, his eyes seemed dim, almost ashamed. "I agonized what to do when I got it," he said. "Connie didn't explicitly ask me to keep it from the authorities. So I had to decide. Give it to her, let her do heaven only knows what with it. Or come to you, let you find out about this woman first. Make sure it's safe for Connie. That's what worried me the most. I thought Connie might take this and get herself in some kind of trouble. She doesn't need any more strain. I hoped you might handle it."

Not sure whether to believe Carver, Tyler shrugged. What Carver said made sense. Connie had already faced enough. She didn't need to run off half-cocked searching for Sandra Lunsford.

"One of us needs to take her the tape," Tyler repeated.

"I'm leaving town in the morning. You want to do it?"

Tyler sighed. "Might as well. I've already told her a woman might be involved."

"What will this do to the investigation?"

Tyler rubbed his beard. "Not sure. But chances are this will pull the plug on it. No reason to waste more tax dollars on a suicide."

Carver stood, his briefcase in hand. "Too bad about Jack," he said. "I've known him a long time. He was a good man. Too bad he got caught up in all this."

Tyler shook his hand, and Carver walked out. Not speaking to anyone, Tyler stepped to an office next door, closed the door, and popped the tape into a video monitor on a rectangular table in the center of the room. Flipping off the lights, he seated himself in front of the video. Using the remote from the table, he clicked on the film. It lasted just over fifteen minutes and showed Jack Brandon and Sandra Lunsford together as he opened the bank account in St. Louis.

Tyler squinted as he watched, trying to interpret the tape. On several occasions, Sandra Lunsford touched Jack's arm or Jack steered her by the small of the back. They talked easily to each other, not laughing but talking seriously, as if they had a secret they needed to keep. More than once, she leaned in close and he did the same with her.

Watching the video, Tyler wished he had audio on it so he could hear what they said. For a moment, he thought about trying to find a lip reader but then decided he had no reason. It was all plain enough. If he had any doubts at all, the end of the video destroyed his misgivings. One picture did it, the last image on the screen. As Jack finished his transaction with the bank, he bent slightly and kissed Sandra Lunsford on the forehead. It was such an act of care that Tyler had no doubt it conveyed love.

Rewinding the tape, Tyler sat still, his hands locked behind his head. He hated the times when he found out bad things about normally good people. It happened far too often for his tastes. A simple, small-town man or woman, moving through life like everyone else, slipping through the stream as easily and naturally as a trout in a river. But then something happens. The man turns forty and begins to feel mortal. The woman sees a double chin creeping up from her neck. An affair begins in the drive to cheat the sands of time. A businessperson, striving to get to the next level, sees the promotion go to a rival. Needing money to pay the mortgage, the young professional dreams up an embezzlement scheme and gets away with it for a few years. But then the hammer falls and prison becomes a permanent address.

Adultery, theft, scams, assault, and yes, even murder. Normal people doing abnormal crimes. Tyler had seen it all.

This one hurt more than most though, he had to admit, because he had come to appreciate Connie Brandon in a way he hadn't appreciated any woman in many a year. He knew he shouldn't feel this way, that Connie faced far too much grief for him to even consider it, but, dadgummit, he couldn't help what he felt.

Connie Brandon deserved better than life had given her lately. But, that didn't change the facts. Life didn't always give us what we deserved. He, the husband of a good woman who died of breast cancer four years ago, knew that better than most. Now, he had to tell another good woman that the man she loved more than anything else in the whole world had most likely spent his last weeks on earth in the arms of another woman.

Reaching into the pocket of his denim shirt for a toothpick, Tyler closed his eyes and breathed a gentle prayer for Connie Brandon, a woman he had come to respect and care for in just a few short days.

CHAPTER
15

T aking care not to wake the kids, Connie quietly opened the side door and left the house at sunup on Tuesday. The air, crisp and clean, smelled pure, like God had just washed it with fresh water. Connie loved this time of day, when everything lay so quiet and serene. Moving out of her yard, she started to lift the weights she carried in each hand, up left, then down, up right, then down. Repeating the rhythm as she walked, she stared toward the Missouri River that ran to her right below the bluffs. The river ran swift but calm today, a snake of mud and moisture. Like everyone who spent any time thinking about it, Connie felt awe when she watched the river. It ran all the time, but it had new water in it every second it ran. Life was like that too—moving all the time, but some things never the same.

Her breath picked up pace. She hadn't walked like this since the day Jack died, and the notion of doing it alone scared her. She gazed at the river and loneliness soaked her. She and Jack loved their walks together, often used them as times of reverent prayer. If not totally silent, they became just the opposite—so talkative they scared the squirrels away.

Connie smiled, remembering their conversations. Jack babbling about the store or the church and she running on and on about the children—a new dress for Katie or Daniel's latest game—or school, a class finished, a class yet to take. If she only had tape recordings of their walks, she could trace their entire married life in them. But now she had no one to talk with her, no one to pray with her, no one with her at all. She had to face life alone, raise two kids alone, deal with the murder of her husband alone.

She didn't know if she could manage it. Especially the last part—finding out what happened to Jack. What looked so simple last night now loomed as an impenetrable black cloud. How could she find out what the police couldn't? They were the professionals, she the amateur. They knew about things like this, she didn't. Jack's death might forever remain a mystery—suspended between the suicide the circumstances indicated and the murder she knew in her soul had occurred.

Feeling herself sinking into self-pity, Connie searched her thoughts for a word of encouragement. Instantly, God provided one. She began to whisper the words of Jesus as she walked.

"Come to Me, all you who labor and are heavy laden, and I will give you rest. Take My yoke upon you and learn from Me, for I am gentle and lowly in heart, and you will find rest for your souls. For my yoke is easy and My burden is light."

As she walked faster and faster, her heart pumping harder and harder, she lifted the weights up and down and repeated the Lord's words over and over. Yes, life became heavy at times and pressed down hard. But Jesus understood that feeling. Jesus could have yielded, given up in the face of it all. But Jesus kept working and serving and acting in the name of God. Through the strength of Jesus, she could do the same.

She pumped her arms faster, her spirits lifting as she walked and prayed. To her right, hundreds of feet below, the Missouri River flowed past, its great gush of water headed toward the Mississippi, which rushed onward to the Gulf of Mexico. Behind her, the sun rose in golden hues, its heat just beginning to lick at the edges of the earth. In that same direction, a quarter of a mile away, a lone man in a red Jaguar kept vigil, his binoculars peeping through the early morning air to keep her in sight. Holding his binoculars with his left hand, he flipped open a cell phone with his right. Another man answered the phone.

"I got the ears into Red's place," said the man in the Jaguar, "when she drove to St. Louis. We'll know soon if she's a threat or not."

"Good work, Brit, keep me posted."

Brit closed the phone and smoothed down his ponytail. Surveillance wasn't his best thing. But who knew where it would lead.

*****

Luke Tyler left his house at just past 8:00 A.M., the videotape of Jack Brandon and Sandra Lunsford laying in the passenger seat of his car and a fresh toothpick in his mouth. Though dreading the encounter with Connie, he nonetheless wanted to get it over with as soon as possible. Sleep had escaped him all night, and he knew he would remain awake until he completed this unpleasant chore.

Heading into town from his white-frame farmhouse ten miles out, he tried to think of some way to make this easier, but no magic solution came to mind. Sometimes, you just had to spill it out. Bad news sugarcoated tasted just as bitter. But, man, what a tough job. He just hoped Connie wouldn't hate him because he was the one who carried the message.

Turning left off Highway 50, he switched on the radio and tuned to a local religious station. He needed that kind of music right now, something to remind him of the good in the world, something to remind him that, ultimately, evil wouldn't win, current facts to the contrary. With the sounds of an old gospel hymn in the background, he turned onto West Bluff Drive and eased toward Connie's house.

Parking two houses down, he paused for a second and cleared his head. Okay, it was just past 8:30. Her kids should have left for school. Just go to the door, tell her you need to talk, show her the video, help her with any calls she needs to make, and then leave. Stay professional. Do your job clean and neat and get out. He glanced in the mirror, then smoothed down his beard. He thought he saw movement to his rear in a red car a hundred yards or so down the road. Studying the rearview mirror, Tyler saw nothing else stir. Just his imagination.

He took one last breath, stepped out of the car, and tossed his toothpick to the ground. A minute later, he rang the doorbell and waited on Connie Brandon to answer so he could blow away what remained of her world.

*****

When Connie heard the doorbell ring, she quickly finished brushing her teeth. Already changed from her walk, she wore the simple khakis that made up so much of her daily wardrobe and a long-sleeved, emerald-green cotton shirt. Her red hair lay on her shoulders. As she glanced at herself in the mirror she decided she looked pretty good for a thirty eight year old suffering the deepest grief a human could feel. Feeling strangely guilty at the notion, she hustled from the bathroom to the front door.

Though startled to see Tyler when she opened the door, she recovered quickly. "Good morning, Mr. Tyler, come on in." Tyler stepped past her into the narrow entry hall.

"Sorry to bother you so early," he started. "And would you *please* call me Luke?"

Connie motioned toward the den, then led him to it. "It's not early for me, I've been up a couple of hours already. Took a walk, got the kids off to school . . . you know, a mom's work is never done."

In the den, she pointed him to a rocker, and he took it. She placed herself on the sofa directly across from the fireplace. Settling in, she noticed the manila envelope under his left arm.

"Hey, it's not even blue," she joked, pointing to the envelope.

He laughed briefly, but she saw quickly his heart wasn't in it. Her spirits sank. Without going any further, she sensed the envelope carried something she didn't want to see.

It didn't take him long to verify her fears. He hung his head over his knees, and she understood that what he had to say caused him great sadness. He didn't want to do this, and for that she felt grateful.

She made it easier for him. "It's bad news, isn't it?" she asked, her voice soft.

He nodded. "I've got a video of Jack at the bank in St. Louis."

Connie raised her eyebrows. "But how did you—?"

"Wilt Carver. Somebody gave it to him. I didn't ask who."

Anger flared in Connie's stomach. "I asked him to get it for me," she said.

"He said he didn't know what to do with it. Wanted to protect you, keep you from doing something you shouldn't do. He had to leave town this morning or he would have come himself."

Connie bit her lip. Wilt's motives sounded understandable. And, she hadn't specifically told him what to do with the tape when he found it. She decided to give him the benefit of a doubt.

Concentrating on Luke again, she wondered how much he knew about her activities over the last few days. Since he had the tape he also knew about the account in St. Louis. Perhaps he knew how much Jack put in it and how much she took out. Even more important, if the state gave him the authority, he might access the account and find out about the check to Reed Morrison, whoever he was. Another possibility came to her.

"Why is the tape bad news?" she asked. "I'm glad to see Jack one more time. Even if he is doing something he kept a secret from me, it's still the last video I'll ever have of him. How can that be bad?"

Luke hung his head and she suddenly felt sorry for him. This hurt him more than she imagined. He really did care about this, about . . . about her.

"Hey, Luke, it's okay," she soothed. "Nothing can be any worse than what I've already faced. Just go ahead and tell me. Whatever it is, I can deal with it. As the saying goes, 'There's nothing too big that the Lord and I together can't handle.'"

He raised his eyes, and Connie saw moisture in them. He choked as he spoke. "He's with the woman, Mrs. Brandon, the woman . . . who told me about the affair. You can't prove anything for certain by it . . . but you can tell they know each other, they touch, you see, not intimately, but like two people who have a relationship. Add to that the fact that she stayed at several hotels in Jefferson City over the last few months. She even came into the store some; Andy saw her there several times. I wish I didn't have to say all this. I'm sorry to bring you such awful news, but that's the way the video shows it, and I just didn't know anything else but to tell you . . . "

His voice dropped, and Connie sat there stunned. Neither of them spoke for a couple of long minutes. Luke stroked his beard, his eyes down, and Connie fought back the tears that threatened to wash away what she had left of her spirit. She nodded toward the video, still held under his arm. "Did you watch it?"

He looked up and nodded.

"Plug it in." She pointed to the television in the corner.

He stood and walked to it, slipping the video into the VCR. Five seconds later, the screen clicked and turned bright and Jack's pleasant face appeared.

Connie watched the video in silence. As the images flickered on the screen, she found herself becoming angry at Jack, then at the woman on the screen, then at herself . . . and finally at God. It all made so much sense now! Jack did have a motive for suicide. Guilt—simple as that. He did have a conscience. He had preached one message all his life—do what's right. If she heard it once, she heard it a thousand times.

An interesting notion popped into her head. Maybe Jack had killed himself, then set up the contradictory clues—the keyboard without fingerprints, the misspelling of Kate for Katie, the lump on his own head. Maybe he wanted it to look like murder so the insurance company would pay off for her and the children. It sounded like one of the mysteries he read from time to time.

But what about this woman? This tape would destroy even his best efforts to make it look like murder.

Johnson Mack came to mind. She would need to sell him the store, get the money, and leave town. If Jack had an affair with this woman, then she wanted nothing else to do with anything he once touched or loved. She would sell the house and the store. Give away Jack's few possessions, purge her life of anything and everything that reminded her of him. The video screen went blank. It took Connie a moment to realize it had ended. She glanced over at Luke. He had his eyes down, examining his shoes as if hypnotized by them. Connie exhaled in a long, cleansing breath.

"Well," she said. "Now I know. The facts keep stacking up. As much as I might want to deny it, Jack obviously had something going on with that woman. The video, the motel charges, the statement she gave you, the fact that Andy saw her in the store. Not much way around it. If it wasn't an affair, it sure walked and talked and quacked like an affair."

She stood up and pulled the video out. "You keep this, Luke. I don't think I want it in the house."

"I can understand that." He took the video.

"I assume this means the investigation stops."

"That's right. I talked to the mayor and police chief this morning. As they see it, the video makes the suicide note sound authentic."

"You agree with them?"

Luke rubbed his beard. "I'm not 100 percent positive, but at this point, I don't see any other logical explanation. I'm open to another look if someone gives me a reason, but—"

"But this video sheds a whole new light on things."

"Exactly. The mayor says this settles it."

Connie wondered if the mayor knew about the insurance. If so, he certainly wanted this declared a suicide. She started to tell Luke but feared her suspicions would sound desperate. Not much chance Luke would act on such a flimsy possibility. She dismissed the idea and moved to another concern. "Can we keep this quiet?" she asked.

Luke nodded quickly. "Don't see why not. With the investigation closed, no reason to say anything more."

"Good, that'll spare my kids a bit of pain."

"Glad to do it."

Connie changed the subject. "Who's the woman?"

"Huh?"

"Her name, Luke. The woman's name."

He gave it without hesitation. "Sandra Lunsford. But you won't need her address. The guys from Columbia called me this morning. They went by last night. This time they found everything gone from the apartment. Cleaned out."

Connie swallowed, gathering herself. Okay. Time to go to Plan B. Though it looked like an affair was indeed probable and she couldn't confront the woman, she could still find out about Reed Morrison. She would too. Though the mystery of Jack's death now seemed explainable, another mystery lay in Las Vegas. Why did Jack pay Morrison such money? Maybe the two riddles had no connection, but somehow, she still thought they did. One way or the other, she planned to find out. If nothing else, Morrison might know Lunsford, tell her why Jack fell for her.

Facing Luke again, she held out her hand. "Thanks for coming," she said. "And thanks for your sensitivity. I know this wasn't easy for you."

"Easier on me than you," he said, his voice sincere.

She sighed. "I'm okay. Just takes some adjustment, you know?"

"I'm sure it does. I'm amazed you're hanging in as well as you are."

"God's grace," she whispered, "is sufficient."

"I pray it will be." He stood, and she led him to the door. As he stepped outside, he turned back to her one more time.

"Look, Mrs. Brandon . . . I don't want you to take this the wrong way . . . but . . . well . . . would you mind if I checked on you every now and again? Just to see if you need anything?"

Not sure how to read the question, Connie studied his eyes. As gray as ever but not intimidating anymore. Kindly, caring. What harm could it do for him to call her?

"That would be fine," she said. "And if I need you, I know I can call."

He smiled briefly, then stepped to his car.

Before he started the engine, Connie ducked back inside. She had to get a ticket to Vegas, and she wanted to catch the next day's 1:20 flight.

*****

Three minutes after Connie finished her phone call to TWA, Brit smoothed down his ponytail and flipped open his cell phone.

"She's headed to Vegas tomorrow on the one-twenty," he said, his right thumb drumming a steady beat on the Jag's steering wheel.

"Get there before she does. You and Lennie take care of business. Don't allow a hook-up."

"On the way."

"Good, don't hurt her unless it's necessary."

"I know the score."

"I'm sure you do."

Brit closed the phone and considered Connie Brandon—Red, as he called her. A smart woman. Maybe too smart. No threat yet. But who knew what the future would bring.

CHAPTER

16

Keeping their normal schedule, Connie called Daniel and Katie into her room about 9:00 P.M. for their devotional. Daniel, still wearing his baseball practice clothes, rested against the headboard of the bed, a baseball in his left hand, his Bible open on his lap, his feet almost reaching the end. Katie wore her pajamas, a Lion King nightshirt that reached to her calves, and she lay in a fetal position beside Daniel, her big brown eyes open but already dulled by coming sleep. She held a Tabasco Beanie Baby in her arms. Just out of the shower, Connie had wrapped a towel around her wet hair and slipped into a pair of full-length beige cotton pajamas.

Climbing onto the bed, she sat cross-legged beside Katie and asked Daniel to read the passage he had selected. He lay aside the baseball, lifted the Bible, and held it close to his face.

"This is Proverbs 3, verses 5 and 6," he said. "Trust in the LORD with all your heart, And lean not on your own understanding; In all your ways acknowledge Him, And He shall direct your paths." With a satisfied nod, he closed the Bible and lay back again.

"Daddy liked that one," Katie said, her eyes barely open. "He read that to us not too long ago."

"That's why I read it," said Daniel. "Because Dad liked it."

"What does it mean?" asked Katie.

Daniel turned to Connie. "Mom, tell her what it means. I could, but I don't want to show off."

Connie smiled at him, then patted Katie on the bottom. "Well, it means that God wants us to depend on him, not think we can figure things out for ourselves. Our understanding can get all mixed up. But God knows what's happening and will take us the right way if we just follow his spiritual guidelines."

"So we just trust God and God takes care of us," said Katie.

"You're mighty wise for seven years old," said Connie, stroking her hair. "Mighty wise."

Several seconds passed. Daniel rubbed his head. "I'm going to let my hair grow out some," he said to no one in particular. "It's so short now it itches."

"I heard Melissa say she liked it short," chimed Katie. "Better not cut it, or she won't like you anymore."

"Who cares what Melissa thinks? I don't like her!"

"Yes, you do. Her sister told me she saw you kiss her!"

Connie moved to Daniel's side and listened as her children picked on each other. It sounded comforting for them to go on this way. What amazing resilience children had! Able to take almost any circumstance and survive it.

"Sit up here," she said to Katie. "Come sit by Mama."

Katie obeyed, and Connie wrapped her left arm around her and her right arm around Daniel. Katie lay her head on Connie's shoulder, and all three of them became quiet, the weariness of a busy day settling in. Connie took a deep breath.

"I'm leaving on a short trip tomorrow," she began.

"Where to?" asked Daniel.

"Can we go?" asked Katie.

"No, I'm going by myself. You guys will do your normal things. I'll see you off to school in the morning. I talked to Mrs. Everhart earlier tonight. She's going to stay with you the first day and night, then Tess the next one if I'm not back."

"Where you going?" Daniel repeated his question.

"Well, you won't believe this, but I'm going to Las Vegas."

"Are you going to gamble?" Katie's brown eyes widened like saucers.

Connie laughed. "No, precious. Mom is not going to gamble. Mom is going to look for a friend of Daddy's."

"I didn't know Dad had any friends in Vegas," said Daniel.

"Not everyone in Vegas is bad. Some of them are normal people, just like us."

"Is Daddy's friend a normal person?" asked Katie.

Connie considered the question. "I'll know soon, I hope."

"When will you get home?" Daniel asked.

"Not sure right now. Maybe one day, maybe two. But, if it takes a little longer, don't worry. Tess and Mrs. Everhart will take good care of you, and I'll call every night."

Katie raised up and squeezed Tabasco to her chest. "Every night, Mommy, you promise you'll call every night?"

Connie patted her red curls. "Every night, precious, every night."

Satisfied, Katie lay back down, Tabasco under her chin. Connie faced Daniel. He nodded. "It's time to pray," he said.

Connie closed her eyes. "Katie, you go first."

Katie yawned, then said, "Jesus, take care of Mommy while she travels. Take care of Daniel when he pitches baseball. Take care of me when I go to school and play. And take care of Daddy there with you. Amen."

Daniel quickly followed. "Lord, we do ask for your protection on Mom. Give Mrs. Everhart and Miss Tess the strength they'll need to take care of us. Continue to help us day by day as we deal with our . . . well, our . . . sorrow over Dad's death. Thank you, Jesus, for being with us in all of this. Amen."

Connie finished for them. "Our Lord, make us aware of your direction. We miss it far too often. We get uncertain of what to do. Show us the way. Mark it plain so even the slow to learn can see it. Give us courage too, Lord Jesus. Courage to do the right thing. Courage to follow your will. Help us to lean on your understanding and not our own. We love you, Lord, and thank you for loving us. Bless Daniel and Katie while I'm away and, like Daniel said, give Tess and Mrs. Everhart enough strength to take care of them. In your holy name we ask it. Amen."

Daniel turned to her and wrapped his arms around her neck. Connie pulled Katie closer. For a long minute the three of them relaxed in the embrace, a warm triangle of love and devotion. Holding her children, Connie's eyes watered and she closed them. "Protect them, Jesus," she prayed silently. "No matter what I find in Las Vegas, protect my babies."

*****

Standing by a swimming pool six miles out of Las Vegas, a lean man in his mid-forties wearing a white suit that cost him a thousand dollars slipped a cell phone from his jacket pocket and pressed it to his ear.

"Hey," he said to the caller on the other end. "What's the news?"

"Listen up, Lennie. She's on the way out there."

"She know anything?"

"Not much, I don't think. But better safe than sorry."

"So what you want me to do?"

"Help Brit if he needs it."

"Brit coming out?" Lennie unbuttoned the white suit jacket.

"Yeah, should be there real soon. Stay close to him. He gets outside the lines sometimes, you know what I mean?"

"Sure, he's a real cowboy. What's she after?" Lennie buttoned his coat.

"More like who. Apparently she's looking for Morrison."

"So who isn't? He disappeared a couple of days ago. Haven't seen him since."

"You know where he lives."

"Sure, but he hasn't been there for a while."

"Keep an eye on his place. He has to come back sooner or later."

"What a great idea! I'll get right on it, right after I finish my swim."

The line fell silent for a moment. When the man spoke again, his voice carried bullets in it. "Don't forget your manners, Lennie. You're not talking to Brit here. Just do your job and make sure it stays clean. You're not indispensable you know." The line went dead.

Unbuttoning his coat, Lennie slipped his phone into his breast pocket and wiped his forehead. How could he be so stupid? A guy could get in deep hooey talking to The Man like that. He'd made it real plain with that last line. Though careful of what he said over the cell phone, The Man made it clear. Do the job or else. Man, how could he be so stupid? He better find Morrison and fast.

*****

Back in Jefferson City, Connie peeped in on Katie and Daniel one more time to make sure they had fallen asleep. Their deep, regular breathing told her all was well. Good. She stepped to her bedroom, slipped into an off-white jogging suit and a pair of cross-trainer shoes. Then, her hair in a Cardinals baseball cap, she stepped out into the dark. She didn't plan to go far, just a couple of blocks from the house, to an empty lot at the end of the road, a lot too steep for anyone to put a house on. It took only a couple of minutes to get there.

Walking to the back of the lot, a spot that overlooked the Missouri, she stared into the sky. From this vantage point, she could see for miles—the bluffs across the river, the sky a canopy of black and silver, and the river shimmering with the glow of moonlight. A light wind whipped across her neck, tickling her under the cap. The moon, almost full, stared down at her like a friendly parent. A barge sat on the Missouri near the opposite shore, its lights warning any passing vessels to give it wide berth.

Connie stood still and took a deep breath. Goodness, what a glorious night. But she didn't feel like celebrating. Today she had learned that her husband had indeed had an affair. The news crushed everything she had ever trusted. She had fought against believing it, but the image of Jack kissing Sandra Lunsford shattered the last of her illusions. She knew Jack loved her and the kids, but something in him had snapped. Other men of God had faltered, and so had he.

Her shoulders slumped, Connie knew she should just give up. Sell the store to Mack, find a buyer for the house, and leave Jefferson City. That would give her money enough to make a decent start somewhere else. With Daniel and Katie, she could survive, maybe even find some semblance of happiness down the road. Skipping the trip to Las Vegas was surely the prudent path. But she knew she couldn't do it. Skipping Las Vegas felt too much like running, and she had decided a long time ago she wasn't a quitter. Her mom and dad had quit on each other and on her, but she wouldn't follow their example. Having never had a home until she met Jack and settled in Jefferson City, she refused to give it up without a struggle. She might lose it eventually, but not because she backed away from the battle.

Reed Morrison might end up a dead end, but she had to make the effort to find out. If he didn't pan out, okay. She could live with that. But she had to try. That's all she could ask of herself.

Staring at the sky, Connie took off her baseball cap and threw back her head. Her red hair, uncombed since her shower, fanned out in the breeze as vibrant as loose fire. With the cap in her right hand, Connie spread her arms as far as they would go, reaching from the east to the west. Spreading her legs and squaring her shoulders, she looked straight up into heaven and screamed as loudly as her voice would carry. "Whhhhhhhhhy?"

The wind picked up her scream and carried it up and down, across and over, a seed darting through the air, lifting it on the breeze, blowing it out over the river, dropping it to the ground, first in this place and then in another. On the barge below, a dog lifted his head and barked. Inside Connie's house, Katie stirred in her sleep and squeezed Tabasco closer. A hundred yards away, if he'd still been sitting in his red import, Brit would have tilted his head in wonder.

Connie, of course, didn't know all this. All she knew was the river seemed oblivious to her scream, and she wondered, for just an instant, if God was also.

CHAPTER

17

A s soon as the kids left for school, Connie dressed quickly, throwing on her comfortable khakis and a white, short-sleeved blouse. Carrying a navy vest in case the plane got too cold, she pinned her hair back in a snug bun and left for the St. Louis airport. Though her ticketed flight departed at 1:20, she wanted to arrive early and see if she could get on the 11:10. The sooner she got to Las Vegas and found Reed Morrison, the quicker she could settle her business with him and move ahead with her life. At the airport, she caught a break—they did have seating availability on the 11:10.

Looking out the window at a sunshine so bright it blinded her, she tried to relax and plan what to say to Morrison. Go with the direct approach?

"Hello, I'm Jack Brandon's wife, and I want to know why he wrote you a check for $10,000, and did that have anything to do with his death?" Or should she come on more subtly? "Hello, I'm Connie Brandon, I think you knew my late husband. Can you tell me all about your relationship?"

No matter how she said it, it sounded too blunt. But how do you ask a man you've never met why he received ten grand from your husband right before he ended up dead in the Missouri River? Blunt it would have to be.

Within two and a half hours, the plane touched down, and Connie climbed off. With no previous experience in Vegas, the presence of the slot machines in the airport terminal shocked her. Was this the destiny of Jefferson City? The destiny of the whole country, for that matter? Slot machines in grocery stores, airport terminals, public buildings? Would the country become so inundated with gambling that no matter where people turned, they would see it? No wonder Jack fought so hard against it. People destroyed their lives with the alluring but evil dream—a quarter buys you a chance for millions.

Hurrying through the terminal, Connie picked up a car and a city map at a rental agency and headed south on Interstate 15. According to the address from the check, Morrison lived at 208 La Toya Drive, a road the map showed running east to west off the interstate a few miles from downtown Vegas. Confident of her direction, she headed toward La Toya Drive, the rental car humming through the arid desert air. Connie tried to imagine Morrison. What did he look like? Would he wear a shiny suit like so many gangsters on television? Was he an elderly gentleman wearing a bolo tie and white shoes? What did he do for a living? Deal blackjack in a casino? Teach school? Run an accounting firm? What about family—did he have a wife and children?

Turning right off the interstate, Connie found herself on a road lined with well-manicured lawns and two-story, Spanish-style homes. Palm trees stood in straight rows up and down the street as far as she could see, and a variety of European cars sat parked in white, concrete driveways. Admiring the attractive neighborhood, she pulled to the shoulder of the road and checked the address again: 208 La Toya Drive. She checked the number of the house immediately to her right: 104. Morrison's house was only one block up!

Connie glanced into the rearview mirror. Her face, though a bit thin, looked fine. No signs of the emotional torrents running inside. A frightening thought dawned on her. Maybe Reed Morrison killed her husband! Perhaps the money Jack paid him was extortion money, blackmail of some sort, money paid to keep an affair a secret?

Her face splotched red. She considered going to a phone and calling the police. Luke Tyler would know what to do. But she couldn't do that. The police had declared Jack's death a suicide. The Las Vegas police would call Jefferson City, get that verified, and shoo her away like a fly at a picnic. She hadn't told Luke about the check from Jack to Morrison. Why would he help someone who held vital information from him? And what if Morrison didn't have anything to do with Jack's death? Then she would really seem crazy. No, she couldn't get help. She had to do this alone.

Guarded by fear, Connie decided to leave the car parked where it sat. No reason to barrel straight into Morrison's yard and ring his doorbell. Better to approach more innocently, walk by the place first, see if she saw anything amiss.

Shaky but determined, she stepped out of the car, gently shut the door, and walked up the sidewalk that ran under the palm trees. She dropped her head lower as if to hide herself in the bright daylight. A minute later she stepped past 208 La Toya Drive. Though she didn't stop, she studied the house as she passed. It looked similar to the other houses on the street. A red, southwestern-style roof covered its two stories and a beige stucco exterior wrapped around it. Palm trees bordered the well-manicured front lawn. A late-model Mercedes with a personal license plate sat parallel to the sidewalk. The house would cost at least $400,000 in Jefferson City. Probably twice that here.

Past the house now, Connie walked another two hundred feet, then pivoted and started back. The house seemed so normal it gave her courage. Even if mixed up in Jack's death, Morrison wouldn't hurt her here. He would wait until later when she least expected it and then strike. By then she could go to the authorities, explain what happened, how she got involved, why she kept this information from them.

Buoyed by her logic, Connie came to the sidewalk leading from the street to Morrison's front door.

Stay calm, she told herself, taking a huge breath. *This guy is the key. Talk to him, find out what happened to Jack. Clear Jack's name. Prove he didn't commit suicide, didn't desert you and the kids.* She took a step up the sidewalk. Then another. Thirty steps later, she stepped onto a white, stone stoop and rang the doorbell.

*****

Inside Reed Morrison's house, Brit and Lennie heard the doorbell ring. In Morrison's bedroom on the second floor, Lennie peered through the drapes and spotted a petite, red-headed woman in a pair of pleated khaki slacks and a short-sleeved, white blouse.

"Who's this?" he whispered to Brit.

Though busy riffling through a desk that sat in a reading arca of the bedroom, Brit instantly shifted his focus and eased over to the window. Spotting Connie, he swore quietly. "She ticketed her flight on the one-twenty!"

"She's a bit early, wouldn't you say?"

Brit sneered at Lennie. "But not early enough."

Both of them looked back at the bed. Reed Morrison, a thick-bodied man in his mid-fifties lay still as a store-window display doll, a small needle prick in the inner middle of his left arm, the spot where nurses always go for blood. His face, though well-tanned, already seemed slightly stiff. Lennie had followed The Man's advice and watched the house all night. Morrison had arrived only that morning, and he and Brit had been hard-pressed to handle their work in such a hurried fashion.

The doorbell rang a second time. "She'll go away in a second," said Lennie. "Then we can search through his papers."

Brit rolled his eyes. "We don't want her to go away, jerk-face. We want to put her to sleep. Just like we did her dearly departed husband."

Lennie rocked back from the window, buttoned his suit coat, and took a step toward Brit. "We didn't get clearance on that," he argued. "I don't do work without clearance."

"Then let me do it," Brit said, his eyes eager, a flick of foam settling in the corners of his thin lips.

The bell rang once more.

"No can do," said Lennie, remembering his orders to keep Brit under control.

They heard a door open. "What the—" whispered Brit, twisting toward the arched entrance of the bedroom, the entrance just past the stairs that led down to the kitchen on the back side of the first floor. "She's coming inside! We have to do her, Lennie, no way out!"

As Brit looked toward the stairs, Lennie quickly unbuttoned his suit and pulled a gun from the waistband. Then, as calmly as if ordering a sandwich from a deli, which he planned to do within the next hour, he cracked Brit across the back of the skull. Catching him as he fell, Lennie snorted. "We'll do her when we get clearance, Bozo, and not until." His arms locked under Brit's shoulders, he slid him across the bedroom, through the arch, down the stairs, through the kitchen, and out the back door.

*****

When no one answered the door, Connie made an instinctive decision. She tested the door to see if it was locked. To her surprise, the handle opened as she turned it. The thought of leaving never entered her mind. One way or the other, she planned to find out about Reed Morrison. Pushing the door open, she took one step onto the hardwood floors of the front entryway. A thud in the back of the house startled her.

"Hello," she shouted. "Anyone home?"

Though not certain, she thought she heard movement, like something sliding, then the sound of a door opening. Without thinking, she rushed ten more steps into the entryway, then caught herself and stopped.

"Mr. Morrison!" she shouted. "Is anybody home?" Her voice echoed through the house, but she heard no answer. Several seconds ticked by. Then, from behind, through the front door, she heard a car door slam, once, twice. Pivoting hurriedly, she rushed back to the front door, then out onto the stoop. Outside, a black Mercedes occupied by two men whipped away from the curb and flew past her, headed toward the interstate. As the car passed, she stared straight at the man nearest to her, the one on the passenger side. His head lay at an odd angle, his mouth sagging open, a blond ponytail behind his head. To her astonishment, he looked vaguely familiar, but she couldn't place him.

Morrison?

She didn't know. Rapidly, she searched through her memory, trying to recall the man's identity. Where had she seen him? Or had she? Was she just imagining she knew him from somewhere? Was it possible he was Morrison and she had seen him in Jefferson City at some point? She couldn't remember. But she had to find out.

Running back into the house, she rushed through the downstairs rooms, searching them for a picture, some evidence of what Morrison looked like and whether or not the man in the Mercedes was him. She found nothing.

Her panic rising, she found the stairwell, paused for only an instant, then rushed up. On the landing, she saw a room to her right. She ran into it. A bedroom. It appeared unused. She hustled out and to a second room, a playroom. Again, no pictures and no signs of life. A third room followed, the room right at the top of the stairs. She ducked her head inside and instantly froze. A man lay on the bed. A man in a white, body-length robe and a pair of navy house slippers. He looked like he had just climbed out of the shower and stretched out for a nap. Connie knew instantly this was no nap. This man wore the face of death.

About to gag, she turned to run back down the stairs, but then realized she hadn't yet identified the man. Was this Morrison? She didn't know. But that's why she came—to find Reed Morrison! She had to know if this was him!

Darting her eyes around the room, she searched for something to identify the man. A wallet? She spotted a desk in a sitting area across from the bed. Pushed now by desperation rather than rational thought, Connie rushed to the desk and yanked open the top drawer. A wallet lay in the middle of the drawer. She jerked it open and found a driver's license. With trembling fingers, she held up the license, then turned around to the man on the bed. The picture matched the face.

She checked the name again to make sure. Reed Morrison. Dead. But why? She didn't know, but she couldn't wait around to find out. The police could take it from here. She would anonymously call in the murder, then fly back to Jefferson City. From there, she would watch to see if the police could figure out the mystery that had become way too serious for her.

Suddenly weak, Connie turned to leave the room. As she did, she stumbled over an ottoman sitting at the foot of Morrison's bed. Falling face forward, she landed by the bed, her eyes at shoe level, staring under the golden dust ruffle that draped almost to the floor. Right before her eyes, she saw a stack of papers. Anxious for any information, Connie grabbed the stack. Then, her feet scurrying to get traction, she pulled herself up, rushed from the room and down the stairs. At the front door, she gathered herself enough to realize that a woman sprinting down the street in an elite neighborhood in broad daylight might attract more attention than she wanted. Though she desperately wanted to run, she forced herself into a fast walk and hustled to the car.

Laying the papers on the passenger side, she gunned the engine and headed the car down the street. Perspiring heavily, but gradually slowing down her heartbeat, she reached the interstate and headed north toward the airport. On the highway, a wave of relief overcame her, and she managed to catch her breath and think rationally.

Okay, she summed up. She found Reed Morrison. But somebody else found him first. But why kill him? Did his death connect to Jack's or not? She glanced over at the papers. Would they tell her anything? Maybe, maybe not.

Spotting an exit just ahead, she pulled off and wheeled into a convenience store parking lot. Her blood still pumping rapidly, she turned off the car, grabbed the papers, and flipped through them.

A piece of letterhead immediately caught her attention. Reed Morrison, Personal Investigator. Underneath the letterhead, a phone number. She recognized it as the one listed on the back of the check Jack had written. Jack had hired a private eye! But why? What was Morrison doing that cost $10,000?

Connie ripped through more sheets of paper, one after another. Without bothering to read details, it didn't take her long to figure out Morrison's business. He did divorce work, missing persons, general surveillance. In addition, he served as a consultant for both prosecutors and defense attorneys in criminal investigations. Typical private detective stuff. His clients paid him handsomely. She read invoices for five, ten, even twenty thousand dollars. He obviously did his job well.

Too curious to feel fear, Connie kept digging at the papers. What about Jack? Anything here about Jack? Near the bottom of the stack, she came to a plain manila folder. She opened it quickly, ready to move on to the next sheet. But there, lying in the folder, she found three pictures. One of Jack Brandon. One of Sandra Lunsford. And one of an elderly gentleman she had never seen in her life.

*****

Headed south on the same interstate, Lennie lifted his cell phone from his coat pocket and punched in his number. Ten seconds later, he got an answer. "Yeah, Lennie here. We had a slight complication with last assignment."

"How slight?"

"First part of assignment finished, job done. But then we got company earlier than we expected from the Midwest— female company."

A pause. "But there was no link up between the company and your assignment?"

"Nope, too late for that."

"Good. But we still got the problem from the Midwest."

"Yeah."

"I was hoping it wouldn't come to this."

"Yeah, well, people get nosy, you know."

"I need to think about the process. This has to go real clean. Anything else will bring down way too much attention. Let's keep an eye on the company for a few days. See if she moves toward anybody. Maybe she'll drop out at this point. If she does, we might can let her go. I'll get in touch in a few days."

"I'll be available."

"Lennie?"

"Yeah?"

"How'd Brit do?"

"Flew off the handle. Wanted to do the company without your clearance. I had to calm him down."

A pause. "I don't know about him."

"I can handle him."

"Please do. Talk to you soon."

Lennie unbuttoned his coat and glanced over at Brit. The guy was still out. What a clown.

CHAPTER
18

When Connie's flight touched down in St. Louis, she decided she couldn't go home just yet. The picture of Reed Morrison, dead in his bed, kept rising up in her mind, and she couldn't throw it out. Her nerves frayed, she tossed her overnight bag into the back of her van and headed to a restaurant on the west perimeter of the airport. She hoped a quiet dinner and a couple of hours of solitude would cleanse the image from her brain before she drove home. Right now, she didn't know if she could concentrate enough to drive.

It took her thirty minutes to get situated at the restaurant, another fifteen to order shrimp and a salad and get served. She started to pick at her food, but she hardly tasted it. The whole day seemed like a jumbled dream, a harebrained, scattered, illogical nightmare. How ludicrous to think she could fly to Vegas and solve something the cops couldn't unravel.

Did she cause Morrison's death? If she hadn't gone looking for him would he be alive tonight, enjoying his beautiful home and whatever family he had? To her sorrow, Connie realized she still knew nothing about the man except his occupation. She had stood over his dead body, seen him in the most intimate of ways but didn't even know if he had a wife.

She took a bite of her salad, followed it with a drink of tea. She probably did cause his death. For Morrison to end up dead on the very day she arrived was too coincidental for the law of averages. While looking for information about Jack, she caused the murder of another human being.

A dim hope came to her. Maybe Morrison died naturally! A heart attack or a stroke! After all, she hadn't examined the body! For an instant, she wondered how to find out. Would the authorities give her the information she needed? But then she remembered the sounds from the back of the house and the two men in the Mercedes. They weren't Boy Scouts, she knew that for sure. They killed Morrison, she knew it in her bones.

Her fork dropped to the table as another truth came to her. Those two men probably killed Jack too! She hadn't really considered that until now, but the connection seemed so obvious. But if they killed Jack, he didn't commit suicide. Which meant he didn't necessarily have an affair! But how did she explain the video?

Connie slumped down, overwhelmed by all the questions. Too many riddles. She needed to concentrate on what she sensed as the most basic fact of all. Push aside the extra details, the mysteries. Focus on what gripped her most completely.

She closed her eyes and let her mind sift through things. What did she believe at the heart of all this? Simple: Those two men killed Jack. Morrison knew something about Jack's death, and they killed him to keep secret what he knew.

Another reality seeped through her. The men might try to kill her. Though she didn't know who they were, she had seen them drive away from a murder. But that didn't prove anything. The men, though, didn't know how ignorant she was.

Connie nibbled at another shrimp. The men might come to Jefferson City. That would place Daniel and Katie in danger. She laid her fork on her plate, and her stomach knotted up into balls of fear. Within seconds, the fear shifted to rage. They had already taken Jack, they would not harm her babies!

But then a wave of helplessness washed over her. How could she stop them? They had already proven their killing skills. To stand up to that, she would need help. But from whom?

She thought of Tick and Tess. They would do anything she asked. But could she bring them into this danger? Quickly, she answered her own question. No, she couldn't. Involving them only widened the circle of those who might get hurt.

Luke Tyler came to mind. He told her to call if she needed anything. But, again, that widened the circle. Worse maybe, she felt guilty for not telling him everything from the beginning. He wouldn't help someone who obstructed his work by not fully cooperating. Besides, he might not see the same connections she saw between the two men and Jack. He had decided to shut down the investigation, and it would probably take more evidence than she had to get it started again. Connie sighed. As far as she could see, this mess lay in her lap and her lap alone. Unfortunately, hers wasn't a very big lap, and she didn't know if it could hold everything the last two weeks had placed there.

Her shoulders sagging, she paid her bill, left the restaurant, and climbed into the van. Two hours later, she pulled into her driveway and eased into the house, exhausted and confused. Mrs. Everhart greeted her at the kitchen door. If curious about Connie's trip, she didn't show it.

"You're back early," she said, her purse on her shoulder as she headed to the door.

"Yeah, finished quicker than I thought."

"The kids are asleep. Best I get home and do the same thing."

"Thanks, Mrs. Everhart, you're the kindest woman I've ever met."

"Don't tell that to Mr. Everhart. He'll expect me to treat him that way." Both women laughed, then went their separate ways.

Changing quickly into nightclothes, then locking all the doors, Connie tumbled into bed. For fifteen minutes, she kept her ears tuned to the night, listening for some threat to emerge from the dark. But then the weariness of the day defeated her fears, and she dropped off to sleep. The hours moved past, one after another, and she slept through them all, the sleep of the depleted, a dreamless sleep marked only by the movement of the hands of the clock by her bed. Outside her windows, the night lay still, not a stir of wind anywhere. It seemed as if the air had worn itself out blowing winter away and now took a respite before another season began.

In her bed, Connie lay still as a stone and never turned over. Only when the sun climbed through the beige and blue flowers on her drapes did she stir. It took more than twenty minutes for her to pry open her eyes. When she did, a cough suddenly shook her body. Clearing her throat, she rolled to the side and sat up. The cough hit her again. She started to lie back down, but then remembered she had to get up and prepare the kids for school.

For the next hour, through breakfast with the kids, through helping them dress, through seeing them out the door to their buses, the cough continued. Weary beyond anything she had ever felt, she took one glance at the dirty dishes on the dining table, then shook her head. The dishes could wait. Another coughing spell rattled her chest, and she headed back to her room and crawled under the covers.

For the next three days, she followed the same pattern. Staggered from bed and assisted the children, did just enough housework to keep the place livable, then climbed back into bed. At night, she fixed supper, then rolled back into bed. She skipped the family devotions at night, claiming sickness as her excuse. She wasn't lying either. Her cough lingered into the weekend, a hacking, empty cough that rejected the remedies of cough syrup and cold medicine. Nothing worked to make it better. She considered going to the doctor but simply didn't have enough energy to drive. The cough, though, didn't keep her in bed. Her depression did that.

Connie recognized the symptoms pretty fast, and though it looked the same as the bout after the funeral, the cause was completely different. The earlier spell had been pure weariness and grief—a season of respite from the world. This one, though certainly tinged with sadness, came more from a sense of utter helplessness. She had seen a murdered man and the murderers drove right past her and she couldn't stop them. If the killers came after her and her family, she would feel equally helpless.

A desire to sleep overwhelmed her, and a dull anxiety jabbed at her soul. The anxiety didn't cause her adrenaline to pump and energize her actions. Instead, it acted as a molasses of the mind and spirit, a sticky weight that pulled and pulled, so heavy it snuffed out hope.

The onset of the depression came as a shock to Connie. To this point, she had avoided the bleak seasons her mom so often endured, the bleak seasons caused by an absent husband and solved by an ever-present bottle. Now, though, the blackness descended on her with a ferocity that seemed bent on making up for lost time. The days stretched out and out, unending hours. She functioned enough to placate Daniel and Katie, but no one else. Tess dropped by every day, and Mrs. Everhart called to see if she needed anything, but Connie hardly spoke. Luke Tyler called once, and Johnson Mack twice, but she knew it only because she heard their voices on the answering machine. She refused to answer the phone.

She didn't cry much, not like in the first days after Jack's death. Crying took emotion, and her body felt devoid of even the energy for that. She lay in bed and slept, or lay in bed and stared at the ceiling, or lay in bed and imagined what death would feel like.

She assumed she would die soon. If the two men in the Mercedes killed Jack and Morrison, they would kill her too. Killers killed, as simple as that.

In an odd way, the idea of death intrigued her. If the men murdered her, she would go straight to heaven and see Jack again. She thought a lot about heaven, a place of joy—no more death or tears or pain. She liked that notion. Heaven meant the end of some things and the beginning of others. Though she couldn't imagine the exact form heaven would take, she trusted God to provide whatever created total joy, whatever offered total completion. Of course, she knew what would do that for her—Jack. Heaven meant eternity with Jack. How bad could that be?

Yet, in spite of her longing to join Jack, she didn't exactly want to die. Even in her depression, she remembered that her children needed her too much for her to seek death. But she didn't see any way to avoid it.

On Saturday Daniel spent all day at a baseball tournament, then asked to spend the night at a friend's house. Breaking the family rule that everyone slept at home on Saturday so they could go to church together on Sunday, she let him go. Why not? At fourteen, he deserved some freedom.

Seeing her brother breaking the rule, Katie demanded equal treatment. Again relenting, Connie walked her down the street to a playmate's home for the evening.

Alone, Connie closed the door, slipped back into a night-gown and headed toward her bed once again. The phone rang. She started to ignore it, but her innate politeness made her pause. Maybe it was Tess. Or even Mrs. Everhart. It rang again.

It seemed so rude to walk away and not pick it up. She stepped to the phone.

"Yeah, Connie, this is Tess. What's shaking?"

"The salt," she said, though without laughter.

"That cough gone yet?"

"Not completely, but it's better."

"You need anything? Want me to come over for a while . . . bring a movie?"

"No, I'm okay, just tired."

"Your Vegas trip?"

"Yeah, it took a lot out of me."

Tess hesitated, and Connie knew she wanted to ask about the mysterious trip, why she went, what she did there, why she had come back and fallen into such a state. But she didn't. "You coming to church in the morning?" Tess asked.

Connie hesitated. She had debated that all day long. Everyone expected her to return tomorrow. This was the third Sunday after Jack's funeral, and she really had no good reason to stay away. Her cough gave her an excuse, but not a very good one. But she didn't want to go. Attending church required so much energy, and she had no reserves in her batteries.

"I don't know, Tess, it still seems too soon. I don't know if I can . . . can do it, you know . . . go sit down and look up there and see the altar where . . . where Jack was . . . in the casket. I don't know if I can go back to our pew and listen to the sermon and not just break up . . . lose it all right there. I don't want to be a spectacle, you know that, have everyone staring and whispering behind my back."

"We'll support you," Tess comforted her. "If you break down, so what? People will understand. We'll help you if that happens."

"But where will I sit? I don't think I can sit in our pew without Jack beside me, but I don't think I can go and not sit in our pew either. You know what I mean? Both choices seem wrong. I guess that's the worst of it, I just can't decide where to sit. Isn't that the craziest thing you ever heard? I don't feel like I belong anywhere." She was close to tears as she finished, and her voice choked up.

Tess sighed. "I would hug you if I was there, I really would. Look, no one can make these decisions for you. You know I'll help if I can, any way you need me. I hope to see you in the morning, but if you decide not to come I won't judge you. Just remember this—the longer you stay away, the harder it will be to come back. An action soon becomes a habit and a habit becomes a way of life. I think you need the church, and I know the church needs you. I know I need you. Okay?"

Connie wiped her eyes on her sleeve and sniffled into the phone. "I know, Tess, I know all that. But I just don't know. It all seems so hopeless, so . . . so confusing. Just pray for me, will you? Pray that I can find my way, find my way . . . back, back to . . . where I need to be."

"I'm already on that job, don't you ever think otherwise. We all are. Now get some rest, and I'll see you in the morning at church."

Connie dropped the phone into its cradle and stepped toward her bed. The phone rang once more. Expecting to hear Tess's voice, she grabbed it.

"Hello."

"Connie Brandon?"

"Yes, this is Connie."

"Your husband got what he deserved. Don't meddle in business that doesn't concern you." The line went dead.

Connie slowly lay the phone down. Who was he? Jack's killer? A hired hand of Blacker or Mack? Sandra Lunsford's husband? Or just a pro-gambling citizen who wanted Jack out of the way?

She sighed, then decided it didn't matter. Whoever the caller was, he need not worry. She didn't plan to meddle in anyone's business but her own for the rest of her life.

*****

Tess and Tick walked into the sanctuary of the River City Community Church on Sunday morning at 10:32 and took their places on the sixth pew from the front on the left side. Tick wore the houndstooth check suit that looked so good with his blond mustache, and Tess had on a burgundy silk blouse and a black skirt. Her mind not yet focused on the worship about to start, Tess craned her neck around and searched the back pews for Connie.

"She's not here," she whispered to Tick, her eyes scanning the crowd. "I thought sure she would come."

"You said her cough was better?"

"Not completely, but that wasn't it anyway. She's all mixed up, you can just tell it the way she talks. All the fire has gone out of her. I knew it had to happen, this getting depressed and all, but I didn't think it would keep her from church. She needs this place, these people, but she's worried about what everyone thinks. She's got this thing in her mind that she won't know where to sit. It's like she doesn't think she has a place anymore. She wants to sit in her old spot, but she's concerned she can't take it. It's tough on her, but I hoped she would—"

A ripple of motion rolled into the sanctuary from the entry of the church. Tess's mouth fell open, and she grabbed Tick by the shirtsleeve and turned him around. From the back, they saw Connie walk through the door, her scarlet hair combed back in a neat bun, her brown eyes staring straight ahead, the same black suit she'd worn at the funeral outlining her petite frame. On Connie's left, Katie held her hand and marched forward, a smile on her face, obviously glad to return to church with her friends. Daniel walked behind Connie to her right, his arm slightly around his mom as if holding her up. Behind the three of them came Reverend Wallace, his well-creased cheeks glowing, a tiny glint showing in his eyes. Tess could see the pleasure written across her pastor's face. A hurting lamb had returned to the sheepfold where the shepherd could care for her wounds.

Tick reached out and took Tess's hand. A hush fell on the congregation as Connie and her kids came down the aisle. Collectively, the people held their breath. Where would Connie and her children sit? It became evident as they passed each pew and headed toward the front. At the third pew from the rostrum, Connie stopped. Tess watched her take a short step toward their old spot, then hesitate. Tess closed her eyes and breathed a short prayer.

"You can do it," she urged Connie under her breath. "You can do it."

For a second, Connie didn't move. She seemed glued to the floor, her feet wedged in concrete. The congregation didn't move. Daniel shuffled his feet, and Katie tugged her mom's hand.

Without thinking, Tess suddenly stood, not sure what she planned to do next. Within a second, Tick stood too. Behind them Mrs. Everhart rose to her feet, her hand on Mr. Everhart's lapel, pulling him up with her. To Tess's right, a pair of church elders jumped up.

Like a rolling stream, the tide quickly overwhelmed the congregation, one person after another, one person after another . . . each of them quietly standing. Now, the whole church stood in one accord, a wave of human support for Connie and Katie and Daniel Brandon.

A tear came to Tess's eye, and she brushed it away, but then another fell, and before she knew it she couldn't brush them away fast enough. Though not known to have ever sung in church, not even on the congregational hymns, Tick Garner suddenly raised his voice and began to sing:

"Blest be the tie that binds, our hearts . . . " and the people instantly joined in, "Our hearts in Christian love . . . The fellowship of kindred minds, is like to that above . . . "

Sniffles echoed in pew after pew, and the men hugged their wives and the wives took their children's hands, and before anyone could think of a reason to stop it, the whole congregation was holding hands and the song continued to ring out. . . .

"We share our mutual woes, Our mutual burdens bear; And often for each other flows the sympathizing tear."

Tess left her seat and, with Tick in tow, moved to Connie's side and wrapped her arms around her. Tick hugged Daniel and Katie, and the whole congregation left their seats and made a series of circles around the Brandon family, a mass and mash of human care, all of them crying and praying and singing their hearts out. "Blest Be the Tie" became "Amazing Grace," and the wonderful echoes of the music and the shared grief and love poured out from the church and into the street.

"Amazing grace, how sweet the sound, that saved a wretch like me. I once was lost but now am found, was blind but now I see . . . "

A jogger passing by the church heard the loud singing and paused for a second to listen. A policeman waiting in his squad car for a light to change tilted his head and wondered what in the world was going on at the River City Community Church.

*****

Feeling the outpouring of love, Connie closed her eyes and basked in the warmth of her church. Her decision to return to church had been a simple one. When she had awakened that morning, she stepped down the hall to wake the children, then remembered they weren't home. That brought her to her senses. Since the day they were born, they had never spent the night away on Saturday, and they had never missed church on Sunday except for the rare instances of sickness. Even on vacations, the Brandon family found a church somewhere and at least attended the worship.

Standing alone in her empty house, Connie started to shake. No matter what happened to her, she wouldn't allow her children's spiritual foundation to go untended. The men from Vegas might come after her, but until they did, she would seize every opportunity to teach her children the ways of God. To honor Jack, she could do no other.

That brought her back. Now, the music still reverberating in the sanctuary, she felt herself in the presence of an angel's chorus. Though she had known it for years, she realized as if for the first time: No matter how tough life became, she belonged here, with the congregation of faith. It came to her that fresh, a revelation so new it made her insides tremble and her face flush. Here, to the church, she could bring her confusions, her awkwardness; here she could bring her questions and her fears, even her doubts and her anger. Here, in the house of God, she could hang out her dirty laundry and leave it to the cleansing power of the Almighty Lord.

The tears streaming, she slowly followed Katie's tugging and moved to her spot in the pew. Deliberately, they moved far enough down the pew to leave the aisle seat for Jack, room for his long legs, he joked, long legs he didn't have. Standing with Katie on the left and Daniel on her right, she listened to the congregation as it continued to sing at the top of its collective lungs. She looked to Reverend Wallace who waited in the aisle behind her. What next? Reverend Wallace motioned for her to sit. She nodded and eased into the pew. Katie and Daniel followed.

Now, everyone else still standing, Connie and Daniel and Katie bowed their heads and closed their eyes and let the sounds of the song roll over them.

"When we've been there ten thousand years, bright shining as the sun, We've no less days to sing God's praise, than when we've first begun . . . "

As the music subsided, the congregation fell quiet, but no one sat down. A scattering of sniffles broke the hush, but nothing else. Gently, so as not to break the whisper of the Spirit, Reverend Wallace lifted his gnarled right hand into the air and began to pray.

"Precious Lord Jesus, we feel your presence in a powerful way today. We feel you as you speak to our hearts, as you nurture our souls, as you reach down and touch us on the spots that hurt. We praise your name today, Lord Jesus, for the love you give us for one another. We couldn't live without that love. Life would be barren without that love, barren as a tree without branches, a day without light, a river without water. Thank you for your love and for giving us the power to share your love with others.

"We pray for each other today, especially for Connie and Katie and Daniel. Continue to dispense holy grace upon their lives. Continue to walk with them through their valleys. Continue to open their eyes to see what you want them to see. Continue to manifest your goodness in big and small ways.

"As we worship in this hour, now, let us never forget your presence. Yes, you are with us always, even to the end of the age. In the name of the Father, the Son, and the Holy Ghost. Amen."

With one voice, the congregation said "Amen" and Connie opened her eyes. As she did, she stared straight ahead, her vision blurred for several seconds by the tears that had just begun to recede. Wiping away the last of the tears, her hand trembling, she leaned forward and pulled a book from the hymnal rack. A black book. Jack's black book, the one they had assumed lost on the night of his untimely death. Sitting right there in front of her, just beside a hymnal.

CHAPTER
19

I t took every ounce of self-control Connie possessed to pay attention to the remainder of the worship. After pulling the black notebook from the pew rack and placing it in her lap, she desperately wanted to open it. But, knowing she couldn't read it in church, she held back. Through the next hour and fifteen minutes, she worked hard to stay focused. As the singing, praying, and preaching unfolded, she kept her eyes straight ahead, not daring to look down. If she looked down once, she feared she would never look back up. More than anything, she wanted to open the notebook and read it, but she realized if she did, she would lose all connection to the events around her.

Sitting rigidly, she clutched the black book like a drowning woman straddling a life vest in the middle of the ocean. To her dismay, Reverend Wallace, apparently inspired by the outpouring of the Spirit brought on by her return to church, preached longer than usual, stretching his normal thirty-minute sermon to forty-five.

Connie fought hard to listen but for the most part failed. Over and over again, she squeezed the book in her lap, wondering how it came to be there. Had Jack lost it? Left it there by accident?

For a moment, she wondered why no one had found it, but then the answer came to her: No one had sat there since Jack's death. And the custodian could have easily overlooked it during the cleaning of the church.

As Reverend Wallace continued to preach, she tried to recall the last time she saw the notebook, but she couldn't. Jack kept it with him all the time, so she became accustomed to see-ing it whenever she saw him. On the passenger seat of his truck, on his cluttered desk at the store, at home on his nightstand. He scribbled in it constantly, working on the story he hoped to get published someday. The idea that he mistakenly left it made no sense.

If not, though, then what? He left it deliberately? That had to be it. Jack left the notebook for her. Without reading a single word, she came to that conclusion. Only Jack would have thought of it—leave his notebook in their pew where she would find it. Yes, he probably assumed she would come back to church sooner to find it, but at the moment that didn't matter. She *had* found it. The day she returned to church, there it appeared.

With a rueful smile, Connie understood the message. A good preacher could make a heck of a sermon from the illustra-tion. When in church, God blesses you in unexpected ways. She squeezed her blessing. Jack's novel. The novel he refused to let her see until he finished it. Now, though she didn't have him any longer, she did have his book. What a treasure!

As Reverend Wallace finished preaching and the ushers moved through the aisles to receive the offering, Connie's mind drifted even further. Why did Jack leave the book? And when?

The ushers moved toward the altar with the offering plates. A disturbing possibility pushed through Connie's head. Why did Jack leave the notebook? Only one reason she could imag-ine: He suspected something might happen to him. The book survived as his way to speak to her one more time.

Already drained of tears, she didn't get emotional at the thought. While he lived, Jack wouldn't let her read his novel. Now that he had died, she would get the chance.

The congregation stood as Reverend Wallace called on an elder to lead in a closing prayer. Connie took a deep breath and rose to her feet. Closing her eyes, she wondered about the novel. Was it a love story? A fantasy saga? A mystery? She didn't know. Jack never told her, and after years of asking, she gave up.

Usually one of the last to leave church, Connie found her-self tense and impatient to go as the prayer ended. But the peo-ple crowded around her, and she found herself shaking hands and hugging necks. She appreciated their enthusiastic welcome home, but she could barely stand it. Time seemed to drag, a turtle crossing a road, but gradually the crowd around her thinned and disappeared. Only Tick, Tess, and Reverend Wallace remained with her and Daniel and Katie.

Tess wrapped an arm around Connie. "You look tired," she said. "How about letting me take Daniel and Katie while you go home for a rest? I'll feed the kids, then you come eat after your nap."

Connie's eyes lit up. At times like this, she wanted to kiss Tess. She could go home and read Jack's book without having to make explanations to the children. Though she wanted them to read it soon, she appreciated the chance to go through it by herself first.

"That sounds wonderful," she said. "I'll bring some clothes for the kids when I come. We can all change and spend the afternoon together."

"Did you fix banana pudding?" Daniel asked Tess, his blue eyes eager.

"Not yet, but for you, I'll see what I can do."

Tess turned to Reverend Wallace. "You and Abby will join us, won't you?"

Reverend Wallace scanned the sanctuary for his wife. "I don't see Abby, but I think I can talk her into banana pudding."

Tick touched Tess on the elbow. "I'll get the car," he said.

Within seconds, Tess had hustled the kids out the door, and Reverend Wallace had walked away to find his wife. Eager to get home, Connie hustled to her van. Twenty minutes later she turned into her driveway and hopped out. The notebook remained in her hands, clutched to her stomach. For a moment, she wondered where to go to do her reading. It didn't take long to decide: the back deck overlooking the river.

Without going inside, Connie circled the corner of the house and stepped onto the deck. Easing into her rocker, she took a long breath and stared out across the Missouri. A hint of breeze rippled across her face, and a hickory tree as tall as a telephone pole picked it up and danced its leaves with it. A bird chirped to her right and the sun, just past straight up, fell through the tree and splashed on Connie's face. Connie stared at the river Jack loved so much. He often said the river was like a human life—always changing and always heading somewhere. She had no doubt she was changing, but she did wonder where she was heading.

She held up the book, then stroked it with her fingers. Jack's novel, written in longhand. She hoped he had finished it. If so, she would do everything she could to place it in the hands of a publisher. She sucked in a deep breath and opened the book. Her eyes dropped to the first words on the first page, instantly recognizing Jack's neat, tiny handwriting. She read the first words. Her heart skipped a beat. The words weren't the first words to a novel. Instead, they were addressed to her.

"My lovely Sunset—"

Connie gulped and bit her lip. She read faster.

> If you find this, then it means something has happened to me. I might not be alive. I simply don't know. If I'm not, please, please know I'm with the Lord. I hope I live to grow old with you, to see your wonderful auburn hair turn gray, to sit in a rocker by the fire in the winter, but I know that might not happen. I might not get to see Daniel go on his first date or walk Katie down the aisle on her wedding day. I might not teach either of them to drive or wrestle with my grandchildren on the floor. If I don't get to do those things, then grieve for me, but not forever. Let God provide and move forward with life.
>
> I'm leaving this notebook where you or Daniel or Katie should find it. No one but our family has sat here for years and if I'm with the Lord and unable to take my regular spot in this pew, I expect no one will sit here at least for a few weeks. So, you or the kids should find this. That's the way I plan it anyway.
>
> As you read this, please know I can't tell you everything I want to say here. Two reasons for that: 1) I don't have but a few minutes before I have to go. 2) There is the possibility that someone other than you or one of the kids will find this. If I write everything here and this notebook somehow falls into the wrong hands, people I care about could get terribly hurt. So, I have to code this, speak in terms only you will understand.

When you finish this and do what I tell you, then you'll understand. So, now, here's what you need to do.

Do you remember the birthday present you three gave me for my fortieth? Along with the black balloons and black underwear? Well, find that birthday present. When you find it, examine it closely. It will give you the information you need to find out what happened to me. As you follow what you find there, remember this, mark it down—appearances can deceive. As the Scripture says, wolves do sometimes clothe themselves in sheep's clothing.

I wish I could make it all plainer. But follow what you find and I think you'll discover why I can't say more. For now, I ask you to stay away from the police. You'll know the reason soon enough. Follow the gift first, then go to the authorities if you need. No one else knows about this gift, so I know you'll be safe for now.

Listen, I have to end this. I could write all night. I have so much I want to say to you and my wonderful kids. You know I lost my parents when I was ten. From that day on, I felt incomplete. But then you came along and filled in the blank spaces in my soul. Then Daniel and Katie put the cherry on the ice cream. I never felt alone again. God gave you three to me and I'll treasure you forever. Now, go. Go and trust the goodness of God. Go and trust the grace of God. Go and trust the promise of heaven God gave us. As you go, remember this—"Now abide faith, hope, and love, these three; but the greatest of these is love." Love endures forever.

I love you,

Jack

P.S. I'll look forward to the day when we can share a bowl of ice cream and you can tell me what you think of my book.

The note ended. Distracted, Connie ignored the pages of the novel behind the letter. Those could wait.

Her heart thumping wildly, she set the book down and slumped forward, as still as death itself. Beyond the deck, the river seemed to slow, too, its current languishing as if in sympathy with Connie. Overhead the bird stopped chirping, and the breeze dropped to nothing. Connie continued to sit still for several minutes. But, even in her stillness, her mind rushed ahead. After her trip to Las Vegas, she had pledged to leave Jack's death in the grave so she could begin the process of moving ahead with her life. But now, from beyond the grave, Jack beckoned her. He wanted her to know the truth. That fit him exactly. Even in death, he wanted to do the right thing.

She raised up and stared at the notebook. Then she smiled and shook her head side to side. Wonderful, honest, precious Jack. The man of her dreams. The father of her children. The joy of her life. What a place to leave his final clue. On the gift they gave him on his fortieth birthday. On a baseball.

The bird overhead chirped again. Connie remained still. The river flowed in the distance. She bit her lip. She had to decide. Leave it all behind or take Jack's final clue and see where it led?

Clutching the notebook, she moved quickly to Jack's closet shelf. There she jerked the box with his belongings off the shelf, then stepped out of the closet. Setting the box on her bed, she opened it and peered inside.

It took only a second to find the baseball. It lay on the bottom of the box, covered by a stack of papers and a number of other odds and ends. Connie lifted the ball out and held it up in the light. It looked like a simple ball—white, stitched, and stamped with the official signature of the president of the National League. Names written in odd squiggles and slashes decorated it, the autographs of the famous athletes who once played for the St. Louis Cardinals. She, Katie, and Daniel paid over three hundred dollars for it, far more than they could really afford.

Connie rolled the ball in her hands, not quite sure what she expected to see. She read a number of the names. Gibson . . . McCarver . . . Flood. The signatures meant nothing to her. She smiled ruefully. With her ignorance of baseball, she wouldn't know the difference between a Cardinal and a killer. But Jack would know about her ignorance. Which meant he wouldn't simply leave a name. No, he would leave something for her to figure out, something no one else would fathom, something to test the logic he always admired in her.

She twirled the baseball over, looking for anything unusual. Perhaps a phone number? Someone to call who could explain all this? She didn't see a number. She held the ball closer to her face, examining it from every angle. In the center of the ball, under the logo of the National League, she spotted it—a circle the size of a small button drawn in black ink. It almost disappeared in the swirl of Orlando Cepeda's signature, but once she isolated it, she had no doubt—the circle didn't fit. It stood out as plain as a woman in a bikini at a church social. Inside the circle, she saw three tiny letters, MHS, and two little numbers, 75.

Her mind plowing through the possibilities, she tried to figure it out. MHS. Initials? Maybe so, but for whom? She mentally ran through a check list of her friends. No close friends whose name began with an "M."

The baseball still in her hand, she searched through the rest of the box's contents. Maybe Jack left something else in here? She scanned through the papers as quickly as she could but found nothing.

For a second, she paused and let herself think. Then, she suddenly turned, ran to the telephone in the den, and flipped open an address book lying beside it. Jack kept a long list of his most called numbers there. She surveyed the list but came up empty again.

Unable to figure out the initials, she focused on the number: 75. What did it mean? An age? She knew some older people but couldn't see how any of them related to this. If not age, then what? An address? But Jack would know the number by itself wouldn't give her enough to find someone.

If not an age or an address, what else? She stared at the number again: 75 . . . 75 . . . A safety deposit box! No, she had already checked hers in Jefferson City and Jack hadn't opened one in St. Louis. If he had opened one at some other bank, he would have given her more direction. 75? . . . 75?

She held the baseball close to her eyes. Just beneath the letters MHS she saw a slight smudge, a touch of ink right at the front of the number. It looked like an accidental thing at first, but as she inspected it more closely, she realized it was an apostrophe. The 75 became a '75, an abbreviation for 1975. The number was a date! 1975.

Now, what happened in 1975? She thought back quickly, running the years through her head. She lived in Ft. Leonard Wood in 1975, the year before her mom and dad divorced, and she moved north to go to school at Lincoln. Jack lived in Miller. She was a junior in high school, still wearing big black glasses and shy as a deer in headlights. Jack was playing second base on the Miller High baseball team, a tough but tiny spray hitter who turned a quick double play.

Connie smiled as she thought of the baseball lingo. She didn't know what it meant, but Jack had described himself to Daniel that way time and time again. 1975 . . . 1975. What happened in 1975? After Watergate and Vietnam. Ford in the White House. Inflation high. She at Ft. Leonard Wood, Jack at Miller.

Miller High School . . . 1975. Jack the senior second baseman. Miller High School. MHS! Instantly, she knew. Miller High School, 1975! Something happened at Miller High School in 1975. But what?

She ransacked her brain, trying to remember. What had Jack told her about his high school years? She automatically answered the question. Nothing. Though married to him for years, he kept his past very much to himself.

Connie thought of his closet again. So sparse, almost empty. A suitcase full of belongings. All her married life, she had thought it a reflection of Jack's simple needs, his lack of concern about material possessions. But now, she wondered. Did he keep himself free from possessions because he had few wants or because he didn't want to get attached to anything he might have to leave behind in an emergency? She didn't know and maybe never would.

Stumped, Connie walked away from the telephone and stepped toward the den, the baseball in her hand. The only thing she had from Jack's high school days was his yearbook and his ring. She had examined the ring only a few days ago and found nothing significant. That left the yearbook.

Though not expecting anything, she moved to the bookshelves in the den. From the bottom shelf, she lifted the yearbook, blowing dust from its cover. A minute later, still wiping dust, she perched herself at the kitchen table, laid the ball down, and began to flip through the pages.

Miller High School. The Wildcats. She examined the cover, but nothing jumped out. Carefully, she opened it and scanned the introductory pages. Typical high school yearbook. Dedication page, pictures of the students in action, the student leaders—Most Likely to Succeed, Best Couple, Most Athletic, so on and so on. She had seen the pictures a few times over the years, nothing unusual about them.

Jack, an A and B student of medium popularity, hadn't won any superlatives. Connie flipped to the next page, the page showing the faces of the senior class. She began to read through the alphabetical listing, again not sure what she should expect to find. Betsy Aaron . . . Bill Abbott . . . Tom Acer . . . nothing jumped out at her.

She moved through the entire class but gained no clue. Exasperated, she dropped the book onto the table and leaned back in her seat. She was missing something here, she just knew it. Jack wouldn't tell her to examine the baseball, then leave her hanging. Somehow or other, she had to figure it out. She glanced at her watch. Almost an hour had passed since church ended. Tess would call her soon, want to know where she was.

Without breaking her concentration, she dialed Tess. She answered in two rings.

"Yeah, Tess," said Connie. "I'm running a few minutes late here. The kids okay?"

"No problem, take all the time you want. Tick's showing the kids the new boat he just bought. We're going to the lake with it soon, and they say they want to go. They don't even know you're not here."

"I shouldn't be much longer."

She hung up and turned to the yearbook again. What had she missed? Sitting back at the table, she picked up the baseball. Had Jack left something more she wasn't seeing? She rolled the ball in her hand. MHS '75, in a circle. He left something else here, she just knew it. MHS, 1975 . . . Wait a minute! In a circle!

Maybe the circle meant something. But what? She bit her lip and closed her eyes, giving the riddle every ounce of her focus. MHS 1975 in a circle . . . in a circle . . . in a rim . . . in an orbit. She considered the meaning of each of the possibilities. Nothing made sense.

She opened her eyes and stared at the baseball again, trying by the very power of her gaze to make it say something she could understand. MHS, 1975, in a circle . . . in a sun . . . in a round . . . in a hole . . .

She gritted her teeth now; she felt that something lay just beyond her thoughts, something crucial, the key to it all . . . MHS, 1975, in a hole . . . in a . . . saucer . . . in a ring, in a—

She knew it instantly. In a ring!

Leaving the baseball on the table by the yearbook, she sprinted to Jack's top right dresser drawer and yanked it open. Pulling his class ring from its box, she rolled it over and over in her fingers examining it for a clue. Nothing obvious came to her. She peered through the glass cutting on top and stared at the "MHS" letters cut into the side. She held it up, inspecting the inside of the gold exterior. She read the initials cut into the inner edge. SER.

SER?

What was that? The initials weren't Jack's! She'd never noticed that.

If not Jack's, then whose?

A strange thought invaded. The ring was so small. Connie slipped it over the ring finger on her right hand. Though snug, it fit. But, if it fit her, how could it fit Jack? Though small, he wasn't that small. This ring definitely fit a woman, not a man.

The ring in her hand, she ran back to the kitchen table, and picked up the yearbook. Not bothering to sit, she flipped it open and scanned the pages as fast as her eyes could move. She had a notion what she would find, but she couldn't know for sure.

Gasping, she came again to the superlatives, the kids voted best in every imaginable category. Hurrying past the Most Likely to Succeed and the Most Athletic, she turned the page to the Best Couple. Her eyes immediately fell on the picture on the right side, the picture of a tall, blonde, senior girl. The female side of the Best Couple.

Connie carefully examined the girl, comparing her to the image she had in her mind. Yes, like everyone else, the girl had grown up since 1975. Her eyes wore some lines at the edges now. But it was her, no doubt about it. For a moment, Connie stood still and tried to figure out what it meant. But, try as she might, she couldn't fathom the riddle. She opened her eyes and focused on the girl again. Absolutely, no doubt about it, the girl voted one half of the Best Couple—a girl named Sandra Richards—was the same person as Sandra Lunsford, the woman in the video with Jack Brandon. The ring belonged to her.

Connie studied the picture. Apparently Sandra Richards had married at some point, became Sandra Lunsford. But one thing bothered Connie. Richards was the maiden name of Jack's dead mother.

CHAPTER
20

C onnie knew how confusion felt. She had practically drowned in confusion since the day of Jack's death. But none of that compared with what now gushed through her. Sandra Richards? Who was this woman? Did Jack date her in high school? Did she give him her ring as a token of love? Did she show up again in the last few months and entice Jack to rekindle a former romance? But Jack had never mentioncd her.

In those times when they kidded each other about their "old flames" he never said a word about her. And what about her name—Sandra Richards? Was that just a coincidence or did she have a connection to his mother's side of the family? No way to tell, unless . . . unless she found Sandra Richards. Which, of course, Jack had deliberately told her to do through the clues left behind on the baseball and the ring.

Connie picked up the phone and dialed information.

"What city, please?"

"Miller, Missouri," Connie said.

The computer connected her.

"Yes, the number for Sandra Lunsford, please."

Biting her lip, Connie waited. A couple of seconds later, an operator spoke. : "I don't have a listing for a Sandra Lunsford," she said.

Connie tried again. "What about Sandra Richards?"

Another wait, then another failure. "No, no Sandra Richards either."

Hanging up, another idea occurred to Connie. She dialed long distance information for Las Vegas. Maybe Lunsford lived there.

But again, she struck out. No Sandra Lunsford or Richards.

Frustrated, Connie laid the phone down. She had come to a dead end. She remembered Tess and Tick and the kids. They were surely wondering about her by now. She decided to leave the mystery for the time being. But, even as she climbed into the van and drove to Tess's house, she knew what she had to do. She had to find Sandra Richards.

Who killed Reed Morrison? If anyone knew, Richards did. Did Jack have an affair? Richards could say yes or no. Did Jack commit suicide? Again, Richards could answer. Who killed Jack if he didn't kill himself? Maybe, just maybe, Richards could give her a direction, perhaps even a name. If not her, then no one could.

Pulling into Tess's driveway, Connie shuddered. Obviously, not everyone wanted her to find the mystery woman. If, as she strongly suspected, someone had killed Reed Morrison to keep him quiet, they wouldn't hesitate to kill her too. Another frightening possibility hit home. Whoever killed Morrison might also want Richards dead. Unless . . . and here the worst suspicion of all came . . . unless Richards and the two men in the Mercedes worked together.

All through the afternoon, even as she talked and laughed and forced herself to function with Tess and Tick and the Reverend and Mrs. Wallace, Connie rolled the different notions through her head. Jack wanted her to know about Richards. But why? So she could answer the riddle of his death? Or to warn her away from her? In some respects, both made sense.

Eating her banana pudding, Connie chewed through her options. She thought back to Jack's words in his notebook. She had stamped them into her brain as a rancher brands a letter on a steer. Jack said, "Remember this, appearances can deceive. . . . " Then, "For now, I ask you not to go to the police. . . . Follow the gift first, then go to the authorities if you need. No one knows about this gift, so I know you'll be safe for now."

She had followed the gift. It took her to Richards. Should she now go to the police?

Connie didn't know. As the shadows of the day became longer, she continued to divide her attention between the party going on around her and the debate churning inside. Jack had told her, "If I write everything here and this notebook somehow falls into the wrong hands, people I care about could get terribly hurt." But what people? Connie and Daniel and Katie? No, that didn't make sense. He would have simply said, "You and the kids could get hurt." He meant someone else he cared about. But who?

Only one answer made sense. Someone she didn't know until now—Sandra Richards. But if Richards meant a lot to Jack, she didn't have anything to do with his death.

Another insight came to Connie. Jack had said, "People I care about could get terribly hurt." "People," as in "more than one." Who else did he mean besides Richards?

Connie remembered the elderly man in the pictures she took from Morrison's house. Who was he? What was his connection? Her head began to throb as she mulled over the questions. To her relief, the party began to break up, and she joined the others at the door to leave.

"Thanks so much," she said to Tess and Tick, forcing herself to concentrate. "This has been great."

"So glad you came." Tess beamed. "Hope this hasn't been too much for you."

Connie shook her head. "No, I needed to get out, back to church and all . . . back with . . . back with my friends."

"The people who love you," said Tick, his bald head glowing.

For a moment, everyone became quiet. Reverend Wallace stepped closer to Connie and put his hand on her back. "You're going to have some more down days," he said softly. "The woods where you're walking are dark and deep."

"I know," said Connie. "But maybe I'm through the first part of those woods."

"I'm sure you are," he said.

"We're walking with you," offered Tess. "All the way."

Grateful for their love, Connie hugged the whole circle of friends, then turned to the van. Daniel and Katie were already in their seats, ready to go.

"I'll call you tomorrow," she said to Tess.

"And I'll check on you before Wednesday," said Reverend Wallace. "Let me know if you need anything before then."

Waving one more time, Connie climbed into the van with the kids and left. Determined to give the children her attention, she shoved aside her continuing questions and took care of their needs for the next couple of hours. Get them into a bath, check on their homework, lead the devotional, tuck them into bed. Leaving Katie's room last, her shoulders slumped in weariness, she changed into her nightclothes and grabbed a couple of aspirin from the bathroom. Chugging them down, she headed to bed. Her headache had gotten worse. She rolled down the covers, then fluffed her pillow. Stretching out, she squeezed her eyes shut and tried to ignore the voice inside her soul. She didn't really want to do what it said.

A sharp pain ripped through her skull. She bit her upper lip and took a long, deep breath. Her head throbbed. She had to find Sandra Richards. As simple as that. Jack cared about her. In what capacity, Connie didn't know. But he wanted her to find Richards. As surely as a lighthouse lit up a shore for a ship in a storm, so Jack had turned the spotlight on this woman, and Connie had to follow that light. As she told herself to relax and go to sleep, she continued to wonder if Jack pointed the light at Richards as a rescue or as a warning.

*****

A hundred yards away from Connie's bedroom window, to the left of her house and just past an oak tree as thick as a refrigerator, Brit pulled his red Jaguar to a stop. As its headlights dimmed, he pulled a cell phone from his pocket and flipped it open. Hitting his auto dial, Brit reached Lennie on the other end.

"I'm situated," Brit said. "I've got Red in sight. She's all settled in after a big day with church and friends."

"She give any signs?" asked Lennie. "Call anybody, anything like that?"

"She's all quiet," said Brit.

"You get ears into Garner's place?"

Brit smiled. The two listening devices he put at Tess and Tick Garner's house had given him access to the whole afternoon's conversation. "Yeah, got the bugs in when they went to church," he told Lennie.

"She said nothing to Garner?"

"Like I said, she's all quiet."

"Nothing to Tyler?"

"What I gotta do, send you an e-mail? She's all quiet!"

Lennie paused. Brit drummed on the steering wheel and guessed Lennie's thoughts. Lennie hoped they wouldn't have to move on Red. But Lennie didn't know her like he did. He'd watched her for several days now. In a strange way, he had come to admire her, the strength she showed, the way she forged ahead, flying out to Vegas all alone. She would move, he knew that. Somehow, she would act. Maybe what she did wouldn't go anywhere, wouldn't mean anything, wouldn't threaten them in any way. But she wouldn't give up. Too bad for her. Since she wouldn't give up, she posed a threat to him and Lennie.

Not that he cared about Lennie. But he did care about himself, and, according to Lennie, she had seen their faces.

"Stay with her," said Lennie, interrupting his musings.

"That's my plan."

"But don't move on her."

"You're the boss."

Brit hung up, rubbed the back of his head, and remembered the knot Lennie laid on him after they finished Reed Morrison. The knot still hurt. Lennie would eventually pay for that. But not now, not until he finished his most pressing business.

He gazed at Connie Brandon's bedroom. She would do something, he had no doubt. When she did, he would move. Lennie or no Lennie, he would make sure she never identified him to anyone who could hurt him.

*****

Stirring in bed, Connie opened her eyes wide and jerked up. It seemed so obvious it amazed her she hadn't considered immediately. Tess worked in the Social Security Department, in the individual accounts division. Her computer held the names and addresses of millions of people, in Missouri and across the country. If a Sandra Richards or Lunsford existed in the United States, Tess could probably locate her. True, if Richards used an alias, Tess might not find her, but chances were, one of the two names would show up on a scan.

Energized, Connie rolled to the nightstand and grabbed the phone. A few seconds later, she reached Tess.

"Hey, this is Connie."

"You okay?"

"Sure, fine. Look, you're working tomorrow, right?"

"If it's Monday, I'm working."

Connie smiled. "I need a favor."

"I'm your girl, whatever you need."

"I'm not sure it's legal."

Tess paused. "How illegal is not legal?"

"Not bad, I don't think. I need you to go . . . go into your computer, see if you can find somebody for me."

"Let me get this straight. You want me to use a government computer to look up a name for you?"

"That's it, as simple as that. I need an address."

Tess hesitated again, obviously making up her mind. Connie figured it would break the law. Neither Tess nor Tick would like that. But would that stop her from doing it? She didn't know.

Tess spoke. "You going to tell me why you need to find this person?"

Connie wanted to tell Tess, knew she owed that much to her. But she just couldn't. To do so would put her in extreme danger.

"I think you know why."

"You're trying to clear Jack's name."

"I knew . . . knew you'd understand, Tess. I don't know if I can live with all the rumors. Jack didn't commit suicide, but too many people think he did. But that's not the worst of it. The worst of it is the kids, they think their daddy killed himself. I don't want that for them. It could eventually make them think Jack didn't love them enough to stay with them. I've got to do everything I can to show them the truth. If I can find a way to do that, then I have to try it, even if it does mean breaking a law in the process. Believe me, I know I shouldn't ask you this, but I . . . don't . . . don't know how else to do it."

"Why don't you let Tick help you? Or Tyler?"

"They've already made their decision about this."

"Tick will help you," encouraged Tess. "Tell him what you know, let him go to Tyler. He'll convince Luke to reopen the investigation."

Connie hesitated. What Tess said made sense. Except for one thing. Luke didn't control the situation anymore. Johnson Mack did. If the major wanted this matter closed, then closed it would stay.

"I can't do that," she protested. "If Luke controlled the matter, okay. But you and I both know he doesn't. For now, I have to do this myself. If it gets dangerous, I'll come to Tick. I promise you that. All I want is an address or a phone number. Both if I can get them."

"Tell me who you're looking for."

Connie started to give Tess the name, then reconsidered. As much as she loved and trusted Tess, she knew Tess might tell Tick. Tess might think that the best thing, and Connie couldn't ask her to hide it from him. That wasn't fair.

But if Tick found out, he would go to Luke, who believed Sandra Lunsford and Jack had an affair. If Luke knew she was trying to find Lunsford, he might try to stop her. Worse, he might even warn Lunsford. For him to know complicated matters far too much.

She said to Tess, "I'll tell you in the morning at your office."

"You sure you want to do this?"

"I'm sure."

"Okay, come to the office about ten. Everyone takes a break then. I'll see what I can do."

"You mean you'll help me?"

"We'll see."

"Okay, see you at ten."

Connie hung up. She felt sure Tess would help her. Though she wouldn't like it, Tess didn't have it in her power to turn down her best friend. Especially if her assistance might help clear a dead man's sullied name and save his children from a lifetime of confusion about the reason their daddy left them.

*****

In his Jaguar, Brit pulled his headphones off and smoothed down his ponytail. Okay, Red wanted to find someone. But who? He had no idea. But one thing he did know. He would follow her when she moved. If her buddy Tess found the address, Brit would go with her when she made contact with the mystery person.

He flipped open his cell phone.

"Hey, Lennie, Brit here."

"What's the deal?"

"Red's on the move."

"What you mean?"

"She just asked Tess Garner to use the good offices of the government to locate someone."

"Her tax dollars at work."

"Exactly."

"Who is she trying to find?"

"Didn't say, but if we can get ears into Tess Garner's office, we'll know in the morning, about ten."

"You stay with Red. I'll get someone moving with the ears. And Brit—"

"Yeah?"

"Stay close to her, but don't act until we get clearance. Since we don't know who she's looking for or why, we need to hold back until The Man gives clearance. You got that?"

Brit didn't answer. Instead, he closed the phone and drummed his fingers against the steering wheel. He didn't know if he'd wait for clearance or not. If Red moved, he might move too.

CHAPTER
21

A t ten o'clock sharp, Connie walked into Tess's office on the second floor and sat down in front of her desk. Tess, her blonde hair showing a few dark roots in the glare of the sun from the window, looked up at her and nodded. "You're right on time."

Connie smiled but felt tension in the room and the smile faded. "Look, Tess—" she started.

"Don't say it," interrupted Tess, resting her chin in her hands, her elbows propped on the desk. "You don't have to apologize. I don't know what's going on here, but I do know you. I stewed over this a lot last night, stayed awake and listened to Tick's snoring. You wouldn't ask me to do something you didn't think absolutely necessary. I know that, so I'll do what you want. But . . . well . . . I've got two conditions."

Connie stared at her best friend and counted her blessings. Not many people would risk their job for someone else.

"Tell me your conditions," she said.

"Simple. First, if you find yourself in any danger, any danger whatsoever, you have to promise you'll contact me or Tick immediately."

"But if I get in danger and tell you, I put you in danger too."

"Doesn't matter," insisted Tess, shaking her head. "If you get in danger, you come to me or Tick. Promise that or I won't help you, your choice."

Connie closed her eyes. She didn't like this. But if that's what Tess wanted . . . She opened her eyes. "Okay," she agreed. "What else?"

"When this is over, you'll tell Tick what you asked me to do and why. Eventually, I'll have to tell him . . . we don't keep secrets from each other. When I confess, I want you with me to explain it all."

Connie leaned over the desk and took her friend's hands. "I'm sorry I have to ask you," she said. "But I didn't know where else to go. When it's over, I'll gladly tell Tick everything. I'll apologize for forcing you to do this. I . . . I know he'll forgive you."

Satisfied, Tess squeezed Connie's hands, then sat up straight and faced her computer screen. "Okay," she said. "Who's the mystery person?"

Connie stood and situated her chair where she could also see the computer. Then, her heart racing, she said, "It's a woman. . . . and I've seen . . . seen two names for her. One possibility is Sandra Lunsford. The other is Sandra Richards. See if you can find either one of them."

"Problem is I'll probably find several, maybe more than that. You got a middle name?"

"No name, but an initial. E. Sandra E. Last address 110 Maple Road in Columbia, Missouri."

Tess clicked the computer mouse. "Okay," she said. "Let's start with just a few states in the search field. Like maybe Missouri, Oklahoma, Arkansas, Iowa, Kentucky, Kansas, and Illinois. Narrow things down a smidge."

She brought up the screen and entered the data. Another screen appeared. Tess clicked the mouse again, then keyed in a password. Another security check came up. She identified herself with another password.

With security clearance that gave her access to all but the most sensitive information in the Social Security system, it wasn't difficult to find what she wanted. Within minutes, a screen full of names appeared. Connie and Tess stretched forward in their chairs, their eyes scanning the list for a Sandra E. Lunsford. Eleven S. E. Lunsfords showed up. One in Ohio, two in Illinois, four in Arkansas, two each in Kansas and Iowa. All but three were men.

"Can you check the ages" asked Connie. "That should narrow it a bit more."

Tess hit a few strokes on the keyboard. "Let's see . . . we got one at seventy-six, one at thirty, and one at nineteen."

Connie shook her head. "Not her," she said. "This woman is around forty."

Tess turned and stared at her. "About Jack's age?"

Connie didn't respond. Tess concentrated on the computer again.

"We got six 'Sandras,'" she said. "Hold on though. Only one of them with an 'E.' initial."

"What's her age?" Connie asked, her face flushed.

"Let's see . . . here it is . . . no . . . not it . . . she's eighty-four years old."

Tess looked at Connie for direction. "You want to stay with Lunsford and increase the number of states we search or you want to try Richards?"

For a moment, Connie didn't answer. Instead, she rubbed her forehead and tried to connect the dots to everything she knew so far. Lunsford came to Jefferson City from somewhere. But where? Not Columbia, probably not even Missouri. If Jack had an old flame or a family member that close, she would have sensed it over the years. Then where?

One answer kept jabbing at her. Las Vegas. Jack wrote a check to a private investigator who lived in Las Vegas. In Morrison's bedroom, she found pictures of Jack and Sandra and an elderly man. If she had to choose one place to look for the answer to this mystery, she would go to Las Vegas, Nevada.

She turned to Tess. "Try Richards," she said. "And try it in Nevada."

Tess rolled her eyes. "Back to Vegas?" she asked.

Connie nodded. "Back to Vegas."

Tess keyed in the commands. The computer clicked in response. Tess and Connie stared at the screen. "We got two 'Sandra E. Richards' in Vegas," said Tess, working to check the ages. "One is twenty-seven and one is fifty-two." She rolled back in her seat, waiting for more instructions.

"Try all of Nevada," said Connie. "She might not actually live in Vegas."

Tess obeyed. Less than a minute later, the screen flipped up a name and an address. "Sandra E. Richards. 5301 Black Canyon Road, Black Canyon, Nevada."

"You got an age on that one?" asked Connie, her blood pressure rising.

"Let's see . . . hang on . . . there it is . . . thirty-nine years old!"

Connie slapped Tess on the back. "It's got to be her!" she shouted. "No doubt about it. Where's Black Canyon? Is it near Las Vegas? Have you got a map in here anywhere?"

"Whoa," said Tess, her tone calmer than Connie's. "Don't go off half-cocked here. This woman sure looks like a hit, but you don't know for certain. Here, let's get a phone number, maybe you can—"

Connie touched Tess on the shoulder. "A phone number is fine," she said. "But I can't call her. She . . . well, she . . . " She paused, not sure what else to say.

"Spit it out, Connie. Who is this woman?"

"I think you know," said Connie, exhaling slowly. "This is the woman who told Luke Tyler she and Jack were lovers."

"But we don't believe that for a second!" protested Tess. "Jack was too fine a Christian for that, he would never—"

"You don't have to defend him to me," interrupted Connie. "But you need to know I found a video that showed Jack with this woman. Plus, and here's the strangest part, I found out she and Jack went to high school together, graduated the same year. So—"

"So you've had reason to wonder," Tess summed it up, not asking about the source of the video.

"Exactly. I've had lots of reason to wonder. That's why I can't call her. I mean . . . how do you call a woman and say, 'Hey, did you have an affair with my dead husband?' You can't do it."

Tess didn't respond for several seconds. But then she stood and walked to her window. The morning sun shone through the glass and lit up her blonde hair as she stared outside. When she turned back to Connie, her eyes were gentle.

"You have to go see her," she said. "No way around it."

Connie nodded. "My sentiments. The only way to the bottom of this is through Black Canyon. Meet Sandra Richards face-to-face."

Tess stepped to her and took her hands. "I know you're going to say 'no,' but I want to offer anyway. Let Tick go with you."

Connie smiled, but not from levity. "You know I can't do that. This is between me and Richards."

"Then let *me* go with you."

"Same answer. Besides, you have to stay with the kids."

"Mrs. Everhart could do that."

"How would you explain it to Tick?"

"I'll tell him I want to spend a couple of days with my best buddy. He'll say, 'Go do it.' Come on, let me go with you."

Connie considered it. She would love to have Tess along to lift her spirits and keep her strong. But, unfortunately, Tess didn't know everything—didn't know about Jack's notebook or the baseball. Didn't know about Reed Morrison's death. She didn't need to know all this. The less she knew, the safer for her. Was going to Nevada safe? Sure . . . maybe . . . perhaps. Connie didn't know. That uncertainty meant she couldn't allow Tess to go.

"I can't Tess," she whispered. "I . . . want to . . . but I just can't."

Tess opened her mouth as if to speak but then didn't. Connie surveyed her shoes for a moment.

"Is going to Vegas safe for you?" Tess asked.

Connie continued to study her sandals. Jack directed her to Sandra Richards. He wouldn't have done so if he thought it dangerous. For now, she felt safe. After she found Richards, she would decide what to do next. She nodded to Tess. "I think it's safe."

"You made me a promise," said Tess.

"And I'll keep it. If I find myself in any danger, I'll let you know."

Tess squeezed her hands, then dropped them. "You better get going," she said. "I know you've got some packing to do."

Connie nodded. "If I can catch an evening flight, I'm going tonight," she said. "No reason to wait. Can you stay with Daniel and Katie?"

Tess grimaced. "I've got a small problem," she said. "Tick wanted to take his boat to the lake for a couple of days. It's been a while since we took any time off."

Connie nodded. "You do that!" she stated. "You two deserve it. I'll send Daniel home with a friend. He'll love me for it."

"Sorry, but Tick has the room reserved already, we're—"

"Hey, don't apologize. After all you've done for me?"

Connie stepped across the room and embraced Tess, a small flow of tears welling up in her eyes. Tess hugged her, too, and the two friends stayed that way for several long moments, their love marked by the tears that flowed like fresh rain onto their faces.

*****

Sitting on Main Street no more than two hundred yards away from Tess Garner's office, Brit flipped open his cell phone and reached Lennie within seconds. "Red's headed to Nevada," he said.

"She going to play the slots?"

"Real funny."

"Then what's her plan?"

"She's going to visit a rival. A woman who claimed an affair with Jack Brandon."

"She got a name?"

"Yeah, Sandra Richards, maybe Lunsford. Why didn't we know about her?"

Lennie paused for a moment, and Brit imagined him buttoning and unbuttoning his coat, trying to come up with an answer. After several seconds, Lennie spoke. "Who said we didn't?"

"You knew about her?"

"Let's just say The Man knew. The Man knows everything."

"But you didn't tell me."

"No reason. She's no threat to us as things now stand."

Brit smoothed down the back of his ponytail and drummed a beat on the steering wheel. Lennie was holding out on him. He didn't like that. When the time came, he would settle things with Lennie. For now, though, he would play it cool. "You want me to go to Vegas?"

"You got that right. I'll meet you at the airport."

Brit hung up and sagged back into his seat. When the time came, he would settle up with Lennie.

CHAPTER
22

At 9:25, Connie settled back and closed her eyes as the 747 left the ground. Goodness, what an incredible day. After leaving Tess, she had picked up some groceries and driven home, pulled $5,000 from her briefcase, packed for a three-day trip, instructed the kids when they came home from school, and stopped by the church for a few minutes to see Reverend Wallace. Not finding him, she spent almost thirty minutes alone in the sanctuary seeking guidance, trying to determine if she had made the right choice. Though no lightning flashed and no voices spoke, the words of Jesus reverberated again and again in her head: "You shall know the truth, and the truth shall set you free."

Content with that word, she decided she had to forge ahead. One way or another, she knew she would never feel peaceful again unless she made this one final effort to find the truth.

Now, comfortably dressed in blue jeans, a dark blue cotton blouse, and walking shoes, she watched the stars whip by in the dark outside the window and wondered what truth she would discover. Who killed Jack? Cedric Blacker through one of his hired gangsters? Sandra Richards's irate husband? Johnson Mack or someone he paid? Or did Jack really commit suicide?

As the flight attendant served her peanuts and a soft drink, Connie turned over all the possibilities. All seemed logical in one moment, crazy the next. She tried to rest, to drop the mystery for a couple of hours, but found it impossible. The jet zoomed through the night, and her mind pushed through the theories.

A major puzzle swirled around Richards. Who was she and what was her relationship with Jack? She tried to imagine Jack in Richards's arms but couldn't. It made no sense. Why would Jack want her to find a woman with whom he had an affair? Nothing made much sense right now.

Her confusion mounting, Connie rubbed her forehead and tried to clear everything out. Simply put, she didn't know the answers to anything. The whole picture seemed as murky as the sky past her window, and she simply couldn't see through it. As the plane began its descent, she realized matters might stay that way. She might live and die without ever discovering what happened between Jack and Richards or what happened the night Jack died. She wondered if she could accept that outcome, wondered how it would feel to live the rest of her days with the dark cloud of the unsolved dilemma looming over her head.

Not sure, she pulled a map from the overnight bag she had under the seat and studied the area around Las Vegas. She had found Black Canyon on the map earlier in the day. It sat about fifty miles southwest of Vegas, a small town not far from the western edge of California.

The wheels of the plane skidded across the runway, and she took a deep breath. Not long now. The plane taxied to the terminal, and she rubbed her eyes. Her body shifted into overdrive, and she moved with deliberate speed off the plane to the car rental counter. After paying for the car with cash, she verified the directions to Black Canyon with the clerk and hustled from the counter into the car. Ten minutes later, she turned onto Interstate 15, thinking about Reed Morrison all the way. Overhead, the stars continued to twinkle and the moon danced a silver waltz, but Connie barely noticed.

Pushing aside her questions, she settled in for the drive and wondered how Black Canyon came by its name. Nothing on the map indicated an answer, and she decided to waste no more energy worrying about it. She concentrated on the road. The white highway stripes cut through the bleak desert wasteland, painted arrows to the unknown. She knew she should feel scared, but she didn't. In spite of everything, the adrenaline pumping through her system pushed fear to the side. Right now she wanted to stand nose-to-nose with Sandra Richards and demand to know what connection she had to Jack Brandon.

The miles disappeared in a hurry, the distance eaten up by the twin mouths of her anger and anxiety. Intent on her impending rendezvous, Connie almost missed the turnoff to Black Canyon. At the last minute, she veered the rental car to the right, up the off ramp and into a left turn. Fifteen minutes and twelve miles later, she hit the brakes as a sign reading "Black Canyon" loomed before her. Two red lights later, she stopped and asked a convenience store operator how to find Black Canyon Drive.

"You're not far from it," said the man. "What address you want?"

"5301 Black Canyon Drive."

"That's Justin Longley's place. No more than sixteen miles up the road. Just keep straight and look for a bit of white fence on your left. Turn there, that's Black Canyon Drive. The road sort of winds down there, a bit of a dip in the desert. You can't miss it. Justin's the only guy out there with any white fence. His house is about a quarter mile into the dip."

Though confused, Connie didn't show it. "You know Justin Longley?"

"Sure, not but about two thousand people in this whole town. I know most all of them, I expect."

Connie considered her next move. Could Longley be the elderly man in the picture she found at Morrison's? Unsure, she hesitated, wondering if she should press the clerk for more details. Did a woman named Sandra live with Longley? Was Longley her husband? If so, what about the name difference? Would the clerk know? Would he answer her if he did? She decided to leave matters alone, not arouse suspicion. She would find out soon enough. She turned to leave.

"Tell Justin I hope he feels better," said the clerk.

Connie faced him again. "He's sick?"

"Sure, don't you know? He's on his last legs. But don't tell him I said that. He's liable to come in here and whack me one with that cane he carries all the time."

Connie smiled. "I'll keep it our secret. Thanks."

Driving slowly through the darkness on the unfamiliar road, it took her over thirty minutes to drive the sixteen miles to Longley's "bit of fence." No more than twenty feet long, the

fence stood unconnected to anything on either side, a distin-
guishing landmark on the bleak road. A mailbox stood to the
right of the white fence, the word *Justin* painted in a fire-engine
red. Connie turned left, and the rental dipped with the road.
Though not more than a few feet, the descent in the road felt like
a steep grade as she drove the quarter mile to the house. Connie
understood now why they called it "Canyon Drive," though the
"Black" part still escaped her.

She spotted the frame house on her right, no more than a
stone's throw from the narrow road. Standing all alone, the
forlorn-looking structure sagged toward the sand. A windmill
flipped its propellers just behind the house and a three-wheel
motorcycle of an indistinguishable color sat to the right of the
windmill. Lights in every room lit up the shabby house and a
couple of rocking chairs rested on the front porch that ran across
the entire front.

Calmer than she expected, Connie slowed the car to a stop,
then pulled to the side of the road. Educated by her experience
at Morrison's, she left the car running and stepped out. A
minute later, she eased onto the porch and knocked on the door.
No one answered. She knocked again. Again no answer. A sense
of déjà vu washed over her. Morrison's house all over again?

She felt her face flush. It couldn't happen twice, could it?
She knocked one more time. No response. For several moments,
she stood and waited, wondering what to do. She just couldn't
go inside this time. The notion of finding another body petrified
her. But could she just leave the place? Leave the place Sandra
Richards listed as her address?

Connie knocked once more. The lights in the house flickered, then switched off completely. The desert shut down on her,
its darkness a blanket of black over her eyes.

Connie panicked. A shriek ripped from her throat, the shrill
sound of a woman in danger. Powered by her fears, she jumped
off the porch and stumbled toward the car, her knees scraping
the sandy ground as she fell. From behind, she heard footsteps.
Her breath choking out in ragged gashes, she jerked herself up
and sprinted toward the car, pushing her legs faster and faster,
willing them to move, move, move. She heard the car idling and
prayed she would reach it before her pursuer reached her.

A roll of perspiration fell into her eyes and blinded her for a second as it flooded her contact lenses. She felt the ground drop beneath her feet, and her right shoe banged into a rock; she tumbled face forward onto the ground. Desert grit dug into her chin. Pushing up, she heard the car engine again; it gave her courage, and she churned toward it.

Someone grabbed her left ankle. She kicked out with her right foot and connected. A man grunted, and Connie screamed. The grip on her ankle tightened, a vise of power like nothing she had ever felt. She kicked again with her right foot, but this time hit nothing. Pain ripped through her left leg as her pursuer yanked her backward.

A second hand grabbed her right ankle, too, and clamped down on it. A man yelled her name. "Connie Brandon!" The grip on her ankles lessened a notch.

"Connie, it's me!"

She twisted her body a hundred and eighty degrees and almost fainted. A bear of a man held her ankles and stared back at her, a look of deep concern etched across his bearded face.

"Luke?"

Luke released his grip, and she scurried away from him toward the car, her suspicions unsatisfied.

"Hold it, Connie!" Luke yelled, gliding across the desert sand. "I'm here to help you."

Connie reached the car and positioned herself on the opposite side from Luke. "But how did you get here? . . . What are you—?"

Luke stopped and held up his hands like a cowboy trying to calm a skittish colt. "I'm a detective, remember?"

"But you said you were shutting down the investigation."

"Sure, that's still where it is, officially at least. But I decided to dig a bit on my own time. No harm in that."

"But how did you find this place?"

"Not that hard since I already had the woman's name. A few computer checks . . . a bit of background searching . . . She's listed as Richards. Lunsford is either an alias or a married name she doesn't use. I found an address. One advantage of being a cop. Some things you can get fairly easily." He took a couple of steps toward her.

"Stay still!" she shouted. "Just stay still for a minute. How do I know . . . how do I know you're not here to . . . to—"

"To hurt you?"

Connie's voice faltered as she tried to answer. "Yes, to . . . to . . . "

Luke softened his tone. "If I wanted to hurt you, why did I let you go?"

Connie shuddered but knew he made sense. He had her by the ankles, could have snapped them in his bare hands, she had no doubt. Luke Tyler could have broken her ankles, then her neck, as easily as a boy snaps a twig in the backyard. But he didn't. Luke had released her ankles and let her go.

Cautiously, she eased around the hood of the car. "Why did you turn out the house lights?" she asked.

"Old police trick. When you don't know what you're dealing with, you put things in the dark. I was inside, heard a knock on the door. Didn't know who knocked, or how many. Darkness confuses things. I hit a breaker, heard you jump off the porch. Of course, I didn't know it was you. I came running." He stepped closer.

She coiled to run again, but then Luke stopped.

"How did you get here?"

"I parked around back."

Though afraid to ask, she couldn't avoid her next question. "Did you find anything . . . anyone?"

Luke took a deep breath. "Somebody tore the place apart. Everything is scattered."

"Any sign of the woman?"

"Not a bit. Nobody there."

Connie's shoulders sagged. "What about a man, a guy named Justin Longley?"

"Who's he?"

Connie shrugged. "Not sure. Husband maybe. Or brother, father, grandfather, or friend. Don't know."

"No sign of him either. Nobody there. Clothes tossed and furniture tipped over and cabinets wide open, but no sign of a human being. You want to take a look?"

Connie considered the offer. Why not? Luke didn't know everything she knew. Maybe he missed something.

"Is that . . . legal?"

Luke smiled slightly. "No, not really. But if you move fast, I won't tell."

"You think it's safe?"

"I think so. Whoever tossed the place left already. I don't think they'll come back anytime soon. You game?"

To answer, Connie opened the door of the rental car, switched off the engine, and marched toward the house, her shoulders set. Luke followed, his big body a comfort against the shadows of the desert. On the porch, she waited while he stepped inside and flipped on the breaker again, flooding the place with light. A couple of seconds later, Luke led her inside. Her eyes adjusted to the glare. She scanned the first room past the door—a living area decorated only with a brown cloth sofa, a couple of rocking chairs like those on the porch, and a fireplace complete with a stone hearth and a dark wood mantle. Whoever lived here had never heard of Martha Stewart.

Carefully, Connie picked her way through the litter on the wood floor—a hat tree, three sofa cushions, several small indoor plants. Nothing broken, just tossed.

"It's got two bedrooms, a kitchen, and a bathroom," said Luke. "That's about it. All pretty much in the same shape."

Connie moved from the living room to the two bedrooms. Luke followed her, his quiet presence more than welcome. The mattresses in the bedrooms lay on the floors, and the dressers, identical pieces of plain wood furniture in both bedrooms, had been ransacked. Bits and pieces of old clothing lay like molted skins all over the place. No pictures decorated the walls. Each room contained a small closet. Connie stuck her head into each closet and found them empty. It looked as if someone had snatched the closets clean, swept them of any sign of human occupancy. Without warning, she thought of Jack's closet. Though not quite as empty as these, it wasn't far from it. Just enough to get by and just enough to snatch away and run if . . . it suddenly dawned on her . . . if someone came searching for you. The similarities scared her, and she shuddered. Then, trying to think of something else, she turned to Luke.

"This place is a bit spare, don't you think?" she asked.

"Didn't keep much extra around, that's for sure."

"You'd never know a woman lived here," she said, moving to the bathroom. "No sign of a feminine touch."

Luke rolled a toothpick from his shirt pocket and followed her. "Maybe Richards didn't live here."

"Then why is this listed as her address?"

"You got me."

Connie found the bathroom as bare as the other rooms and quickly walked out. The kitchen told the same tale. Pots and pans thrown here and there, but no clues to anything. Puzzled, Connie left the house and stepped onto the front porch. There, she stared into the darkness and weighed the possibilities. Luke stood beside her, his toothpick working.

"You're right," she said. "Richards didn't live here, at least not recently."

"So who did?"

"Justin Longley, whoever that is."

Luke nibbled his toothpick. "Wonder if she came and got him?"

Connie stepped toward Luke. "Or *they* came and got him . . . or him and her." Her voice sounded as a whisper in the desert stillness.

Luke's gray eyes widened. "Who got them?" he asked.

Connie shook her head. "I don't know who they are. But . . . but I saw them . . . saw them in Las Vegas last Wednesday."

"You went to Vegas?"

Connie almost smiled at the irony. It did sound crazy. A small-town, tiny woman like herself flying in and out of Las Vegas, searching for . . . well . . . searching for some conclusion to the tragedy that had invaded her life.

"Yeah, I went to Vegas. And . . . when I did . . . I found a man named Reed Morrison . . . found him . . . dead. That's when I saw them, two men in a black Mercedes. I can't prove a thing, but I know . . . I know, somehow, they're tied up in all this. If we can find them . . . well, if we find them, we'll know who killed Jack."

"You've been a busy girl," said Luke, a hint of admiration in his words.

"I had no choice. You closed down the investigation."

"Johnson Mack closed it down."

Connie started to speak, then hesitated.

Luke asked, "What next?"

"You tell me."

"Back to Jefferson City, I think. I want you to search through some mug books. You think you'd recognize the men you saw in Las Vegas?"

"One of them for sure, a blond one."

Luke nodded toward her rental. "I'll follow you to the airport."

Connie stepped off the porch.

"By the way," said Luke. "Who's Reed Morrison?"

Connie pivoted back to him. "I'll tell you on the plane."

She hustled to the car, climbed in, started it, and shifted into gear. A minute later, Luke pulled up behind her, and the two of them moved back down Black Canyon Road, up the dip to the highway, and back toward the interstate. Driving by the convenience store, Connie flicked her eyes toward the clerk who gave her directions to Longley's place. Through the glass of the well-lit building, she spotted him behind the counter, talking to a man standing next to a magazine rack. Her eyes on the clerk, Connie failed to see the silver Lexus parked in the shadows by the side of the store. If she had seen the Lexus and the blond man with a ponytail behind its wheel, she would surely have screamed.

CHAPTER

23

Looking at the mug shots at Luke's office the next afternoon produced nothing—no leads, no names, no possibilities, a big zero. Connie raised her eyes from the last page of the final book and shook her head.

"They're not in here," she said to Luke.

Luke, his broad back nestled in his chair, nodded and twisted a toothpick in his teeth. "Okay, it was a long shot anyway. We don't have a huge collection of pictures here in Jefferson City. Maybe the computer will pick up something later."

"You think the description I gave will do any good?"

"It's possible. We'll get a sketch artist from K.C. or St. Louis to make a drawing. I'll enter that in the computer, then pass it around in a few spots. See if it stirs up anything."

Connie breathed deeply and looked at Luke. Worn out from last night's trip, she rubbed her eyes and wondered what to do next. So far, her best efforts had led to nothing. She had no proof of anything she suspected, and the police had no real reason to reconsider their verdict of suicide. Yes, the disappearance of Sandra Richards and the trashing of Longley's house caused some concern. But a trashed house provided no evidence of anything worse than a prank. With nothing more to offer, Luke hadn't even bothered to call the authorities in Black Canyon.

Frustrated by the dead end, Connie's energy plunged. When she spoke, her voice was frail. "We've done all we can, haven't we?"

"I think so, for now at least. But that doesn't mean we give up. I'll keep nosing around, see if I can find out what happened to Richards."

Connie slumped. She felt so weak. "The insurance won't pay in the case of a suicide," she said.

Luke stayed quiet.

"It's for a million dollars," she said. "If Jack killed himself, it won't pay. I'll have to sell the store."

"Johnson Mack wants it." Luke said it matter-of-factly.

Connie's eyes widened. "You know that?"

"Sure, I'm a detective, remember. It's not like it's a secret. He's buying up half the town."

"That gives him motive for murder."

"Sure it does. But motive doesn't mean proof. I've nosed around some on Mack, but he comes up clean so far. Nothing except motive connects him to Jack's death."

Connie sighed. She understood how it worked. The law. The law she loved and would soon embrace as her career. Even with the sale of the store, she would still have to get a job, probably full-time. The investment of the money from the sale of the store would earn a tidy sum but not enough to get two children through school and on into college.

"I don't know if I can stay in Jefferson City," she said. "Too many people with too much gossip."

"People here care about you," said Luke.

"I know, but not all of them. I don't want the kids growing up in a town where half the people think their daddy killed himself. A clean start might do us all some good."

Luke rolled his toothpick in his mouth. "I know you'll make the right decision," he said. "But, I want you to know . . . well . . . I want you to know I hope . . . hope you'll stay."

Connie noted the care in his tone. "Thanks, Luke . . . you've been a big help . . . I'm glad you're here to keep an eye out in case anything turns up."

"Glad to do it," he said. "Just call me if you need anything."

She stood to leave. Luke stood too, walked around his desk, and reached out to shake her hand. She extended hers, and he took it, his huge fingers swallowing her whole hand. His hand was gentle, warm. She noticed his breathing, so soft and soothing. Luke placed his left hand on her elbow, a gesture of kindness and protection. Connie's face suddenly flushed. This was more than a handshake to Luke! It was a touch of affection, of . . . attraction!

Stunned, she jerked her hand from his and twisted away. A feeling of shame ran through her. Had she done anything to encourage this? Had she, so soon after Jack's death, given off any signals that invited Luke Tyler to care for her? Though not sure, she felt certain she hadn't.

She sputtered as she spoke. "I . . . need . . . need to go . . . to get home . . . to—"

"Let me know if I can help in any way," insisted Luke, his tone relaxed, apparently unaware of her confusion.

"Yes, I'll . . . I'll call if . . . if anything . . . " She fled the room and rushed through the building back to her van. In the front seat, she gulped in huge mouthfuls of air and began to cry. She loved Jack more than anything in the world. To have another man consider her attractive seemed like such a betrayal. No matter what she thought, she must have done something to make Luke see her that way. But that wouldn't do! She had to stay away from Luke. Give him no occasion to mistake her friendship for anything more. Whatever happened in the next few months, she wouldn't go back to Luke. To do so might make him think thoughts he simply shouldn't think. So determined, Connie bit her lip and started her van. No matter what, she would avoid Luke Tyler like the plague.

*****

Six hours later and just over 130 miles away, Sandra Richards stepped across the narrow space of Justin Longley's one-room trailer and kissed him on top of his gray head. A tank of oxygen sat beside the small, bunklike bed where he lay, and a green, snakelike tube ran from the tank up the side of the bed and into his nose. A stubble of white beard stuck out in uneven tufts along his chin, and a series of brownish age spots ran like broken steps up both cheeks. His breath coming in short gasps, Justin lifted his head off his pillow and panted his words out. "You . . . go . . . to her," he said. "Bring . . . her . . . back . . . to me. Before she gets . . . gets herself killed."

Sandra picked up a gym bag and slung it over her shoulder. "I'll get her," she said. "Are you going to be all right for a couple of days?"

Justin smiled as best he could and reached out his right hand. She took it, and he squeezed hard. Though thin and bony, the hand still felt strong. "I . . . made it . . . a long time," he wheezed. "I guess . . . I'll last a few more . . . days."

"I put a big chicken casserole in the refrigerator. Just warm it up on the stove, you'll have enough to eat."

He dropped her hand. "Just . . . go." He waved at her. "I can manage."

Sandra inhaled sharply. He looked so frail. Last night's narrow escape and all-night drive had taken too much out of him. Their good friend at the convenience store had done exactly what Justin had asked him to do years ago—call him if and when anyone came asking for directions to Black Canyon Drive.

When the two men in the silver Lexus stopped in for gas and directions, he gave them both. Then, the second they pulled out of his parking lot, he called Justin's house. Sandra pretty much took it from there. She grabbed the oxygen and the few belongings they kept in the closets. Loaded it all in the small trailer home Justin had bought years ago for just this purpose. Hooked the home to her truck. Drove down Black Canyon in the opposite direction from Rudy's store. Parked behind an outcropping of bare black rocks and waited and watched until the intruders left.

Everything followed the plan Justin had made since the day he moved to Black Canyon almost twenty years ago. The intruders, faceless men with unknown names, came as Justin told Sandra they someday would. Though managing to escape them for almost half a century, he had long anticipated the day they would hunt him down.

Well, now the day had arrived, and Justin, with Sandra's help, had managed to stay one step ahead of them once again. Staring at the pencil-thin man, she didn't know how many more days he had left, but if she had anything to do with it, his days would end naturally, not when a couple of hired thugs decided to take him out.

Through a set of worn but serviceable binoculars, they had watched the two men from behind the black rocks. When the thugs finished, Sandra and Justin started back toward the house, planning to pick up a few more belongings before making their final exit. But then another car arrived, then a third. The binoculars identified the driver of the third car as Connie Brandon.

Sandra felt like crying when she saw Connie. This meant the worst possible scenario had played itself out. Not only had Jack died, but now his wife had placed herself in grave danger. Unable to leave the tragedy alone, she had kept picking at it and picking at it until she had uncovered the sore and made it worse. Her persistence created danger for her, but she either didn't know or didn't care. It didn't slow her down any. Sandra had to do something to make her stop.

"Your cane is right here," she said to Justin. "Right by your head."

Justin snuggled deeper into his pillow. "I know where my . . . my cane is," he said, his voice just a bit short. "Now . . . go. She needs . . . to face it. Bring . . . bring . . . " He couldn't continue.

Sandra leaned over him again and ran her hand over his cheek. She kissed him one more time. For far too long he had kept the burden to himself—the burden of knowing too much, the burden of hiding from those who wanted his secrets dead and buried. Only within the last year had Sandra learned what Justin knew. Only within the last year had he turned to anyone but himself to survive. Now, because of that, he blamed himself for Jack's death. Worse still, he feared Connie might die too. If he didn't reveal the truth to her, she might stumble into the wrong place at the wrong time and die like her husband. It almost happened last night. If she had come to Black Canyon a couple of hours earlier, she would have met her end in the Nevada desert.

Her bag secure over her arm, Sandra pivoted and headed to the door. Only she could prevent Connie's death. But to prevent it, she had to bring her to Justin.

Opening the camper door, Sandra turned back for one more look at her granddaddy. "You take care now," she said. "I'll see you soon."

"If that casserole you made don't kill me, I'll be fine."

Laughing, Sandra left him, unhooked the trailer from their truck and climbed into the cab. Heading down the dirt road from the grove of hickory trees where the camper sat, she considered praying for Justin. But then she shook her head. Prayer didn't do much for her. Since high school, she had given up much praying. Turning off the dirt road onto the highway, she decided she better keep on depending on herself. So far, that had gotten her along just fine.

*****

All day long, Brit watched Connie. Refreshed from a few hours sleep on the plane and powered by the best amphetamines money could by, he had no trouble staying awake. When she disappeared into her house after seeing her kids onto their buses, Brit sat in his red Jaguar, drummed a steady beat on the steering wheel, and waited. When she came out just after nine o'clock and drove downtown, he drummed and followed. When she came back home, sat down on her back deck, and stared out over the Missouri River, he drummed faster and waited some more. When the kids traipsed in all noisy and busy after school and the sun went down and the smell of chicken frying drifted out her kitchen window, his drumming and waiting reached a fever pitch, and he didn't know if he could wait much longer. Then, when darkness fell and Connie stepped out of the house in a jogging suit and started walking down the road, Brit stopped drumming and decided to wait no more. As he figured it, he had waited too long already.

Lennie had held out on him about Sandra Richards. Now she and that sickly old grandfather of hers had disappeared. After leaving Richards's place, he and Lennie had come back to St. Louis without doing a thing about Connie Brandon. If he waited any longer, she might do worse than disappear. She might go to the police, find his picture in a Nevada computer check, identify him for what he was, a rogue operator who hired out to the highest bidder to do odds and ends on the dark side of the law. He couldn't wait for that to happen. Regardless of what Lennie said, the time to act had come.

Watching Connie stride down the road in her white jogging suit, her hair pinned back in a ponytail, he made a snap decision. It would happen so quickly she would never know what hit her.

Brit's eyes lit up at his simple plan. Connie Brandon walked almost every day—either morning or night. Everyone knew that. Her stroll took her down a steep narrow road, a road that bordered the cliffs that hung over the Missouri River several hundred feet below. From time to time, she came within a few feet of those bluffs, close enough to stop and stare over them. During his surveillance, he had seen her do it. If he knew, then surely so did others. He could knock her over the cliffs and everyone would assume she fell . . . or maybe jumped.

He switched on the car. It purred like a big cat. Brit smiled and smoothed down his ponytail. He flicked on the lights and saw Connie up ahead of him, her slender frame disappearing as she pumped her arm weights and moved around the curve of the road. Slowly, he eased away from the curb. The car seemed to leap under his hands. He pressed the gas pedal more firmly. The car darted across the road.

Connie disappeared around the curve. He smiled wider. He knew the spot. A quick twist in the road, a narrowing of the shoulder on the right side, a few short feet to the bluffs that dropped down to the river.

The car took on a life of its own. He slammed the gas pedal to the floor. The headlights of the car grabbed into the night, a cat's paws seeking prey. He slid around the corner and spotted Connie Brandon no more than twenty feet ahead, her red hair bouncing in its ponytail. The front fender of the Jaguar cut to the right and reached for Connie's left hip. In a half second, it would—

Brit's smile died on his face. Connie Brandon moved with the agility of an antelope avoiding the big cat. Without ever looking back, she made a quick leap to the right, avoided his car, and tumbled away from him toward a thicket of deep green underbrush. Something crashed on his hood, and he spotted one of Connie's arm weights as it thumped off the car onto the road.

As fast as he had tried to run her down, Brit gunned the car away, down and around the twist in the road and across a bridge that sat a quarter of a mile away. Cursing under his breath, he turned left past the bridge and darted up the highway. Though certain she hadn't seen him, he made a couple of calculations usually beyond his ability to make. He concluded, first, that he needed to switch cars if he wanted to continue his surveillance and, second, that he had to do her in a hurry. If she had by some chance seen him just now, she would know beyond any doubt that he wanted her dead.

CHAPTER

24

L eaping off the ground, Connie steadied herself and peered down the road at the back of the car that had almost hit her. Seen in the glow of its taillights, the car looked foreign, a bright red European model. For several seconds, she stayed poised behind a huge hickory tree, ready to dodge again. To her back six feet of Missouri soil separated her from the bank that dropped toward the river.

A frown crossed her face. Did the driver of the car deliberately try to run her down? She didn't know. The pavement curved sharply at the exact point the car almost hit her, and it was dark. Maybe it was an accident. But why didn't the driver stop and check on her?

Her left elbow throbbed, and she realized she had landed on it when she fell. By the streetlight, she checked the arm, saw a scratch running from her wrist to her elbow. To her relief, nothing else hurt.

She stepped past the hickory tree and hurried onto the road. Forgetting her weights, she hustled back to the house and ran inside. Carefully, she locked the doors and checked on Daniel and Katie. Both were sound asleep.

In her bedroom, she left the light on, grabbed her Bible off her nightstand, and climbed under the covers without removing her walking clothes. Not wanting to close her eyes, she opened the Bible and began to search it, reading each and every passage she could find that told a Christian what to do with fear.

*****

At just past eleven o'clock, Sandra Richards parked her truck in the shadows at the side of a grocery store off Missouri Boulevard, smoothed down the front of her blue jeans, and climbed out. After scanning the front of the store for unfriendly faces, she held up a slip of yellow paper and studied it for several seconds. Then, mumbling the numbers to herself, she hopped out of the truck and walked briskly to the pay phone by the side of the store. At the phone, she tilted her head into the metal box that housed it and dialed Jack Brandon's house. It took five rings before anyone answered.

"Hello?"

Sandra squeezed the phone and exhaled. Okay, now or never. "Yes, Connie Brandon?"

"Yes, who is this?"

Sandra closed her eyes briefly, then spat out her message. "This is Sandra Richards. I knew your husband."

Silence came onto the line. Then Sandra heard Connie choking. She decided she better speak before Connie hung up or collapsed from shock.

"Connie!" she shouted, forgetting her need for caution. "You need to know this right now! I didn't have an affair with your husband. I made that up—if you'll let me see you, I'll make it all plain to you. I've known Jack a long time . . . but not in the way you think. Connie, I'm Jack's cousin! His father and my mother were brother and sister, you've got to believe me . . . I can explain it all . . . just let me see you—"

Sandra stopped, panting from her effort, hoping Connie wouldn't slam down the phone. Above her head, a storm of insects buzzed at a light, and she glanced up at them as she waited for a response. For a second, she thought Connie had fainted, but then she heard a deep breath and knew she hadn't lost her.

"Connie, I need to see you," she pleaded. "I'm your only hope of knowing the truth about Jack." She waited again, knowing she should now leave it alone. Connie would accept or reject her offer, and she would accept whatever she chose. If she said no, then so be it. She and Justin would disappear. To do more placed all their lives in danger.

She heard Connie clear her throat. Her long fingers gripped the phone tighter.

Connie said, "I knew Jack stayed faithful, I just knew it."

"He did, Connie, he did. Never doubt that, not for a second. Can I see you? I'll tell you everything."

"Where are you?"

"Real close."

"I'll meet you."

"That may not be best. People are looking for me."

"Then how do we do this?"

"Let me come to you."

Silence came on the phone again. Sandra guessed the reason for the hesitation. Connie didn't trust her. Why should she?

"It's okay, Connie," she assured her. "Look, I'm not here to hurt you, or the kids either. I'm here to help, to give you some answers. You've got to—"

She stopped as a black car slowed down and pulled into the parking lot. The car's driver gazed at her as he came to a stop and climbed out. Sandra exhaled softly. The man wasn't one of the two who ransacked Justin's place in Black Canyon. She focused again on Connie.

"I've got to get off the phone," she said. "I'm . . . well . . . I'm in some danger here. Can I see you?"

Another second passed. Then Connie asked, "When do you want to meet?"

"Tonight, right now."

Connie didn't hesitate this time. "Okay, I'm home, it's—"

"I know the address. I'll get there in ten minutes."

"Okay." The line went dead.

Hanging up, Sandra surveyed the parking lot, then crawled back into her truck. For better or worse, she had to convince Connie to go with her to Justin.

*****

The instant Connie opened the front door and looked into Sandra Richards's eyes, she felt certain the woman had told her the truth. Her eyes, up close like this, mirrored the eyes of Jack Brandon. Slightly narrow at the edges, deeply set under the brow, and covered by eyelashes long enough to catch a spider. Almost as tall as Jack, her frame matched his, too, slender but not frail. Connie stepped back and motioned Sandra inside. As she eased past, Connie noticed her hands, long and tightly clenched by her sides. Seeing the tension, Connie almost smiled. She knew the feeling.

"Let's go to the kitchen," said Connie, hoping she sounded calm. "I've got some tea brewing." She led Sandra through the entryway.

"Have a seat," she said, indicating the table by the back window.

Obeying, Sandra pulled out a chair and sat down, her slender hands resting on the table. Connie poured two cups of tea, carried them to the table, and took a seat beside Sandra.

Connie dropped a cube of sugar into her tea and stirred it slowly. Her heart thumped, and she squeezed the spoon to keep her hands from shaking. After several seconds, she raised her eyes and faced Sandra. "Tell me all you know," she said.

Sandra took a sip of tea, then set the cup down. "I don't know everything," she said. "But I do know Jack and I didn't have an affair. I need to say that first thing, get it cleared up between me and you. Like I told you, Jack and I, we're—well, we were cousins."

"Why did you tell the police you and Jack were lovers?"

Sandra sighed. "I had to do it," she said, matter-of-factly. "I did it to protect you."

"You'll need to explain that one."

"Well, it's simple really. I didn't want you hurt. The more you dug around into Jack's death, the greater the danger became. Whoever killed him certainly wants the police to write it off as a suicide. But, if you found something that indicated murder, they couldn't do that. I figured it better for you to think it a suicide than for you to end up a victim. I didn't want your kids to end up orphans. So, I gave Jack a motive for suicide, a guilty conscience, you know how that works."

"But an affair ruins his reputation."

Sandra lowered her eyes. "I had to make a choice," she said. "A tough one. Help you stay alive or . . . "

For several moments, Connie let the silence linger. Then she said, "But what were you even doing here? What brought you to Jefferson City in the first place?"

"I came to get Jack."

"You'll have to explain that too."

Sandra studied the beige tablecloth for a moment. Connie could see her thinking, trying to decide what to say. She lifted her tea to her lips and waited. Sandra inhaled slowly, then faced her. "Jack's grandfather," she whispered. "He's dying."

Connie almost dropped her cup. Jack's grandfather! Still alive? According to Jack, his grandfather died the year he started college at MU!

"But he's dead!" she insisted. "Jack wouldn't lie about that! Jack wouldn't deliberately make up a story, hide the truth from me. It's not—"

Sandra held up her hand, interrupted her. "He would, and he did. Justin is alive and waiting for me about three hours from here. Waiting for me to bring you to him."

"But why?" moaned Connie. "Why would Jack lie . . . why?"

Sandra touched Connie's hand. "I think you know why," she said.

Connie tilted her head, and it dawned on her, as clear as a rock-bottomed riverbed. Jack would never lie unless . . . unless he did so to protect someone he loved. She ran the dilemma through her mind. As a believer, she tried to tell the truth in every situation. So did Jack. But what if the truth hurt someone? Maybe even brought physical danger? If a German soldier asked a farm woman if she had any Jews hiding in her barn, should she tell the truth and thereby condemn the Jews to death? Or should she lie, thereby giving them the chance to live? Which of the two represented the greatest good or the worst evil?

Shaking her head, Connie decided she couldn't settle that moral issue right now. Obviously, Jack had faced a similar question and had answered it on the side of protection. Working to control her emotions, Connie took a sip of tea, then spoke. "He did it because he had to do it."

Sandra nodded. "His grandfather has been on the run for years. Powerful people want him dead. For years at a time, he did just fine. Every time his enemies came too close, he simply moved away, established a fresh identity, settled down somewhere else. Jack lived with him in Miller for about ten of those years. I came the last three, our high school years. My mom died of cancer. My dad was already dead, a car accident two years earlier.

"At the time, Jack and I didn't know about Justin's enemies. Heck, we didn't even call him Justin then. He was Hal Wilson. But then, the summer after we graduated high school, Justin got wind his pursuers were closing in. This time he told me and Jack the story, wanted us to understand why he had to leave us. We needed to get on with our lives, he said. We couldn't go into hiding with him, it wasn't fair to us or to any family we might have someday.

"So, Justin made Jack and me promise to leave it alone, not try to find him."

"And you agreed?"

"What choice did we have? Though we didn't know everything, Justin told us people wanted to kill him, told us if his enemies connected us to him, they would come after us, too, make us reveal his whereabouts."

"So he disappeared to protect you."

"Sure. Left us enough money to begin college, faked his own death—drove an old truck into the Missouri River—and cut out from Miller."

"They never found a body?"

Sandra smiled. "None to find. Justin wasn't in that truck."

"But it fooled his enemies?"

"For a while."

Connie took a sip of tea, pondering Sandra's story. Something in it didn't add up. "But you and Jack," she said. "Why didn't you two stay in touch? Isn't he your only relative?"

Sandra dropped her eyes, and Connie noticed her grinding her teeth.

"We did keep in touch for a couple of years," she said. "But I drifted off. It was my fault, not Jack's. He tried to communicate with me, but he went to college and I moved to California. He wrote, but I never answered his letters and . . . well . . . we just lost track, that's all."

Something in her voice made Connie suspicious, and she pressed further. "But that makes no sense to me, you lived together with your granddad for three years, then you disappear and won't keep in touch with your only relative? How—?"

"That's not for discussion right now!" Sandra said, her jaw clenching and unclenching. "That's a whole different matter. Right now, I'm trying to tell you what happened to Jack, not what happened to me!"

Connie decided to let the subject drop. Maybe later, when she knew Sandra better and circumstances had improved, she could find out what had happened between her and Jack. But for now, other matters demanded her attention. Like the most obvious question of all.

"Why is your grandfather on the run?" she asked.

"That's not for me to tell. It's his story."

"You say he wants me to come to him to hear it?"

"Exactly. He believes his story ties in with what happened to Jack."

Connie looked toward the bedrooms where Daniel and Katie lay sleeping. Since Jack's death, she had neglected them in some ways, not so much in time as in focus. Even when she gave them her time, she knew her attention had drifted far too often. She had done the best she knew how, but she worried her best hadn't been good enough. Now, a woman she had never seen before tonight sat in her kitchen asking her to leave them one more time.

She faced Sandra. "Do you know who killed Jack?" she asked.

Sandra placed her tea on the table. "No, I don't. I have some suspicions, but I'm not sure."

"Who do you suspect?"

Sandra shook her head. "I'm not the one to tell you."

Connie's eyes narrowed. "Jack's grandfather is?"

Sandra took a deep breath. "It's not that he knows for sure either. But . . . he knows some people who had good motive. That's what he wants to tell you, what he knows. If it takes you to Jack's murderer, then so be it. If not, well, he's done all he can. That's really what he wants to do, get it clean before he . . . before he dies."

Connie thought of the old man's picture she found under Reed Morrison's bed. Obviously, it was Justin Longley. The man had a strong face, a face lined with years of struggle. Now that she knew his identity, she could see some resemblance between him and Jack. The square jawline, the eyes tucked under a thick forehead.

All these years, Jack's grandfather lived, but grandson and grandfather could not see each other. Daniel and Katie couldn't know their great-grandfather. Her heart ached for what her family had missed. Her family didn't see each other either, but that estrangement came from choices made, the choice of a father to desert a wife and daughter, and the choice of a mother to lose herself and her daughter in a bottle. At least Jack's family had a reason for their separation.

Connie sipped her tea. "Jack paid a man named Reed Morrison $10,000," she said, moving back to matters at hand.

Sandra nodded. "Yes, he did. I came and told Jack that Justin was dying. I wanted to give him one last chance to see his grand-dad. Jack, though, wouldn't hear of letting it go at that. He wanted to do more. He wanted Justin to get more extensive med-ical treatment, go to a hospital. Justin refused, not just because he didn't have the money, but because he wanted to sit on his porch as long as he could and watch the sun go down over the desert. But Jack insisted. When I wouldn't deliver the money, he hired Morrison to find Justin, funnel the money to him."

"But didn't Jack know where Justin was?"

Sandra laughed slightly. "Nope, Justin wouldn't let me tell him. When Jack came to see Justin, we met him in Las Vegas."

"Jack came to Nevada?"

"Sure, for three days the second week of January."

Connie exhaled. "I remember the trip. Jack seemed pretty vague about it. I didn't pay much attention. Trusted him, you know what I mean?"

"No reason not to trust him. He was the best man I ever knew, next to Justin, of course."

"How did Morrison find Justin?"

"He didn't. We found him. Figured we better confront him quietly rather than have him running all over the place stirring up dust. Dust shows people where you are, sometimes people you prefer to avoid. We took the money from him, then left."

"How did you know he was looking?"

"Oh, Justin knew. He will tell you how. A private investi-gator snooping around for a guy in Vegas creates some notice."

"Morrison had pictures."

Sandra shrugged. "Jack gave them to him. Took them when he came out in January."

"He took a picture of you."

"I know. He said he wanted to show his kids someday."

Connie slowly shook her head. Jack didn't lie about his trip. Just didn't say much. Didn't say much, then went to Nevada to take money he didn't have to help a grandfather he hadn't seen in years.

"Morrison is dead," said Connie, her eyes on her tea but not really seeing it.

Sandra groaned. "Sorry to hear that," she said. "Seemed like a nice enough man. Guess he didn't tell them what they wanted to hear."

"Or he did tell them, and they killed him anyway."

"He didn't have anything to tell," Sandra said. "He didn't know where we were."

"So Morrison died for nothing."

"That's about the size of it."

Connie sipped her tea. Two good men dead. For the first time in several days, her grief welled up inside her chest again and a rush of tears ran to her eyes. Men like her husband came along far too rarely. For a moment she held back the tears, but then she gave up and let them pour out. She felt so tired. The tears ran over her chin and dripped toward her teacup.

Sandra took Connie's hands in hers. Connie continued to weep. She had worked so hard trying to hold it all together, to do her best to clear Jack's name. He deserved that. With so few like him, it seemed wrong to leave people with the impression he took his own life. But in her effort to clear Jack's name, she had placed herself in danger, maybe her kids too. And it had led to this. Justin Longley might know enough to steer her in the right direction. But to find out, she had put herself in harm's way once again. For Jack, she had no other choice.

Her tears still running down her chin, she smiled at Sandra. For Jack, she concluded. For Jack she would take the step.

"I'll come with you," she said, her voice choked but determined. "For Jack's . . . sake, I'll give it . . . give it one more shot."

Sandra smiled at her. "Good," she said. "We'll go in the morning. He's not far from here. If all goes well, you can get home for supper."

Connie sniffled and held tighter to Sandra. Into the hours of the night, the two women sat together at the kitchen table and talked, their fingers intertwined and their hearts softened by their common love for a good man.

*****

Almost two hundred yards up the street, Brit pressed his earphones tighter to his head and leaned forward in the driver's seat of his new van. The conversation between Sandra Richards and Connie Brandon at the dining table greatly disturbed him. Red and Desert Two had just joined forces. He didn't like that at all. Even worse, he didn't know if Lennie had the stomach to do anything about it.

Brit drummed his fingers on the dashboard, trying to decide what to do. If he acted and succeeded without advising Lennie, he would get a healthy bonus and a pat on the back. If he acted and failed without advising Lennie, he might end up in concrete boots swimming with the fishes. That idea didn't please him too much. He stopped his drumming and flipped open his phone.

"Yo, Lennie. Brit. Trouble in River City."

"Fill me in."

"Red and Desert Two just had a cup of tea."

"Desert Two is in River City?"

"Arrived just a bit ago. Looks like a family reunion."

Lennie paused. Brit waited, his fingers thumping the steering wheel.

Lennie said, "They got further plans after tonight?"

"Looks like it. Going to see Granddad."

"Sorry we missed Justin last night."

"Looks like we'll get another chance."

"Follow them."

"That's my plan."

"Keep me informed. Don't act without clearance."

Brit stopped drumming but said nothing.

"Brit, you hear me? Don't act without clearance."

"I heard." He shut his phone and started thumping again. If he waited for Lennie, he might miss his opportunity. He wouldn't let that happen. No way. If the opportunity came, he planned to grab it.

CHAPTER
25

A t just past eight-thirty the next morning, Connie and Sandra climbed into Sandra's pickup truck and backed out of the driveway. Connie had made all the necessary arrangements—Mrs. Everhart would arrive about two to meet Katie. The mother of one of Daniel's teammates would pick him up and bring him home after baseball practice. If all went well, she should get home before dark.

Before she left, Connie contemplated calling Tess, then remembered she and Tick had taken their new boat to the lake for a couple of days. She had promised to call if danger arose. Well, the worst of the danger had surely passed. With Sandra beside her, she felt more secure than at any time since the funeral.

Satisfied with matters at home, she settled into the pickup and tried to relax. She and Sandra had stayed up late, and she needed to rest if she could. Headed west out of Jefferson City, however, she found rest almost impossible. Far too many ideas bounced around in her head and far too many feelings churned through her stomach. Sandra had told her so much about Jack's high school days.

Other students liked Jack immensely, in spite of his gentle demeanor. They listened when he spoke and followed when he led. A .280 hitter on the baseball team—not great but always quick to get a walk, steal a base, lay down a sacrifice bunt. He didn't date a lot, but the girls he did date inevitably thought him wonderful and kind and smart. As comfortable with Sandra as a friend at a slumber party, Connie enjoyed the evening more than anything since the funeral. Stoked by the memories of Jack, she had trouble sleeping when they finally rolled into bed, Sandra on the sofa in the den.

Now, talked out from the previous night, Connie and Sandra rolled down Highway 50 in virtual silence. Enjoying the quiet, Connie thanked God for the blessing of meeting someone from Jack's past. Without realizing it, she had wanted to hear all of this history so badly. In the weeks since his death, she had discovered just how little she knew of his past, and that lack of knowledge had haunted her, made her feel incomplete.

Sandra's stories filled in some of that blank space. Hearing them, she felt like she had a bonus added to her years with Jack, extra cash to spend for her own pleasure. In days to come, she planned to have Sandra sit down with the children and tell them all about their daddy's teenage days. Daniel and Katie would love the stories. Yes, it would bring their grief to the surface again. But, in the long run it would make so much difference. Sandra's tales added so much color and detail to Jack's life, and the kids would value them forever.

As the first hour became the second and the second moved toward the third, Sandra pulled the truck off the highway and onto more narrow Missouri roads. Conversation remained at a minimum. Concentrating on her own thoughts, Connie paid little attention to their location. To her, only one thing mattered. In a short while she would meet Jack's grandfather.

What a life the man had lived! A fugitive for years. But bright enough to avoid those who wanted him dead. Compassionate too—loving enough to separate himself from his family in order to protect them. Without ever meeting him, Connie liked him. How could she not? He raised Jack. Jack loved Justin. How could she not love him too?

She wondered about Justin's health. Sandra said he had cancer. The last doctor he saw refused to name a time frame, but Sandra and Justin knew he couldn't last much longer. Connie hoped he lived long enough for her to hear his story. After that, if God allowed it, she wanted him to meet Daniel and Katie. What a joy for that to happen!

Sandra pulled off the pavement and onto a gravel pathway. The truck bounced through a series of small gullies in the washed-out road. Tree limbs covered with fresh green clicked the sides of the truck as they passed.

"Not far now," said Sandra.

Connie raised up straighter. Sandra turned the truck once more, this time onto a dirt road. Connie rubbed her eyes. "Where are we?"

Sandra smiled. "It's a little piece of land Justin bought years ago. Not far from Miller. We used to come here to fish."

The road snaked up a long incline, then twisted to the right into a thick blanket of trees and shrubs. At the top of the incline, the path broke into a clearing. Connie saw a silver camper trailer nestled under the trees in the center of the small glade. To the right of the trailer stood an unpainted shed.

"He's here?"

"Yes, in the trailer home."

Connie told herself to stay calm. Sandra backed the truck up to the trailer. Then she faced Connie. Connie smoothed down the front of her jeans. She felt so strange, like she was on a date and about to meet Jack's parents for the first time.

"It's okay," said Sandra. "This is the last step."

Connie nodded. "I know," she said. "It's just, well . . . you know . . . I didn't know Jack had any living relatives. It's such a shock. I feel like I need to make a good impression or something."

Sandra patted her hand. "Believe me, Justin is more nervous than you are. He's wanted to meet you for years, wanted to see you and the kids, to hold his great-grandbabies in his arms."

"He knows about the kids?"

"Sure, he's even seen them once or twice."

"But how—?"

"He's a pro, remember. Moves like a shadow. In, then gone. You see him, then you don't. That's what kept him alive all these years."

Connie started to ask more about the mysterious man. But she knew Sandra wouldn't answer. Justin would. He waited less than twenty yards away, a sick man wanting to tell his story before he died.

She nodded to Sandra. "I'm ready," she said. "Let's go."

"I need to do one thing," said Sandra. "Hook the trailer to the truck. Justin taught me to stay prepared."

Without another word, Sandra climbed out and Connie followed. Waiting for her to do the job, Connie tried to relax. She inhaled slowly, listening to the chirping of a score of birds, their twills and peeps and twerps filling the shade-covered glen. Mesmerized by the sound, she felt a sense of peace, almost as if God had given her these few minutes to calm her soul. Still listening to the birds, she watched as Sandra finished with the hitch, then led her up the one wooden step to the trailer home and into the only room.

Connie's eyes widened. There, lying on a bed in the corner, rested Jack's grandfather, a thick wooden cane in his left hand and a pistol the length of a small hair dryer in his right.

"Justin!" snapped Sandra. "It's me, put down that gun!"

Justin squinted, then lowered the weapon. Sandra rushed to him and grabbed it from his hand. "It's okay now, Justin," she soothed. "I'm here. And look who I've brought with me."

She turned to Connie and motioned her closer. Though momentarily stunned by the weapon, Connie quickly gathered herself and stepped to Sandra and Justin. Sandra kissed Justin on the cheek. Obviously still confused, he kept his cane in his hand, his knuckles white from gripping it. Connie, her face red with nerves, waited for more instructions.

Sandra gave them. "Move closer," she said. "He doesn't see so well right now."

Connie eased past Sandra and stood directly over Justin beside the small bed. Though certainly sick, he had not allowed himself to become sloppy. Wispy gray whiskers sprouted on his chin, but he had tucked his blue shirt into his khaki slacks. His eyes were a bit glassy and the skin under his chin sagged on his neck. But he had his hair combed. Even the oxygen tubes that ran into each nostril seemed straight and in place.

Staring into his eyes, a wave of joy rushed over Connie. This man raised Jack! Forgetting she didn't know him, she touched his hand, the one with the cane, and patted. His fingers relaxed, and the cane slid from his grasp. Taking the cane, Connie said, "Mr. Longley, I'm Connie, Jack's wife."

For several seconds, he didn't say anything. Then, his lips turned upward as if considering something pleasant.

"My cane," he said, his voice stronger than Connie expected.

Unsure what to do, Connie glanced at Sandra. Sandra nodded, and Connie placed the cane back in his hand. Taking the cane, he lifted his hand slowly, and Connie wondered for a second if he planned to use it against her. But then he pushed the cane to the floor and pressed his weight against it. Connie reached to help him, but he grunted and jerked his head from side to side. She took the cue and stepped back half a pace. Using the cane for leverage, he raised himself up and squared his shoulders. Sandra stepped past Connie and fluffed his pillows behind his back. Situated, Justin smoothed out the front of his shirt and lifted his eyes to Connie.

"So," he said, his voice weak but clear. "You came to see me."

Connie smiled at his dignity. So much like Jack. "It's my pleasure," she said. "I loved the boy you raised."

Justin smiled too, his teeth still white in spite of his age. "He was . . . a good . . . boy. I've missed him."

Connie's eyes glistened. "I miss him too."

Justin grunted, then tapped his cane on the side of the bed. "Why don't you sit . . . down? I've got a story to tell, and I don't know how long I'll last. So . . . you better . . . sit down and hear it."

Connie glanced at Sandra. Sandra nodded, then said to Justin, "I'll get you some water. I expect you'll need it." She turned and moved away.

Justin tapped the side of the bed again. "Sit," he said.

Connie obeyed this time, squeezing onto the narrow slice of bed unused by Justin. Sandra came back and handed him the water. He sipped it for several long seconds, then handed Sandra the glass. She placed it on a small table beside his head.

"I don't know if I can . . . can tell it all at once," he said. "I'm a mite weak these days."

"You sound strong enough to me," said Sandra, smiling at him.

"I saved up the last twenty . . . twenty-four hours," he said. "Knew . . . knew you'd bring Connie." He wheezed slightly.

Connie looked at Sandra, worry in her eyes.

"He's okay," Sandra said. "Just loses his air at times. Usually, he's fine, can talk for good stretches without much trouble. He'll know when he needs to stop."

Connie faced Justin again. He placed his cane on the floor and pushed up a bit more. "Now," he said. "Where to begin?"

Connie repositioned herself. In spite of the tragedy of the last three weeks, she felt like a child on Christmas Eve. Finally, the time had come to learn what happened to Jack. Justin cleared his throat and adjusted the oxygen tubes running into his nose.

"Now . . ." he began. "Let's get one thing straight. I don't for certain know who killed Jack. But I . . . I do have a theory. My theory comes from some things that came to pass a long time ago, back when you and Jack were two little sprites. As I tell you this, you're going to think it's all crazy, that it has no connection . . . to what you've just suffered. But stay patient with me for a few . . . few minutes. Listen to what I say. Then make up your mind." He stopped for her to respond if she wanted. She nodded quickly, and he continued.

"Of course . . . you never knew Jack's daddy. But I got to tell you something about him. He was my son-in-law and he was a good man, but . . . well . . . he had himself a weakness. Not the bottle, nor any other drug. And he didn't chase other women either. So far as I know, he stayed faithful to Jack's mama, God rest her soul. But Bill couldn't say no to the lure of the gamble—cards, blackjack, roulette, the slots—you name it, that boy couldn't walk by it without giving it a try.

"I don't know when the bug bit him—neither he nor Barbara ever explained any of that to me. But out in Nevada where he grew up, the bug bites a bunch of folks. So, as soon as he graduated from high school, he headed to Vegas. That city drew Bill like syrup draws an ant.

"He met my baby Barbara there. She worked at a hotel I owned. Bill stayed at my hotel from time to time. From the beginning, she knew he loved to gamble, but that didn't seem to matter much—you know how love can blind us.

"Anyway, she and Bill got married, and it looked for a while like he would stay home and do right. He took a job as a maintenance supervisor at a high school outside of Vegas. He always did well with his hands, mechanical and all. He and Barbara had Jack the second year of their marriage. But within a couple of years, the wheels fell off. Bill lost his job, never quite understood why, a problem with a union or something. After that, everything crumbled—from bad to worse.

"Instead of finding another job or coming to me for help, he took what money he had and tried to make a quick score at the blackjack table. He lost like usual. Trying to make up what he lost, he borrowed money from the wrong people—a couple of brothers who ran the sharking racket in and around Vegas. With the borrowed money, he kept on playing. Playing and losing. His debts piled up higher and higher.

"For several years, he stayed about one step ahead of the collectors. He'd win just enough or work just enough to pay down a bit of his debt. From time to time, I gave Barbara some money, too, but he never asked for it. He had his pride that way.

"But then he'd lose again, and the mound of debt would get a little deeper. Finally, the debt grew so big, the sharks couldn't let it go anymore. They had to collect or lose credibility with everyone else who owed them.

"They found Bill . . . and called in the loans. He couldn't pay."

Justin stopped and waved his hand at the glass of water by his head. Connie grabbed the water, handed it to him, then waited as he took a big drink. Handing her the glass back, he licked his lips, adjusted his oxygen tubes, then pressed on with the story.

"Most times, in situations like this, the guy in debt ends up with a two-paragraph obituary in the Las Vegas newspaper. But not this time. The sharks offered Bill a deal he couldn't refuse. They offered him a way to pay back all his debts in one fell swoop."

He swallowed, and Connie could see the talking had taken a toll. His breath began to come in shorter gasps, and his face dropped a notch in color.

"Are you okay?" she asked. "If you need to rest—"

He patted her hand. She noted the purple veins in his wrist.

"I'm all right," he said, a tiny smile on his face. "I know I look like death warmed over, but like . . . like they say, appearances can deceive. So . . . as I was saying . . . the sharks offered Bill a deal . . . a business transaction. Do one job for them and they . . . they would tear up all his notes . . . clean up his debts in one fell swoop."

Justin closed his eyes and clenched his fists. Connie noted the veins on his hands seemed thicker, and she sensed a tension seeping into the room. His eyes still closed and his voice softer, but no less intense, Justin pushed on.

"They told him to kill a man. As simple as that. Kill or be killed. He got to choose. Pay them off with the hit and go back to his wife and baby boy or never see the light of day again."

Justin opened his eyes and stared at Connie as if to test her reaction.

She touched his hand. "What did he do?"

"He decided to take the offer. Didn't see any way around it. He . . . he agreed to the deal. They gave him the name of a hotel in Vegas, told him the target would be in room 312 on August 22. They handed him a key to the room and a gun with a silencer on it."

Justin nodded for the water again. Connie handed it to him, her neck splotching with red, her teeth digging into her upper lip. Justin sipped the water as if he had all the time in the world. Connie wanted to pour it down his throat to make it go faster but resisted the temptation. Finally, Justin finished the water and passed the glass to Connie. She placed it on the table and faced him again. He continued the story.

"August 22 came, time to do the deed. In the middle of the night, Bill drove to the hotel, took the elevator to the third floor, slipped the key in the lock, and eased into the room. The lights from outside the windows lit it. With the gun shaking in his hand, Bill stepped to the bed. The man in the bed raised up and stared Bill right in the eyes. Bill pressed his finger on the trigger. The man never said a word. Bill suddenly started to cry. He couldn't do it. No matter the danger he would face later, he couldn't go that far. He was a gambler, but he wasn't a murderer. He threw down his gun and ran from the room, never turned back for even a second. . . . "

A glow of satisfaction showed on Justin's face, and Connie read the pride in his eyes. His son-in-law had weaknesses, but he hadn't given in to the worst weakness of all.

"What happened to him?"

"He ran . . . left Vegas with Barbara and Jack. I don't know to this day where he found the money, but he stayed out of sight for almost two years. Lived all over the place, the West, the Midwest. But, like always, they eventually found him . . . found him in southern Illinois and burned . . . burned down his house, him and Barbara and Jack, barely ten years old, asleep inside. You know that much. Jack escaped, but Barbara, my . . . my baby . . . " His voice broke, and tears rolled to the corners of his eyes and slid down his face onto his blue shirt.

Connie twisted and faced Sandra. She stood and brought a wet towel from the sink and brushed it over Justin's face.

"You need to rest a while?" she asked. "Just lay there a bit?"

Justin pushed away the towel. "Let . . . let me . . . finish," he said, finding his voice again. "I need to get . . . this done."

"I know you've been holding this a long time," Sandra agreed. "Just don't make yourself any sicker."

"That's not possible," he said, his face lighting up. "You can't . . . can't kill roadkill but once."

Sandra grinned briefly, then sat back down.

Justin faced Connie again. "Give me your hand, child," he said. "Let's get it said."

Connie offered her hand, and he gripped it in both of his. She felt his pulse thumping. He cleared his throat.

"The police called the fire an accident, but I know better. They killed Bill and Barbara, pure and simple. He owed them big money from his gambling, and the code said they could show no mercy. Thank the good Lord Jack got out. He had this dog, see, a mutt no bigger than a healthy rat. That dog slept in his room, started barking at the smoke and woke him. Jack stumbled outside, then passed out. When he woke up, the flames had gutted the house, his mama and daddy in it."

Justin stopped and adjusted the oxygen tubes in his nose.

"I know now why Jack hated gambling so much," Connie said. "It killed his father."

"It certainly led to his death," agreed Justin.

"I'm puzzled by one thing," Connie said.

"I expect you . . . you are," he said. "I bet I know what it is. You want to know how I know all this, am I right?"

Connie nodded.

Justin adjusted his oxygen once more, then cleared his throat. "It's simple, really. I know the story because I'm the man Bill almost murdered."

Connie gulped. What kind of madness was this? A son-in-law sent to kill his wife's father? But why? Justin quickly answered her question.

"The sharks Bill owed were Mob guys, that's no shock. They needed someone to do a dirty piece of work—kill a guy protected by the FBI. I don't think we called it witness protection back then, but that's what it was. I was the guy, had been in the system for almost eleven years. Entered it after a six-year stint as an undercover agent with the Bureau.

"In my last assignment I turned up a murder-for-hire scheme by the wise guys in Atlanta. We got our man, but not before he flushed out my cover. The Bureau had to protect me, so they put me in the witness protection. I decided to set up my new life in Las Vegas. Pretty cute, huh? Go where they least expect you. It worked for a long time. I grew a beard, shaved my head, blended into the city as a transplanted southern boy. But then somebody identified me, a wise guy in town from Atlanta for a recreational weekend. He sent word up the line. They came after me through the sharks who had their hooks into Bill. Figured if the Feds caught him, they hadn't lost anything."

"Did he know it was you from the beginning?"

Justin sighed. "I don't know. Never got to ask him, but I don't think so. When he saw me that night in the hotel, the look on his face told me he didn't know."

"You never saw him again?"

Justin shook his head. His eyes seemed weaker to Connie, less focused. He licked his lips, then spoke again. His voice floated from his throat, whispery words. He stared into space as he talked.

"Bill . . . took Jack and Barbara and disappeared. They wrote me from time to time, I had moved too. Here to Miller, took another name, opened up a grocery store. Word about the fire came to me a few days later. Folks from Social Services in Carbondale, Illinois, called me, said they found my address on a scrap of envelope in the trunk of Bill's car. Jack told them he had a granddaddy in Missouri, and he wanted to live with him."

"That's when you got Jack."

"Two days later. A couple of FBI buddies picked Jack up and brought him down. We settled down in Miller."

"Jack lived with you until he graduated."

"Exactly. I raised my grandboy, giving . . . giving him . . . the best upbringing I knew . . . knew how . . . " His eyes fluttered, and his voice trailed away.

Noting Justin's weakness, Connie turned to Sandra. "You came along when?"

"Oh, about five years later. When my mom died of cancer, I had nowhere else to go. Before she died, Mom told me about her brother. Justin had stayed in touch with her over the years, a phone call here, a letter there. When he found out she was sick, he told her to send me to him. The day of her funeral, he called me. Two days afterward he drove to Little Rock, picked me up, brought me to Missouri."

Her head spinning, Connie closed her eyes. Okay, she knew how Jack's parents died. She knew how Sandra came to live with Jack. She knew why Justin disappeared the year Jack graduated high school. But she didn't know how any of this related to Jack's death.

Opening her eyes, she started to ask Justin the rest of her questions. To her chagrin, she saw he wouldn't answer any more questions for a while. His head tilted to the side and his mouth gaped slightly open. He had dozed off. In that pose, he appeared ancient and sickly to Connie, and she wondered if he would finish his story before he died.

CHAPTER
26

He'll sleep a couple of hours," said Sandra. "Does this everyday, as regular as clockwork. You hungry?"

Connie glanced at her watch. Almost three o'clock.

"Not really," she said. "But I guess I need to eat something."

Sandra walked to a small refrigerator in the opposite corner of the tiny room. "I'll make a sandwich," she said, pulling out a tomato. "Turkey okay with you?"

"Sure, that's fine."

"Good, that's all I have."

The two women laughed, and Connie sighed in relief. As bad as things were, she at least now knew a member of Jack's family. Even in the worst of times, God could do a good thing.

"You and Jack were close?" she asked Sandra.

"Like brother and sister."

Connie remembered Sandra's refusal to explain the breach in their relationship. She fought the urge to probe deeper and changed gears to another confusing issue.

"Did Justin tell Jack about his father after high school?"

Sandra sliced the tomato, her long fingers nimble with the knife. "Yeah, as I told you, the Mob found him again. They may go slow, but they do make progress. The Bureau had picked up the word, and they tipped him off. Set him up with a new name again, a new place to live. But he had to leave us behind that time. Before he did, he told us about his work with the Bureau, why he was under witness protection, why he had to leave. We protested at first, but it didn't take long to accept it. His way made sense. Though we hated it, we had to let him go."

She dropped a slice of turkey onto Connie's bread. "Mustard is in the refrigerator," she said. "Or mayonnaise, whichever you prefer. You want some chips?"

Nodding, Connie pulled out the mustard. A couple of minutes later, they placed their sandwiches on paper plates, carried them to a small table by the refrigerator and sat down. Connie nibbled on her sandwich.

"How did you get back with your grandfather?" she asked.

Sandra munched on a chip. "He called me about a year ago," she said, her shoulders slumping. "I hadn't heard from him since the day he left. He said he had cancer, didn't have long to live."

Connie stopped chewing, trying to recall last spring. "Did he call Jack too?" she asked.

Sandra shook her head.

"Why you and not Jack?"

"Easy, I had never married, had no family to hold me back. I could go to him without worrying about anyone else."

"But you told Luke Tyler your name was Lunsford. That's not a married name?"

Sandra smiled. "No, it's not. I thought a false name might help if he started searching for me. And, I didn't know if you would put two and two together if I told him my name was Richards."

"I doubt if I would have been that smart. Why didn't you marry?"

A scowl darted across Sandra's face. Sandra swallowed a bite of sandwich and gritted her teeth. "That's personal," she said. "And it's not important."

Connie wanted to press but knew from the set of Sandra's jaw that she couldn't. She let it pass and returned to the subject at hand. "So Justin called you. Told you he was sick. Wasn't he still worried about putting you in danger?"

"Sure, but he said it wouldn't matter soon. If we could stay out of sight for just a few more months, the chase would end. I could go back to my normal life, and no one would know the difference. In the meantime, he needed my help."

"His sickness?"

Sandra smiled. "Oh, no, nothing like that. Justin never worries about that. He's a man of Christian faith, came to that commitment right after he entered the protection program. Death doesn't worry him."

Before thinking, Connie blurted, "What about your faith?"

Sandra shrugged but didn't seem to take offense. "Can't say I have any. Not hostile to it, just haven't seen much proof of the kind of God Justin trusts. I've seen too much pain to believe in all that 'God is love' stuff."

Connie started to probe, but Sandra shook her head as if in warning and she held back. Later, she promised herself, she would ask Sandra about the pain she had seen.

"If not his illness, then why did Justin contact you?"

Sandra placed her sandwich on her plate and wiped her mouth with a paper towel. "Easy. He came across some information he had wanted for years."

The half-eaten sandwich in Connie's hand began to shake. She kept her eyes on Sandra, her heart notching up its pace. For a couple of beats, she waited on Sandra to continue. When she didn't, Connie pressed her.

"What kind of information?"

"Information to convict the men who killed Bill and Barbara."

"Then why didn't he call Jack?"

"Easy again," said Sandra. "Remember the kind of man Justin is. He didn't want to put anybody in danger until he knew for certain he was right. He knew if he told Jack his suspicions, Jack would try to do something about it, he would . . . you know, try to do the right thing, no matter what. He didn't want Jack acting until he had all the facts. To make a mistake meant almost certain death.

"So, thinking he might die before he verified what he suspected, Justin called me, told me what he knew. He didn't want to die with the information, but he didn't have the strength anymore to do what needed doing. He needed my hands to do his business. That's what I've been doing for almost a year, trying to find out whether Justin is right."

Connie's voice fell to a whisper. "What have you decided? Do you know who killed Jack's parents?"

Sandra shook her head. "You'll need to ask Justin that question," she said. "He wants to tell you."

Connie glanced at her watch. "When will he wake up?"

"Oh, another hour. As regular as clockwork."

"You came to Jefferson City."

"Yes, even though Justin told me to stay away. I didn't want him to die without Jack seeing him. Knew Jack wouldn't forgive me if I did."

"That's when Jack went to Vegas."

"Exactly, then borrowed the money to give to Morrison."

"He borrowed twenty-five thousand."

"Guess he planned to have enough for anything."

Connie lifted a chip from the bag and stuffed it into her mouth. She didn't know how to ask the question, but she needed to do it. "What did Justin do with the money from Jack?"

Sandra stood, walked to a drawer by the refrigerator, opened it, and pulled out a cigar box. She handed the box to Connie. "It's right here. All but about $2,000. Morrison kept that for fees and expenses."

Connie flipped open the box and stared at the money. Sandra sat back down. For several long seconds, the two women remained quiet. The air hung heavy in the small trailer, and the heat of the sun baked down on top. The long night and emotional day caught up with Connie, and she suddenly felt claustrophobic. Silence reigned in the hot trailer and nothing sounded from outside either. It struck Connie that something had changed. The chirping of the birds had ceased.

A sense of unease seeped through her, and her stomach rumbled. She felt faint, and she focused on Sandra to stay alert. Sandra jerked up, her long hands pushing off the table and her blue eyes darting to the one window in the trailer.

"Somebody is out there!" she yelled, darting toward Justin. "Get to the truck! I'll take care of Justin!"

Connie obeyed instantly, her mind shutting down on everything but obeying Sandra. Flipping open the door, she jumped to the ground and sprinted to the pickup five steps away. She climbed inside and started the engine.

Poised at the wheel, she scanned the clearing, trying to see what had disturbed Sandra. Nothing moved. That spooked her. What happened to the birds?

She stayed still, her body tense, coiled. The sound of a shot popped off to her left, and she instinctively ducked. The bullet zinged off the truck's left fender, not more than four feet from her face. A second shot fired, this one at the trailer, and Connie hit the gas. The truck plunged forward through the thick grass and onto the dirt road. The trailer bounced behind her, its square body crunching the undergrowth around the narrow pathway. Her hands glued to the wheel, Connie jammed the truck ahead, not bothering to look for the shooter. Biting her lip, she concentrated on one goal—reaching the highway. She would run over anything that separated her from Daniel and Katie.

Directly ahead, she spotted a brown and tan all-terrain Humvee. Beside the vehicle stood the man with the ponytail from the Mercedes at Morrison's house. Crouched in a firing position, he pointed a rifle straight at her. Connie pushed the gas pedal harder and screamed.

The rifle fired, and the truck windshield shattered, glass spewing back into Connie's face. She screamed again and slammed back against the seat, but her hands never left the wheel. The man appeared larger in her vision, no more than ten feet away, now five, now—

His eyes widened, and Connie saw fear in them. Her truck reached out for the man, the grill almost smashing him. The man dropped his rifle and threw himself into the bushes on the left of the dirt path.

Connie never slowed. She kept her foot jammed to the floorboard. Her right fender smashed into the back of the Humvee and spun it out of the way. The crash jarred Connie's bones, but she didn't stop. Her face red with adrenaline, she let out a whoop as she spun past the crash, the truck lurching over the bumps and gullies. For a second, she wondered about Sandra and Justin, but knew she couldn't slow down if she wanted them to survive.

Up ahead, the road snaked to the right and onto the blacktop of the highway. Heavy on the brakes, Connie swerved out of the woods and onto the road. Keeping her eyes peeled in the rearview mirror for the Humvee, Connie pressed on, desperate to put some distance between herself and the man who wanted her dead.

*****

Brit rolled over in the thick bushes and sat up. Brushing himself off, he stood and mentally checked himself out. Nothing hurt that he could tell. He walked out of the bushes and back into the clearing where his transportation sat. For a couple of minutes, he did a survey of the damage. A crunched back left fender, but not enough to jam the tire. The front grill pushed into a tree, but no liquids dribbling to the ground.

Finished with the inspection, he hopped into the seat and tried the engine. It started, and he exhaled. With the engine running, he jumped back down and picked up his weapon, a semi-automatic Remington he had only recently bought but not yet mastered. The rifle cradled to his chest, he climbed back into the Humvee and wheeled it out of the clearing.

He began to drum on the steering wheel. "Lennie won't like this," he mumbled. "But what Lennie don't know won't hurt him."

Determined to make sure Lennie never found out, Brit left the woods, turned onto the highway, and headed toward Jefferson City. Though not sure Red and Desert Two were going that way, he knew eventually they had to return. Red wouldn't stay away from her precious children too long.

Smoothing down his ponytail, Brit licked his lips. Maybe he had approached this the wrong way. Maybe he shouldn't chase the woman. Maybe he should make the woman come to him.

*****

A half hour after crashing past the Humvee, Connie pulled off the road and parked outside a truck stop. Sandra jumped out of the trailer and ran toward her. Hopping out, Connie opened her arms, and the two women embraced each other like two teammates who had just won a Super Bowl. Her adrenaline finally leveling off, Connie began to tremble. This had gotten far too dangerous. The incident last night scared her, but she hadn't known for sure that the driver specifically tried to hit her. Now she had no doubts. The man in the ponytail wanted her and Sandra and Justin dead.

Stepping back, she willed herself to stop shaking. Her eyes searched the parking lot but found nothing suspicious. She motioned to the trailer home. "Is Justin okay?"

Sandra exhaled. "Yeah, thank goodness. Justin's fine, just mad that you bounced him out of his nap. You all right?"

Connie nodded. "I just can't believe I'm mixed up in something this bizarre! I'm just a plain, small-town woman trying to raise a family . . . trying to deal with the death of her husband!"

"It's a strange world sometimes."

Connie scanned the parking lot again, her nerves on edge, thinking someone might take a shot at her at any moment.

"Let's get out of the open," she said, nodding toward the small restaurant attached to the truck stop. "No reason to give someone an easy target. You think Justin will be okay if we get a cup of coffee?"

Sandra surveyed the parking lot too. "We'll sit by a window near the door," she said. "If the guy shows up again, we'll see him before he can do anything."

Satisfied, Connie walked to the restaurant, Sandra beside her. Within a couple of minutes they had taken a booth by the front window and ordered two cups of hot coffee. Blowing on the coffee, Connie moved to the subject that had occupied her thoughts since she bounced out of the woods and onto the highway.

"I got one big question," she said. "What next?"

Sandra leaned back against the booth. "I think that's up to you," she said. "Justin can tell you the rest of the story, or you can drive away right now and leave it all with us. Justin will die with what he knows. No reason for the Mob to come after you if you don't know anymore than you do now. It's your call."

Connie blew her coffee, then said, "You know it's not that simple. That guy in the clearing—I've seen him twice now. Once outside of Morrison's and again today. And, now that I think back, yesterday I about got run over by a car. I thought it was an accident. Now, I'm not so sure. If I didn't know better, I'd say he was upset with me."

Sandra smiled, but only for an instant. "Then we have to deal with him," she said. "No way around it." She sipped from her coffee, not bothering to blow it cool.

"But how? What do you do with a guy who's trying to kill you?"

Sandra placed her coffee cup on the table. "I guess Justin can answer that better than me," she said. "He's been dealing with that question for years."

Connie tried to drink her coffee, but it was still too hot. For several minutes, she didn't say anything else. She just couldn't think anymore. Everything sagged in on her, a weight heavy enough to crush an anvil. Right now, she simply wanted to get home, snuggle her children in her arms, and go to sleep. With that in mind, she blew on her coffee and pushed away the decision of what to do next. Just get home, she decided. Worry about the future after that. Right now, just get home.

CHAPTER
27

At just past nine o'clock, Connie parked Justin's truck and trailer on the street in front of her house and breathed a huge sigh of relief. No matter what happened now, she had others to help her deal with it. Tess and Tick, Reverend Wallace, the members of the church—all would support her through this crisis. She thought for a second of Luke Tyler, but then pushed the idea away. He would help if she asked, but she couldn't ask.

Sandra stepped out of the trailer, and Connie smiled. Sandra and Justin agreed they should all three deal with the man in the Humvee. He wanted them all, so they should stay together through whatever came.

Behind Sandra, Connie saw Justin edge to the door of the trailer. His cane in his right hand, he eased himself onto the wooden step Sandra set below the door and walked down. Though unsteady, he made it onto the driveway. Sandra grabbed him by the left elbow and ushered him toward the house.

"Hold on one second," said Connie as they reached the door. "Let me see if anyone is still up."

No one was. Rubbing her eyes, Mrs. Everhart met Connie as she walked into the den. "I guess I dozed off," she said. "Kids went to bed about thirty minutes ago. Both of them worn out."

"Great," said Connie. "They asleep?"

"I think so. They had a good day from what they told me. Daniel says he's supposed to pitch tomorrow. Wanted to get a good night's rest."

Connie patted Mrs. Everhart on the shoulder. "You're so good," she said. "The kindest woman who ever lived."

Mrs. Everhart shook her head, but Connie knew she liked the compliment. "I best get on home," said Mrs. Everhart. "My back is kicking up on me a bit."

Connie escorted her to the door. "I've got some company," she said as they stepped outside. "These are friends of mine. Sandra Richards and Justin Longley. This is Mrs. Everhart, the best baby-sitter who ever lived."

Mrs. Everhart appeared confused, but she didn't question anything. "Glad to meet you both," she said. "You from out of town?"

Sandra answered for them. "Yeah, from Miller."

Mrs. Everhart started to speak again but then dropped it. "Well, enjoy your visit in Jefferson City," she said. "It's a good town."

"I'm sure it is," said Sandra.

Mrs. Everhart headed to her car. Connie motioned Sandra and Justin to follow her into the house. Inside, she left them in the den to go check on the children. She found them both asleep. Though careful not to wake them, she kissed them both and headed back to the den.

Justin and Sandra had taken seats on the couch, Justin stretched out, his cane in his left hand, his legs dangling off the edge.

"You okay without your oxygen?" Connie asked him.

He cleared his throat. "I can go for a while without it when . . . when the weather isn't too hot. I'm fine for now."

"You need anything?" she asked, looking first at him, then to Sandra.

Both shook their heads.

"Just sit down here," said Sandra, indicating the rocking chair by the sofa. "You've got to be worn out."

Connie obeyed, easing into the rocker. She relaxed her shoulders and rolled her head around on her neck. Goodness, it felt wonderful to sit down in her own home. Though she had been gone for only the day, it seemed like weeks. So much had happened so fast. She raised herself and faced Justin and Sandra.

"Sorry the kids aren't up to meet you," she said. "They'll make up for it about six in the morning. This place will sound like an army moving after somebody yells 'charge.' Never heard two kids make so much noise."

"I know you're proud of them," said Justin.

"You got that right."

"I'll look forward to the morning."

Connie smiled and noticed again how Justin resembled a much older version of Jack and Daniel. No one could ever question the connection among these three males. She wondered about Jack's father. Did Jack look like Bill as well? What a shame she would never know. He was dead, and Jack had once told her that the fire that killed him destroyed all the family pictures. Her shoulders slumped.

"What am I going to do?" she asked.

No one answered for a moment. Justin picked up his cane and laid it across his lap. "Your choice," he said. "I'll tell you the rest of my story if you want to hear it. Or Sandra and I can meet your kids in the morning and then leave here like we came, quiet and easy. Whichever you want."

Connie nodded. She'd already thought this out. She had to protect Jack's name, and she had to know the rest of Justin's story. One way or the other, she had to know. Like Justin said, it might not lead her to the killer, but it would lead her to the truth. If his theory proved incorrect, at least she would know it. If it proved true, then justice could yet occur and Jack's influence could yet survive.

She began to rock. "Tell me," she said. "Tell me the rest of the story."

Justin wrapped his cane in both hands and cleared his throat. "Okay," he said. "Let's get this done." He coughed lightly, then began.

"With the help of the Bureau, I've stayed one step ahead of the wise guys all these years. It's not been the best life, but it's . . . I don't know . . . it's been okay. The worst of it has been the separation between me and Sandra and Jack. That's been hard, awful hard. At times I've felt like . . . like giving it up, throwing in the towel. But one thing always kept my oil pumping. I wanted to know who set my Barbara's house on fire, who murdered my family." He paused and touched his cane to the side of his face, and Connie watched him fighting his emotions. He coughed again, and Connie noted the rattle in his throat. He bent forward, grimaced, then continued.

"The years rolled on by and I did okay. Bought the place in Black Canyon. Not much, but the big sky and a few buddies I made after a while made it home. Then the cancer got a toehold in me. I started to think I'd pass on without ever finding out anything. But I got a break. One of the brothers surfaced, one of the two sharks who tried to hire Bill to kill me. His picture showed up in a Vegas newspaper on page three, just as pretty as you please—"

"You saw one of the men who wanted to kill you?" Connie couldn't believe it.

Justin laughed, then started to cough again. His coughing deepened and his body almost convulsed. Connie jumped up from the rocker and ran to the kitchen. A minute later, she rushed back into the den and handed Justin a glass of water. Taking it, he swallowed half the glass before he regained control of the coughing.

With Sandra rubbing his back, he straightened up and touched his cane to the floor. Her eyes wide, Connie eased back into the rocker.

"You need your oxygen?" she asked.

He waved his cane at her. "No . . . it's not that. Just got choked. Can happen to anyone."

He cleared his throat, then lay back again. "I'm almost done," he said. "Let me . . . let me finish."

Connie nodded. Sandra continued to rub his back.

"I saw his picture. He's much older now of course, but I'd recognize him anywhere. He has this birthmark on his chin, looks like a banana. He's a legitimate businessman now. Big in legalized gambling and living in Kansas City, developing riverboats all over the United States."

Connie thought of Cedric Blacker. But Casino Royale ran out of Las Vegas, not Kansas City. Did the two companies have some kind of connection she didn't know about? She would check.

"How did you know what he looked like?"

Justin smiled. "These guys have been after me for years. After Bill backed out, they came for me themselves. We almost met a couple of times, narrow escapes and all that. Over the last twenty years or so, they've sent other guys, but I haven't forgotten."

"Are you sure the guys who hired Bill to kill you killed him?"

"Sure, that's the way it works. Bill owed them money, and he knew they hired him for murder. If Bill lived, the sharks lost two ways. One, other guys with bad loans might think they could get away with it. Two, so long as Bill lived, they couldn't know for sure he wouldn't go to the authorities."

Connie nodded. It made sense. "But how does it all tie to Jack?" she asked. "Why would they kill him? He didn't know about Bill, you . . . "

Justin tapped his chin with his cane. "Easy," he said. "I told Jack about the man in Kansas City. I didn't want to go to my grave with it on my head."

"You told Jack you thought you knew who killed his mother and father?"

Justin swallowed. "I'm sad to say it, but yes," he said. "When I did that, I guess I got him killed. But I didn't see any option. I knew I was too sick to go after the guy, but I didn't think it right to let it go unpunished. The Bureau might get him, but I didn't know about that. Still don't. I figured Jack could keep after it; he and Sandra together could find enough to go to the authorities."

"Why didn't you go to them yourself?"

He gripped his cane tighter. His knuckles turned white, the veins purple. A glisten of water formed in his eyes and pooled at the base. "I did," he moaned. "But I don't have enough evidence yet. The guy is a prosperous citizen now, clean as a whistle. The story I'm telling is nearly forty years old. It's my word against the sharks. I told a couple of guys in the Bureau, but I'm an old coot to them now, nobody took me very seriously. So, I . . . I told Jack and now he's . . . " His voice trailed off.

Connie stopped rocking and leaned toward Justin. Though his decision may have led to Jack's death, she didn't feel angry with him. How could she? Jack would have done the same thing. He, too, would have tried to bring to justice those who murdered his loved ones. Justin had to do what he thought right, regardless of the results. She reached to touch Justin but then drew back as a puzzling idea came to her.

"How did the man in K.C. know you told Jack about him?" she asked.

Sandra answered for Justin. "We don't know that he does. That's why we're not sure he had anything to do with Jack's death. If he doesn't know about Jack, then he had no reason to go after him."

"Jack might have contacted him," suggested Connie. "Tried to set up a meeting or something."

"Would Jack do that?" Sandra asked.

Connie considered it, then realized it didn't feel plausible. "No, he would go through the authorities, the police, let them do their jobs."

"If that's what he did, then the theory sort of falls apart," offered Sandra.

Connie followed the logic to its conclusion. "Unless . . . unless the police . . . "

Justin, his emotions in control again, finished her sentence. "Unless Jack went to the authorities and someone there tipped the guy off."

"But who?" asked Connie. "Who would do that?"

"That's easy," said Justin. "His brother would."

"His brother?"

"Sure, the brother of the shark in Kansas City is the mayor of Jefferson City."

CHAPTER
28

Connie almost bolted from her chair. Johnson Mack involved in the death of Jack's father? That made no sense.

"But . . . but how?" she sputtered. "Why would he come here, choose this place to settle?"

Justin tapped his cane on the floor and a fresh surge of energy seemed to pump through his veins. His voice took on new power. "Think about it. The gambling interests have worked hard over the last decade to spread their vice all over the country. With Nevada saturated, they needed to expand, make it legal everywhere. They've managed to do that in lots of places. But a lot of states in the Midwest and South—your conservative, religious strongholds—remain closed to them. If the gamblers can get a foothold here in the state capital, they can move almost anywhere.

"You may find it hard to believe, but this small town holds the key to gambling's expansion in the next ten years. Stop gambling here and you put a big dent in the momentum of the gambling forces. But if it passes here, the door swings wide open. It doesn't surprise me they sent Johnson Mack out here a few years ago to soften up the community. They plan decades in advance. Their long-range plans make corporate America blush. That's how organized crime works."

"Did Jack know about Mack?"

"No, he didn't, not so far as I know. I didn't know about him until Jack's murder. I saw him at the graveside of Jack's funeral. Bold as brass."

"You came to the cemetary?"

Justin shrugged, and Connie nodded. Little surprised her anymore. She rocked slowly, her mind spinning. The gambling forces in Vegas sent Johnson Mack to Jefferson City seven years ago to get in position to influence the community. These people had vision. If she didn't hate what they did so much, she would have to admire their ingenuity.

No wonder Mack wanted to buy her store. With that much property in his control, he could bend the entire town to his will. In fact, with that much property, he could dictate every condition for the construction of the convention center. Even with her limited knowledge, she knew Jefferson City had only two options about where to build it. Who knows—Mack might own land in or around the other sight as well.

She concentrated on Justin again. To her surprise, she saw he had closed his eyes and stretched out even more on the sofa. His breathing suddenly sounded labored, and he had dropped his cane to the floor beside the sofa.

Leaning forward, Connie whispered, "You okay?"

Justin waved his hand, dismissing her question. Connie turned to Sandra. "Is he all right?"

Sandra nodded. "I think so, just tired. He's talked enough today to fill up a normal month. Just let him rest."

Connie shrugged. Sandra knew best. She focused again on her situation. If Johnson Mack was involved with Jack's death, she couldn't go to the police. Not even to Tick. He would simply report to Luke Tyler who would report to his chief who would report to Mack.

She faced Sandra. "We need help with this," she said. "Someone outside of Jefferson City influence."

"You know someone?"

Connie nodded. "I sure do. A good friend of Jack's. The attorney general. Wilt Carver. He'll know—"

"How well do you know him?" Sandra interrupted, a scowl darkening her face.

Connie shrugged. "Not that well, he's a friend of Jack's."

"You think you can trust him?"

The question puzzled Connie. She had no reason to distrust him. Why was Sandra so suspicious? "I . . . I don't know, don't see why not."

Sandra's lips curled in disgust. "He's a politician, Connie, just like the rest. Chances are good he's in the gamblers' pockets. You'll need someone else, someone you know well enough to have no doubts whatsoever. Promise me you won't go to Wilt Carver, promise me that right now!"

Her ferocity stunned Connie, and she didn't know how to avoid the promise. Sandra seemed irrational to her, yet maybe she had a point. Wilt did take the video to Tyler without asking her first.

"I tell you what I'll do," she offered, deciding to compromise. "I won't go to him except as a last resort. And I'll let you know if and when I do."

Sandra gritted her teeth, but she didn't fight Connie's decision. Instead, she became very quiet. The room fell silent for several seconds, and both women shifted away from the confrontation. Connie wondered why Sandra disliked politicians so much. Unable to answer, she glanced past Sandra to Justin, resting on the sofa. He remained quiet, his breathing—

To her horror, she realized he had stopped breathing!

"Justin!" she yelled.

As if fired from a pistol, she jumped from the rocker and rushed to him. From behind, Sandra appeared, her larger frame nudging Connie to the side.

"Get his oxygen!" she yelled to Connie.

Sprinting, Connie ran to the door, pushed through it, and bolted outside to the trailer home. Less than a minute later, she lugged the oxygen tank through the door of her house. She saw Sandra leaning over Justin, her hands massaging his chest. She had ripped open his shirt and the bare white of his hairless chest glared in the lights of the den. Driven by fear, Connie lugged the oxygen to Sandra, unhooked the twin tubes that ran into his nose, and handed them to her.

Grabbing the tubes, Sandra shoved them into Justin's nostrils and nudged up the gauge on the tank. Justin gagged and took a deep draught of the air, but he didn't open his eyes. Sandra continued to press on his chest, massaging it firmly with both hands.

"Is he—?"

Justin gagged against the oxygen. "I need to get him to a hospital!" shouted Sandra. "I think it's his heart. His rhythm is all off, his pulse weak. Where's the nearest hospital?"

"Ten minutes from here! Come on, I'll drive you!"

"What about your kids?"

Connie bit her lip. Should she wake them up, tell them what was happening? Take them with her? But that would take too much time. She couldn't call Tess; she was out of town. Could she call Mrs. Everhart back over? She looked at Justin again. His face had turned blue.

"Get him in the van!" she shouted. "I'll call Mrs. Everhart from the hospital. Ask her to come back. She's only a few minutes from here."

Sandra instantly obeyed, grabbing Justin under the shoulders and motioning Connie to grab his feet. Grunting and straining, the two dragged him from the sofa, out the door, and into the backseat of Connie's van. Hustling back to the den to grab her keys, Connie thought of leaving a note but then decided against it. No time.

Slamming the door, she jumped into the van and backed out. Justin lay prone in the backseat, Sandra kneeling on the floor in the middle of a stack of baseball equipment, her hands working Justin's chest.

"Move all that junk," Connie shouted. "Push it all away."

"Hang in there, Justin," Sandra urged. "The hospital isn't far."

Connie gunned the van down the street. The ride didn't take long. Within ten minutes, she screeched to a stop under the canopy of the emergency room, hopped out, and sprinted inside. With three medical personnel and a gurney in tow, she reappeared within a minute and pointed them to the van. The medical team moved into high gear, pushing Sandra aside to get to Justin. Hurriedly, they did their work—a quick examination, a series of questions fired at Sandra, a transfer from the van into the emergency room. The whole process took less than five minutes, but to Connie it seemed like forever. Here she had finally met two people from Jack's past—and one of them teetered on the verge of death.

She found her mind shifting toward Scripture. Bits and pieces of the Psalms flooded her head, the words building up on one another as if forming a brick wall.

"The Lord is my shepherd . . . "

"I will lift up my eyes to the hills—from whence comes my help? . . . "

"The Lord is my rock and my salvation . . . "

The medical team rolled Justin behind a white curtain, and a nurse came to Connie and Sandra and escorted them to a waiting room a few feet down the hall.

"You can wait here," said the nurse, her open face reassuring. "We'll call you as soon as we know what's going on."

Neither Sandra nor Connie protested. They knew the way things worked. The doctors needed to do their jobs.

Sandra eased into a plastic chair. Connie started to sit down beside her, but then remembered her children. She started to search the hallway for a phone, then decided not to call Mrs. Everhart just yet.

"Let me run back home," she said. "I'll wake Daniel, tell him what's going on, then call Mrs. Everhart. She'll come over, then I'll come right back."

Sandra smiled thinly. "You don't need to come back," she said. "We're fine. He's had a couple of spells like this in the last year. Take care of your family. I'll call you when—"

"No, you won't either," insisted Connie. "As soon as I get things situated at home, I'll head back. It shouldn't take more than forty-five minutes. You hang in there until then, I'll be right back."

Sandra's eyes rimmed with tears. Connie wrapped her arms around her new friend and hugged her. "I'm praying for you," she said. "The Lord can do things the doctors can t even comprehend."

Sandra nodded but didn't speak.

Connie started to say more but, not wanting to press Sandra in such a vulnerable moment, decided against it. No matter what happened to Justin, she would have another opportunity with Sandra. Right now the woman needed love and companionship, not hard-sell preaching.

"I'll be right back," Connie assured her. "Just hang in there." As she hustled to the van, it suddenly hit her: Love and companionship were hard-sell preaching. They were the proof of the product. If she wanted to sell Jesus to other people, she had to show them who Jesus was, what Jesus did. What she did served as evidence of what she said.

In her van, she headed home. Sometime soon, she would tell Sandra more about her faith. When she did, she hoped and prayed Sandra would listen.

*****

Brit had traded in his Jaguar and Humvee for a more sedate vehicle, an egg-white, four-door sedan with black tires. He smiled as he followed Connie from the hospital, thinking how official he looked in the new car. From all appearances, he might as well be a policeman.

As Connie pulled into her driveway, he drummed his thumb along the steering wheel and tried to anticipate the next few hours. Lennie had called just a few hours ago and given him his instructions: set up a meeting with Connie Brandon. Nothing more, nothing less. Lennie had insisted on that—do nothing else except make the call. Set up the meeting, then wait for him to arrive.

Brit glanced at his watch. Lennie would arrive within the next two hours. He had to wait until then. Though he disliked the waiting part, Brit knew he couldn't disobey orders again. For all he knew, he'd already disobeyed one too many times. Last night, he had tried to run over Connie Brandon. Today he tried to shoot her and her new companions. Tonight? Well, tonight he had removed all the evidence of his presence in her house and guaranteed she would make the meeting Lennie told him to set up. He couldn't go any further without clearance. Even now, if Lennie found out about the first moves, he might face severe penalties.

Frustrated, but not foolish, Brit decided to do what Lennie told him. Make the call, set up the meeting, then wait on Lennie. Anything else would go too far, even for him. Content, he stopped his drumming and stared at Connie as she stepped from her van.

"Get on inside," he muttered. "Get on inside so I can make the call." A gleam burned in Brit's soft, colorless eyes. He would set up the meeting, and she would come. No doubt about it, she would come. Then, sometime before the sun came up on the Missouri, he would put a finish to all this.

*****

Walking into the house, Connie rubbed her eyes and realized how tired she felt. The last few days had taken a toll on her, a toll marked by both physical and mental fatigue. Not accustomed to such emotional ups and downs, her body felt stretched—as taut as a high-wire with an acrobat on it. If anything stretched her one more inch, she thought she would snap.

Headed toward Daniel's bedroom, she pledged she would tell Tick Garner the whole story the minute he and Tess came back from the lake. With Tick, she would go to Luke and from there to Wilt Carver. Wilt would know how to handle this, and it seemed, in spite of Sandra's protests, going to him made more sense than anything.

Connie opened Daniel's bedroom door. Behind her, the telephone rang. She hesitated for only a second, then turned around. Must be Sandra. She left the hallway and stepped back into the den. Picking up the phone, it startled her when she heard a man's voice.

"Connie Brandon, we need to meet," said the man.

The voice sounded familiar. Connie ran the sound through her mind for an instant, then remembered—the same man had called and told her Jack got what he deserved. Confused, Connie concentrated on his voice. "I'm . . . not sure what you mean," she said.

"It's a simple notion. We need to meet."

"Who are you?"

The man laughed. "Oh, you know me. Black Mercedes, Humvee in a forest glade, blond hair, snappy dresser, red Jaguar. I've been around the last few days."

Her neck splotching red, Connie squeezed the phone and tried to stall, give herself time to think. This man murdered Reed Morrison, probably Jack! Now, he wanted her dead too. She couldn't meet with him!

"Who are you?" she shouted. "Who do you work for? . . . It's Cedric Blacker, isn't it? Or Johnson Mack. They're in this together, aren't they? Both of them with the gamblers . . . you're—"

"You think you're a smart lady, don't you? Well, maybe you are and maybe you aren't."

"I know it's the gamblers! They—"

"I got no time for this," interrupted Brit. "Just do what I tell you."

His sullen tone slowed Connie's outrage. But she didn't dare do what he said. "I don't . . . don't think I can meet you," she stammered, hoping to get help before this went any further.

"You have no choice."

The man sounded awfully sure of himself, and the arrogance made Connie's blood boil. How dare he barge into her life and try to harm her and the only relatives Jack had left! She wouldn't meet with him! She would call Wilt Carver the minute she hung up the phone. She would tell Wilt everything, and he would start a search for this man, and they would find him and punish him like he deserved! Her anger fueling her courage, Connie minced no words.

"You can forget it!" she shouted. "I've had enough of this! You think you can just . . . just terrorize someone . . . stalk them . . . stalk them and . . . try to . . . to murder them, then call out of the blue and expect them to do what you say? No way will I meet you. You won't—"

The man laughed, and goose bumps sprinkled across Connie's forearms. He sounded so cocky and sure of himself.

"You better calm down, lady," he said. "Calm down and listen to me, if you know what's good for you."

Though not sure why, Connie did what he commanded. She forced herself to calm down so she could listen. Something in his voice told her he had the upper hand and knew it. Biting her lip, she waited for him to continue.

"You'll meet me at midnight," he said. "No cops, nobody but you. At the Katy Trail, by the overpass where the trail runs under the highway. You know the place."

More confused by the second, Connie wondered how the man knew of her familiarity with the Katy Trail. "I know the place," she said, hoping she sounded stronger than she felt. "But I can't meet you. I have kids here, I can't leave the house."

The man laughed, and a pang of fear shot through Connie's guts. Dropping the phone, she sprinted into the hallway and popped open Daniel's bedroom door. His still form, lanky and quiet, lay stretched out on his bed. Relieved, but only momentarily, Connie backed into the hallway again and sprinted toward the last room on the left. Praying she had jumped to the wrong conclusion, she slowed down, then stopped at the door. Her heart thudding so hard it almost hurt, she popped open the door and took three quick strides inside. There, on the bed, she spotted a Tabasco Beanie Baby. Beside the stuffed animal was an empty spot. An empty spot where Katie normally slept!

Pushing back the scream in her throat, Connie hurtled back through the hallway and into the den. Grabbing the phone, she shouted into it, "You hurt my baby and I'll kill you! I'll . . . " Her voice failed as anger and fear snuffed it out.

"Easy, lady," said Brit. "The little girl is fine. What a pretty thing. So much like you. You should feel proud."

His arrogance prodding her, Connie found her voice again. "Okay!" she shouted. "You want your meeting. You've got it! Midnight. Just make sure you bring my baby."

The man laughed again. "Good," he said. "You make sure you're alone. I see any sign, and I mean any sign you brought company, and you'll never see your girl again. You got that?"

"Don't you hurt my child!"

The line went dead. The phone still in her hand, Connie sagged against the counter and started to tremble. In little more than an hour, she had to figure out a way to save her life and that of her baby girl. Tears began to roll down her face, and she wondered where to turn. Tick and Tess were forty miles away at the lake. Sandra had to stay with Justin. Who could she call? Wilt Carver? But the man had warned her to come alone. Would calling Wilt jeopardize Katie's life?

Though uncertain, she turned to pick up a phone book to find Wilt's number. She saw Daniel standing in the hallway in his gym shorts, his sleepy eyes wide with fear.

"Mom?" he asked. "Is someone going to hurt Katie?"

Opening her arms, Connie stepped toward Daniel and embraced him.

"How much did you hear?" she asked.

"Enough," he said, his voice firm. "Mom, what's going on? You've been gone so much lately. I haven't said anything, but I've wondered . . . Is there something . . . something about Dad's death I should know?" He stared straight at her, so mature and caring, she wanted to cry. She realized he deserved the truth. Though she hated to disturb his young world with such painful news, the time had come to tell him what was happening.

"Get dressed," she said. "Then come back in here. I'll tell you on the way."

"We're going somewhere?"

Connie hesitated, not sure what to do. Leave him home? But look what happened to Katie when she did that. Who knew what this man might do next? If she didn't stop him somehow, he might come back to her house, take Daniel like he did Katie and disappear.

"Just get dressed," she said. "We've got to hurry."

Without another word, Daniel disappeared down the hall. Connie leaned against the counter and breathed deeply. She knew she couldn't handle this alone. Since Jack's death she had discovered reserves of strength she never knew she possessed. But this situation demanded more than she could possibly muster. Her hands at her sides, she tried to figure out what to do. Go it alone? Call for help?

Feeling faint, she stepped to the breakfast nook and opened the door leading to the back deck. She eased onto the deck and stared past it to the river below. A sheen of silver moon raked over the water.

A passage of Scripture popped into her head. "Trust in the Lord in all your ways and lean not on your own understanding. In all your ways acknowledge Him and He will direct your paths."

For several seconds, she pondered the words. Goose bumps appeared on her forearms, and the hair on the back of her neck stood up. Her ears seemed to prick higher, and her eyes widened. A sense of God's presence flowed through her in a way she had never before experienced.

"Trust in the Lord," the words repeated. "He will direct your paths."

She inhaled deeply. The smell of the river rose up to her, the smell of water flowing, yet always constant. The river—so much like God, always moving, but always there.

As if drawn by an invisible magnet, she raised her hands from her sides and extended them toward the sky.

"I'm listening," she whispered.

Trust in the Lord. He will direct your paths.

Her palms tingled, and a light touch of night breeze fingered her face.

Trust in the Lord.

Goose bumps played on her neck and her hair fluttered in the breeze.

He will direct your paths.

Just like that, she knew who to call. As the name flashed into her head, she almost rejected it.

"No way," she thought. "What can—?"

Trust in the Lord.

The moon played with her eyes. She stood on tiptoes, her hands open heavenward.

Trust in the Lord.

She couldn't deny the message. She knew who to call.

Her palms suddenly felt normal. The hair on her neck lay down again. She dropped her arms, and the sense of awe disappeared. She lowered her hands and looked around. Everything appeared normal.

For another few moments, she stayed still, not sure what had just happened. Had God truly spoken? If so, the message made little or no sense. But nothing else did either. The time to act had come, the time for faith.

Walking back into the kitchen, she closed the back door, picked up the phone, and dialed a number. Daniel suddenly appeared beside her, his blue jeans and Cardinals jersey loose and his tennis shoes untied. She motioned him closer. She placed one hand around his shoulders, the other on the phone.

"Listen in," she said. "That way I won't have to say this but once."

When a voice answered on the other end, Connie immediately began to talk.

"This is Connie," she said. "I know it's late and I hate to wake you up with this, but I need your help."

"No bother about the time. You know I'll do anything I can."

"Then listen to this. It's complicated and it's crazy, but it's the truth."

"I'm listening."

With a sigh of relief, Connie poured out the story, abbreviating where she could to save time. As she covered the gist of what had recently happened to her, leaving out what was already known by them both, a sense of peace overwhelmed her. She had held so much to herself—to release it felt liberating, as if removing a stone from her back. Her listener didn't interrupt, just let her speak without comment or question. Within ten minutes, the account came to a close, and Connie relaxed even more. No matter what happened now, she wouldn't face this by herself.

"So I'm meeting him in about an hour. He told me to come alone."

"But you called me anyway."

"I didn't know where else to turn. I've got an idea, thought you could help. Tell me if you think I should do something else."

"I'm listening. And you know I'll tell you if I disagree."

Her gaze on Daniel, Connie began to speak, her brown eyes lit with a strange glow. Her idea seemed ludicrous as she said it, but somehow it seemed right, too, as right as anything she had ever done in her life.

Daniel tilted his head as she talked, and a line of concentration appeared on his young face. She smiled, knowing what she suggested sounded bizarre. But Daniel had missed the instant of inspiration when God spoke to her. If he had experienced it, then he would most certainly understand that ideas like the one she had didn't come from anywhere but above.

CHAPTER
29

Glancing at her watch, Connie ushered Daniel through the emergency room and asked a nurse where to find Justin Longley.

"Three-oh-one," said the nurse. "They just took him up."

Connie hurried Daniel to the elevator. In less than an hour, she had to be at the Katy Trail. The whole thing seemed unreal to her, but she knew just how real it was. A maniac had Katie, and she had to save her. She punched the button to the third floor and rested her head momentarily against the wall.

"This man is my great-granddad?" said Daniel, his eyes big.

Connie raised back up. "Yes, your dad's granddad. He talked about him from time to time, but not that much."

"I thought he was dead."

"So did I."

The elevator slid open, and Connie followed Daniel out. Grateful Justin had stabilized enough to go to a regular room, she hustled to the room and knocked. Sandra answered immediately, and she and Daniel quietly entered. Sandra greeted them with her arms open.

Connie opened her arms, too, and the two embraced, stayed together for a second, then stepped back. Daniel waited, his gaze scanning the room, his blue eyes intense as he focused on the man lying in the bed.

Connie faced Daniel. "Daniel, this is Sandra," she said. "Sandra, this is Daniel." She pointed to Justin. "Daniel, that's your great-granddad."

Daniel stared at Justin, taking in the tubes and machines attached to him.

"Is he all right?" he asked.

Sandra extended her hand to Daniel, and he shook it.

"He's comfortable," Sandra said. "Out of danger for the time being."

Daniel said, "Mom told me about you on the way over here. Said you and Daddy were cousins, knew each other a long time ago."

Sandra laughed gently. "Maybe not that long. But yes, I'm your dad's cousin. We knew each other back in Miller."

"Dad never took us to Miller."

"Maybe I can take you someday."

Daniel nodded, apparently satisfied with his new relative. Connie put her arm around his waist. "I wish we didn't have to rush this," she said, urgency in her tone. "But we've got trouble."

Sandra started to speak, but Connie held up a hand and stopped her. "Just listen," she said.

She rushed through the story, telling Sandra about the call and the demand for a meeting. Though anything but calm, she kept her tone even as she told her the man had taken Katie. Sandra's mouth dropped open, and she started to interrupt, but again Connie refused to let her speak.

"Let me finish," she said. "I've called for help, the only person with the power to do something about this, I called—"

"You didn't call Wilt Carver, did you?" Sandra broke in this time before Connie could head her off, her voice shrill and panicky.

Confused by her reaction, Connie hesitated. Why did Sandra show such a violent reaction to a politician? It didn't make sense. What did she know—?

Wait a minute! Carver went to school with Jack! That meant he also went to school with Sandra. But what did that matter? Did Sandra dislike Wilt so much she would refuse his help, even in a desperate situation like this? Connie didn't know, and she didn't have time to find out. Less than a half hour remained for her to get to the Katy Trail. Less than half an hour separated her from knowing if her scheme came from God or heaven only knew where else.

"Look," she said to Sandra, "there's no time to argue this. Don't worry about who I've called. I did what I had to do, you'll have to trust that. I've got to go. I want to leave Daniel with you."

"No way, Mom!" argued Daniel, his hands on his hips. "I'm going with you!"

"I am too," said Sandra, apparently willing to put aside her concern about Wilt Carver. "Justin is stable. He'd want me to go."

Connie stared over at Justin. His breathing appeared steady. But her plans didn't call for company.

"You can't," she said. "Neither of you. It's too dangerous."

"Doesn't matter," said Sandra. "I'm coming."

"Me too," insisted Daniel.

Connie stared first at Sandra, then at Daniel. Their jaws were set, their eyes narrowed in determination. But she couldn't give in on this. She stepped to Daniel, put her hands on his shoulders, and stared directly into his eyes.

"Look," she said, her voice shaky. "I've already lost your dad. And this man now has Katie. I just can't take a chance that anything could happen to you. Do you understand, Daniel? I want you to stay here with Sandra, stay here and pray as hard as you've ever prayed in your life. Can you do that for me? Can you?"

Daniel's eyes trickled tears. "But I don't want you to go by yourself, Mom," he sobbed.

"I won't be by myself," she soothed. "You know that. God is with me. You pray. That's what I need. You stay safe and pray."

Daniel nodded, and she turned to Sandra. "Stay with him," Connie said.

Sandra nodded, then reached behind her back and pulled something from the waistband of her jeans. "Take this," Sandra said. "It's Justin's. You may need it."

Connie bit her lip and studied the gun. Its coal-black barrel looked comforting, much more so than the crazy plan she had concocted in a matter of seconds standing on her deck. She started to take the weapon but then drew back. Taking the gun meant she had no faith in what she thought God instructed her to do. Taking the gun lowered her to the level of those who killed Jack. Though she felt foolish, she shook her head and refused the weapon.

"I can't go that way," she said. "No matter what happens, I can't go that way."

"But what about Katie, Mom?" asked Daniel.

Connie stared at Daniel and saw the anguish in his face. A gun made more sense than her scheme, no doubt about it. But she knew nothing about guns. Even if she carried it, she probably couldn't hit anything, not even if her life depended on it. Which, of course, it would.

"I'll take care of Katie," she assured Daniel. "But I'll do it without a gun."

She faced Sandra again. "You'll take care of him . . . if anything happens to me . . . "

"Nothing is going to happen to you," said Sandra, slipping the gun into her jeans. "Just go. I'll take care of Daniel."

Connie kissed Daniel on the forehead. "Pray," she repeated. "I'll see you soon."

*****

Fifteen miles away, Lennie kept one hand on the steering wheel, flipped open his cell phone, and hit the autodial button. Within ten seconds, Brit picked up on the other side.

"You in place?" asked Lennie.

"Not quite, but almost. Had to pick up a couple of things at her place first."

"What things?"

"Oh, you know, the listening devices, a few pictures, a couple of canceled airline tickets."

Lennie nodded and buttoned his suit. Brit had removed the bugs and taken the pictures of Morrison and Richards as well as Connie's ticket stubs to Vegas from her house. After they finished this, they didn't want any odds and ends floating around to make the cops curious.

"Good work," he said.

"How far out are you?"

"Ten minutes, no more than fifteen."

258   A CAPITAL OFFENSE

"The Man coming?"

"Don't know, he didn't say."

"You think he'll come?"

Lennie unbuttoned his suit coat. He really didn't know.

"He might," he said.

"You tell him where?"

"Absolutely, he always knows where."

"Anything else?"

Lennie buttoned his coat. "Don't do the deed until I give the go-ahead."

The line fell silent. Brit had hung up on him. That cowboy! Lennie cursed and unbuttoned his coat. A lot rode on tonight. He just hoped Brit didn't slop it up for everyone.

Lennie touched the Glock pistol he kept holstered to his left hip. If Brit got out of line, The Man had given him permission to put him out of business. Permanently out of business.

*****

Her heartbeat notching higher, Connie pulled her van onto the gravel surface of the parking area of the Katy Trail and rolled it to a stop. Overhead, she saw a bank of clouds climb over the moon. The night became darker, and she breathed a touch easier. What she planned needed as black a night as possible.

Slowly, she scanned the scene. To her right, probably a hundred yards away, she saw the dim outline of the Highway 54 overpass, the bridge where the mysterious caller had said to meet him. Somewhere over there, the man held Katie.

Her face flushed, and she noted her body heating up. Her heartbeat revved up even more. *Steady yourself,* she thought. *"Be anxious for nothing, but in everything by prayer and supplication, with thanksgiving, let your requests be made known to God." Steady.*

She focused again on the overpass. Though she couldn't see it, she knew that another section of trail rolled on from there, the section that ran toward St. Louis. Nearer to her, she noted a square building, no larger than a double phone booth with windows halfway up and on all four sides. Though she didn't know the purpose of the building, she did know it had come in handy once when she, Jack, and the kids got caught on the trail during a thunderstorm. Just across from that building, a bathroom building sat empty of customers. By the bathrooms, a small ditch ran parallel with the gravel trail, and a number of huge trees lined the parking lot behind her. Grateful she knew the area so well, she told herself to stay calm.

Then, moving before she changed her mind, she grabbed the door latch and snapped it open. Dropping her feet onto the trail, she heard gravel crunch under her shoes. She took a deep breath, then stood still for a second. In the darkness, she felt so small, so alone. A shudder racked her body. Everything boiled down to this.

One woman. One gamble. One chance. One plan she hoped came from God.

Biting her lip, she stepped away from the van and began walking toward the bridge.

*****

Lennie leaned against one of the concrete pillars that supported the overpass and peered through the inky night toward the parking lot where a van had just driven up. Katie sat on the gravel beside him, her eyes blindfolded and her ears stuffed with plugs. Two steps ahead of them, Brit cupped his forehead with his right hand as if shading his eyes from too much sun.

"I can't see her, Len," he complained. "But that had to be her van."

"Relax, Brit. Sure it's her van. She's getting up her courage. Give her a minute."

A light suddenly glowed in the dark, and Lennie recognized it as the interior light of a vehicle. He heard a door slam, and the light blinked off.

"She's coming, Len," whispered Brit.

"She said she would." Lennie reached for the top button on his coat and unbuttoned it. Behind the button, he touched the handle of his Glock. Though planning to use other means for this business, the touch of the weapon gave him comfort. If worse came to worst, he had the gun available. Buttoning his coat again, he turned and glanced over his shoulder at The Man hiding in the shadows. Unusual for him to show up, but everything about this case was unusual.

Lennie heard feet scratching gravel, and he twisted back toward the sound and saw Connie Brandon emerging from the shadows, her head erect, her posture steady.

For several seconds, Lennie studied the woman. He'd only seen her the one time in Vegas when she showed up at Morrison's house. Though that episode had been brief, he felt like he knew her pretty well. Everything she had done since then only verified what that one encounter suggested. She demonstrated a number of qualities he admired—resourcefulness, persistence, bravery, compassion. A heck of a woman. Not bad-looking either. Too petite for his taste, but hair so bright you could cook on it and eyes that created dreams.

Watching her stride his way in her denim jeans, knit top, and tennis shoes, a touch of regret ran through him. Tough he had to do a job on her. He touched the breast pocket of his suit. The needle, encased in a plastic bag, rested against his chest. Enough cocaine to kill her five times waited in his car, less than a hundred yards away. At least she would die like her husband.

Connie Brandon walked within speaking distance now, and Brit slithered out of the shadows and appeared like an apparition before her. Lennie stayed hidden under the bridge.

"That's far enough, Red," said Brit.

Connie stopped in her tracks. Lennie heard her breathing. It was rushed, panting, but her body stayed still.

"Where's my daughter?"

Her voice, though a bit forced, sounded pretty strong, considering the circumstances. Lennie wondered if she had a weapon hidden somewhere on her body. He hoped she did. A weapon would at least give him an excuse. If she drew a pistol on him or Brit, he could do her and claim self-defense to his conscience. Otherwise it became cold, hard killing, and his stomach churned at that.

Brit twisted halfway around and flipped his thumb toward the darkness under the overpass. "She's back there."

"I want to see her!"

Brit laughed, and Lennie decided he never wanted to work with him again. Brit took too much pleasure in his work. Lennie, though successful at what he did, never truly enjoyed it. He did it because that's what he was, but it pained him every time, especially when it meant hurting someone as innocent as Connie Brandon.

*****

Hearing the man's high-pitched laughter, Connie's heart fluttered, and a sense of doom ran through her. The man lived for this kind of experience! He had no intention of letting her leave with Katie!

Connie locked her knees and gritted her teeth. If everything unfolded as planned, she and Katie would survive this.

"You're in no position to make any demands," said Brit, his voice devoid of emotion.

"You said you'd give me my daughter."

"So I will." He turned halfway around but kept his eyes on Connie.

Five seconds later, a blindfolded Katie popped out of the darkness under the bridge, her little body struggling to stay upright as she stumbled forward. Someone had evidently pushed her away from the bridge. Noting the presence of the second person, Connie reached for Katie and gathered her into her arms.

"Mommy!" Katie cried, burying her head into Connie's shoulder.

"It's OK, Katie." Squeezing her baby, Connie felt a twinge of fear. Whoever pushed Katie could cause problems in the next few minutes.

Concentrating on the unseen person in the darkness, Connie almost missed it as Brit lifted a pistol from the waistband of his slacks and pointed it at her.

For a moment, she didn't say a word, but her breathing became even faster. In the night's silence, it sounded like someone inflating and deflating a tire, up down, in out, breathing it in, breathing it out. Her legs quivered, but she refused to give in to her fear.

"You're not going to let us go, are you?" she asked, her voice holding.

Brit laughed again. Connie almost choked. This guy sounded one step short of going over the edge.

"Your girl, sure. No reason to hurt her. I'm not an animal. But you, Red . . . you're a different story. You know too much."

"I know you killed my husband."

"See, that's what I mean."

"I know you work for the gamblers."

Brit laughed again, but with less energy. "You think you're a smart woman. Well, maybe you're not so smart as you think."

Connie hesitated. Brit's words made her wonder. Did everything add up here or not? Brit didn't give her time to settle it.

"Leave the girl," he said. "It's time for us to move."

Connie studied his face but kept her hands on Katie's shoulders. How tragic to see a man end up so evil, so far from what God wanted. He appeared so normal, but in a few minutes she might be dead at his hands.

"Hold it, Brit!" A deep male voice erupted from the shadows, and Brit turned toward the noise. Connie looked, too, squinting to see the speaker. Her eyes widened as big as saucers as she saw him step away from the bridge and walk toward her. Brit stepped to the side to let him pass. He stopped no more than four feet away from Connie. Though she knew Brit still had his gun trained on her, she completely ignored him. The man in front of her demanded her whole concentration.

"I want you to know I'll take care of your children," the man said.

Connie started to speak, but her voice deserted her. She stammered, but nothing came out. Her thoughts, though, jammed rapidly ahead. This made no sense at all! Why—what—?

"I don't want you to die worried about your children. I'm not a vicious man."

Her astonishment passing, Connie found her tongue and choked out a response. "I don't understand!" she said. "What are you—?"

"This isn't about gambling, Connie."

She bit her lip, her hands still on Katie. "Then what is it about?"

"Haven't you figured it out? You've done so well with everything else. This is about my son."

"But how? I don't understand . . . How does he—?"

"Think about it."

Her mind twirled as she tried to put it all together. Bits and scraps of the days since the funeral jumbled up like so many pieces of a mixed-up puzzle. She twisted and jammed the pieces into each other, trying to find some that fit together.

If she had to die, she at least wanted to know why. Why did Jack die? With the man's promise to keep Katie and Daniel safe, that's the only other thing she wanted. Just let her see the whole picture before he sent her to heaven.

Her head hurt from thinking, and she couldn't figure it out. She gave up and closed her eyes. Okay, if she had only a few seconds more, she would use them to pray for her family. Daniel and Katie, God bless their sweet souls. And now Justin and Sandra, God give them joy in the days ahead—

Wait a minute! Sandra.

A picture suddenly popped into her mind, and it fell into place all at once, the obvious answer. Jack and Sandra at Miller High. Sandra in the picture of the "Best Couple" standing arm in arm with a handsome boy. Something happened during high school between Sandra and a young Wilt Carver. It all made sense. Sandra's intense dislike for Wilt. The scar on Wilt's chin that no one ever explained.

Connie opened her eyes. "What happened with Wilt and Sandra?" she asked, staring hard at Robert Carver, his thick torso standing sturdy as a refrigerator on the road. "Something Jack found out, planned to tell?"

"Bingo. Sorry about the term." He smiled lightly.

"What happened between them that you couldn't let the public know?"

"You can imagine."

Connie's mind clicked through the possibilities. Only one thing made sense, explained Sandra's hostility toward him.

"Wilt did something to her, something no boy should do."

Carver shrugged, and his voice dropped a notch. Connie leaned forward to hear him better.

"Wilt loved her, at least as much as an eighteen-year-old can love. Wanted to marry her, told her they would get married some day. One night, after dating for almost a year, he became a bit . . . well . . . overexuberant, shall I say. He got carried away. She told him to stop. He didn't. He wasn't accustomed to anyone saying no to him. She fought him, scratched him badly. You've seen the scar. He lost control. Hit her. Knocked her out, or she fainted . . . I don't know. Then he . . . well, he . . . "

"You don't have to say anything else," said Connie. "I know what happened."

Carver took a deep breath. "I regret it has come to this. But you leave me no choice. Just like Jack."

Connie moved Katie around behind her legs, talking as she did so. "But all that happened a long time ago. Why should any of that matter now? Sandra hasn't said anything all these years."

"I made that exact point with your husband the night I met him out here. I said to him, 'Let it go.' But he couldn't. He said he 'had to do the right thing.'"

"How did he find out about it?"

Carver shrugged again. "I suppose his grandfather told him. Or Sandra. I don't really know. I just know he couldn't let it rest. He came to Wilt several months ago. Told him to drop out of politics and he would let that end it, punishment enough, that sort of thing."

"But if Wilt refused?"

"Jack said he would have to report it, let the public decide it from there. I couldn't let him do that. I had to deal with it. A father's love for a son, you can understand that . . . "

Carver's voice dropped even lower, and he seemed to lose track of his surroundings. He mumbled as if talking to himself, and Connie strained to hear the rest of what he said.

" . . . My boy might make it all the way, someday. I couldn't let something that happened so long ago keep him from his destiny. If Jack had just practiced some of that forgiveness he talked so much about, everything would have been fine. But no, he couldn't do that. He had to do the right thing. Too bad . . . too bad for all of us. Too bad for him . . . for you . . . for all . . . of us."

His head down, he turned away and sighed. "Do her, Brit," he said. "But don't make her suffer."

Connie's heart thundered and her knees shook. Her plan seemed so stupid now, so out of place and impossible. Hoping to forestall the moment of testing, she shouted at Carver. "What about my children? You said you would take care of my children!"

Carver faced her once more. "That's right. I'm not a spiteful man. I'll take care of them, like I said. That's why I came here tonight, to let you know that. I'll send Wilt to provide for them. A friend giving financial support to his dead friend's children. It'll make wonderful copy for the papers."

One final question dawned on Connie. "Does Wilt know?" she asked.

Carver stared at her. "No," he said. "He's not involved. I set up the meeting with Jack, you see. Told him to meet me. I wanted to talk to him, make a deal. But your husband didn't make deals. Too bad. But Wilt had nothing to do with it, too risky for him."

"But not for you."

Carver smiled, then began backing away. "Nothing is too risky for me to protect my boy's destiny. Do her, Brit."

Carver walked toward the bridge. "Make sure, Lennie."

Lennie stepped away from the bridge, hurrying down the path, his right hand holding his pistol at chest level.

"Hold it, Carver!"

From the ditch three feet below the trail to her left, Connie heard the voice of Reverend Wallace cutting through the darkness. Carver froze in place, and Brit and Lennie stopped too. But neither man lowered his gun.

"Drop the guns," called a second man, his voice coming from Connie's right. She turned to the square building where she and her family had once waited out a summer storm. Tick Garner emerged from the building, a pistol in his hand. Connie's heart skipped a beat. Reverend Wallace had called him at the lake!

Brit shifted his feet and pointed his gun at Tick. For a split second, Connie thought he was going to shoot, but then a third voice rang out, stopping him.

"I wouldn't do that!"

Luke Tyler stepped from behind a hickory tree twenty feet from the building, his massive form standing sideways to Brit, the largest gun Connie had ever seen steady in his huge hands.

"We're here," yelled a fourth man's voice.

"And here," called another.

From every side, Connie heard the voices, the voices of the elders of the River City Community Church, the voices of the people Reverend Wallace had called after she called him. From the ditch that ran along the trail to her left, from the trees that bordered the bridge just ahead, from the bathrooms near her car, person after person appeared from the darkness, apparitions of rescue, human angels, willing to risk their lives for their friend. Connie's heart rose up in her throat as she saw what her simple scheme had created—a wave of people surrounding her, supporting her, protecting her. That's what she planned all along, an army of God facing down one lone kidnapper. Yes, now they had to face three, but even three couldn't stop them all. Seeing the odds against them, surely the killers would give up! They couldn't shoot them all, so why shoot even one? Any reasonable person would understand that.

"Drop the guns," shouted Luke. "It's all over."

"You're putting a lot of good people in danger here," said Carver. "All I have to do is give the signal and these two will make an awful mess."

"You won't do that." A voice from the right surprised Connie, a voice she hadn't expected to hear. She turned and watched as Wilt Carver eased out of the black night into view.

"Stay out of this, son. It's not your business." Robert Carver held up his hand to stop Wilt.

"It's all my business, Dad. I started this a long time ago. I'm going to finish it tonight. Luke Tyler called me. Said Connie needed my help. I promised her I'd help her if I could. So this has gone far enough. I'm going to do what Jack asked me to do, get out of this political nightmare. I should have stepped out when he first came to me, but I didn't have the courage. He didn't want to hurt me, he said. Just wanted me to get help. He knew what I needed, a way to cleanse myself of the guilt that stained me, the guilt that stained everything I did, everything I wanted to do."

"How did Jack know about it?" asked Connie, her voice shaking.

Wilt dropped his head for a moment. Everyone stayed frozen in place, anxious and poised.

"Sandra told him. When she showed up back in January and took him to Justin, he found out about Joseph Mussina, the man in Kansas City. He wanted to come to me, ask me to start an investigation. But Sandra wouldn't let him. He asked her why. She refused to answer. He pressed her. Finally, she broke down and told him. Then Jack came to me with all of it."

"Do you know about Johnson Mack?" Connie asked.

"I know he's the brother of Mussina. Just found out a few days ago. I've found out a lot of things in the last two weeks. The last thing I plan to do before I resign is begin an official inquiry into Mussina and Mack and their activities in the gambling industry. I don't know if I can get them for the murder of Jack's parents, but maybe I can pin something on them. Get them out of the gambling business anyway."

"You're in over your head, son."

Wilt faced his father. "I'm sorry, Dad," he said. "I have no choice. Jack was right. I have no right to lead others after what I did. I know that now. I have the guts to leave this fishbowl, go back to something normal. Try to repair my family, save my marriage.

"If I had known you would go this far, I would have acted on Jack's advice the instant he came to me. But I didn't. Didn't have the courage. Then, after his death, I didn't know what to do. I had no idea you had anything to do with his murder, thought it was the gamblers. But tonight it ends, all of it. I ruined things once, I'm going to fix them this time."

He stopped talking and took a step toward his father. Robert Carver remained still, stunned into rigidity. Someone coughed, but everyone else remained in place, as if waiting to see what father and son would do next.

Suddenly, one person moved. Twenty feet from Robert and Wilt Carver, Brit shifted his feet and shouted. "Nothing ends!" he screamed, aiming his pistol. "Nothing—"

He fired into the dark and the bullet ripped through the quiet. He sprinted to his left as the bullet popped into Wilt Carver's side and knocked him to the ground, a quick spurt of blood gushing from his white shirt. Everyone but Brit hit the ground as the gunshot exploded in their ears. Brit continued to sprint, his feet skipping across the gravel.

Prone on the ground with Katie beside her, Connie looked up just as Brit rushed past. She grabbed at his ankles, but he jumped over her outstretched arms and she missed him.

"Get him," yelled Luke, pushing up from the ground.

To her right, Connie spotted Tick moving low along the trail, his gun ready. Furious that she missed Brit, she jerked herself up and dashed after him. Her heart jumped into her throat. Brit was running toward Reverend Wallace! Opening her mouth to scream, she saw Luke Tyler suddenly stop and take dead aim with his pistol.

"No!" she shouted. "No!"

Reverend Wallace fell to the ground and rolled to the side toward the ditch.

Brit rushed ahead, his stride picking up pace, his blond ponytail streaming out behind his head. From Connie's back, a shot rang out.

Brit kept running, no more than fifteen yards from the van. He raised his pistol, and Connie knew he would shoot Reverend Wallace within seconds, and she could do nothing to stop him. Too horrified to scream, she stopped trying to get up. Her eyes on her pastor, she began to pray.

Connie watched the next few seconds pass in slow motion and every movement etched itself forever in her mind.

Brit pointed his pistol directly at Reverend Wallace.

Reverend Wallace closed his eyes.

Brit's finger twitched on the trigger.

A shot fired. Brit's gun kicked upward as it fired too. He toppled toward the ground, his gun falling from his hand and onto the gravel trail.

Everything shifted into normal speed for Connie, and she rushed toward Reverend Wallace. At his side, she threw her arms around him and hugged him close. Luke stood over Brit, his gun cocked. Brit lay motionless on the gravel, a pool of blood dripping from his shoulder.

Wilt Carver suddenly appeared, his shirt stained with blood and his father, his head down in shame, at his side. Tick showed up, too, with Lennie in tow.

Katie, blindfold and earplugs gone, stood holding Tess's hand. Connie grabbed Katie with one arm and left the other wrapped around her pastor.

Her eyes glistening with tears of joy, Connie found herself surrounded by a circle of friends, all of them hugging and shouting and celebrating together. Squeezing her daughter with every ounce of strength in her body, she stood in the center of the circle and began to laugh and cry all at once. Her friends reached out to her and to each other, each of them laughing and crying too. The circle firmed up as arm linked with arm and friend embraced friend. There they stood in the middle of the trail on a moon-hidden night, a circle of praise and joy, each person touching another and everyone feeling the touch of God.

CHAPTER
30

T wo days later, on Friday afternoon at just past 5:30, Connie parked her van and stepped out. A hint of a breeze played across her hair, and the last of the day's sun warmed her back. Reading the headstones as she walked, she picked her way through the cemetery to the spot where Jack rested. Just ahead, a cardinal flitted into the hickory tree that draped over Jack's burial plot. Connie stopped for a moment, watched the bird, and took in the beauty of the quiet place. Blinded by grief, she had seen so little three weeks ago when she buried Jack, had missed the towering hickory trees and gentle slope of the green grass. Moving again, she reverently approached his gravestone.

It seemed impossible that so much had happened since Jack's death, that her whole world had changed. But then she realized death did exactly that to the survivors, changed their whole world, shook it up, reconfigured their hopes and dreams, their attitudes and opportunities. She sighed. Jack's death had certainly done that to her. Everything had changed.

She ached inside as she climbed into bed at night, an ache she suspected she would feel for a long time to come. But strangely, she felt stronger, too, stronger to face the ache and whatever else life threw into her path. She knew that Jack's constant encouragement had started the process of growth in her, had birthed the notion that she could achieve certain things. But his death speeded up that process, thrust her forward out of necessity, made her act when she might have hesitated. The cardinal chirped, and Connie smiled. A cardinal. Jack loved the

Cardinals. How appropriate that one of the gorgeous birds kept vigil over his spot. She stepped to Jack's grave and knelt down beside it. She placed her hand on the grass that covered him. A tear dripped from her eyes.

"It's been three weeks," she said. "I've wanted to come back, but couldn't for some reason, too painful I guess. But I'm here now." She stopped and wiped the tears from her face.

"Sandra and Justin are still with me," she sniffled. "And Wilt . . . he's okay. Spent one day in the hospital then went back to his office. Started an investigation of the men who killed . . . killed your mom and dad, started it before he resigned last night. He's trying to do the right thing, Jack, just like you taught. He's talking to Reverend Wallace, too, trying to figure out his life."

The cardinal chirped again and Connie lifted her head and stared at it. It peered back at her for a moment, then darted down from its perch in the tree and landed on the top of Jack's gravestone, no more than four feet from her.

Connie looked at the gravestone, reading again the epitaph written on it.

JACKSON LEE BRANDON
1957-1997
A HUSBAND AND FATHER WHO DID THE RIGHT THING

She shifted positions, moved closer to the gravestone, ran her fingers over the words. The stone felt cool to her touch. Her tears fell heavier now, a gush of water down her cheeks. She closed her eyes and pondered what the next day would bring. What was the right thing for her to do? A rush of ideas flooded her mind.

She needed to see her professors at law school, postpone her final exams until the fall. She needed to decide how to invest the insurance money, money the company had promised would come to her within a week. She needed to read Jack's novel, then send it to some publishers. She needed to throw her assistance to the men and women still working toward the June vote on gambling in Jefferson City. She needed to clear the air with Luke Tyler, thank him for his help, but tell him she couldn't imagine anything more than friendship. She needed to do all that and more.

She opened her eyes and ran her hand across the ground. Her tears slowed, then stopped completely. She took a deep breath and patted the ground.

"I promise to teach the children," she whispered. "With the Lord's help, I promise to teach them what you believed, your faith and your love for the Lord. I promise to raise them in the truths of Jesus. That's the right . . . the right thing for me. No matter what, I'm going to do that."

She stopped talking but remained seated for several seconds. Then, her eyes dry, she stood and sighed heavily.

"I'm going to leave now," she said. "Time to get on with it. The kids need supper, and then we're going to see Justin at the hospital. He says he has some stories about you he wants to tell. Seems he watched you play a lot of baseball and eat a lot of ice cream. I have a feeling he'll live until he gets all those stories told. I hope it takes a long time."

She paused and bit her lip. Then she said, "I love you, Jack Brandon. I always will. Thank you for loving me." She twisted away to leave. The cardinal chirped. She turned back for one more look at the grave. The cardinal jumped off the headstone and whirled up into the sky, its wings flapping in the direction of the Missouri River.

Connie smiled and left the grave, her face toward her van, her face toward the future. With God's help, she knew she would make it. That was the right thing to do.

LOOK FOR THESE OTHER GREAT THRILLERS
BY GARY E. PARKER

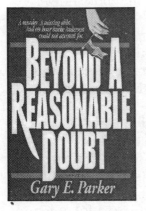

Beyond a Reasonable Doubt

A young pastor is implicated in a homicide—but he can't remember where he was at the time of the murder. This fast-paced thriller follows Pastor Burke Anderson on a trail through temptation to the liberating truth. The first in a series that has Anderson solving a crime that baffles the police.

0-8407-4148-0 • Trade Paperback • 256 pages

Death Stalks a Holiday

Four women are murdered on four consecutive Sundays, and only as the case gathers momentum does Burke Anderson reluctantly become involved in the investigation. While sifting through the evidence, he sees a connection. As a former pastor, Anderson can tell that the wounds the women have sustained are identical to the wounds of Jesus from the crucifixion. Now he must uncover the identity of the killer before another woman loses her life.

0-7852-7784-6 • Trade Paperback • 288 pages

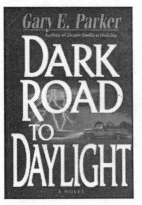

Dark Road to Daylight

When a young girl is kidnapped during a messy child-custody battle, the girl's mother is the key suspect. Another fast-paced mystery that has Burke Anderson piecing together clues and solving a baffling crime, while repairing the lives of the shattered family.

0-7852-7785-4 • Trade Paperback • 256 pages